The
Gypsy's
Daughter

Katie Hutton

ZAFFRE

First published in the UK in 2021 by
ZAFFRE
An imprint of Bonnier Books UK
80–81 Wimpole St, London W1G 9RE
Owned by Bonnier Books
Sveavägen 56, Stockholm, Sweden

A CIP catalogue record for this book is
available from the British Library.

ISBN: 978-1-83877-037-2

Also available as an ebook and in audio

1 3 5 7 9 10 8 6 4 2

Typeset by IDSUK (Data Connection) Ltd
Printed and bound in Great Britain by Clays Ltd, Elcograf S.p.A.

Zaffre is an imprint of Bonnier Books UK
www.bonnierbooks.co.uk

The
Gypsy's
Daughter

Katie Hutton is Irish but now lives in northern Tuscany, with her Italian husband and two teenage sons. She writes mainly historical fiction on the themes of love and culture clash. *The Gypsy Bride* was her debut novel in this genre, with *The Gypsy's Daughter* following. Katie is a member of the Historical Novel Society, the Irish Writers Centre, and the Romantic Novelists' Association, and reviews for Historical Novel Review. In her spare time she volunteers with a second-hand book charity of which she is a founder member.

Also by Katie Hutton:

The Gypsy Bride

For my parents, Brian and Serena Hutton
Nottingham 1952–1957

CHAPTER ONE

French's Farm, Patrixbourne, Kent
September 1942

'My hands is all black still,' complained the smaller of the two girls. The Loveridge sisters were standing at the edge of a hop field, but the feverish activity of the morning was suspended, as the hoppers sat around in a companionate murmur amidst a bee-buzzing haze of heat, eating sandwiches and drinking lemonade. They were predominantly women – of all ages – and children. Close by every hopper, no matter what age, sat a small rectangular gas mask box, a reminder that death could come even out of a clear blue sky. The few men present were almost all middle-aged. Too old for conscription.

'*Are* all black, Harry,' said the older of the two. 'Let me see.'

Six-year-old Harry held her palms up. A shiny dark patina covered them.

'I scrubbed and scrubbed them, my Flora, before we went to chapel. I'd to put my winter gloves on to get my clothes on. I didn't want marks on my new dress.'

'You wouldn't mark your dress,' said Flora, with a twelve-year-old's authority. 'It's not like mud. The hops do that to your

1

skin, but two weeks after the hopping's over, that'll have rubbed away. Your skin makes new, all the time. *I* learned that in the big school.'

'Oh. So can I touch my dress then?'

'Of course, silly. But we'll need to change our frocks soon. We've to help Daddy after dinner.'

Harry took hold of the printed cotton of the skirt by the tips of her fingers, not quite trusting Flora about the hop stains. 'I love this dress,' she said quietly, more to herself than her sister. Flora smiled tolerantly, and looked down at her own. It was made of the same material, a pattern of baby elves sitting on branches talking to brightly coloured birds.

'They're pretty, aren't they? But a bit babyish for me,' said Flora.

'*Not* babyish,' retorted the little girl. When her mother had given her the dress, Harry had laid it reverently on her bed and spread out its skirt, tracing with her finger the plump little elves perched on the branches, giving them names, and eventually inventing conversations for them. Walking along the road to the tin chapel in Bridge that morning, she'd lagged behind the others, in her imagination listening to the twittering of the birds in the folds of the fabric and the laughing babble of their elfin companions. It was one of the few garments she had that hadn't been worn by Flora first. Harry knew that her little dress would be washed and pressed and given away to one of the village children once she was too big for it. She hoped that whoever that child was would be able to hear the elves too. A consolation would be that Flora's dress would come to her in time.

'Mother let me sew the hems,' said Flora.

'Will she teach me?'

'I expect so. When you're bigger,' said her sister. 'She had to cut out the fabric really carefully. It was damaged, you see. Daddy went down to Canterbury after the air raid with his helmet on, and the man who'd lost his shop wanted him to have it. He said, "Can't sell that now. But if your wife can make something out of it for your little girls, we'll have cheated Jerry of something, won't we?"'

'The elves made it. And they saved it for us,' said Harry, obstinately.

'Well perhaps they did . . . oh look, Daddy's coming. Mr Ackleton's with him.'

Harry's eyes followed her sister's pointing finger. Behind where the hoppers sat over their sandwiches and apples, the stripped hop poles marched up to the horizon. Human beings had swarmed over them for the past three weeks, pulling down the bines like great ropes, flickering fingers plucking the hops into the bins. Even though it was Sunday, they would work on until six or seven, until Harry's father Sam would call out 'Pull no more bines,' when the last hops would be stripped from the tough skeins and the hoppers would make their way back to the row of brick huts that were their temporary homes. Small as she was, Harry felt a pang of regret looking at the bare hop poles. She knew that in a week all this would be over, and though she half-longed for the fields to be her own again, she knew she would miss the laughter, the smell of evening sausages grilling over improvised fires, the feeling that French's Farm was briefly the centre of the turning world.

The two men were close enough now for the girls to hear their conversation.

'Do you understand what they say, my Flora?'

'Daddy and Mr Ackleton? A bit. That's Gypsy talk, that is.'

'Mother doesn't speak that way.'

'She wouldn't. She's not a Gypsy. We're *diddakoi*[1] remember.'

Harry did. Her mother's position in the village school had saved all the Loveridge children from teasing, but when her brother Tom had gone to the big school in Canterbury he'd knocked down another boy for name-calling. Sam and Ellen had gone to see the headmaster, and there'd been a long, murmuring talk that evening with the still protesting Tom.

'Uncle Vanlo can talk that way too.'

Flora smiled. 'Uncle Vanlo's funny. Lives all the year in his wagon on his own in the back field, 'cept at the hopping when the Scamps and the Hildens and the Ackletons bring theirs too. Except he's not there this year, of course.'

'Where is he, Flora?'

'Fighting Hitler in Africa somewhere.'

'He'll win, then. I love Uncle Vanlo. He's never been to school but he knows everything,' said Harry. '*Daddy!*' She ran to the tall man in shirtsleeves and battered hat, and threw her arms around him as though she hadn't seen him in days, though they'd walked back from chapel together only two hours earlier.

---

[1] Romani: mixed blood.

'My maidy!' said Sam Loveridge, scooping her up. 'You're heavy!' He turned to his older daughter, and passed his hand over the top of her chestnut head. 'My Flora.'

Wester Ackleton tipped his hat to the two girls. 'Your mother's kindly asked us to Sunday dinner,' he said, raising a little cloth bag he held in his other hand. They heard a chinking sound. Both girls knew why he carried it. In their home, when 'Daddy people' came to eat with them, they brought their own cutlery and plates. Anyone else was served on their mother's Willow pattern.

Walking down the lane to the Loveridges' cottage, Wester Ackleton murmured to Flora, 'My Nelson's friend wrote him a letter for us. Your mother read it for me. He asks to be remembered to you.'

Flora blushed furiously, but remembered her manners enough to mutter, 'Thank you.' She didn't manage to utter another word until her mother led them in saying grace. For all her 'big school' superiority with her little sister, Flora's head was full of her last sight of the illiterate Nelson Ackleton, calling at the cottage with her elder brother Tom, both of them proudly showing off the uniform of the 'Buffs'. Later that day, the two girls had found their mother, Ellen, in a corner of the kitchen garden, crying into her apron.

'I couldn't stop Tom, but poor Nelson didn't need to go,' sobbed Ellen. 'Nor did your uncle Vanlo. One's too young and the other's too old.'

'Couldn't they have said so?' asked Flora.

'They fibbed,' said Ellen, drying her eyes. 'Neither of them have birth certificates, so they couldn't be found out.'

Harry frowned, digesting this information. 'Have me and Flora got them . . . stiffkets?'

'Yes you do . . . and your brothers.'

'And you and Daddy too?'

'Just me. Daddy hasn't,' said Ellen.

'That's why Daddy doesn't have a birthday, Harry,' said Flora. 'You have to have a certificate or you can't have one.'

*

Harry never did wear Flora's dress. In December that year, what had first looked like the feverishness of flu had been followed by Flora screaming that her head hurt, and to please close the curtains for she couldn't stand the light in her eyes. With trembling hands, Sam Loveridge had opened the drawer in the dresser and brought out the Friendly Society certificate for his elder daughter. Dr Titterton was fetched and, twenty minutes later, Ellen ran to the vicarage, the nearest house with a telephone. An ambulance came, and a week later a dark car came back, travelling slowly, and there was no celebration at French's Farm that Christmas.

It was Harry who got Flora's elf dress out of the wardrobe and took it to her weeping parents.

'Can she wear it, so's they can keep her company?'

*

Flora's headstone was in place six months later, close to the flint wall of the churchyard. Harry knelt and ran her hand gently over the tiny carving of a horse above her sister's name.

'What's the horsey's name?'

'You think of one for 'en, my Harry,' said her father.

'The other people haven't got one,' she said, looking round at the other graves.

'They ain't travellin' people.'

'*You* don't travel, Daddy. You're always here, with us.'

'Not now. I used to, always. Me and your uncle Vanlo. Then when your gran died – my mother – I put her in a place like this, near a hedge it was, close as I could get her to the road. That was near Maidstone – on the way up to London. After that I stopped moving, like her, only I wunt dead. I came back here for your mother – and for Tom and David. They was in Canterbury, waiting for me, you might say. An' I've never gone anywhere after. I'm used to house-dwellin' now.'

Harry sat back on her heels, and lifted the lavender plant out of her trug. She stuck her trowel in the earth and, frowning with the effort, moved it back and forth to break up the soil.

'Want me to do that?'

'No . . . I can.' The child worked the trowel back and forth, then scrabbled out small fistfuls of earth.

'Do you still go to places in your head?' she asked, without looking up.

'Yeah! I do,' replied Sam, surprised. 'Do you?'

'Always and always,' said Harry. She patted down the soil around the plant, and sat for a moment looking at her work, her head on one side. 'I go to the places I read about at school,' she said, 'but when I'm bigger, I want to *really* go and see them.' She scrambled to her feet. 'I need to water this now.'

Sam watched her carry an empty tin to the tap near the gate. She was wearing her elf dress from last summer, her favourite, but he could see even at a distance how it tugged across the shoulders and under the arms.

'Oh my maidy,' murmured her father.

'When Hitler's caught,' said the child, coming back, 'and Tom and David and Uncle Vanlo come home, we could all go to London and see Uncle John and Aunt Amy. And after that, *your* family.' She lifted the tin and, in a circular motion, tipped the water out onto the plant.

'My family's here, my Harry. Ain't got nobody else. Don't need 'en.'

CHAPTER TWO

Kimberley, Nottinghamshire
September 1945

'Bye, Mam,' said Ned, his hand on the door handle.

His mother took her hands out of the clatter of breakfast things and dried them on her apron.

'Yow'll be ah' raight, Ned,' she said. His face, pale but determined, was almost on a level with hers, but she hesitated to embrace him, for he was neither boy nor man. At Ned's age, her own father was already going down in the cage at Digby Colliery, protected only by newspaper stuffed inside his cap, returning sweating and black every evening, to a zinc hip bath. Ned's father now travelled to Eastwood, wore a helmet and came back from the pithead baths smelling of Palmolive. Sarah Stones settled for stroking her son's hair.

'Remember, lad, it's your way to a job in daylight, the schoowel.'

'I dint pass exam, Mam.'

She smiled hesitantly; she wasn't going to let go of the brave face she'd decided on when she woke that morning.

'*Yow'll* be back for your dinner, yowthe. Grammar school lads can't manage back from Bulwell for that.'

*

'Any of you lads know anything about France?' asked the Geography teacher.

Ned's heart thumped. This was his moment. He raised his hand, conscious of his new shirt clinging cold to his damp armpit.

'Stand up then, boy. Remind me of your name again.'

'Stones, sir.'

Ned got to his feet, suddenly feeling that the gouged and grooved slope of his desk was a vertiginous distance away. Some twenty or so moons of faces swivelled to gaze up at him. He cleared his throat.

'*La sors aitch pee est un melang de hort qualitee de fruits orientox de pieces et de vineggrer ne conteent nye colorants artifiseels nih—*'

For a long minute the only sounds in the room were the scuffling of Ned's feet as the teacher dragged him by the collar to the front of the classroom. His companions, most of them boys he already knew, watched the struggle in sweaty-palmed silence.

'I have never – in twenty years as a teacher – encountered such impertinence.' Ned felt the spray of spittle from the man's mouth and screwed up his eyes and pursed his lips. A blow landed on his left ear. Ned cupped a hand around the pain, heat radiating against his palm. The teacher shoved him away then. Ned staggered sideways, but before he could regain his balance, the man had seized the blackboard pointer and brought it down across his shoulders. Ned shouted in pain, bending forward with his hands fluttering upwards. The next blow landed across his spine; it was surprise and shock that winded him. The stick whirred again, and with it the boys in the room stirred like saplings in a breeze; someone at the back started to cry. Ned had dropped to his knees and was trying to crawl to the shelter of the nearest desk when he felt the air displace, and out of the corner of his eye saw a pair of trousered adult legs enter the room.

'What on earth is this?' he heard. It was the same voice that had delivered a solemn and bewildering address to the entire new first year that morning in Assembly. All Ned could remember of it now was the phrase 'industry expects'.

The rest of the lesson was taken by the headmaster himself, with a monotone explanation of the canvas-backed map of France hanging from the picture rail. Ned stared dully at the movement of the stick that had bruised his back as it darted from Paris to Lyons to Marseille, whilst rage, resentment and pain cooled around him like amber, leaving a hard smooth surface with the child Ned Stones curled immobile at its heart.

At dinner-time he said little, feigning tiredness when his mother asked him how his first morning had been. When she turned her back, he swivelled the HP Sauce bottle so he could no longer see the French words that he had so painstakingly, so proudly learned off by heart. He'd so wanted to impress at school, to do something to make up for the disappointment his mother had so quickly smothered when he'd failed the eleven-plus. He was too young still to understand the contempt that teacher felt for himself and the children he no longer wanted to teach, who took every sign of independence in the classroom as a personal affront.

Ned felt the months and years to come loom over him as long as a war; the school-leaving age had just been raised to fifteen.

CHAPTER THREE

Patrixbourne
November 1947

Harry and her mother walked in uncharacteristic near silence to the village school in Bridge. Ellen hunted for something to say to end the tension and distract her daughter from what she knew consumed the girl's every waking thought.

'How are you getting on with that book – the Steinbeck?' she asked tentatively.

'The one you thought would be too old for me?' muttered Harry.

Stung, Ellen's eyes flared, but all she said was '*The Pearl*. That one. I just thought—'

'I've finished it. It was brilliant,' said Harry, with energy. 'The poor fisherman should never have had to pay the doctor to help his little boy. He's only nice to the family when he thinks he's going to get a good fee. All the badness starts when there's money involved.' She took her mother's arm. 'Sorry I snapped. It's just . . .'

'I know.'

'How will I be told if I've passed, Mother?'

'You'll be called to the headmistress's office.'

'Will you be there too?'

Ellen hesitated. 'You won't need me there, Harry. And you know the infants can't be left.'

*

Tension crackled in the small classroom. Miss Holgate had given the older pupils a composition to do, the ones who had been prodded to sit the eleven-plus and who were now waiting to know the direction their lives would take.

That didn't really work, did it? thought Miss Holgate, wishing she'd just gone to the piano instead and distracted everybody with a lively singalong. From what she could see, most of the little group were staring at blank, lined pages, ink coagulating on their nibs, absently playing with hair, or gazing unseeing towards the windows. Harry Loveridge, though, was scribbling furiously.

*

'Flying colours,' said Miss Ward, smiling at the solemn dark-haired girl sitting opposite her desk. 'You'll be going to Simon Langton Girls. The world will be your oyster.'

Harry thought of the poor fisherman in the book she had just read, hurling the cursed pearl, cause of so much joy and suffering, far into the waves, and murmured, 'It shan't be like that. I shan't let it.'

'I'm sorry?'

'Oh . . . *I'm* sorry. It's just a bit of a shock.'

'It shouldn't be. A bright girl like you.'

Harry blushed. 'Am I the only one?'

'There are some schools where they read out the news you've had today in Assembly, so everyone knows. But imagine the humiliation of those who had hopes and whose names aren't read out? No, you're not the only one. We've done well this year. But when you go to the big school you'll meet new friends, just as they will.' The headmistress got to her feet, and Harry also stood. 'I'm going to let you go home for the rest of today – go and tell your father. I shall let Miss Holgate and your mother know. You'd better run along now . . . I've good news for a few more.'

*

Harry found her father and Uncle Vanlo pulling up the last of the wurzels in a field behind the house. She stood watching the stooping men from the gate – both were in shirtsleeves though it was a cold day, yet wearing mufflers – and remembered her attempts to help as a smaller child, when she hadn't been strong enough and had only got in the way. Neither man had complained – on the contrary, she'd been praised at the tea table although there'd been little to show for the stubborn half-moons of dirt beneath her nails. Harry's eyes prickled. Flora had been there . . .

Harry knew even then that Miss Ward's news meant that stooping to grub roots for animal feed from the resisting ground was not in her future. Sam Loveridge looked up then, and smiled. 'Bruv!' she heard him say to Vanlo. 'Our maidy's done it.' They straightened up, wiping their hands on old suit trousers, and walked across to congratulate her, the two men at the centre of Harry's world, neither of whom had ever been to school a day in their lives.

CHAPTER FOUR

Kimberley

October 1948

'Fancy the Top Cut comm Sunday?' asked Henry Stones, addressing Ned but with half an eye on his wife.

'Just uz?' said the boy. He didn't want his younger brother there, nor his sister – not that he thought they'd be interested, except to thwart him. Neither had the patience to sit waiting for the tug on the line, not understanding that even talking too loudly could alert the fish.

'Just uz. Unless yuh wannt to play football instead wi' Jimmy an' his mates.'

*

Carrying their tackle in an old canvas bag, Ned ambled beside his father along Main Street in the direction of the Eastwood Road. The boy was so used to the scarring on his father's forehead that he was barely conscious of it now, but Ned knew that Henry preferred to walk on his son's right so that his injury was less visible. Glancing at him, Ned now wondered when it had happened that his height had outstripped his father's. It could only have been a few weeks since they'd walked this same route. Had the warmth of the summer – his last as a schoolboy – somehow heated and stretched his bones, or was it that the stocky Henry, down the pit since he was younger than his son was now, had stooped and shrunk?

Father and son didn't speak, as if they were in training for their long vigil by the canal. Henry nodded to men he knew, workmates. Faces he had known since they had all been in short trousers.

As the Midland Railway bridge reared up above them, the two of them turned left, following the path by the abandoned railway embankment, a place where Ned had played often enough, though he couldn't now remember the last time he'd done so. His long stretch at school was coming to an end. This was the last October he'd have to spend there. Within a few weeks, he'd sing in his man's voice in the last school carol service. He wondered if there was anything he'd miss, or anything he'd recall of those chalk-dusted rooms and ink-stained desks. Only once could Ned say he'd enjoyed himself, with a young supply teacher who'd covered for the loathed 'Hairy' Hewitt when he'd had his fall – an idealist who'd invited his temporary pupils to imagine the Peterloo Massacre and the Chartists gathering on Kennington Common as having happened in Slab Square in Nottingham. Something had stirred in Ned then, a green shoot of understanding that he and others like him could be part of something much bigger, but it had been trampled on as soon as Hewitt returned, bruised and irritable.

'Noat,' Ned muttered, under his breath, then added with contempt, 'nothing,' as he'd been told at school that 'noat' was not correct English. Henry shot him a look, but said nothing.

They were passing by the old army building that had been taken over as the kitchens for those hated school dinners. Though it was a Sunday, Ned was convinced he could smell stewed beef and cabbage, seeping through the brickwork and the metal-framed windows. Ned had begun at the big school by going home for his midday meal, but had been teased for being a mummy's boy. He'd not forgotten the hastily suppressed look of relief on his mother's face when he'd asked if he might stay at the school all day after all.

Then came the playing fields, with the air-raid shelter that now served as changing rooms. It still seemed extraordinary to Ned that anyone would have wanted to bomb Kimberley. They hadn't really; Nottingham was the real prize – that and the pits. Beyond the football pitch came the council dump, and then at last the sweeter air and longer grass of the country. Ned heard Henry take a deep and satisfied breath, as if he wanted to remind his coal-blackened lungs of what clean air really felt like. Their feet thudded, almost in unison, over the old railway sleepers that made up the little bridge over Kettle Brook, before they followed the path down to Awsworth Lane. Henry went over the stile in an odd, crab-like motion, familiar to those who moved underground. The endless span of Forty Arches viaduct was before them. Ned reminded himself that one day he would come down here and actually count all those loops across the landscape. Some childish fear of their height and mass remained, and he walked more quickly as he passed underneath a brick arch, refusing to look up.

'Not long now, yowthe,' said Henry, as they followed the path along the viaduct's shadow, and then turned into the musty little brick-lined tunnel under the disused embankment. As the vault closed over them, Ned felt his heart speed up despite himself, and kept his eyes on the pale autumn sunlight framed softly by the undergrowth that dripped over the far mouth of the tunnel. Not for the first time, Ned feared the pit-cage drop, the loss of light, the coal seams narrowing . . .

'Ah don't wannt yow gooin' underground,' said his father, as if he'd read the boy's thoughts. His voice was louder in the enclosed space.

'Dad?' Ned said, his voice shaky with surprise and gratitude, so sure he'd been that his future lay in the mine.

'Never 'ave. Not sin' th'accident. Ah thought that, when me 'ead was gettin' battered. Not for no son o' mine. Don't be a miner, Ned.'

'No.' They were almost at their destination, and the boy knew that his father had an almost ceremonious way of setting up the rods that tolerated no conversation. Ned followed his father's movements, a step behind him. He was clumsy with happiness, though, dropping things. *We've allus bin miners,* he thought, looking up at the open sky as though the world was his for the taking.

*

'Yow got ote yet?' asked Ned, half an hour later, shifting on his fold-up stool. The canvas creaked and he felt the flimsy metal frame sink a little further into the soft earth of the canalside.

'There's a reason they call it fishing, yowthe,' said his father. 'Yuh don't allus get.'

Ned had expected that answer. He'd really only asked the question because he wanted to reopen the conversation they'd been having when they arrived, to check that it was real. Yet he appreciated Henry Stones's delight in the near silence of the fine autumn morning, the buzzing of insects and twittering of birds in the hedgerows. His father could name the songsters too, and imitate them with his sibilant whistle. Ned thought again with a kind of horror of the maze of tunnels beneath the ground where they sat, those black seams where filthy bare-chested men hacked and dragged, almost afraid to believe he was going to be spared their fate. The days were shortening, and soon Henry would go to work in darkness, and rise in the cage to darkness.

'They've comm to the schoowel,' said Ned. 'Abaht factory jobs.'

'Who?'

'Blokes in suits from Personnel. Free smokes if yer go to Player's,' said the boy.

'Laight mi one, Ned. Ah'll hold yur line steady. And tek one for thissen, only say noat to yer mother.'

Ned put the cigarette in his own mouth to light it, then placed it in his father's. That, and the conversation about work, made him feel suddenly adult.

'It's good when they comm abaht the jobs. Better'n lessons, anyroad. Ah liked Raleigh best.' He pronounced the firm's name Rally, as he'd always heard it, though the man in the suit had said Rah-ley.

His father eased his cigarette to the corner of his mouth. 'Yow'd 'ave to be up sharp. To get into Nottingham.' He named the city in the same tone as when he occasionally mentioned London, as if it was just as remote.

'Showed uz a film. Talked abaht bein' an apprentice. Said there'd be prospects.'

'Folk'll allus wannt bicycles,' said Henry. He glanced sideways at the boy. 'Lasses'll work there too, ah bet.'

'Doin' the fancy work. Them stripes and finishes an' that – in the film.'

There was a pause as his father stared out at the still water. 'Bit young yet for lasses, yow,' he said.

Ned coloured, his sense of his adult self deflated. His father coughed, and spat out the stub into the grass.

'Yow oughter know abaht 'em though. So's they don't catch yer when y'arnt lookin'.'

Ned looked down at his hands holding the rod, and thought about the promptings of his adolescent body, the things he'd heard older boys say – rumours about women in Nottingham and lurid stories of 'knob-rot'. Then he remembered that at school he was one of the older boys now, as hardly anyone stayed on, and felt suddenly frightened, much as he was longing to get out of the place.

'Catch me?'

'Ah've said too much, mebbe. It's just yow'll be aht o' the schoowel soon enough. Mebbe we'll talk then.'

Ned pushed aside the thought of 'lasses', convinced anyway they were unattainable, and thought of Nottingham, the factories, the crowds, the shop windows, all of this to him as thrilling and exotic as an extended Goose Fair, fresh in his mind from the previous weekend – only without the dodgems and the candyfloss. Some of his companions had truanted to go to the fair on a weekday with the express purpose of finding girls. Ned hadn't gone only because he didn't think he could bear the look of disappointment on his mother's face when the inevitable note from the school came. The hunt for girls had failed anyway, so the boys had taken their frustration out on a squealing kid in the uniform of Nottingham High, giving him 'a raight pastin' until a woman with a rolled-up umbrella had intervened. Briefly, the shadow of National Service darkened Ned's musings; he tried to reassure himself with the thought that *mebbe by end of my apprenticeship that'll a' be over.*

Henry's finger tapped the back of his hand. 'Look to yer line, lad.'

CHAPTER FIVE

Patrixbourne

November 1954

Sam Loveridge heard his daughter's voice before he saw her – she was talking animatedly to her mother, but he couldn't make out what either of them was saying, Ellen's responses sounded cautious. He put down the rat-trap he was making and walked out of the barn to greet them, wondering why Harry was late home from school.

By the time he got outside, Harry Loveridge was twirling around in the yard, evidently pleased with herself. Sam always marvelled at how his only daughter could make 'even them dull *togs*—' his term for her gym-slip school uniform '—look fetchin',' though he could never understand why every 'little maidy' had to dress exactly like her companions. *Too much like being in the army – or in stir.* Ellen was standing in the cottage doorway, a dishcloth forgotten in her hand, looking anxious.

Sam stopped dead. 'What've you gone and done to your pretty hair?' he cried.

Harry tossed her neat head of soft black waves.

'Oh *Dad!*' she said. 'It's the latest thing – the Italian look, you know. Just like Ava Gardner in *Mogambo*.'

'What's that, then?'

'*You* know! The pictures – at the Odeon. I showed the hairdresser a photo in a magazine. I'm the sixth girl this week, she said.'

'What'd she do with all she cut off?' said Sam, finding he was close to tears.

'Oh that?' said Harry, airily. 'They've someone to sweep it up, Dad.' Though in truth there'd been a horrible moment of near-regret when she'd seen the first swathe of her long black locks hit the lino. She'd breathed deeply, met her eyes in the mirror and fixed a smile on her face. Fifteen minutes later she'd squealed with delight at the result.

'It'll be a lot easier to wash, I expect,' put in Ellen.

'Soap ain't on the ration now,' Sam said. Defeated, he passed the back of his hand over his forehead. 'It's your hair, Harry,' he said. 'But don't you go doing the same thing, my Ellen.'

His wife smoothed her own silver-streaked light brown hair, tied back from a still clear brow and looped into a loose bun at the nape of her neck, a style not changed in almost three decades. 'I wouldn't, Sam. But she does look nice.'

*

Sam turned down the oil lamp as he got into bed, but didn't extinguish it entirely.

'She's a fine neck, our little girl. Like yours, my Ellen. Couldn't really see it before.'

'It's not a permanent wave she's had either.'

'What's that?'

'I mean it curls that way naturally, now the weight of her hair is gone. The hairdresser said so.'

'Makes her look more grown up. She'll mebbe be wanting her Sunday name now.'

'No, I think she'll always be Harry, even if she knows how to say Harmony properly now.'

Sam laughed. 'Remember, my Ellen, how she'd come out with "Harromie" instead?'

'She was only a little dot then, wasn't she?' said Ellen, smiling. 'That was when she used to say sick people went to "hostible".'

'Eh, well, she ain't little anymore,' he said, his mood sinking again. 'An' hostible didn't do her pore sister no good.'

Ellen reached for his hand. 'God rest our little girl,' she said.

'You said your prayers?'

'Yes, Sam. And you were in them.'

'I need that.' Stretching out, he extinguished the wavering light. 'Harry'll be wanting them trousers next,' he said in resignation into the darkness.

'She's eighteen, Sam. They call them slacks.'

There was a pause before he said, 'Never seen a travellin' girl in trousers.' He heard his wife catch her breath. 'I'm not sorry for leavin', my Ellen. Never have been. There's things I miss from the Gypsy way o' things, o' course there is, but them's nothing compared to bein' with you. I ain't sorry how we've brung up Harry either. I'm proud of her – proudest I am of anything.'

Ellen stroked the cheek she couldn't see and said, 'I've never underestimated what you gave up for me, Sam, never. And Harry knows where she's come from; you and Vanlo have helped her understand that, even though you told me that the day you walked away from the camp you knew you walked away from that life forever. Don't you see, Sam, that even with her new haircut, and whatever she's wearing, she knows who she is. She mightn't be a "travelling girl" in a wagon, but she won't stay put. I've known that since long before she went to the grammar school. She's in a waiting room for a journey to the entire world. Harry will leave us, and it won't be because she's getting married – though of course I hope and pray that one day she will find someone she loves and who loves her—'

'Like we did,' said Sam quietly.

'Yes, like we did. And whoever he is, wherever he comes from, we must welcome him with open arms – give him and her what wasn't given to us, Sam, by the people who said they loved us most. But I think she'll leave us well before then.'

'Oh . . .'

'No, don't be sad. Remember what she said to you that day by Flora's grave? That she wanted to escape to the world she read about in books? We mustn't stop her, Sam.'

'A Gypsy girl,' he said slowly.

'Yes. The most of all our children.'

'She is, ain't she? But it's late. I'll stop my worryin', Ellen, so's you can get some sleep.'

'Goodnight, Sam.' Ellen turned on her side. Sam rolled round and moulded to her body, putting his arm over her, nuzzling into the back of her neck. His wife was soon asleep, but Sam lay awake for more than an hour, listening to the rise and fall of her breathing.

*

The following Sunday the three of them, along with a handful of Methodist neighbours, had made their customary short walk to the next village to what was affectionately called 'the Tin Chapel'. Ellen had prepared most of the Sabbath meal before going out, refusing Harry's help on the grounds that 'it's better you should be studying.'.

Now, at just after half past twelve, Ellen called up the stairs. 'Harry? Your brother's here!'

With a whoop of delight Harry dropped her pen and scraped back her chair. Nevertheless, she was still declining a particularly sticky French verb in her head as she thundered down the stairs. The scent of the Sunday roast grew richer with every step.

Her elder brother Tom was at the foot, waiting for her. Her middle brother David, a Methodist minister on the Birmingham Circuit and the father of her only nephew, couldn't manage to get back to Kent often, but Tom being in Faversham came to Sunday dinner regularly – though not Sunday worship.

'Hello, sis! Oh my, look at you!'

'Like it?'

'You look like a film star, you do.'

'And you look like a matinee idol, big bruv! Do you think we've missed our true calling?'

'I think I've found mine. I wouldn't give up the drays for anything. Dad like your new look?'

'He's getting used to it,' said Sam, from where he was sitting at the table behind them.

Ellen carried the roasting dish over to the table and settled it on the trivet.

'Hello, Uncle Vanlo,' said Tom, taking his place next to the sturdy figure of the man everyone thought of as his father's brother.

'Hello, my Tom.'

Tom fingered the faded red and white checked tablecloth with affection. It was familiar: it had been on the table on Sundays since he was a boy. He knew there was a separate bowl for the washing of that tablecloth, for when his parents had finally been able to marry, his mother had asked his father to teach her the travelling people's ways. *What you wear and what you eat off should never be washed together.* He'd said this to the woman who had been his wife and she'd laughed. 'What, two machines in the laundromat? It all gets clean anyway! Since when were Gypsies known for their hygiene?' That had been the beginning of the end for them.

There was a moment's silence as they all waited for Ellen to sit down.

'Be present at our table, Lord. Be here and everywhere adored. These mercies bless and grant that we may feast in fellowship with Thee,' she said, and handed Sam the carving knife.

'Amen' they all murmured, and conversation erupted around the table.

'How are the *grais*,[2] Tom?' asked Sam.

Harry had expected this question, for her father invariably asked about the horses her brother cared for. Tom had risen to be head ostler at Shepherd Neame brewery. Sam listened attentively as his eldest son recounted the news of each animal, occasionally interjecting advice about how to deal with ailments (this usually involved Epsom salts), or what was the best route to take a horse who was feeling his years. Tom had a paddock behind his cottage where there was always at least one old nag he'd not had the heart to consign to the knacker's. The first horse Harry ever sat upon was a piebald her brother had brought to French's Farm. The animal had twitched an ear and continued to crop the grass, ignoring the feeble drumming of her small heels against his sides.

'How long do you think they'll keep the drays?' asked Sam.

'Can't see them going of out fashion. The horses showed their worth right through the war. And can you see a lorry trying to get through the lanes to all the village pubs, stopping and starting and giving off all them fumes? The beer wouldn't taste right.'

'Well, as long as there are still village pubs . . .'

Tom laughed. 'They'll never close, will they? The pub and the chapel. Without them what village would you have?'

'One like this,' said Sam. 'His lordship's that tied to the parish church that there's never been no chapel in Patrixbourne. It's as well it's a nice walk to Bridge.'

---

[2] Horses.

'Talking of the chapel, Tom, your brother David is going to try to get down before Christmas, if his congregation can spare him,' said Ellen.

'That baby'll be on his feet by now.'

Sam looked down at his plate. 'You still alone, son?'

'Yes, that's me. Fancy free,' said Tom, but didn't sound it.

'Ever see Mavis?'

'As a matter of fact, yes. In Ashford, about three weeks ago.'

Ellen had got up to clear the plates but rested her hands on the back of the chair, listening.

'I ducked up an alleyway before she could see me,' went on Tom. 'She looked well. She had a little girl with her.' He saw the sag of his mother's shoulders. His father made a small sound he recognised as 'dordi!'[3] Harry patted Tom's forearm; with his other hand he caught hers and held it. 'Oh well,' he said, 'just another casualty of war. Perhaps one day we'll get our own monument. "To all those divorced in the line of duty!" Anyway, what about *you*, sis? Anyone you're thinking of making an honest man of?'

'Haven't seen anyone I like well enough. The men in books are better than the real ones!' Harry said, wrinkling her nose to general laughter.

'*I* can't think of nobody as would be good enough for our Harry,' said Sam.

'Harry's got time enough. She's got school to finish first,' said Ellen.

_____

[3] Exclamation, something like 'oh dear'.

'Miss Shaw thinks I should try for a scholarship, Mum. She says I'm university material. It would mean another year at school after this one.'

Ellen put down her fork.

'My maidy at a university . . .' began Sam.

'She only said I should try,' said Harry. 'I haven't decided if I want to, yet.'

'Oh Harry, that would be marvellous!' said Ellen.

'What's the scholarship amount to?' asked Tom.

'It's not a fortune, but enough to live on if I'm careful. They've things called "Exhibitions" as well, but they're a bit less money.'

'Exhibitions? Sounds like one of them rude shows they have up in the Windmill Theatre,' said Tom. 'Kept going right through the Blitz: "We're never closed – we're never clothed."'

'Shut up!' laughed Harry.

'That's enough, Tom,' murmured Sam. 'Not at Sunday dinner.'

'Sorry, Dad.'

'What do you think, Ellen?' said Sam. 'Will we go up to the school and see Miss Shaw?'

'No need to yet,' said Harry. 'I need to think about it myself first. But thanks.'

'Where would this university be, then?' asked Vanlo.

'That depends . . . could be anywhere. London. Scotland. I'd have to see which'd have me.'

'Just you, then, in a strange place?' said Sam.

'Not just me. Hundreds of other girls all in the same boat.'

'Boys too, I s'pose.'

'Well, yes. Only Miss Shaw said they'd live in different buildings. Perhaps you *should* go and talk to her, Dad. So you'd see it's all right, really.'

'Boys go away for National Service. David went away to college,' said Ellen softly. 'And there were girls in uniform in the war, Sam – you remember the Land Girls – all of them far from home.'

Sam shifted in his chair. 'It'll be whatever you want, my Harry. Your mother and me'll help you whatever way we can. Dunt mean we won't miss you, though – nor stop worryin' about you. As long as you know home is always here.'

'Oh Dad!'

'Same goes for you, my Tom.'

*

In a draughty barracks just outside Nottingham Ned shivered in a queue of other young men, waiting to be inspected by a doctor and a middle-aged nurse with an efficiently bored expression. He was completely naked, his hands held over his crotch. His only comfort was that all the other conscripts were in the same situation. He wanted a pee, though he'd gone in a pub outhouse just before presenting himself for the medical.

'Ah'd hoped it'd all be over,' he'd said to the personnel officer at Raleigh, the same man who'd come to his school all those years earlier.

'So did we, to be honest. But we'll keep your job open for you, Stones. We'd have to anyway, but you're a good worker.'

'Thank you,' Ned had answered, realising to his surprise how much he was going to miss the place.

'Two years'll go by quickly, you'll see. There's no shortage of places British servicemen are needed. Perhaps you'll get sent somewhere warmer than Nottingham.'

Now, shuffling forward in the queue, his eyes on the stubby vertebrae of the thin youth in front of him, two years felt like a long stretch, but it wasn't Raleigh he was worrying about now. The factory would still be there.

I can't write to Dora. What if her husband reads mi letters?

'Next!'

CHAPTER SIX

Forty Arches Viaduct

December 1954

Ned scraped his bowl clean of his mother's apple crumble and told his parents that he was going for a walk.

'Ah'll comm with yow, lad,' said his father, pushing back his chair.

Gathering the plates, Ned's mother darted a look from her son to her husband, and said, 'No, Henry, he's mebbe wanntin to go on his own. An' the washin' line is dairn, remember? Ah'll need that put raight fer Monday.' She retreated into the cramped kitchen before either could respond.

'A pint o' pale mebbe when I comm back, eh?' said Ned. 'An' a proper long walk in mornin', if yuh'd laike?'

'Ah' raight, yowthe.' Henry turned round in his chair and called out to his wife, rinsing the plates under the tap, 'Mek us a brew, will yer, plaise?'

'Not me, Mam,' said Ned, reaching for his old donkey jacket on its peg behind the door. His leave would end the following afternoon, but whilst he was home he doggedly wore his own clothes, refusing to let his father show him off to neighbours and friends in battledress blouse and beret. 'Ah'm not a real sowjer,' he'd said.

Seconds later, Ned was outside in the wintry air with its threat of worse weather to come, scrunching his fists into his pockets. He walked briskly out of the town, taking the route he and his father had followed on his boyhood fishing trips, aware that his stride had lengthened with all the marching he'd been made to do over the last few weeks. He looked at every familiar landmark as if he was afraid he might forget it. *I'll even miss bein' this snatched wi' cold,* he thought.

When he reached the path alongside the viaduct, he slowed his pace, his face turned towards the arches as he walked. At the third, he stopped, then moved briskly forward under the vault, his hands out, and went into the arms of the woman waiting there.

'Dora,' he whispered, his face in her neck. 'They're sending me to Malaya. I don't even know where it is.'

*

He said bitterly, half an hour later, 'It int raight, like this. Ah wannt you a' naight, not out in cold wi' yow against them bricks.' He held the edges of her coat, then reluctantly helped her button it. Dora was crying softly. Ned brushed her tears away, then lifted her fringe from her brow, as he liked to do. She flinched.

'The bastard!' The bruise was close to the hairline.

'Allus where yuh can't see it,' she said. 'Ah'll give him that – he wunt show me up.'

'Hissen, you mean.' He touched his mouth to the bruise. 'Where're the nippers today?'

'At Mam's. Where ah'm meant to be. Ah'd better go, Ned. We've said our goodbyes.' She kissed him, hard, desperately, then turned and walked off without looking back, as he knew she would. He didn't try to follow her. Her action was as decisive as the way she'd met his admiring gaze and held it, that night in the taproom at The Gate.

Ned leaned against the brickwork, at the place where he had held Dora.

She'll write to me, but I can't write back. He had no idea when he would see her again, and a year and eleven months of army life stretched out into his future.

CHAPTER SEVEN

The Hopping
September 1955

What's the matter with me? thought Harry. *I always used to enjoy the last night of the hopping.* She slipped away from the raucous crowds, the greasy aroma of the roast, the tang of beer and cigarettes. The air was still warm, the dark sky cloudless, the rows of stripped hop poles marching up the field almost phosphorescent in the light of the full moon. *But why shouldn't the hoppers enjoy themselves? They've got London tomorrow – no grass and fields for another year.*

In the distance, an accordion came to the end of a tune in a discordant, jangling burst of sound, greeted with shouts and laughter. The party had started to break up before Harry had moved off into the darkness, wives helping staggering husbands back to their huts, children heavy with sleep lifted and laid against shoulders. Love, she had seen, had come to some amongst the bines, though there were boys, for all their bravado, who hadn't had the courage to declare themselves until this night, fortified with beer and the knowledge that if they didn't speak now, they might well never do so.

'I've seen them,' her mother Ellen had said, 'courting one year, back here wed the next, a baby the one after that. Some families grow faster than the hops! Good workers always want to come back to a good farm – your father sees to that.'

I want something else, though, thought Harry, *not to be always on this endless wheel of the land ... harvest, hops, turnips, ploughing. Places I've read about in books. I see it in Dad, sometimes – he can be restless too. But he's like me – travels by reading.* Tears pricked her eyes then. She knew her father didn't like to be observed with a book in his hand, and would lay whatever it was by and say, 'Must get on!' if he was. Just once though, on a rainy day, Harry had glimpsed him from the doorway to the parlour. He'd sat, his lips moving silently and his finger tracing the words. He'd looked up, and said, 'See this, Harry?' He'd shown her the endpapers of the volume he was holding. '"Everyman I will go with thee" it says here,' he said, without looking at the words. 'I like that.' He got up to return the book to its place on what he called 'your mother's shelf', so Harry never saw what it was.

'It's Mr Hardy I like best, though,' he'd said, coming back. 'Dunt care for Mr Dickens. He writes about them people so's we can laugh at 'em, mostly, and there's so many anyroad I forget who they all are. But Mr Hardy's kind about country people – respects them. An' he knew us Gypsies was there too.'

She'd thought to herself then, *I could put that in an essay, what he says. My dad, who couldn't write his own name until he went to prison.*

'We was there all the time,' he said, 'always have been. Even if we get blamed for *chorrin'* a *grai*[4] when we hadn't, in that book where the lady has trouble with all them husbands.' He peered out of the kitchen window. 'Looks like the rain is letting up a bit,' he said, reaching for his boots.

That day something official came in the post, the Agriculture Ministry men wanting their statistics, and the quiet reader of *Far from the Madding Crowd* handed the paper to his wife with the words, 'Write this for me, would you, my Ellen? You've such a fine hand.' Harry watched her parents, remembering a science lesson. *That's it . . . Dad's like a planet that circles around another one – like the earth around the sun. Mum's fixed. Without her, he'd always be on the go, but he can't and won't break away from her.* Yet her joy as a small child had been sitting on her father's lap and leaning her head against his chest, so that she felt as much as heard him speak, as he talked to her of his own childhood, an impossibly remote world. 'If you'd had enough of a place, or the people hadn't been kind,' he'd said, 'or there was richer pickings in some other place another travellin' family told Father about, well, you'd put the horse in the shafts and pick up the reins and *coor* the *drom*[5], you know, take to the road again. I loved that,

---

[4] Stealing a horse.

[5] Travel the road.

hearing them hooves striking the ground, watching the *grai's* ears, and his mane in the breeze.'

'Can't we live like that?' she'd asked.

'No, my maidy, we wouldn't be let to. It's got worse, see? Good *atchin' tans*[6] fenced off, though they're not getting used for anything else, the *gavvers*[7] always on to you for "loitering", though all they make you do is go and loiter somewhere else. I wunt want that life for your mother neither. If you ain't brought up to it, it's hard work – it's hard enough work if you *are*. And you and your brothers can read and write, and I'm proud that you can. Tom takes after me, of course, likes working with his hands and bein' outside and that, but David always liked his books – no surprise to me he went to be a minister.'

Alone with these thoughts in the soft darkness, Harry prodded a tussock of trampled grass, then froze, now fully in the present. Nearby she'd heard someone strike a match.

'Who's there?'

Nothing.

'Come out, then! Afraid I'll bite?'

The silence seemed to hold its breath. The sweet tang of tobacco wafted on the soft air. Not a brand she recognised. Not her father's Old Holborn – the cigarettes he rolled himself and that Mother had at last succeeded in getting him to smoke outside.

---

[6] Stopping places.

[7] Gavengros=policemen.

The thud of footsteps. Harry turned, but too late. A hand wrapped around her waist whilst another clamped over her mouth. Years later she was still able to describe the feel of that hand, greasy with pork fat, that tobacco stench.

Hot breath at her ear, and something stood dark between her and the moon. *Oh God, there are two of them!* A scrape of metal.

'Be a good girl. Bert's got a knife, see?' The mouth was so close to her that the man's breath was hot and damp against her ear. His body was close against her – and Harry knew, having been around horses for as long as she could remember, what it was that pushed at her. 'Go through that lovely face of yours like it was butter.'

Something cold pricking beneath her chin. *Lift it higher!*

'Make ourselves comfortable, shall we? Ground's dry, ain't it? Won't even get grass stains on that pretty dress.'

'*How dare you!*' she said, against the hand.

'Forgot what I said, did yer?' said the voice against her ear. 'Best not annoy my friend here!' He pulled her back, away from the knife, but then forced her onto her knees.

'First dibs to me,' said the second man. 'That's what we agreed.'

Harry was pushed backwards; her head jarred on the ground.

'Bert!' she cried. 'You've known me for years . . .'

'Time we got better acquainted, then,' said Bert. 'Stop 'er noise will yer?'

The other one forced a rag into her mouth, pushing it so far in she thought she would suffocate. Her chest tightened. Bert and George. Her mind raced, suddenly seeing with crisp clarity all those clues, one behind the other. There had been hoppers, of course, who'd gently tried to flirt with the foreman's beautiful daughter as she'd grown from child to young woman, only to be met with polite disinterest. Bert hadn't ever approached her, but worse, he'd stared, each year more than before. She remembered him earlier that afternoon muttering something behind his hand to his friend George, who'd looked, and sniggered. Harry had put her nose in the air and walked off.

'Nah, don't kill 'er though! We can't say she asked for *that!*'

The rag was pulled partly out, and her burning lungs gasped for air.

*

How much longer? Harry sobbed, her teeth sunk in that dirty rag. But one moonlit leering face was replaced by another. From a distance the shouts and laughter of the dregs of the party reached her – the people who didn't want to let go of the closest thing they ever had to a holiday – people having the best night of their year, whilst yards away she was caught in the worst of her life.

'You done now?' came Bert's voice, anxious, urgent.

*

Harry rolled onto her side on the stubbly grass, and curled up like a hedgehog. She trembled, yawning incontrollably. *I am so blessed cold!* Turning her face upwards, she moaned at the stars. They blinked back at her indifferently. *Oh God, what's that noise – they can't be coming back!* Something blurry moved amongst the hop poles but before she could lift her head it rushed at her.

'Oh Digby, Digby!' she howled, and buried her face in the lurcher's musty pelt.

'Harry! Harry!' The voices – there were two of them – sounded a long way off. Digby set up a whine. Lying curled on the ground clutching the dog, Harry felt the reverberation of boots on the dry earth.

'She's over here, Sam! Hurt!' Vanlo dropped on his knees beside Harry and leant over her, touching her shoulder, another hand on her forehead. Harry released Digby and tried to push Vanlo away.

'It's me, Harry. Your uncle Vanlo. What happened?'

'*Oh Vanlo!*' She felt her entire body go into spasm.

Sam charged up.

'My maidy!'

'*Dad!*' She tried to say Bert's name, but couldn't get it out. 'He ... they ...' She turned her head and retched into the grass.

'Oh no ... no ...' murmured her father, kneeling beside her. 'I'll get 'em, Harry. I promise. They'll pay. I'll make 'em pay!'

'Let's get her home, Sam!'

'Home?' wept Harry. 'This was home.' Her father put one arm under her shoulders, the other under her knees and lifted her limp body, grunting with the effort.

'No, put me down,' wailed Harry, slithering out of her father's arms. 'They've gone! They've gone!'

'Who was it?'

Harry gulped for air. 'Bert – that one you had words with about the tally – and George.'

'Harry! Wait!'

She'd fled, screaming amongst the stripped hop poles.

*

Harry was still trembling as a weeping Ellen bathed her scratched and bloodied feet, for she had run off leaving her sandals behind. For a long time afterwards Harry could not remember anything of how she got back to the house – but when the day at last came when she stood up and told the scores of faces silently turned in her direction everything of the events of that night, she was able to describe all of it with absolute clarity. But then, at one o'clock in the morning, she found herself in her own bed, the only one she had ever slept in but for occasional visits to her Uncle John's manse in Euston, or her brother's in Birmingham, muffled in her warmest pyjamas despite the mild night. Ellen was sitting on the bed crying. Harry vaguely remembered now crouching in the kitchen in the old hip bath, brought in from the outhouse, clutching the bar of Sunlight until her mother had gently taken it from her, and rubbed it on a flannel with which she'd washed her back.

'You're bruised even here, Harry, all along your spine,' she'd said.

'Where are my clothes?'

'I've folded them and put them in a bag. So we can show the police.'

'The police,' said Harry, and shut her eyes.

'I've called the doctor.'

CHAPTER EIGHT

French's Farm

At half past one in the morning Harry sat on the edge of the bed and looked up at the doctor she had known all her life, a dedicated member of the chapel and the man who had delivered her, in Ellen's final, frantic and shortest birthing.

'I'm sorry to say it won't just be me,' said Dr Titterton. 'If you go ahead with this there will be a police doctor who will examine you too. I'm afraid . . .' He hesitated.

'Go on,' said Harry.

'They don't much like it if you wash first, I'm told.'

There was a silence.

'I can understand absolutely why you did so, Harmony. I am not a woman, but for any self-respecting one, it seems to be the most instinctive thing to do. Like baptism, being reborn.'

'I stank,' she whispered. 'I stank of them.'

Titterton took her hands. 'I shall write all of this down – all my observations, I mean. Nobody—' he moved her hands up and down for emphasis '—nobody could be in any doubt of the violence done to you. The bruising to your spine, to your face, not just the . . . tearing. I can give all of this to the police surgeon in Canterbury. He's a sensible enough chap. For now, I'm going to give you a bromide. Then, in the morning – I mean later this morning – if you wish, your father has said he can take you to to make your report.'

'Where *is* Dad?'

'He's gone with Mr Buckland and the rural constable to try and find the culprits. Along with that fine dog of yours. But it looks as if the two of them are long gone. Probably hitched a lift home with a lorry, would be my guess.' He released her hands, and took a syringe out of his bag. 'Any preference as to which arm, Harmony? Grit your teeth.'

'Here . . . ahhh!'

'Brave girl. You *are* a brave girl.' He wrapped the syringe in a clean handkerchief and snapped his bag shut. 'Harmony, just one thing I will say, as an old friend.'

'Yes?' said Harry, feeling the numbing effects of the injection already.

'Not all men are brutes. There are many who are good and kind.'

'Mmm . . .'

'Lie down, now. Is that the cat I can hear scratching at the door?'

'She's not allowed . . .'

'Perhaps tonight is an exception.' He got up and softly opened the door. Mittens chirped, and in a blur of tabby fur landed on the bed, where Harry's eyes were already closing.

*

A few hours later, Sam watched Harry's slim figure disappear down a corridor of the police station, a policewoman at her left shoulder, a policeman at her right. Someone behind him cleared his throat.

'Mr Loveridge?'

'That's me,' he said, turning round, to look into the face of a man of about his own age. His glance flickered over the officer's uniform, noting the three chevrons on his sleeve.

'Sergeant? What are they doing with my daughter?' said Sam.

'She'll see the doctor first. Then she'll be interrogated.'

'Interrogated? She ain't done nothing.'

'Wrong choice of words. Interviewed, is what I mean. Only . . . if she goes ahead with her complaint, then interrogation would be the right word to use about the men's lawyers . . . I'd be remiss if I didn't warn you of that. Look, come in here. Better not to talk about these matters out in the corridor.'

*

'I'm a father too, Loveridge,' said the sergeant, across the table. 'The problem is there were two of them, and she knows them both. One of them for some years.' Seeing Sam's expression, he added: 'I'm just anticipating the arguments the defence would use.'

'Them bruises, and all the rest.'

'They'd just say they were being a bit lively.'

'*Lively?*'

'I know this is going to sound mad, but her case would've been stronger if they'd used the knife on her, even just a bit.'

'I dunt believe I'm hearing this.'

'I've never found it easy to say. A stranger up an alley is a different matter. They'll want to know why she was wandering about in the dark on a night when everyone was making merry.'

'Her own hop garden. She was at home, Sergeant.'

'You told my colleague there'd been a row earlier, over a tally.'

'That's right. That – Bert—' Sam said the name as though he held it at arm's length, in pincers '—he'd been cheating and tried to blame another hopper.'

'Were there witnesses – to the row, I mean?'

'Oh yeah, plenty of 'em. Only they've gone home. Ellen'll have their addresses. Only not for Wester Ackleton. He didn't say where he was going on to next.'

'A Gypsy, is he, this Mr Ackleton?'

'Yeah. What's that matter?'

'It's the kind of thing a defence barrister, never mind a jury, would pick up on.'

'I got thrown out of a pub in Harbledown just a year into the war. Landlord said, "I'm not serving none of you lot in here" though my money was as good as anyone else's. I'd occasion to go back there, when I was in the ARP, 'cos they wasn't observing blackout properly. This time there was a notice in the window saying we wasn't welcome. In I went in my uniform and helmet, and the fellow tried to bribe me with ale – we'd had to warn him before, see. I took my helmet off, and fetched his notice from out of the window and tore it up. "I can read," I said, "and so can my son what's in the Buffs in Italy at this very moment." I wished I'd had Ellen's little Brownie with me 'cos his face was a picture. Each time they've a war you think everything's going to change. Does for some.' He sighed. 'Harry was meant to go to the university. I've played by the rules, Sergeant. We all have. So I dunt know that I can say what you've just said to my Harry, though I understand why you said it. It's up to her, not me.' He paused. 'How long are they going to be with her, though?'

The sergeant glanced up at the clock on the wall behind Sam. 'It's only been twenty minutes. The surgeon mightn't even have finished with her yet.'

'Wunt our own doctor enough?'

'Um . . . our man probably sees more of this . . . knows what to look for.'

Sam flushed.

'There'll be a nurse with her. And a woman officer when she's questioned.'

'This feels like the longest twenty minutes of my life.'

'And it will be for her, too.'

'I know. She tole her mother she thought she was hours there . . . with them brutes. She said she didn't know why we hadn't missed her earlier, but it was only about half an hour.' Sam covered his eyes.

'She should say that – in court, I mean. It's another reason to believe her.'

Sam looked up, his face distorted. 'I was at the feast, see, sayin' goodbye to them all. Everyone was in such a good mood, and not just because of the beer. That Bert's old aunt – a decent old soul, bin coming here for years, apologised for her nevvy's causing trouble over the tally, said she wunt let him come again even if I was to say it was all right. I thought then he'd already took hisself off home, only she said something like "Where's the blighter got to anyway? I tole him he'd a cheek showing up for the feast after all that but he said something to me I shan't repeat – to mind my own business, in a manner of speaking." That was when I started to wonder, Sergeant, and it was like someone had forced me to drink something so cold it burned my insides. Harry had been at the feast earlier, but she must've gone off. That wasn't anything to be surprised about. She likes people, but she's always said she likes being alone too – what I mean is that she gets on with people but she dunt always need 'em. Bein' alone helps her think, she says. An' then Digby comes up – that's my old dog – making them whickery noises and pawing at me. He's a clever beast. Always knows when something ain't right. That's when I went to get my brother Vanlo out of his wagon – he ain't partikler keen on big gatherings. What you might call shy. And him and me went off with Digby to find her. I'll never forgive myself for not doing that earlier. Only, Harry's always tole me I fuss her too much. When I was her age – and younger – I was never alone; that's the Romani way. Somebody'd always know what I was up to.'

'You cannot blame yourself. You must remember you weren't at fault, and nor was Harry. *She* has to believe that. Otherwise no jury will.'

At last there was a discreet knock at the door, and a young constable came in, handing the sergeant a note.

'They've finished with her.'

*

A door clicked open at the far end of the corridor where Sam and the sergeant were standing. A tired-looking middle-aged man in a too-tight utility suit came out first, putting an elastic band around his notebook.

'Couldn't you have done the talking?' whispered Sam.

'Hills is a good chap. Thorough.'

'Oh *dordi*, look at her!'

The slight figure that emerged with a uniformed policewoman directly behind her looked diminished, defeated. Even at that distance Sam could see Harry's eyes were puffy, her shoulders sagged. The crisp white blouse she had put on that morning looked crumpled, as if she'd been in a struggle. She caught sight of Sam, and rushed towards him, her hands held out.

'*Take me home!*' she howled into his chest.

'You aren't going home on the bus.' Sam heard the sergeant say, more as a statement than a question. 'I'll run you back myself.'

Harry looked round.

'That's kind of you . . . only I don't want anyone seeing me in a police car,' she said.

'I was thinking of my own Austin Seven,' said the sergeant. 'I'll leave you on that bit of road between Bridge and Patrixbourne. So nobody will know.'

*

'Hello, Mum.'

'Harry!' Ellen put down her pen on the pile of primary four compositions, and got to her feet. Her daughter looked over the too-big, childish handwriting and smiled.

'I've homework to do too,' she said. 'I'm going back tomorrow.'

'Are you sure?' said Ellen, coming forward to embrace her daughter.

Her voice muffled in her mother's shoulder, Harry said, 'I've never been surer of anything. I'm not letting them get in the way of my books. Where's Mittens, Mum?'

'I've not seen her come down. She's probably still on your bed.'

'I'll go up then.' Harry gently but firmly extricated herself from Ellen's arms and went upstairs before her mother could see her cry.

*

As soon as she heard Harry's door close, Ellen collapsed into her chair. Sam came and stood behind her, his hands on her shoulders. She started to weep.

'Dunt let her hear you, my Ellen.'

'She's so calm!'

'She wunt calm in the station. She was crying like a five-year-old, when they'd finished with her.'

'What if she has a child, Sam? Not knowing which of those beasts gave it her either.'

'Oh, Ellen . . . if that happens we'll have to help her, whatever she decides. Here . . .' He took out his handkerchief and gently dried his wife's face.

'I'll make some tea,' she murmured.

'You wunt. I'll do it. You go on handing out stars to them kiddies.'

'I'll take a cup up to her, though.'

*

Sam looked up as Ellen came slowly down the stairs.

'Well?'

'She's got her books out, but she's sitting in front of them wetting the cat's fur.'

'*Dordi!*'

'She said we're not to talk about it again, before the sergeant comes back with whatever the next step is, or if there are "other developments". But she wants her day in court. Those were exactly the words she used. I don't know, Sam, which is better – for her to bottle it all up the way she seems intent on doing, or talking about it so she's reliving it all over again. I'd do anything to protect her from any more harm, but I don't know *what* it is I should do.'

'No more do I, my Ellen.'

'She's quite extraordinary, though. She's always known her own mind, even when she was little.'

'I remember,' said Sam, smiling in spite of his misery.

'When I was talking to her just now, it was as if I was the young one that needed comforting, and she was the older, sensible one who knew what to do. She said: "I'll know what's what in a couple of weeks." She had her diary out, and had worked out – well, you know – when her monthlies were due. She's asked me if I'd go up to the school though and talk to Miss Shaw. Let her know how things are and to tell her that provided everything is . . . all right . . . then she wants to go for this scholarship.'

'Well, that's good, ain't it?'

'Yes – and no. She's determined to go away from here.'

Sam's shoulders sagged. 'Then mebbe so mun we, my Ellen.'

'We should let her make her move first.'

CHAPTER NINE

Old Dover Road, Canterbury
October 1955

'Sit down, Harry,' said Miss Shaw, hitching the shoulders of her chalk-dusty teacher's gown.

'I'll be late for French . . .' said Harry, gazing at the chaos of Miss Shaw's desk.

'From what I'm told, you of all girls can afford to be late for one lesson. I've squared it with Mam'selle.'

'What does she know? What do any of them know?' flared Harry.

'Only that there was a disturbance on your father's farm and that you were needed to give evidence to the police. The only ones who know the truth are myself and the headmistress. We shall keep it that way unless you tell us otherwise, Harry.'

'The truth?' said Harry. 'Miss Shaw, I haven't even told Mum and Dad about what was really said in that room. I catch her crying into the dishes or when she's correcting homework . . . and he's gone all quiet – a man who talks to everyone, dogs and horses included. I don't want to burden them further when I can see they're trying to be strong for me. The truth is that going to the police was like having it all happen again near enough. The truth is that I wasn't believed, Miss Shaw, or rather, that even if I was believed it didn't matter. There were two of them and one of me, and I was "wandering about in a hop field in the dark where there were men present" and who did I think the jury would listen to? The man told me, "We're saying this for your own good, Harry." I *hate* it when anyone says that—'

'So do I.'

'He said, "They'll just think it was some high spirits got a bit out of hand," and looked at me as if I should be grateful to him for saving me from more trouble. There was a policewoman with him, but I think she was just there for show, as she never said anything and barely looked at me, just went on making her notes. When she went out at the end she never even said goodbye to me.'

'Oh, Harry . . .'

'I don't want anyone's pity, Miss Shaw,' said Harry, starting to cry. Miss Shaw retrieved a box of tissues from somewhere within the pile of papers on her desk. Harry noticed the words 'man size'. She blew her nose vigorously.

'You do not have my pity. You have my rage.'

Harry stopped wiping her nose, but still held the tissue to her face.

'I hope, Harry, that you never lose your own rage. I simply wanted you to know that I am here whenever you need someone to listen to you, someone to whom you can express whatever you are feeling. At any time. Here,' she said, handing over a folded piece of paper. 'This is my address, and my telephone number. I know I don't need to ask you not to share them with anyone else. But remember your mother and father want to be there for you too. They've told me that they think *you're* trying to be strong for *their* sake, when a good shout and bawl might be good for all three of you.'

Harry lowered the tissue. 'Thank you,' she said, taking the note.

'May I say something, Harry?'

'Yes . . .'

'What I think you should remember is that what was perpetrated on you was an act of violence, an exercise of power. Those two demonstrated what they thought of as their superior strength, with the added assurance that, unlike other forms of physical assault, they could defend themselves by insisting you'd wanted them to do what they did. From what your mother said, they were attacking you to attack your father, as though you were his property – like setting fire to a hayrick or stealing his bicycle. That's what's so monstrous – one of the many things that's so monstrous – about what happened to you. But do try to remember that there are some decent men in the world, men who would be revolted and horrified by what happened to you.'

'But they might think differently of me. Like poor Tess of the d'Urbervilles and Angel Clare.'

'Angel Clare was a fool!' said Miss Shaw. 'There are fools like him, unfortunately, who aren't just in the pages of a book. But *you'd* never settle for a fool, I trust. A practical question, if I may? When is the curse due?'

'In about ten days.'

'Trauma such as you have undergone – I call it trauma advisedly, as much as if you'd been injured in a serious motoring accident – might interfere with your cycle. You could say that our bodies shut down, to defend ourselves against further harm.'

'Like those poor women in the camps?'

'Ye-es, like them, though starvation played its part, not only fear. You must distract yourself – easier said than done. A bracing game of hockey—'

Harry wrinkled her nose.

'I forgot you dislike team sports. Something energetic though.'

'Cycling?'

'Ideal . . . only, did you propose to do that on your own? I worry about you being left alone with your own thoughts.'

'I'd like to go to Whitstable. Sea air, you know?'

'Not alone, Harry.'

'No, I know I can't. That's something else they took from me, Miss Shaw. I used to enjoy being on my own. But I daren't now, even in the safest places. Only in my bedroom, and only if I know there's someone downstairs.'

'My old Armstrong is heavy but serviceable still . . . do you think you could bear the company of an old woman clanking along on such an embarrassing machine?'

'Oh Miss Shaw! I should love that!'

'Why don't we cycle down, I'll treat you to tea and cakes at the Red Spider and when our tummies are full we could push the bikes back along the track where the Crab and Winkle Line used to be.'

*

Her fingers on the door handle, Harry turned back to the room. 'Miss Shaw?'

'Yes, Harry?'

'How is it you knew the right things to say?'

Miss Shaw smiled. 'You mean that as a middle-aged, middle-class, unmarried lady I shouldn't know? When one has the care of young girls, one must be forearmed, on their behalf. And in wartime one learns a great deal one did not expect to learn. Most of all, I think, a girl should be able to talk about whatever has happened to her, and be believed.'

*

A week later, at about six in the evening, the little Austin Seven puttered to a halt in front of the farmhouse, and the sergeant got out, dressed in civvies. Ellen answered his soft knock.

'I'm sorry for disturbing you at teatime, Mrs Loveridge,' he said.

'Do come in,' said Ellen. 'Will you eat with us?'

'Perhaps a cup of tea,' said the sergeant, taking off his hat and ducking slightly to get under the low door frame. 'My wife will be expecting me. Is Mr Loveridge at home?'

As if on cue, Sam followed him in. 'Sergeant!' he exclaimed. 'Sorry I wunt here. Me and my bruv have been out shooting those pore blind rabbits. Did you want them skins, my Ellen?'

'I don't think I could even bear to look at them, Sam.'

'I'll bury the lot then. Where's Harry?'

Hesitant feet came down the stairs.

'Hello, Sergeant,' said Harry, putting out a hand.

'Dunt know why we're all standing. Sit yourself down, Sergeant,' said Sam. 'You'll have news?'

'Not good news,' cut in Harry. 'I can see that in your face.'

There was a stiff silence. Finally, the sergeant said, 'I'm sorry. It wasn't my decision.'

'They're getting off scot-free, is that what you mean?' said Harry.

Ellen uttered a small scream, and stuffed her knuckles into her mouth. Sam struck the table so hard that the teacups rattled.

'I've read the notes,' said the policeman. 'It's not the approach I'd have taken, but I know why my colleague spoke to you as he did. If this had gone to trial, pretty much what he asked you, Harry, would have been asked again across a courtroom, with scores of people gawping from the public benches. He wanted to test your mettle. It's probably no comfort, Miss Loveridge, but he believed you. Otherwise the suspects would not have been interviewed.'

'They were?'

'Yes . . .'

'And?'

'They denied everything.'

'*What?*'

'I would rather spare you the details, Miss—'

'Don't,' said Harry. 'After what I went through, I don't think "details" can trouble me much.'

'Very well. Bert Parker said you'd met him by arrangement,' said the sergeant, unable to meet her accusing eyes. 'He claimed you'd been flirting with him every weekend he'd been there. And the other one backed him up.'

'Flirting? What about my bruises?'

The policeman remembered the words of Parker's testimony, jeering even on the page: '*She wanted it rough. So I did it the way she wanted. Some of 'em like it that way.*' 'He said the ground was hard.'

'*What?*'

'Harry . . .' said Ellen, putting her hand over her daughter's clenched fist.

'Don't, Mum, I'm all right,' said Harry in a voice that was anything but.

'What did the other one say?' said Sam quietly.

'He denies even having been there.'

Sam struck the table again. '*This is all wrong!*' he shouted and, scraping his chair back on the flagstones, looked round as though he wanted to break something.

'I agree, Loveridge,' said the sergeant.

'What's that you say?'

'I agree with you. And so, by the way, did the police surgeon. But they don't think they'd get a conviction, and your girl would be destroyed in the witness box.'

White-faced, Harry got up and rushed out through the scullery. The back door banged shut before anyone could follow.

'I'll go, Sam,' said Ellen. 'Sergeant, I appreciate your going to the trouble of coming out to tell us personally. Harry isn't shooting the messenger. It's just that the idea of seeing justice done has been what has kept her going.'

*

Half an hour later, Ellen returned to find Sam sitting alone at the table, his head bowed. She put a hand on his shoulder.

'Sam,' she said softly, 'there is one bit of good news today.'

'Oh?' he said, looking up.

'Yes. There isn't going to be a child.' His shoulders sagged, as if invisible strings that had held him taut had suddenly been cut. He reached up to the hand. 'Sit here a moment, my Ellen.'

She reached for a chair.

'No, here, on my knees.'

'Oh, Sam, we've not done that for years!'

'Well, we oughter. Just so's I can hold you. There . . . Remember how it was, Ellen? How we was going to leave all of 'em behind, years ago . . . just go up to the road and wait for the carrier for Oxford?'

'But there was your mother, and mine.'

'And then I was taken off by main force.' He shut his eyes, his head resting on her breast. Ellen's lips brushed his wiry, greying hair.

'When I found you again, Ellen ... and we was locked up 'cos of poor Harold, an' after I got out we got this *kenner*[8], an' Vanlo turned up – everything seemed like it turned out, you know, *kushti.*[9] We was happy.'

'But?'

'I'm not sayin' it was easy – settlin', I mean.'

'I know.'

'Only, in the travellin' life, when there was trouble, with the *gavvers,* or on account of the poaching, or the horses bein' out to grass and a farmer not liking it, well, you'd pack up your bits and sticks an' move on. Now the trouble's come to us, to our Harry, an' we can't go. An' I dunt know how to face them other poor hoppers when they come round again, though they done nothing wrong.'

'Do you want us to leave here, Sam?'

'I dunt know ...'

'You warned me years ago I'd be a poor man's wife. We thought we'd have lots of children. How easy it was for me to fall pregnant ... remember? And how easy to lose the poor mites too.'

Sam's arms tightened around her.

'Well, I said I'd go anywhere with you then, and I still would. Only, it's a comfort to me to tend Flora's grave and talk to her there.'

'And to me. You've the teaching too. You always wanted that.'

---

[8] House.

[9] Good.

'I did. I do. But there are children everywhere, Sam. And Flora's in our hearts. Only, it's Harry we've to consider. She's afraid of the dark now, which she's never been. We've to lock everything up when we never did before. Would she feel safer somewhere else? Or is it here that matters, the place she knows, even though she – and it – have been trampled in this way?'

'We mun ask her.'

'But not yet. Let her come out with it herself.'

CHAPTER TEN

Vanlo's wagon, French's Farm

Harry was sitting opposite the stove in Vanlo's *vardo*.[10] It had not been harnessed to a horse in years, but sat on hard standing within sight of the Loveridges' cottage. Yet Harry's uncle maintained his home as carefully as if he was going to take to the road the following day. The interior was immaculate, the engraved glass panels that hid the built-in bed polished with newspaper, not a speck of dust on the shelves at Harry's back. Vanlo was pouring tea into the cup kept for his niece.

'I dunt know what they've said to you, the doctors and that – your teachers mebbe,' said Vanlo.

'Only my housemistress knows, her and the headmistress,' said Harry.

'What's a housemistress? Funny way to talk about a teacher, ain't it?'

'She's sort of in charge. A bit of a mother hen to her girls.'

'Kind lady, is she?'

---

[10] Wagon.

'Oh yes. I love her – nearly as much as I love Mum.'

'That's lucky. Harry . . . well, you know I never had no proper schooling, so my suggestions mightn't be as good as what others say. I know plenty of other things just by doing 'em, that and adding a bit of oil here and there. There's nothing I dunt know about how to get an old tractor going, or a reaper-binder, or any of them things. You just know that all the bits come together somehow, like your own body does, and if something is out of shape then it'll make everything else pull out of whack too. You can tell what's wrong with an engine by listening, same as you can tell what's up with a horse by looking at his teeth or his eyes or his coat. If I'd to study all that in a book I think it'd make too much noise for me, if you see what I mean, and get in the way of my thinking. I'm sorry, Harry, I'm maundering . . .'

'Books help me to think, though, Vanlo. It's as if I can walk into them and into another world. I'm never alone, you see, if I've something to read. The only problem is when they take over.'

'What do you mean?'

'I read this book once about a girl who had near enough the same thing happen to her. The man ruined her life. She was good for no one after that. So many years after she killed him.'

Vanlo smiled. 'Good for her!'

'It wasn't, Vanlo. They hanged her.'

'*Dordi!* That ain't real life though, is it? You said it was a book.'

'The wrong things do happen, though, don't they? That poor woman they hanged in the summer though there was a big petition got up to save her – she'd killed the man who kicked her baby out of her. I sat up there crying, not just for me, but for that woman in London, and the girl in the book. A girl who never existed except in that writer's head, but who felt like me.'

'That's what I was trying to say, only I'm not good at explaining myself the way you are. When I'm working on something, you see, it's as if I get out of my own head and walk around a bit. I can forget what I'm doing and that I should be eating my sandwiches, because the time's gone by without my noticing. What I mean is, when you was little, Harry, before you went to the school, you used to scribble pictures on any scrap of paper you could get your hands on. Well, I wondered if you'd like to do that again, mebbe? Help get you out of yourself a bit.'

'I love art at school . . .'

'I bin to that art college place in Canterbury, Harry. It was when you was there with the *gavvers*. I couldn't get them to understand what I was after to begin with. They thought I was looking for work, or rag and bone. I was, in a way.' He rushed on. 'But they was nice people. Not the usual *gauje*[11] kind. A bit like the vicar. It was him said to try there – no I never said nothing about what happened to you, only that I wanted to make you a present. Anyway, them students gev me this broken easel, and tole me what other bits and pieces you'd need. I've fixed the easel. I'd to replace a piece and the wood wunt quite the same as the rest so I sanded it all down and varnished it and you'd never

---

[11] Non-Gypsy.

know ... I've put some new hinges on and now there's not a squeak in any of 'em. It's a clever thing, Harry, it all folds up like a piano accordion. I bin to get paints and brushes and that and cleaned up a canvas bag and put a bit of webbing on it for a handle. If you'd like to see ...'

*

The October day was mild enough that the woman and the girl were able to sit out beneath the overhanging roof of the café, and look out across the shingle. Harry's housemistress watched her pupil's eyes, transfixed by the ebb and flow of the water.

'Another scone?' asked Miss Shaw.

'Oh yes please. That ride has made me ravenous.'

The teacher watched as Harry intently and carefully spread the butter, then the jam, then the cream, and tested how far she could push down the top of the scone without the mixture oozing out.

'Penny for them, Harry?'

'I was just thinking about Mum and Dad. About how happy they are. I was wondering if I will ever be like that.'

'In time. You'll find a man you like, and who likes you, and when you do you'll just know. As they must have known.'

'Even now?'

'Especially now. Because everything you do from this time on will be on your own terms.'

'You sound so sure. About knowing when you've found someone you're meant to be with. Yet you aren't married.'

'I found that person all right, Harry. But he died. He has a pristine white headstone amongst scores of others in a place called Châlons-sur-Marne. I went there some years ago with his mother. And his name is on a plinth beneath a statue of a soldier leaning on his rifle in the village he grew up in.'

'I'm sorry . . .'

'We don't learn much though, do we? That was meant to be the war to end all wars. I'm so glad you've decided you want to study History, Harry, because historians are prophets. The only snag is that they're not always believed.'

'You mean like the cause of the second war being the peace of the first?'

'Precisely.'

'How did you get over it – losing him, I mean?'

'I haven't. Not really. I think about Stan every day. He wasn't Stanley, but Athelstan. His father was an avid reader of Walter Scott. Yes, I can see from your face you think Scott boring. So do I, to be honest, but he was very popular once. My way of coping was to throw myself into a cause. I marched for the vote. It was more or less won by then, because with all the men who could be spared, and those who couldn't being at the front, women were doing men's jobs. There was a terrible scene at home. My father tried to thrash me, only I wouldn't take the thrashing, so he tore around his study after me, knocking everything over. I was nineteen, and I was bereaved, but he was a Victorian patriarch through and through.'

Harry gazed at Miss Shaw in astonishment. 'My father has never hit me. I don't think he's ever even dreamed of it, no matter how annoying I can be.'

'That's because he's never wanted to break your spirit, as my father wanted to break mine. And in my view, though perhaps not many of my colleagues would agree with me, much less the great British public, I don't think any child deserves to be hit. Anyway, on that occasion I finally refused to do what Father wanted. He gave up when his arm was tired of waving his cane about and his face was all red and shiny – my goodness, I can see it now! I escaped to my room and locked myself in. Only then did I let myself cry.'

'Didn't your mother have any say?'

'Dear good soul. She was terrified of him. But she came upstairs and knocked softly at the door, so I let her in. She'd brought me a glass of warm milk, just as she used to do when I was little. She put it down on the bedside table and then hugged me. She said to me: "I am so proud of you!" Father died six months after that, and then we found that he wasn't as good at making investments as he claimed to be. To me that was a liberation. It meant there was no argument about me having to earn my living. Mother sold that pretentious, uncomfortable house, and bought a nice little flat, and with the difference there was just about enough money to support me through university and then teacher training. I'd found my cause, Harry, and I have never regretted fighting it. Educating young girls to become young women is the purpose of my life. And now you must find yours.'

'I have no idea what that should be. You and those others have done all the work. We can vote . . . and . . . we don't have to have those enormous families anymore.'

'That's true, in part at least. But there are plenty of girls whose colleagues do a whip-round for them when they marry, and then those blushing brides find themselves sacked by the boss. There are many jobs a girl could do but her trade union brethren will prevent her, because a woman's wages are usually less than a man's. Whether that becomes your battle or something else, Harry, there is still much to be won.'

'I know I can sense in my bones when something's right or wrong, but I feel I don't have the arguments, only the emotions. I mean, I hate that money is spent on developing atomic energy when it seems to me to be a chained dragon just waiting to break free, but I also feel for men who toil underground to heat cities where people breathe soot from the day they were born. I am sure there must be other ways, but I don't know what they are.'

'Take things one step at a time, Harry,' said Miss Shaw, handing her a napkin.

'Oh, thank you,' said Harry, wiping away the stickiness of jam and cream.

'Just don't dampen down your fire. You have a splendid suite of A levels and now the scholarship exams ahead of you. You'll break through that tape as quickly as Dr Bannister. Start with your education – the rest will follow.'

*

Two weeks later, Vanlo came up to Harry when she was working intently in charcoals in the yard at the back of the house.

'Ssh. I'm doing his portrait. Don't wake him up,' and she pointed at Digby, apparently asleep on a pile of sacking. The lurcher opened one eye and obediently shut it again.

'You've got him,' marvelled Vanlo in a whisper. 'You could put your hand on that an' feel how rough his coat is.'

'Don't though! You'd smudge it.' But Harry was delighted. 'I want to give it to Dad.'

'I'll make a frame for it, Harry.'

'You were right, Uncle Vanlo. This does take me out of myself.'

'I've something else for you, mebbe. I'll be in the barn.'

*

'There's a bit of work to do yet,' said Vanlo, 'the old girl ain't looking her best at the moment.'

They stood in the entrance to the barn. In the far corner, something lay long and low beneath a tarpaulin. *Too small for farm machinery,* thought Harry. Vanlo went over to it and uncovered it.

'The auctioneer's man said I'd have to paint them letters out. Otherwise everybody'll think you're the postman. Do you want it red still, or some other colour?'

Harry stared at the little motorbike, her lips parted. 'Red, Vanlo, but maybe a bit of something – decoration. As if it was a *vardo,* I mean.' She hugged him. Her voice was muffled in the old battledress blouse he wore for jobs on the farm; on market days he dressed up in shirt and waistcoat and *diklo.*[12] 'How was it you knew just what I needed? First the easel and now this!'

---

[12] Neckerchief.

CHAPTER ELEVEN

Scholarship year
December 1955

'Thank you for coming to see me, Mrs Loveridge,' said Miss Shaw. 'On such a cold day too.'

'Harry isn't having problems with her schoolwork?'

'Problems? Far from it. She is one of the brightest girls I have ever had the pleasure to teach. If anything, she is almost *too* single-minded. She is utterly determined to succeed. She works as if her life depends on it. I wish, almost, that she would relax a little. I am no psychiatrist, but I'd say it is her way of sublimating what happened to her. Getting her own back, almost.'

'And I wanted to thank *you*, for all you have done for her. I think it's you who has brought her back from the brink.'

'You flatter me. She's a remarkable young woman in her own right, but in all the conversations I have had with her the thing she stresses again and again is the unconditional love and support she has from you and her father – and her uncle. It was a stroke of genius of his to get her those painting things. I sometimes think – with no disrespect to my colleagues in the art department – that our curriculum obliges us to be a bit narrow, to produce excellent draughtswomen but to lose some individual verve in the process. It would seem that Harry has both gifts.'

'I wish, though, that she could recover some happiness.'

'That may come in time. Regrettably, this is not the first occasion in my teaching career, or indeed in my wartime service, that I've encountered outrages like Harry's. There doesn't seem to be a way to anticipate how a girl will deal with it. Some turn in on themselves, going out of their way to make themselves as unattractive as possible, as if what has happened is their own fault. I knew one though who went in the opposite direction – flinging herself at men who could only do her harm, with no regard for her own well-being or even her health.'

'Dear God . . .'

'In that dark place perhaps she thought she was exercising some sort of control – choosing who would exploit her rather than letting others choose for her. These are only my observations, of course. A lot can depend on the legal process, or lack of it. For Harry that will always be unfinished business. Yet she refuses to be beaten, as if she regards any failure on her part as a victory for her attackers. Next month she will need to travel to the universities for which she'd like to obtain a scholarship. This year is dedicated to supporting and coaching her to that end.'

'She's certainly taking it seriously. Her nose is never out of her books. She barely goes out now, not even to go to hops with her friends. "I've more serious things to do than dance with pimply boys," she says, "treading on my feet and smelling of their dads' aftershave.'"

'She's bright enough that she may end up with a choice of where she goes. Personally, I hope she favours one of the younger universities. History is her driving passion, and there's a good department at Nottingham. It's a city, bigger than anywhere she has lived before, but the university sits on its edge, in beautiful parkland. Yet she wouldn't be shielded from the smoke and toil of a modern, working community, with all its energy and all its inequalities – a city hopeful for the future after all we have gone through.'

'You speak as if you know it well.'

'I was at Oxford, but one of my contemporaries has been warden in a women's hall at Nottingham for the last fifteen years. Margaret Spellman is an able and compassionate woman who would appreciate Harry's qualities and be a true mentor and friend to her. Harry can by all means sit for Oxbridge too, and she could certainly take their academic demands in her stride. There is, however, as you rightly say, the question of her happiness. She might find the other girls in the older institutions to be somewhat entitled in their attitude, their academic community existing at some distance from how the masses toil – I know that a number of my fellow students at Oxford were astonished to learn that there was a car factory on their doorstep. Unlike them, Harry strikes me as having a very strong sense of social justice. Many young people do, of course, and that's one of the charms and attractions of teaching – but you know that.'

'Indeed. I teach tiny children, and I think they have an instinctively stronger sense of right and wrong than many intelligent adults. It's the world that teaches them to be self-serving and cynical.'

'Unless they are given different examples, as you and Harry's father have done. The difference is that Harry wants to do something about her imperfect world. One might say that she's searching for a cause – a calling. She's not merely indignant – about the presumptions of empire, about the Bomb, about the opportunities or lack of them open to us women – and about the injustices meted out to her father's people – she wants to do something about them, and is seeking the tools, the knowledge to enable her to do so. Harry is capable of great things, and does honour to her upbringing.'

'We cannot claim the credit. Harry is who she is.'

'Even so . . . That is why I am suggesting Nottingham, and not just because my dearest friend could look out for her. As an institution it has been there some seventy years or so, but as a university with its own charter it's a fledgling. It hasn't been endowed by monarchs and prelates but by an industrialist – a Wesleyan, I believe – son of a farm labourer, grandson of a herbalist.'

Coltsfoot and thyme, Miss Quainton. Brew it like tea, like it was nettles, or sage – the leaves, not the flower. Ellen heard again a young man's voice, saw herself standing before Sam on a country path beside a wood, as though three days and not three decades had intervened.

'You are smiling.'

'Yes. We live in a world where these things are possible at last.'

'To arms, Mrs Loveridge.'

'To arms!' said Ellen, with tears in her eyes.

*

'Nottingham,' said Harry.

Sam put down his fork. 'Dunt even know where that is. Dunt know no one there.'

'Further up the country. I looked it up in the atlas at school. About fifty miles from Birmingham. About forty miles from Lincoln.'

'Lincoln I've been in,' said Sam slowly, 'but not for a long while. Didn't get to see much of it.' His fist curled beside his plate. His first prison, for evading conscription – where he was punished for looking out of a window. Where a warder beat him so badly he came round in the infirmary.

'Dad?'

'Sorry, my maidy. What was you saying?'

'I have to go there for an exam. If I pass it then they'll give me a scholarship. Nobody'll need to pay for anything. Miss Shaw says I should walk it.'

'But have you got to go so far?'

Harry got up and came around the table, and put her hands on her father's shoulders. She spoke to the back of his head. 'Dad, I love you and Mum. I love this place and it'll always be in my heart, and I'll always want to come back here.'

Sam's eyes met Ellen's across the table.

'I just can't stay here *now*,' went on Harry. 'I want to be somewhere where nobody knows me. Where I can start again. Miss Shaw said, if I get my degree, nobody – nobody – can take that away from me. That's mine forever.'

Sam twisted round, looking up into his daughter's determined face.

'Someone'll go with you.'

Harry frowned, making a small impatient movement of her shoulders that Sam recognised as Ellen's.

'Just this time – for the exam,' he said. 'Just to see you to the door of the place. If you dunt want me, there's your uncle Vanlo. He's good at following people around.'

*

'So this is Nottingham?' said Harry, looking up at the rearing Victorian buildings, the castle crouched on its hill, the vista of factory chimneys. 'It's so big, and noisy, and sooty. Strange after Canterbury. I thought going up St Thomas's Hill was steep, but here everything is up hill and down dale . . . the buildings can't be taller than in London, but they seem so because the streets aren't as wide.'

'Where've we to go to now, my Harry?' said Vanlo.

'It says here we can get a bus – we've to walk down to Old Market Square – just down here . . .'

Ten minutes later, Harry and Vanlo learned from a housewife at the stop that 'Nobody, mi duck, calls it Old

Market. It's Slab Square, that's what it is. Only we just call it the Square.'

*

'I'll wait for you down there, then, in front of that *rai's*[13] head on the stand. When you come out tomorrow.' Vanlo pointed down to the gates on University Boulevard, the two eagles poised either side, and Jesse Boot's bronze bust on its plinth.

'But where will you go?'

'Dunt you worry. I'll find somewhere. You go back in there an' do yourself an' your parents proud. Think about all the places round here you're going to go on that little Bantam.' Vanlo kissed her forehead briefly.

'Thank you, Uncle . . .'

'No tears, now.' He picked up his little canvas bag and slung it over his shoulder.

Harry watched Vanlo's loose-limbed stride as he descended the slope. He took the countryman's shortest route, across the mown grass. As he neared the bottom, he waved, without looking round. Then he was out through the gates, glancing up at Boot's head on its plinth, and swinging left, back in the direction of the city that smouldered on the horizon.

*

---

[13] Gentleman.

'Thank you, Miss Loveridge, for coming to see us today,' said the eldest of her interviewers. 'We expect to make our decision within a fortnight.'

Harry stood up, not sure if she should shake hands. The three gowned figures on the other side of the long table also got up, and the one woman among them reached out her own hand.

'We've enjoyed hearing what you had to say, Harmony. I hope there may be more opportunities for such lively discussions.'

'Oh – thank you. I'm often told I'm a bit too direct.'

'Refreshing.' The woman smiled.

Harry hesitated.

'Was there something else?'

'I . . . I hope very much that you do give me a place. Until I came here I'd never been away from home – I mean, apart from to stay with relatives. And now in a way I don't want to go back, though my mother and father are very dear to me. I've loved every minute of being here – talking with that other girl in our room last night, making our cups of cocoa, even doing the exams. I would promise to work very hard. It would save me – I mean, I think it would transform my life.' Harry flushed. 'Sorry.'

'You have nothing to be sorry for, Miss Loveridge,' said the third academic, a theology lecturer in his fifties. 'I am sure I speak for my colleagues when I say that your enthusiasm does us honour.'

'More than that we cannot say at the present time,' said the older man. 'We promise to be prompt. Try if you can to think of something else for the next two weeks.'

*

Vanlo watched the little figure bounding down the hill, swinging her holdall back and forth. He thought of Harry when she was a little girl, in the park by the River Stour, on days he had taken her into Canterbury, of how she would run at him, small hands flexed as she butted her head into his diaphragm and he would theatrically stagger and pretend to be winded.

She had slowed to a walking pace now, but he could see that this took an effort of will. Even at a distance he could tell she was bursting with excitement.

'You look different,' he said, as she took his arm.

'I *feel* different.'

'More in charge, like.'

For a moment her expression changed, to that of an anxious child. 'I do hope they'll take me. I can't think what I'll do if they don't.'

'They will.'

'What about you? Did you find somewhere?'

'Me? Oh – yes. Somewhere to doss.'

'The rooms here are beautiful. Big and airy. I'll be sharing with another girl. We'll all have meals together, like school, but breakfast too. Sometimes the dinners are formal, and you have to wear a gown – a bit like the ones teachers wear – and a proper frock. There's a JCR – that's a common room – a big sitting room. It must be twice the size of our little tin chapel. And a library! A lovely room, with French windows looking out on to a lawn, and a little alcove with a fireplace. They've a piano in there. It's a much better piano than Mum's, but you mustn't tell her that. There's a laundry, with big machines you put money in, and a sewing room, and a bar. It's a little world of its own. Oh, Vanlo, what if they say no?'

'They wunt. Now, shall we go for the train? There's people at that stop so there must be a bus due.'

'Is it a long way on foot? It seemed quite a journey when we were on the bus.'

'That's 'cos you didn't know where you was going. Took me an hour on Shank's pony.'

'Shall we walk then? It might calm me down. And I want to see something of this city, if it's going to be my new home.'

Vanlo smiled. 'Time was, I never had a home, because all the world was home. Wherever we stopped. Home came with us instead.'

'Dad hankers for that life sometimes, I'm sure of it. Only he'll not say.'

'All he has to do is look at your mother and that settles 'en.'

'Do *you* miss that life?'

'At times. But I'd miss living by you an' Sam an' Ellen more.'

'I've always envied you having your wagon. Ever since I was a little girl. Even if you never went anywhere in it. It was the thought that you could.'

'I did try livin' in the house – long before you was born. But I couldn't take to it. Sam was already used to living that way, what with the army, an' the gaol an' all. And I can see it's easier, having a tap indoors and that.'

'A tap? That's all there is. Dad wants it that way. The other houses in the village have mostly got inside toilets. I asked Mum once why we didn't, why the bathtub had to be in the outhouse, even though we've a washing machine now – it's not as if Dad's against mod cons, especially if, as he says "we've more time for talking that way" – but she said Dad said lavatories are dirty and shouldn't be in the same place as you sleep and eat. But the privy is always spotless, and it would be easier to keep that way if it wasn't out the back.'

'That's not just Sam's way, Harry, it's *our* way – the Gypsy way. How can it be clean to be making and eating your dinner with all that going past you through the wall?'

'That makes sense . . .'

Vanlo smiled. 'But p'raps we should talk about other things – where you're going you'll have three years of inside jakes!'

'That's if they take me.'

'Your Miss Shaw wouldn't have put you up to it otherwise.'

'If they do, I'll share a room with another girl. I've not done that since Flora died.'

They fell silent, listening to the synchronised tread of their own feet.

'I always shared,' said Vanlo eventually, 'until I left my brothers and threw in my lot with Sam and Ellen. We was all pell-mell in the *vardo* or outside in the bender tent if it was warm enough.'

'Didn't you ever want to marry though?'

'That? Oh no. Never found anyone I could marry,' said Vanlo. 'What if she'd've wanted an inside toilet?'

*

They settled into their compartment. 'Here, I got us something for the way back,' Vanlo said, reaching into his bag. 'Just bread and cheese and beer. Keep us going till we get to Aunt Amy and Uncle John's. You eat something. I'm going to get a bit of kip first.'

A moment later, Vanlo was fast asleep, his head propped against the headrest, his large hands loose between his knees. Harry chewed her bread and cheese as quietly as she could, feeling a stab of pity for the sleeping man. *I talked nineteen to the dozen all the way to the station. I never asked him what he did or where he went. He looks as worn out as if he'd slept on a park bench.* Vanlo's mouth was slightly open, revealing the gleam of strong, uneven teeth. His Adam's apple, above the knotted *diklo,* looked vulnerable, though his throat was strong. The dark brows drew together in his sleep. He was huddled deep in an old airforce greatcoat, which still bore the signs of where various insignia had been unpicked; the heating in the carriage was fitful on that January afternoon.

He's a fine looking man, is Uncle Vanlo. But he's never given that diklo *or any other to any woman that I know of so that everyone would know she was his.* Harry got up as quietly as she could, and drew her holdall down from the rack. She unzipped a side compartment and took out a pad, and a tin box. For the next hour she worked intently with her stick of charcoal.

CHAPTER TWELVE

A fatherly warning Patrixbourne

February 1956

'Postman was early,' said Sam. 'Look.'

Ellen took the sheet of lined writing paper, and read from it an address in Poplar.

Dear Mister Luffwidge,

As you may know tho p'raps they don't like to say so, the police kem round to my sister's on account of her Bert and his doings when he was down at French's Farm on the last hopping. My sister and me have had words becos she thinks the sun shines out of him and it's my view she has him spoiled and so he gets away with murder and always has done. My sister and him don't know I'm writing to you but I am shamed after so many years coming to the hopping as you know and there's never been no trouble before and would not be if people just got on with their work and not go on as if they was doing you a favour. Not content with doing bad things with that lovely girl of yours and bosting about it he've persuaded another young woman to marry him and I think she deserves better actually any woman does. She is a decent young woman this Ada she works as a barmaid at the Resolute but it's not true all they say about barmaids. I wouldn't wish him even on them naughty ladies in Paddington tho they might know better how to handle him or at least them fellows that man-nidge them would sort him out if he tried anything them girls don't like. Forgive me for writing in this frank way Mr Luffwidge but I am very sore and angry with him for we are a respeckable family but for him and I just wanted to say how sorry I am from the bottom of my heart specially as Bert is full of himself as he says they aint going to take him in charge after all and I hope I can come back next time as I look forward to the hopping all year round.

Sincerely yours

Enid Lasseter (Mrs)

Ellen looked up. 'I can see from your face that you're going to do something, Sam. What?'

'Go there, o' course. Speak to this young woman if I can. I'd guess that's what Mrs Lasseter is after if she's telling me where to find 'er.'

'Don't go alone, please!'

'I wunt. I'll take Vanlo. I'll need to square it with young Mr French, 'specially with everything slowed up with the freeze. Soon as the trains are back to normal.'

*

Sam rang the bell in the private bar of the Resolute. 'Two pints of bitter please, lady,' he said, when the older of the two barmaids appeared at the hatch.

'When you goin' to ask?' asked Vanlo, as he brought the glasses over to their table.

Sam got out his tobacco pouch and started to fill a paper. 'Make one for you, bruv?'

'Nah, I like my Black Cats,' said Vanlo, pulling out a packet. Sam struck a match and lit his companion's cigarette before lighting his own. Vanlo watched it burn down rapidly, and knew that nerves had made Sam roll it too loosely.

'I'd rather find out than ask,' he said. 'Mightn't be that she's working tonight, and I dunt want no one else knowing our business.'

Half an hour later a clerk, impatient at the time he'd waited at the hatch, shouted out into the din beyond, 'Oi! Ada! I've ivy growin' up me legs through 'ere!'

'Same again, is it?' bawled a voice.

'See?' murmured Sam. 'Now all we've to do is wait till closing up.'

*

Sam and Vanlo stood on the corner under the street light, and watched the lights dimming one after the other in the windows of the Resolute. At last two women came out, and the door was shut and barred behind them. As Sam had guessed, the landlord lived above his premises. The next thing was to see if the two went home separately.

'Smoke before you go, Ada?'

'Not sure I feel like one, Glad, but thanks anyway. Doesn't taste the same at the moment.'

There was the flare of the match as Gladys lit up. 'Told 'im yet, 'ave you?'

'Nope,' said Ada. 'Don't know if I should. Oughtn't ter make any difference, either way. He says he wants us married quick anyway.'

'Still going to be Bow Road, is it?'

''Fraid so. I'd've liked a nice church wedding – something a bit more special, historical sort of. But he wouldn't 'ave it. Told me to think of the expense – as well as saying something nasty about girls wearing white.'

'Oh well, it's only that day, ain't it? You've to think about what it's going to be like all the years after that.'

Ada paused before answering. 'Yes. I expect you're right.'

'You love 'im, doantcher?'

'Wouldn't matter if I did or not, would it, not now? Baby has to have a father.'

'Spect it'll be all right. Well, must get 'ome, dear,' said Gladys, grinding her cigarette butt under her heel. 'See you tomorrow then.'

''Night, Gladys.'

'G'night.'

As Ada passed the two men under the lamp, Sam threw down his own cigarette, but waited, as he had discussed with Vanlo, until the girl was thirty yards or so ahead, her heels clipping the pavement with a sound not unlike a pony's iron shoes. The two men followed her at a swinging pace, talking, as planned, about a spavined horse.

'It was one of them blind ones, right inside the hock.'

'How'd you spot it, then?' said Vanlo.

'The way she dragged the leg. I made the fellow walk her up and down so's I could look properly. Too much load on 'er back when she was still growing, I tole 'im.' Sam touched Vanlo's arm then, for they were about to overtake the girl, fortuitously just as they reached a lamp post.

'Miss Ada?' said Sam.

She spun round. 'Whatchoo want?' The whites of her eyes gleamed yellow in the light. Sam spread his hands.

'Only five minutes of your time, miss. Right here under the light. Seein' as you is soon to be married.'

'What business is that of yours? Don't care for it much, people sticking their noses in.'

'It's about him – Bert Parker.'

Ada stiffened, but waited silently, knowing that she'd not mentioned Bert's surname to Gladys.

'Go on,' she said, wary still, but not aggressive. 'Only keep your voices down.'

'I'd prefer that anyroad,' said Sam. 'This here is my brother Vanlo. We come up from Kent this morning—'

'You're from that hop farm, aintcher?'

'You know about it, then?'

'It's all lies,' said Ada, her voice shrill with uncertainty.

'T'ain't lies,' said Sam. 'I'm the maidy's father.'

'Look, it's got nuffink to do with me. The bluebottles said there was no case to answer.'

'And they're always right, are they?'

'No, but . . . How'd you know where to find me?'

'A concerned member of the public.'

Ada's eyes flickered from Sam's face to Vanlo's, and her face hardened.

'I don't know what the people down in Kent are like, seeing as I've never bin, but you two look like gyppos to me.'

'Guilty as charged. But your father would've done the same as we're doing if what happened to my little girl had happened to you, I'm sure.'

'My old man? Even Mother don't know where he is. Thinks he might have gone to sea to avoid the payments. Anyway, like I said, what's all this got to do with me?'

'You want to marry a man as can do that?' Ada's expression reminded Sam of a cornered rat's. He could see how her tawdry prettiness would fade, how quickly she would grow pinched and hard – and disappointed.

'You 'eard everyfink back there,' she said. 'A bit late for second thoughts now, ain't it?'

'What if my girl had been having a baby too?' said Sam.

'Well, 'e can't marry two of us, can 'e? Sounds like she ain't, anyway.'

'If she was, I'd not want her marryin' your Bert, baby or no baby. She deserves better, see.'

Ada's eyes widened. 'I don't know if you're insulting me, Mr whatever your name is—'

'Loveridge. Sam Loveridge. I've written it down on this bit of paper, with my address. And there was no insult intended, miss. Only what you might call fatherly concern.'

Ada took the piece of paper with its few printed lines, and for a moment Sam thought she was going to crumple it up. Instead, with a popping sound, she undid the catch of her handbag and placed it inside.

'I think your girl is lucky,' she said.

'*Lucky?*'

'That's what I said, didn't I? She 'as a father and a nunkle to take 'er part. I've got no one 'part from my old mother and a little sister. So I've just got to make the best of it. And I've got to go now. They'll be wondering what's happened to me.'

'Can we walk you home?'

'I – no – thank you though. I can look after myself, see?' She raised her head defiantly, but Sam could see the trembling of her chin. She turned aside, hunching her shoulders, and marched off, heels clicking defiantly.

'What now?' whispered Vanlo.

'Nuffing. What *can* we do? The young lady knows already, but as she's in the family way she's squarely caught.'

'We could go after *them*.'

'I promised Ellen I wouldn't – I tole you. She says I mustn't swing for what she calls my principles. But that poor kid, that Ada, *can't* look after herself, no matter what she says. She's jumping out of the cooking pot and into the fire, and knows it. Look how she's walking. She's crying, she is.'

'So that's it, is it? We just go back to John's and home on the early train?'

'Let's go and see Mrs Lasseter. I need a cup of tea anyroad – that beer's gone sour on me. Give me a look at that map again.'

In the pool of yellow light he searched for the two crosses Ellen had marked for him.

*

The tenement had an outside staircase, recessed into the block, so they could see, when looking up, that no one was ascending the stone steps before them.

'Cleaner that way,' said Vanlo. 'Rubbish blows in, but blows out again. More chance of bad smells getting out too. Mun be cold though.' They started to climb.

'Remember that place we was in in Wandsworth?' said Sam.

'Don't I? How many years ago was that? I'd like to say I hope the bombs got it, only that if they did they'd have finished off more than bricks and mortar and them rats.'

'Third floor left . . . here we are. Bless 'er, she's even got a *biti*[14] brass plate, all polished up, like that letterbox. 'Ope she won't think it's too late.' Sam put his ear to the door, straining his hearing against the clip of nailed boots on the street below, the fractured song of a drunk, the rumble of a distant car on uneven asphalt. 'Somebody's there.' He knocked softly. The shuffling he'd heard turned into wary silence. 'Mrs Lasseter?' he said. There was a thump close by, then a rattle of a chain, and the letterbox squealed on its hinges.

'Wotchoo want?'

---

[14] Little.

Sam bent down and said quietly into the opening. 'It's Sam Loveridge from French's Farm. And my bruv, Vanlo.'

The door opened almost before Sam had straightened up, and his arm was seized.

'Come in, will yer? Afore any of them nosy beggars sees you.'

*

As she bent over the thin fire, setting the kettle on its hook, Sam glanced round Mrs Lasseter's room. His heart lurched with pity. She straightened up, a hand in the small of her back. There was a tiny creak – of old-fashioned stays.

'Nice to 'ave a bit o' company,' she said. ''Specially when I wasn't expecting it. I'm only sorry I didn't reckernise your voice. It's you bein' in a strange place did it – strange for you, I mean. Well, you can see now why coming down to the hoppin' is something I look forward to all year round.' She gestured at the worn patches on the lino, the narrow iron-framed bed pushed up against a disintegrating wall. 'I used to put pitchers up,' she said, 'only there was no point. They got damp that fast. All soft like slices of bread. That little hut down at yours is cosier. I miss that little hut.'

'It'll be there for you next hopping, Mrs Lasseter.'

'Let's hope *I'll* be, then. This place does my cough no good at all. The whole lot's condemned, they tell me, and I'm on the list for a new place, but I don't know as I'll get to be with fam'ly. Only with the fam'ly split over Bert, mebbe it's better we're all broken up. *He* wants to take Ada away in any case. One of them new towns, a place with a bit of garden front and back. Not that I can see 'im bothering about that. *She'll* have to do all the work. An' she'll 'ave no one to turn to if 'e treats 'er bad. There's a baby, ain't there?'

'Not for me to say, only—'

'That's what she told you though, ain't it? I think it's a crying shame, doing what 'e did to your pore gel then getting this one in the fam'ly way so's she's trapped good and proper.' She reached into a cupboard and took out three cups and saucers, gleaming in that dreary room, and put them on the table beside the tea caddy and the tin labelled 'National Dried Milk'.

'I'm sorry I ain't got nuffink else to offer you, no biscuits nor nuffink. With it just being me now, I daren't buy 'em. I'd 'ave 'em all ate in one go. Do you mind the powdered stuff?'

'Not at all,' said Sam, again grateful that deep in the country he had missed the worst of rationing.

'Take my advice though and don't go after Bert,' said Mrs Lasseter, pouring the steaming water into her battered teapot. ''E ain't worth you getting into trouble for, because you'd get taken up for it even if 'e never was.'

'That's what my wife says.'

'That lovely lady. Such a pretty face even if she ain't a young 'un no more. I 'preciate you coming all this way to try to talk sense into pore Ada. If anyone could've, it was you, but things has sort of decided themselves all the same if there's a baby coming. I will say this though, if the bluebottles ever do change their minds, and you need my pennyworth there in court, I'll be there for you.'

*

'Poor old soul,' said Sam, shoulders hunched against the drizzle. 'Kind of her to make that offer about speaking up for Harry. Not that she'll ever have to make it good.'

'Hope that bastard dunt work out it was her got you up here.'

'I'm mebbe wrong, but I think Ada's not even going to mention it,' said Sam.

'P'raps you're right. Are we too late for them trains?'

'If we are we've a bit of a walk to John Quainton's.'

'You've the key though, Sam?'

'Yeah. But I'd rather not have been late. If it was me, I'd be lying in bed waiting to hear the key in the lock.'

'Wait for me here, would yer?' said Vanlo. 'There's a jakes. Too much beer and tea.'

Sam watched Vanlo descend into the dimly lit white-tiled interior, then walked some paces away to escape the gritty stench of dried urine that made him wish it hadn't stopped raining. He amused himself by reading the names above the shuttered shops, recollecting the day nearly thirty years earlier when he had walked out of the prison at Winchester with his newly acquired literacy. Shopfronts and names on carts – the first things he had read as a free man. The street was now watchfully quiet, in the way that country lanes were not. It was then he heard a subterranean cry.

Where's my bruv got to? He looked back towards the mouth of the public toilets. There was a scuffle of boots and then Vanlo burst out onto the pavement, running towards him.

'*Jal!*[15]'

Sam did as he was told, and ran too, dodging down into the warren of terraced houses, their nailed boots striking loud on the asphalt. Most of the buildings were in darkness, though here and there a pale light gleamed in an upstairs room. After they'd turned left, then right, then left again, Sam cried 'Stop!', clutching his chest and wheezing.

A distant rattling of a bus was all they heard.

'I'm all out of breath – Ellen keeps telling me I got to cut down on the smokes,' said Sam.

'We've lost 'en, anyroad,' said Vanlo, looking back to the mouth of the street.

'He never came after us, I think, though we'd've been easy enough to follow. Them boots is all right on good country earth, but here they're as good a warning as an air-raid siren. You going to tell me what happened?'

Vanlo looked away. 'He came on to me. He was waiting in one of them stalls. Came out when I was about emptied and stood too close to me. Asked me if I wanted something. I said I didn't and to leave me in peace. He got closer, so I knocked him down.'

'*Dordi*, bruv, that's why he's not come after us. You've done for him.'

---

[15] Run.

'He's a bloody nose, that's all. He was getting up when I *jalled*.'

'You sure?'

'Yeah, that I'm sure of.'

'All right. We'd best shift, anyways. Just let me go to the end of the street first and check nobody's there.'

*

Two days later, and the encounter with Ada and then the tea with Mrs Lasseter had been sombrely gone over at the kitchen table in Patrixbourne. Harry's response had been brief: 'Well, I should be glad I'm not Ada. She's got him for life, poor girl.' And she'd picked up her easel and painting things. 'I'm going out for a while.'

As the door closed, Ellen lifted the lid of the teapot and peered inside. 'Want another one, Sam?'

'Please.'

She put the milk into the cup only Sam used, and poured, added sugar and stirred, before giving it to him, and then made herself half a cup.

'Thank you,' he said.

'There's something else, isn't there, Sam?'

He took a swig before answering. 'Yeah, there is. But nothing to do with Harry – with that business. It's Vanlo.' He recounted their flight through the near-dark streets.

'There are such lonely souls, Sam. There's a case in the paper at least once a month. Last year they even locked up some lord and his friends.'

'I met men like 'em in the gaol. It's not that. It was Vanlo. He wouldn't look at me. He was lying, Ellen. Only I dunt see why.'

'You think he might have really hurt the man?'

'No. That's the only bit I'm sure of.'

'Then I think, Sam,' she said slowly, 'we just have to leave it at that. Vanlo will have had his reasons.'

CHAPTER THIRTEEN

Leaving home

1956

Harry cannoned into the kitchen. 'I've got it, Mum!' Ellen got up from the kitchen table where she had been correcting compositions from eight-year-olds.

'I'm going to Nottingham! A full scholarship!' Harry capered about the room, unable to keep still. Mittens crouched down and tunnelled across the floor to escape up the stairs.

'Careful! You'll knock the plates off the dresser – hold still a moment while I cuddle you. My darling girl. You have no idea how proud I am of you!'

'You'll come and see me, won't you?' said Harry into her mother's shoulder, breathing in her familiar lavender scent.

'Of course – but after a while you won't want us to. You'll have your own life to lead.'

'Of course I'll want to see you!' Harry relinquished her mother and went out to the scullery to fill the kettle, calling over her shoulder, 'Where's Dad?'

'Feeding mangolds to old Chubb's herd.'

'How is Chubb?'

'Getting worse. It'll kill him to give up the farm, but he knows that's coming.'

Harry came back in holding the filled kettle. 'Poor old man. Will you have a cup too?'

'I will, thank you. But when your dad gets in you and he should have something stronger to celebrate.'

'No point in asking you to join us, I suppose?'

'Habit of a lifetime, not having that habit. I'll toast you with my own elderflower cordial.'

'Oh, *Mother!*' Harry spooned tea into the strainer. Ellen's silence made her look up. 'I will miss you – and here – you know. But I must do this.'

*

Ellen brushed out her hair as Sam watched her from the bed, in a little ritual consolidated over the years.

'Can't she stay here and learn to be a teacher from you?' he said.

Ellen stopped brushing, looking at her husband's reflection in the mirror on the dressing table. Her heart lurched with pity. She put down the brush and turned around. Sam sniffed – in the light of the oil lamp Ellen could see his eyes shimmering wet.

'Sam . . .'

'I couldn't protect her, Ellen, not even in our own backyard. How can I protect her when she's with strangers?' He pushed back the covers and swung his legs over the side of the bed. He was naked, a youthful habit interrupted only by prison and by a stay ten years earlier in the new hospital in Canterbury to have his appendix out. Ellen saw that his long legs were corded more than muscular now, the hollows of his throat deepened, but he was lean, and loveable, and hers. Yet he was so tense that she wondered if he was about to pull his clothes back on and go off for a walk in the moonlight.

'Come here, Ellen,' he said. She came over to where he sat. He put his arms around her where she stood, and pulled her towards him, resting his cheek on her breast.

'I've not seen her this happy since before *that* time,' he said. 'If it's what she wants, she mun have it.'

Ellen threaded her fingers into his hair.

'Will you put off your nightie, Ellen?' she heard him say. 'I need your skin next to mine tonight.'

*

Eight months after receiving the letter, Harry stood outside the door of what was to be her room in Florence Boot Hall. She checked her key again, to be absolutely sure she had the right place, but paused before knocking. Someone was blundering about inside. *I want to remember this moment always. My new life starts here.* She'd cried when her mother and father and Uncle Vanlo had seen her off, and all the way on the train to London had felt the tug of home, made worse when fields of cows and oast houses and hedgerows had given way to ribbons of semi-detached homes, and the countryside expired in smoke-stained brick and noise. Crossing the Thames on the train going into Charing Cross this time had felt like passing a frontier.

The journey north had been easier. A friendly guard had asked her if she wanted to stay in his van, 'to keep your nice motorbike company'. Companionable cups of tea followed in the stretches between stops, whilst gentle chatter about the routes he worked each week, the busiest stations, the competitions for the best kept ones, and a mutual hatred of the ravages of Beeching both passed the time and made Harry realise that, really, home was only ever a punched ticket away.

There was a lull now in the thumping and dragging going on behind the door. Harry held her keys in one hand, and knocked.

'Come in, then!' cried a voice. Harry walked into an airy room, much like the one she had spent the night in at her scholarship exam, with long graceful windows, and clean-lined, pale-wood furniture. In the midst of this stood a tall, ungainly girl in cat's eye glasses, an overlarge pullover and a pair of rather loud plaid slacks. A suitcase lay disembowelled at her feet.

'Hello, happy camper!' she said, sticking out a bony hand with vivid red nails. Harry wasn't surprised at the firmness of her grip. 'Anna Segal.'

'Harmony Loveridge, but everyone calls me Harry.'

'Cry God for Harry, England and St George then. Your trunk's arrived. I haven't picked the lock yet. Any preference as to your berth?'

'None whatsoever,' said Harry, glancing at the two beds. 'But shouldn't it be first come, first served?'

'I've tried 'em both. I'd say both are good for one's back. Hard, in other words.'

'Oh . . . I don't know then. Maybe that one?' said Harry, indicating the one to her right. 'I haven't shared a room for years.'

'Only girl, are you?'

'Now I am. With two brothers.'

'I've just the one, the brute.'

'Sounds like you're fond of him the way you say that.'

'Oh, I am, rather. A barrister, no less. So it's up to me to save the family honour. Yours?'

'One's a brewer's drayman. The other's a Methodist minister.'

'That's quite a contrast! You a God-botherer, too? Oops – sorry.' Anna pulled a face.

Harry laughed. 'That's all right! I go to the chapel, but to be honest with you, I'm not sure what I believe these days.'

'Well, I'd describe myself not so much a Jew as Jew*ish*.' She scrutinised Harry's face for a moment, then said, 'Mind, you look a bit . . .'

'No. Dad's a Gypsy.'

'Thank heavens for that. Last thing I'd want is someone reminding me of my religious obligations. Hmm . . . you don't suppose they deliberately put us ethnics together, do you, like a sort of Indian reservation?'

'I doubt it. I don't think I put it on any of their forms. My brother Tom says it doesn't help if you do.'

'No Gypsies, no coloureds, no Irish, you mean?'

'That sort of thing. Mind you, they've taken those signs out of the pubs he supplies. He politely informed the landlords concerned that it would be impossible for him to put the barrels in their cellars otherwise.'

'Good man!' laughed Anna. 'I could sink a beer right now, but the bar isn't open. There's a kitchenette down the corridor, though, and I've a packet of tea and some milk in the fridge. Join me?'

'Yes please!'

*

'What's your father do?' asked Harry.

'Administrator for the Home and Hospital for Jewish Incurables – known as the Incurable Jews for short – Tottenham. But you ought to have asked me first about Mother. Much more formidable.'

'Oh?'

'A surgeon at Whipps Cross. Specialises in women's problems. A pioneer and won't let you forget it. Loves the National Health Service – she's a picture of Nye Bevan on the desk in her study. You can imagine the fisticuffs at home when the Ministry wanted to bring the Incurable Jews into public ownership. In the end the board got the better of the mandarins, so Dad still has to be nice to the benefactors if he's going to get paid. Pity you weren't on an earlier train. They only left an hour ago. You could have asked Mother to fit you a cap. She asked me if I wanted one, but I said I'd other things to think about. Embarrassing, one's parents, aren't they?'

'Fit me a cap?' said Harry, wondering if she hadn't listened properly and the conversation had somehow veered to washing machines.

'I'm sorry. I clank on like a train without looking at the signals. Nerves, probably. More tea, vicar?'

'Thank you.' Harry held out her cup.

'Tell me about your two then. They can't be as embarrassing as mine.'

'Dad's a foreman on a farm where he used to go every year to pick hops. He settled when he married Mum. She's a schoolteacher. I'm what you might call their late flowering. It was always thought a bit odd at school having a mother who worked – by the other girls, I mean – but I'm proud of her. Nearly as much as Dad is. Even though he never went to school himself. He learned to read and write first in Winchester, and then she kept him at it.'

'Never been to Winchester – seen a nice railway poster of it.'

'Dad didn't see much of it.' Harry paused. 'He was in the gaol.'

Anna whistled. 'Heavens! Am I allowed to ask what for?'

'Sorry, I've probably said too much already. Stealing a horse. He hadn't done it though. It was a family feud of some kind, and they made him pay.'

'You've not said too much. We're going to be falling over each other in here from now to June if not longer so it's not as if we're going to have many secrets from each other. Poor man, though.'

'Poor man, indeed. They flogged him until he fainted.'

Anna shuddered. 'Bloody hell.'

'Tell me more about you, though. Being Jewish. Are there things you can and can't do because of that? Dad has some rules, you see. Mum's learned them too.'

Anna laughed. 'Well, there was the time Dad and Nathan and I went to Frinton. We sat looking out to sea and had a jar of cockles each, only he told us not to tell Mum, because that food's forbidden. Everybody else was eating them though, and *they* weren't dropping dead.'

'We have some rules other people don't have too. Not so much about what you eat but how you eat it. Hygiene things. Everybody is supposed to have their own plate and cutlery, if they stick with the traditions. My uncle Vanlo has his own still, but Dad doesn't bother, apart from his cup. What we eat off and what we wear always has to be washed separately though. One of the old ways was also a husband and wife sleeping apart during the curse.'

'We've got that too! Perhaps your lot and my lot are really long-lost cousins,' said Anna. 'My two have never done that, though. Mum says that a lot of the traditions are to do with keeping clean and eating safely in a Middle-Eastern climate with no running water or Prestcold fridges on the never-never, which oughtn't to be a problem for anyone living within spitting distance of the Piccadilly Line.'

'Mine don't either, but I think it's only because Dad would never want to let Mum out of his sight.'

'On the food business, though, I'm opting to eat vegetar-ian in Hall – you can, you know, and it might be advisable. I've heard they're so kind to animals here that they let them die naturally before eating them. Sorry – terrible joke. Mum and Dad go to *shul* – that's synagogue – and so does Nathan when he thinks somebody's looking. And we observe the main feasts. Dad likes *Purim* best – he says it's his religious duty to get so drunk he can't tell the difference between Haman and Mordecai.'

'Oh gosh! It all sounds much more fun than the chapel . . . tea meetings and cricket matches. I feel mean saying that, though, because the people are very kind. They gave me a little send-off in the village hall . . . oh . . .'

'Here you are, Harry,' said Anna gruffly, pulling out a clean man's handkerchief.

'Sorry.'

'Don't be. I bawled after my lot had gone.'

'Dad likes a pint, of course, and so does Tom, though neither will take one on Sunday. Tom says the horse will always get him home if he can't remember how to get there himself. But Mum is t-t. She's a bit old-fashioned, in the kindest possible way. Her grandfather was a blood and thunder preacher of the old school, apparently. Believed in crying out God's message in the market-place and the fields more than in a building.'

'And you?'

'I've an uncle in London who is a minister, like my brother David. I went with him and Aunt Amy and Mum once to hear a preacher at Hyde Park Corner. He said something I've never forgotten, and I try to live by – about the miracle of the loaves and fishes . . . that story, you know—'

'I do. We've got the New Testament in N17 too.'

'Of course. Anyway, he was talking about how we shouldn't be judgemental. He said that Jesus wasn't – his friends were the kind that many respectable people mightn't want for neighbours – tax collectors, prostitutes, fellows smelling of fish guts and so on. This preacher was particularly cross about the idea of there being deserving and undeserving poor, in the minds of some people who call themselves Christian. He said Jesus didn't feed all of those people because they were *good* people. He fed them because they were *hungry*.'

'Sensible chap. The spirit not the letter.' Anna started counting on her fingers. 'So, we've covered family, religion, or lack of religion – what else? Politics. Men – or lack of. I've never even asked you what you're here to study. Mine's Eng Lit . . .'

*

Lying in their respective beds later, Harry said, 'I feel as if I've known you forever, Anna.'

'Likewise. And that we'll always be friends. Sorry, and all that, Loverish! Shall I put the light out, even if we'll probably be talking till the birds wake up?'

*

A week later the two girls had established their nightly ritual of cocoa and confessions. Harry looked at Anna sitting slumped on her bed and thought, *I want us to be friends forever.*

'I don't know about you, Harry, but I'm all in,' said Anna. 'And that's only the first seven days.'

'It went by in a blur, didn't it, but I feel as though I've been here months.' Harry got up from her chair and walked over to her wardrobe, opened it, and inhaled deeply.

'Whatever are you doing?' said Anna.

'Those things smell of home. Even the water is different here.'

'I'm homesick too,' said Anna, sniffling. 'Oh dear, please excuse me.' She blew her nose loudly.

Harry went and sat beside her friend. 'First impressions, Anna?'

'Hmm. Well the men aren't up to much.'

Harry laughed.

'No, seriously. A purely anthropological observation. The male of the species is quite definitely wet behind the ears, looks younger than us, and in lectures huddles as far away from us as he possibly can. They're all scared of us girls, Harry, even though they outnumber us here.'

'*Them,* scared of *us,*' said Harry pensively. 'I think, in a way, I've come here to avoid men.'

'You say that now, but just think, Harry! Somewhere out there in the dark – well, in his room probably – at this very moment, lurks the man who'll be your husband one day.'

Harry stifled a cry.

'Whatever's the matter?'

'Sorry, it's just the way you said it.'

'Hmm,' murmured Anna, looking over her glasses. 'There might even be someone for me. Not that I've come here looking for him either, though from the conversations you hear down in Hall, some girls obviously have.'

'Oh, I know what I wanted to tell you,' said Harry, eager to change the subject. 'I met Professor Chambers today.'

'Who's he?'

'Economic and Social History – but his sister was D.H. Lawrence's first sweetheart.'

'Ah!' Anna sat up straight. 'Marvellous writer – vile man. Do tell!'

'Your reaction, only milder. I got the impression he admired Lawrence but didn't like him. They've a big archive here and they want to make more of it, even though the library used to keep his books under lock and key.'

'Unsuitable for maidenly eyes, of course. Which is why I've read all of 'em myself, apart from the banned one. Mother insisted on it.'

'If you'd like a spin on the Bantam we could go out and see his birthplace. In fact, I think we should . . .'

'Why the frown?'

'Lawrence was a miner's son, wasn't he? It's just that I can't get over how lucky you and I are being here.' Harry gestured at her desk. 'We have the luxury of study, first-rate people to teach us, books, a beautiful airy room to sleep in, meals prepared for us that we don't even have to wash up after. But in Nottingham, people pour in and out of factories every day, making everything from bicycles to bridal veils, whilst all around it, miners are tunnelling underground to keep all of that industry fired up and all of us warm. They might be down there right now for all I know. Do miners work at night? I don't know. I'm *ashamed* I don't know . . . Sorry, I'm ranting . . .'

'Don't be,' said Anna. 'Never mind a husband. Find yourself a cause here, Lover. You're unstoppable.'

CHAPTER FOURTEEN

Trent Building
November 1956

'*Non, Mesdames et messieurs,*' the speaker cried, running a hand through his untidy mop of dark hair, 'one cannot regard my country as a light in the darkness. Yes, it is true that France no longer interferes in Vietnam. Yes, it is true that both Morocco and Tunisia are at last free of the colonial yoke, but it is also true that the imperial occupation of Algeria continues though that country cries out for independence – and now we see the home of *liberté, egalité, fraternité* go meekly side by side with another decaying colonial power to tell the Egyptians that they may not nationalise their own canal!'

'Nasser's just a darkie Hitler!' yelled a voice from the back of the hall, to a chorus of booing.

'And all this will do is make his people support him more!' retorted the young man on the podium.

'Hypocrite, aren't you! Taking English money!'

The speaker glowered. 'I *earn* your English money. I *teach* your English students.' He looked around the packed auditorium.

'My case, *chers camarades*, I have made. I urge this house to vote in favour of the motion, that British and French forces should withdraw from Suez immediately!'

The assembly erupted in cheers and foot-stamping. Sitting in the front row of the lecture theatre, Harry felt the boards beneath her feet shake and the voices rise behind her as loud as the roar of a waterfall. She looked at Anna, sitting beside her: her friend was hunting for her cigarettes, knowing the debate was all but over.

'Excuse me . . .'

Harry lifted her head to find the proposer of the motion looming over her.

'I wonder, *mam'selle,* if I might have a word . . . once the proceedings are over.'

What fierce eyes he has! 'Certainly . . . I—'

'Good.' And then he was gone, and the convener was asking for a show of hands. Harry and Anna raised theirs for the ayes, and, twisting round, saw that three-quarters or more of those present were with them.

'Not that it'll make any difference,' drawled Anna.

'But we *must* show what we believe. Otherwise . . .'

'Not a wasted evening, anyway, Loverish. Monsieur le speaker is pretty taken with you.'

'Nonsense. I wonder what he wants though . . .'

'Anyone could see what he *wants,* Lover. He didn't exactly *ask* you, did he? Sounded more like an order to me. He's a looker, though, and with that accent. Here he comes now,' said Anna, pulling on her mackintosh. 'I'll see you back at the ranch.'

'Anna, *wait!*'

'I am Max Arago,' he said.

'I know. You were introduced.'

Max looked momentarily wrong-footed, but recovered quickly. 'I do not know *your* name.'

'Harry. Harry Loveridge.'

"Arry? It is a boy's name, *n'est-ce pas?*'

'It's *my* name.'

'*Certainement* . . . 'Arry, would you have dinner with me?'

'What, now?'

'If you are hungry, yes.'

'All right. As long as you see me home afterwards.'

'I am a gentleman.'

*

'It was not so bad, I think, for English food?' he said, as the waitress took their empty starter plates away. Harry watched the girl's retreating back, noting the slight twist of her shoulders. *I'll give you a decent tip, whether you heard him or not.*

'I'm grateful for anything someone has taken the trouble to prepare for me – and it *was* good,' she said.

'Let's see what Nottingham does with Tournedos Rossini then.'

'You find this place a bit of a backwater after Paris, I expect.' Something in her tone made him look at her closely.

'It is true that I need a British university on my record,' he said. 'I see myself teaching in the United States next, but eventually I shall return to the Sorbonne.' Harry loved the way he pronounced the name of his university, the first syllable soaring on his rolled 'r', the second a long descent. *I can't go on saying Saw Bon then.*

'I admit though that I have been pleasantly surprised.'

'What do you mean?'

'Please, I think I offend you. I mean that the standard of the students is 'igh. I note too that they – all of you, I should say – are drawn from all over society, that you are all here on merit.' Some of the verve that had characterised his speech at the debate came into his voice. He topped up her glass. 'A country needs that. Europe needs that. Education. Social mobility. The *mélange* of class, breaking down the old barriers. Otherwise, our old continent . . . it cannot grow.'

Harry laughed. 'There's some way to go there, though. What's your dad do for a living then, Max?'

'He's a professor – of Philosophy.'

Harry imagined this man, spectacles on his nose, a neat, grey beard. A book-lined study. And she saw her own father, taking off his boots at the farmhouse door, hanging up his jacket on its usual nail, sitting at the kitchen table and unfolding the *Daily Mirror,* and fumbling in his pocket for his tobacco tin before he remembered Ellen's new rule about not smoking in the house.

'And your mother?'

'*Mais non!* Maman does not work. She was his student, and now she supports him – proofreading, dealing with his correspondence. And yours?'

'Mum is a teacher – in a village school. My father works on a farm.'

'Why did they call you 'Arry? It is not so . . . 'abitual, I think.'

'My father's mother's name. It was Harmony. I decided myself I was Harry.'

'I have never heard of an Englishwoman – any woman – with such a name.'

'Well, you can't know everything, can you, Max? My father's Sunday name is Sampson. He's a Gypsy. They – we – have a liking for names like that.'

Max raised his eyebrows, and his glance flitted over her face. Harry saw him reading her countenance, noting her thick black hair, her glossy dark eyes, the line of her jaw – the inheritance of Sam Loveridge, born in a field somewhere north of Oxford.

'Ah! I had thought *juive* . . . Jewish. Now I see . . . but you do not travel? You are educated?'

'No, *we* do not travel. That way of life is made so difficult now. And yes, I am educated. So is my father, though he might not describe it that way.' She watched Max's face as she said, 'He learned to read and write in prison.'

Max couldn't disguise a slight start. 'As I said, education is essential. So that we can all move – I don't mean like your father's people—'

'—my people.'

'*Bien sûr.* I mean, that there's a choice. One does not stay in the station in which one is born.'

'Though there might be nothing wrong with that station.'

'*Absolument*. As I said, a choice.'

*

The taxi idled while Max stood under the light at the door to Florence Boot Hall.

'I have enjoyed your company, 'Arry. I am not convinced that you have enjoyed mine. I pride myself on finding the right things to say – on that platform tonight, putting words on a page – but I do not think I have been so successful with you.'

'Oh, I don't know about that.'

'May I see you again?'

'If you like.'

'Saturday?'

'Provided I finish my essay – yes, why not?'

'I shall hope that you do then,' said Max, and put out his hand. When Harry took it, he leant forward and went to kiss her cheek. She pulled away sharply.

'*No!*'

Startled, Max held up both hands. 'I'm sorry. It is just the French way. A kiss on each cheek – and then anuzzer – that is all.'

'No, I'm sorry. You weren't to know.'

'Weren't to know what?'

'Never mind. Go on then. Your French way.' She stood still as Max kissed her cheeks with courtly formality.

'Your perfume?' he asked, although he knew.

'Tweed.'

'*Naturellement – parfum français*. Sleep well, 'Arry.'

*

'*Well?*' said Anna, pulling her dressing gown cord tighter.

'He's funny.'

'Made you laugh, funny?'

'Odd, funny. No, that's unkind. He's just very formal. Old-fashioned even. I was a bit sharp with him.'

'Put him to the test, did you?'

'Sort of. He's a bit full of himself. Sniffy about Nottingham, turns his nose up at English food, though even he had to admit the meal was good. He wasn't very impressed with the wine though.'

'Where did he take you?'

'The George.'

Anna whistled. 'A scholarship wouldn't last long there!'

'I think he's quite rich. He wouldn't let me see the bill but whatever it was he didn't blink at it. I insisted on leaving the tip though. I don't think the waitress liked him much. But you saw him this evening – fiery in defence of a cause. I'd bet though he doesn't meet many of the people he'd go in to battle for.'

'Easier to campaign for Algeria than for injustice on his own doorstep, you mean?'

'Partly that. But he has his principles. He likes that people like me can get to university on merit – and no, he wasn't being patronising. He talked about meritocracy well before I told him my dad couldn't write his own name until he was in prison. Anyway, he's asked to see me again and I said yes, sort of.'

'Sort of?'

'I'm a bit scared, if the truth be known.'

'Want a nightcap?'

'A cup of tea. That food was rich.'

'Sit there, I'll get it. Then if you want you can tell me why you're scared.'

*

Half an hour later, the two girls moved on to Anna's cognac.

'Does anyone else here know what you've just told me, Harry?'

'In Nottingham, no.'

'I'll not abuse your trust.'

'I knew you wouldn't. It's a relief to have told you.'

'How on earth do you feel about it now?'

Harry passed a fingertip around the edge of the glass.

'Cheated out of my day in court. Angry, that I hadn't been able to stop them.' She shivered and, after putting down her glass, pulled the edges of her cardigan closer. 'I mean, they're out there somewhere. Maybe doing to another girl what they did to me – right now.' She sniffed loudly, and lifted her head as her eyes brimmed.

'*Hey!*' said Anna, leaving her chair to sit beside Harry on her bed, putting an arm around her shoulders.

'Sorry,' said Harry, and blew her nose. 'I have nightmares sometimes . . .'

'I noticed.'

'*Did* you?'

'You cry in your sleep sometimes. I always get up and come over to see if you're all right, but you've never woken.'

'Oh, Anna,' said Harry, trying to smile. 'I love you for that. It's always the same dream, but it's been happening less since I came here. I'm running along a row of hop poles, trying to find the way out, and they're coming after me. I can't hear them, but I can *smell* them. I'm afraid of the dark, which I never used to be. You'll think this sounds daft, but afterwards, at home, I started using a potty again, like a child. Our jakes is plumbed and everything, but it's out the back – you have to go outside. Here, there's always a bit of light – under the door, or from the lamp post out there. And always a bit of noise.'

'Out with it. Tell me I snore.'

'You don't. But your breathing is a comfort. And the fact that everyone under this roof apart from the porters is a woman.'

'Max isn't, though.'

*

'Where is it tonight, then?' asked Anna, a fortnight later.

'The Playhouse. *The Importance of Being Earnest*. Max was crowing about our English doublethink. "This country destroyed Wilde's spirit but you go in droves to see his plays."'

'And I'll bet you're not going to be up in the gods.'

'We're not. He said the play deserves better . . . and so do I – me, I mean – he says.'

'Hmm. He stumps up for everything, doesn't he?'

'I tried to stop him. I've budgeted for fun too, though not much more than matinee tickets at the Gaumont.'

'Exacts payment in kind, does he?'

'Um, not exactly. He's very French . . . I mean, not that I have any more experience than a school trip to Calais. But hand kissing, cheek kissing. I take his arm, not his hand.'

'No need to go so red, Lover. He sounds very chivalrous and not a bit Anglo-Saxon.'

'Yes . . . only . . .'

'Only?'

'I don't know if I didn't scare him off, that way, after he took me to dinner at the George, and he thinks I'm like one of those medieval ladies guarded by a unicorn. Oh, hell, Anna, I don't know what I'm trying to say. It's not as though I'm an expert. A few slobbery attempts from pimply youths when we had joint hops with Simon Langton Boys, when I wondered why I hadn't stayed at home with a good book.'

'Ahem . . . do you want him, Harry?'

'You mean . . . I don't know. I don't think I want anyone, that way.'

'Does your heart beat faster when he's near you?'

'Well, *yes*.'

'Does his gaze penetrate to your soul? Sorry, too much Lawrence.'

'I don't know that I have a soul – I mean, not the kind of soul you probably mean.'

'What *do* I mean, then?'

'I mean . . .' Harry hesitated. 'You remember that book we read because the newspapers said it was disgusting?'

'Kinsey and female humans.'

'That one. Well, you remember Kinsey said ten per cent of married women are frigid. They go through their whole lives like that, and their husbands either don't realise or don't care.'

Anna leaned over and put the back of her hand on Harry's forehead. 'Nope, you don't seem to have a fever, Harry, so maybe the problem's just him. Despite all his manifest charms you just don't get the vapours about him. Does he smell funny, by any chance?'

Harry laughed. 'Of course not! Maybe it's just that I've been vaccinated. Perhaps what happened in the hop field has left me immune. Only I won't know, unless I expose myself to the disease again, so to speak. He hasn't kissed me – not here,' she said, brushing her fingers across her lips, 'so I have no idea.' She paused, frowning. 'That night . . . *they* never kissed me – let's just say they bypassed all endearments.'

'I don't believe you've been immunised, Lover, and nor should you. Give yourself time, or you'll let the bastards win. But promise me something: don't, for heaven's sake, stick with Max unless you're absolutely sure you want to be with him.'

'I'm *not* sure, but how would I know if I was? How do I know it's not just because I'm frightened?'

'Have you told him about the hop field?'

'I don't intend telling anyone but you. It's my way of coping. That was there. This is Nottingham. But I suppose I'll have to.'

'Why?' asked Anna, quietly.

Harry took a deep breath, and exhaled slowly. 'Because he asked me my thoughts on marriage.'

'Gordon Bennett! Help me back onto my perch, Harry! And it's not even Christmas yet. What did *you* say?'

'I said I had none. I said I had to get my degree first. I do.'

'And how did he take that?'

'He was amused. "Naturally," he said. "I could not marry a woman who is not a graduate."'

'So he *was*, as the lady novelists say, "making you an offer". Crumbs, Loverish, you've beaten all the husband-hunters to it. The ones who want a degree as another bourgeois wifely accomplishment, like knowing who to put next to whom at their dinner parties, and how to write a nice thank-you letter to the wife of her husband's boss.'

'Well, *I* didn't come for that!'

'I know. That would never be enough for you. But just think, those nice respectable girls have to sift through all the gauche grammar school boys on offer – that or take on some entitled survivor of a Dotheboys Hall of a minor public school with a penchant for having his bottom whacked. Once they make their choice, they know that the army is going to haul him away God knows where for two years the moment he's finished posing for a graduation photo. Yet they've got to hang on to him, hoping that they really have got the reliable accountant, the Tudorbethan detached and membership of the right tennis club that they were planning for ever since they donned their first Maidenform bra.'

'How grotesque! The suffragettes were force-fed so that we could settle for that?'

'That's my girl. But you got him without even trying. He's older, he's a dish, rich, sophisticated. He has a killer of an accent. He's presumably already satisfied his military obligations for Queen and country – well, for country, anyway – best not mention queens given he's French. Out of interest, Harry – spontaneous answer, please – could *you* marry a man who wasn't a graduate?'

'Of course! If I loved him. If he was kind, and made me laugh. If I felt as though there was no one else on earth I'd like being with more.'

'And that's Max, is it?'

Harry paused. 'I don't know. It's too early to say, probably.'

'It's Sunday tomorrow. Will you spend it with him?'

'Oh, I . . . well, no. You see, I said I'd got Dr Fryer's tutorial on 1848 to read up for.'

'And have you?'

'As a matter of fact, I do – have the tutorial coming up, I mean. I've already done the reading. But I was going to ask *you* if you were free in the afternoon, if you wanted to catch a bus into town to look at the Art Gallery. I still haven't been there yet.'

'So Max is *not* the one person on earth you want to be with more than anyone – it seems I have that honour – but *is* he kind, and *does* he make you laugh?'

'Oh, gosh, Anna, that stings. I could say that he is *generous,* with me anyway. He hasn't made me laugh, at least not deliberately, not yet.'

'Well, I would like to look at pictures with you tomorrow afternoon. And a coffee afterwards. As long as it's somewhere with those shiny Formica tables, that doesn't have waitresses with squeaky shoes and chests like pigeons.'

'Oh God, Anna, you're priceless! Kind *and* you make me laugh. I ought to marry *you!*'

'Harry, I thought you'd never ask!'

*

Max led Harry down Queen Street after the performance.

'Thank you,' she said, looking up. 'I enjoyed that.' He was frowning slightly. 'Didn't you, Max?'

'Yes, only I am perplexed. Everyone laughed – you also – when Lady Bracknell said, "A handbag?" It is not so *drôle,* I think?'

'It's the way she said it. But perhaps it's just one of those things that English people like to do, same as standing up for the "Hallelujah Chorus", or saying "How do you do?" and not really expecting an answer.'

'*Évidemment,*' said Max, raising his eyebrows, and Harry could see it wasn't evident in the least.

They were strolling across Slab Square in the direction of the Council House when the first spits of rain fell.

'Come, 'Arry, under the columns.'

They hurried over, and up the few steps into the portico. They were not alone; at least two other couples murmured in the shadows. Max turned, so his back was towards them, hiding her from their view. He loomed up dark and indistinct, but a solid presence. Harry could hear his breathing. *Calm yourself. This is a public place.*

'*Pardon,*' he said and, putting his hands on her upper arms, he kissed her.

*

'I'll never tell him this, Anna, but when I saw his face coming down at mine, the first thing that came into my mind was that test they give you to find out if you need the tuberculosis jab – that six pinprick thing in your forearm to see if you've natural immunity.'

'And were you – immune?'

'No, I had to have the jab afterwards.'

'Not what I meant.'

Harry averted her face.

'Sorry, Loverish . . . hey, you're smiling! Not immune, then.'

'No,' said Harry, going pink. 'I liked it.'

'"You should be kissed and often, and by someone who knows how."'

'What . . . ?'

'*Gone With the Wind.* This calls for a celebration I think.' Anna parked two slightly smeary glasses on the desk and unstoppered the cognac.

*

Three days later, Harry came out of a lecture, shrugging off her undergraduate gown. She'd been astonished to learn that wearing one to lectures was compulsory only for History students.

Every student had one, but most had to wear them only for formal dinners.

'Miss Loveridge? Do you have a moment?'

Harry turned round to see a pale young man with lifeless brown hair and short-sighted grey eyes and suppressed a sigh.

'I'd really like to continue that argument we had earlier.'

'But it's just as Dr Holt said, Bill. You have to look at the evidence. I know we'd love to think of Magna Carta as an early declaration of the rights of all freeborn Englishmen, but really it was just about the barons protecting their own interests. The same kind of people who put down the Peasants' Revolt.' Harry paused, as she wasn't entirely sure about this assertion. That lecture wouldn't take place until the following term.

'I *am* looking at the evidence. Here are the earliest arguments against the divine right of kings, that underpin Cromwell's challenge—' Bill broke off, looking over Harry's shoulder.

'You will please come with me, 'Arry,' said Max, taking her elbow and steering her away from the open-mouthed Bill.

The moment they were out of the boy's earshot Harry shook herself free.

'What do you think you're doing, Max?'

'I could ask you this also,' he retorted. 'Who is that *radis pelé* and why do you talk with him?'

'Not that it's any of your business, but Bill is another student in my year, it is unkind to call him a peeled radish, and I shall talk to whoever I like, *whenever* I like.' With that, Harry stomped off, her shoulders stiff, clutching her books tightly; the gown slipped to the floor without her noticing. Max hurried to scoop it up, and rushed after her. Harry spun round at the sound of his running feet, about to tell him to go to blazes, when she saw the black material in his hands.

'Thanks!' she said between gritted teeth, and forced herself not to snatch.

*

Two evenings later, as a still simmering Harry came down to dinner with Anna, Tim Davies, one of the porters called out to her.

'Ey up, Harry. Yuh've a delivery. I'll help you girls up with it later if you like. It's raight heavy. Bowks it'll be – from Sisson & Parker's.'

Harry frowned. 'I've not ordered anything . . . thanks though. I'll be back as soon as I can get my pud down.'

*

The three of them had got the delivery upstairs by opening the parcel and dividing its contents between them. Heavy volumes in pale blue dust jackets nearly covered the entire surface of Harry's desk.

'It looks like the entire set,' she said, 'ten volumes or more.'

'There's a docket in this one, and it's got your name on it,' said Anna. 'But the bit with the price on it's been cut off.'

'*The Oxford History of England*,' said Harry. 'I can't afford this.'

'I expect M'sieur le Professeur could. I think this is a peace offering, Lover. Did he choose well?'

'I . . . oh . . . well, yes he did, actually. There's a set in the library, but only for reference. It gets fought over, just about.' She felt her face heat up. 'Max would have had to ask someone what I'd find most useful.' She could see him in her mind's eye, picking up the university telephone and dialling . . . who? Dr Holt? Dr Fryer?

'This is so humiliating, Anna. What if he's mentioned my name?'

'Hmm. Perhaps all he had to do was go to the department secretary and consult a book list.'

Harry's face cleared. 'Yes, perhaps you're right.'

*

Tim Davies handed Harry a note the following morning. It was an invitation to a coffee bar in the city centre. 'They are Italians,' wrote Max, 'so one must hope to find something drinkable. I hope you will give me an opportunity to explain myself.'

He was there when she arrived, and stood up to formally kiss her on both cheeks. He ordered for them both.

'*Je suis desolé,* 'Arry. I pray you will forgive me.'

Harry eyed him over the rim of her cappuccino.

'There's no harm in Bill Bolton, really there isn't.'

'I did not like how he looked at you, 'Arry.'

'He only peers because he's short-sighted, Max, and because he gets himself worked up. He's far more interested in history than he is in *me.*'

'I cannot believe that. But do you like your present?'

'Oh Max! I do. Those are books I shall keep forever, and read often. I *am* grateful, but you didn't need to make such a grand gesture.'

'I do not like that you must handle books that so many others also have touched,' he said.

Harry felt her scalp prickle. 'I'm not a sensitive plant, Max.'

'Forgive me. But you give me an idea. It does not rain, so shall we go to the arboretum and have a walk?'

'I'd like that,' said Harry. She buttoned her coat against the December cold.

*

By one of the cannons beneath the Chinese Bell Max kissed her. Like Rhett Butler, Harry had to admit, he was 'someone who knew how'. But she broke away early, holding his hands back. 'Before you kiss me again, there's something you have to know.'

'*Oui?*'

'No point in going round the houses, is there—' she said, addressing his shirt buttons.

'—the houses?' Max looked bewildered.

'Forget the houses. It happened the September before I came up – my last year at school. I was attacked by two men – on the farm where I grew up, where my father works. It could just as well have been in my home.' She felt his hands stiffen in her grasp.

'*Tu as été violée?*'

'Yes . . . that is a good way to put it. Better than English. I was violated.' She let go of his hands; she couldn't bring herself to look at him. There was a short silence.

'This explains . . . ' he tailed off.

'Explains *what?*'

'Sorry, my 'Arry. I have put my feet in the plate again. I meant, when I wanted to kiss your cheek. Our first evening.'

Despite herself, Harry laughed, and looked up at him. He was frowning, a muscle twitching hear his mouth, but there was concern in his eyes.

'I am sorry, 'Arry. *Vraiment.* I did not expect . . . I thought you were just being English. I thank you for telling me this. Who else knows it?'

'In Nottingham, just you, and Anna.'

'Then you honour me.'

He was silent though, as they walked back towards the entrance. As Waverley Street came into view, he said, 'It is *très joli,* this little park. I hope one day you will also walk with me in the Bois de Boulogne.'

*

'The problem is, Anna, that I don't know who he was sorry for,' said Harry, cradling her evening cocoa. 'I think it might have been himself, as if he'd just found out that I wasn't quite what he thought I was.'

'But he still wants to stroll with you through Paris.'

'Yes. But just before he put me on the bus home he blurted out something like "Did you fight back?"'

'Ah!'

'I said, "There were two of them, Max," and let go of his arm. I got on the bus and didn't look round at him.'

'All this for a membrane.'

'I wish I'd never told him,' said Harry, and started to cry. 'Like bloody Angel Clare and Tess of the D'Urbervilles.'

'I think we need something stronger than this wretched cocoa,' said Anna, putting an arm around Harry.

*

The journey home for Christmas was as different as it could have been from Harry's journey north. She travelled with Anna, and Max came to see them off. Anna shook Max's hand, businesslike, and retreated into their compartment, leaving Harry by the lowered window, looking down into Max's dark eyes.

'It is good you have her company,' he said, 'but after London you will be alone.'

'I'll be on the bike to Charing Cross, and then I'll sit with it in the guard's van to Canterbury. So stop worrying.'

The guard's whistle shrilled, and the train belched steam. Max held her hand, until the train began to move and her fingertips were pulled away. He stood there and Harry waved until she couldn't see him anymore, then went along to her compartment, wondering what it was she ought to be feeling.

*

At Loughborough, the elderly couple who had shared their compartment got out. Harry and Anna were alone.

'Has he ever mentioned the hop field again?' asked Anna, unwrapping her sandwiches.

'It's as if I'd never said anything. He's a bit . . . I don't know whether to call it chivalrous or possessive. But he was always that way – he made a bigger fuss over that Bill Bolton business. He only asks me when he can take me to Paris.'

CHAPTER FIFTEEN

Southern Region

December 1956

Harry sat on a packing case near the door of the guard's van, watching through the horizontal bars of the window as London died away into vistas of frosty-grey fields, church towers and oast houses. They looked to her like places in a book, the smaller, quieter world of the past. *I've only been away three months.* She thought of the long windows of the room she shared with Anna, the ramped seats of the lecture theatre, Dr Holt's voice urging his students to insist always on evidence, and finally her own fingers released from Max's hold as the train drew out of Nottingham Victoria. *I miss it, all of it . . . only I'm not sure how much I miss him.*

Then Chilham came, then Chartham, then Sturry, and Harry stood holding on to the window bars as the train went over the level crossing as it pulled into Canterbury West, and she saw the road stretching up to St Dunstans, the cars and cyclists waiting for the train to pass and the barrier to lift.

And there they were on the platform, her mother and father, his arm around Ellen's shoulder, a bag of shopping by her feet.

They've come to meet me even though I've got the Bantam. It came to Harry suddenly why they'd done so. *Since I've gone they've been alone in that cottage, for the first time ever,* and she felt humbled by her own importance.

*

The following day, Harry was standing at the sink in the house in Patrixbourne scrubbing potatoes when her mother asked, 'What does it feel like to be back here, Harry?'

'It's lovely – of course it is.'

'But?'

'I thought my heart would break when I left you behind in Canterbury. But I'm happy in Nottingham. I can't tell you how much. I'm sorry, that must sound ungrateful.'

'No. It's transformed you. Your father said so last night. You're confident, in charge. That makes him happy, you know. He worried so when you left.'

'I did miss everybody here.'

'You'll see them all on Sunday. They've been asking about you. Dare I ask, do you go to chapel at all?'

'Ye-es. Not every Sunday. Derby Road Methodists. It's a lot grander than the Tin Chapel. Powerful red and yellow brick. Mum, come and see me up there. Nottingham isn't perhaps a pretty place, but it's *proud,* somehow. And lively. We go to the cinema, and the theatre – there's something new every week.'

'We?'

'Me and Anna. Sometimes.'

'And the other times?'

'Oh, Mum . . .'

'Will we get to meet him too?'

'Maybe . . .'

'Aren't you going to tell me about him?'

'His name's Max. He's a bit older than me. French. A lecturer. Everybody seems to think he's a catch.'

'Do you?'

'I . . . I don't know. How *does* one know? How did you know with Dad?'

'Because I would have died for him,' said Ellen quietly. 'I still would. I know he'd have done the same for me. And still would.'

'When?' said Harry. 'When did you know?'

'Oh . . . very quickly.' She paused, carrot in one hand, knife in the other. 'I thought about nothing else. I'd go to the chapel and bow my head, and all I could see was him. I thought I was the worst sinner on God's earth. He wasn't what anyone else would call "a catch", though I had never seen anyone as good-looking as him – I still haven't. He couldn't even write his own name. Everyone but everyone was against us. In its way it was worse than what Princess Margaret had, and at least her man was divorced.' Her voice dropped. 'You see, your father already had a wife.'

There was utter silence in the kitchen until Ellen dried her hands on her apron. 'I'm not ashamed of loving your father, but the world thought I should have been.'

'Not Uncle Vanlo though?'

139

'No, not him. Harry, he's always stood by us. But that's another thing you don't know. He's not your father's brother. He's *her* brother. Your father's first wife.'

'Vanlo's not my uncle?'

'There's no blood relationship. But we are his family, and you couldn't have a better uncle – don't forget that. He *chose* us – he didn't have to. You too have choices, Harry. Including about this man. But I will say this: if you choose a man without being absolutely sure that you love him – as well as him loving you – you will be the loneliest person in the world.'

*

Ned Stones faced the personnel manager across his varnished oak desk, the roar of the factory muffled by the heavy door.

'Welcome back, Stones. Very brown and lean, I see, from your time in the tropics. Christmas Dance on Saturday – the girls'll go for you.'

Don't wannt any of 'em. 'Not sure I'll comm, sir.'

'No? Pity . . . bit early, maybe. You'll feel different come the New Year. Then there'll be the Skegness outing to look forward to.'

Ned pushed a piece of paper across the surface of the desk.

'What's this? Not leaving us already, are you? Oh . . . change of address. Good thinking. You'll not have to get up so early if you're living in Nottingham, will you? You might want more shifts then – easier for you.'

Nobody cares abaht me yellin' over Dora in the dark in Chippendale Street.

'Yeah.'

The man got to his feet, signalling the end of the meeting. 'So apart from your Reservist training, you're back in Civvy Street, Ned. It'll soon feel as if you've never been away.'

I 'ave bin away. I'll never feel I wurnt. 'Yes, sir,' he said, standing up.

Something in Ned's expression made the personnel manager hesitate. He patted the younger man's shoulder. 'You'll be all right. I was in the last dust-up – the navy. Ship was torpedoed and a lot of the chaps didn't make it. I just have to keep reminding myself I was lucky. You look as if you got away with nothing worse than sunburn and insect bites.' He opened the door, and Ned walked out into the crash of noise.

CHAPTER SIXTEEN

Nottingham

April 1957

'I've got time off for good behaviour, Anna.'

'Meaning?'

'Max is going to be away next academic year. Some sort of research exchange. In Grenoble. "The distance is to love what the wind is to the flame," he says.'

'Provided the wind doesn't blow it out. I can't tell from your face if you're relieved or sorry.'

'There *is* something I want you to help me with first.'

'Go on. I'm your man.'

'He wants to meet my parents before he goes.'

'Will *I* get to meet them too?'

'Oh God, of course. They've heard more about you back there than they have about him. Anyway, they're coming, and Max wants us to go out for dinner . . .'

'So what are you flapping about? You're not embarrassed by them are you? They can't be as awful as my two.'

'It's just that I can't see them in the same room as him, that's all.'

'He's not making noises about marrying *them* though. But if it gets that far – and you ask yours truly to be your bridesmaid and all that – it'd be your dad that hands you over, wouldn't it?'

'I hadn't even thought that far . . .'

'Well, *Max* certainly has. But if you aren't daydreaming about spending your life with him and having his babies, Harry, then I'd even go so far as to say you're being unfair to him, that's all. And I'm *your* friend, not his.'

'He knows he's not getting an answer until I have my degree.'

'You've said that, but that's two years away. You ought to be enjoying your time here and looking forward to graduating without having a decision like that hanging over you the whole time. Have you talked at all about what you'd actually *do* with the degree?'

'He asked me what I wanted to do, and I said . . . I said I wasn't sure.'

'Didn't you tell him Dr Fryer had been encouraging you to stay on here?'

'Not only Dr Fryer . . . I didn't only because that's sort of private . . . and it's only my first year . . . well, you know how competitive Max is, even though we're not in the same field. I'm not sure he'd be pleased.'

'Ah!'

'You see, he told me there was enough money that I wouldn't have to work anyway. I could be like his mother. I could just help him – or run a *salon,* bring people together, that sort of thing . . .'

'A gilded cage, but still a cage. But you said he *does* make your heart beat faster. Is that wanting-to-rip-his-shirt-off beating faster, or what?'

'Oh . . . it means I'm not sure I can breathe. Panic . . . or fear.'

'Bloody hell. You know what? I hope he finds some other pash when he's in Grenoble, I really do. More than that, I wish *you'd* meet someone else. None of the callow youths here have had a look in yet, because Max is always glowering in the background, whilst *you're* behaving like a Jane Austen heroine who thinks she mightn't get a better offer – in 1957.'

*

'I shall book somewhere suitable for your mother and father then,' said Max.

'*You?* I think I can manage that, Max. They won't want anything fussy, knowing them – so no, not the County Hotel. If I'd given them more notice, they'd have gone and found some Methodists to stay with. I should have been able to do that for them, but I've been pretty lazy about chapel attendance lately, so it would have been an awful cheek to take advantage of someone's generosity. A pub with rooms would do, even if my mother is teetotal.'

'So your mother is a Methodist who does not drink and your father a *manouche,* who presumably does?'

'He likes a glass of ale, yes, but he's not a "drinker". He smokes too much, and Mother doesn't at all.'

'Your parents are quite . . . how shall we say . . . original?'

'I've never thought of them that way,' said Harry.

'No, no, of course not. I am sure they are *charmant,* and I shall be likewise. The Flying Horse then. They have a restaurant too, I believe, though I can make no claims as to its cuisine—'

'Max!'

'*Comment?*'

'Don't be sniffy! We are going to eat with my parents, not write a review for that Egon Ronay thing.'

'I apologise, Harry. I am sure it will be a delightful occasion.'

'Only if you promise to be nice to the waitress. Oh, and one more thing. I should like to bring Anna.'

'*Anna?*'

'She *is* my best friend, and she wants to meet my parents. I can pay her part.'

'Don't be silly. The money is nothing. I just don't see the need for this chaperone. It is a little . . . *de trop.*'

'I'm glad you said it because I didn't know how to,' lied Harry. 'It's a Gypsy thing. Our girls shouldn't meet a man without one. Dad would be surprised if I did.'

'I understand then. No need for you to blush.'

*

Harry bought herself a platform ticket under the great cast-iron filigree cage of Nottingham Victoria. *I want to be as near as possible the first person they see here.* Though the London train was not due in for at least five minutes she ran over the clanging bridge. She spotted another girl further up the platform looking anxiously down the line by which the train would come – unlike the other knots of people bound for the further stations of Sheffield or Manchester, she had no luggage. Harry noted her freshly waved hair, the neatly buttoned box-jacket above her wide skirt with its stiff petticoats, the fake lizard handbag and thought, *she's got up in her best. She's waiting for a man.* She tried to imagine herself one day doing the same for Max.

The train was pulling in now, in a great cloud of steam and clanking of pistons. *How dirty that girl's lovely clothes are going to get.* She looked down at her own pea coat, slim-cut trousers, moccasin shoes, and too late remembered her father's resigned grumble about 'them slack things'. The fact was she felt safer in them. As the steam cleared for a moment she could make out the driver high up in his cab, his cap pushed back on his head, and then suddenly in a shriek of brakes and a relieved hiss of steam the train came to a dignified stop. The hitherto smooth line of carriages bristled as their doors opened, and slammed closed again with a noise like pistols going off. A national serviceman got down, dropping his holdall to swing the waiting girl off her feet. For a moment she looked like a doll in his arms. Harry's eyes prickled. And then just beyond the couple she caught sight of a tall man wearing an old fedora at a jaunty angle, arm in arm with a slender, neatly costumed woman with a little brown felt hat above the gentle, contented face of one whose life has long been lived in love. Harry's first thought was: *what a handsome couple they are.* The second was: *I'm sorry, Max.*

*

'It's a pub, with rooms above,' said Harry, walking them down to Slab Square.

'Oh, we like places like that, don't we, my Ellen?' said Sam, tucking his wife's arm more closely under his.

It's nearly embarrassing, thought Harry, *seeing how much they're in love. It's more obvious here, because it's a strange place for them both.*

Finally, they stood before the creaking gables of the old inn, and Sam let out a joyous laugh. 'Flying Horse? Oh, Harry, your man couldn't have chosen better. I like him and I've not even met him yet!'

Harry looked from one to the other, perplexed. Her mother's face was half-turned away, wearing a girl's smile. *There's a pub of that name in Canterbury. Must be some secret of theirs.* She felt a sudden surge of melancholy overwhelm the anxiety she already felt about the forthcoming meeting. *They were young once, and now they're not. Will I ever find happiness like theirs?*

*

'Looks like a nice place,' murmured Sam, as they entered the res- taurant, taking in the wooden panelling, the hunting prints, the horse brasses nailed above the fireplace. 'The way taverns used to be, only you can eat more private-like. And with carpets.' They were following a black-skirted waitress in a frilly cap, wearing an apron too small to be anything but decorative.

Anna saw them first, pushed her glasses back up her nose in a gesture her friend loved, and stood up. Max quickly followed suit. Harry made the introductions, glancing anxiously from one man's face to the other. She took her place flanked by Max and Anna, on one side of the table, Sam and Ellen opposite. The starched waitress reappeared with menus; Harry bristled as the woman hesitated, frowning at Sam before scurrying off.

Moments later, the waitress returned accompanied by 'this is Mr Baines, the manager'. Baines bowed stiffly, then brought his mouth close to Max's ear as Harry watched his eyes widen, first with surprise, then with amusement. All she caught were the words 'we have our standards to maintain . . . I am sure you understand, sir,' as Baines pressed something into Max's hand.

'You English,' said Max, his mouth twisted in delight. 'You never cease to surprise.' He waved his arm at the other tables, the scuttling waitresses. 'So much effort to create an old world 'ostelry, yet they have the petty snobberies of some gentlemen's *académie*. Myself, sir,' he went on, speaking to Sam, 'I find your appearance most *distingué*. But for this little man, you will not do. You do not wear a tie. He requests that you replace that charmingly knotted strip of silk with this object of decidedly inferior quality.'

'Well, I think we should just tell them what we think of them and walk out of here!' spluttered Harry.

'*Ma chère*, did you not warn me not to be – what was it? – "sniffy" with people?'

'I'm *not* being sniffy. My father is worth ten of that creature. I'd love to know if *he* went out under the bombs in an ARP helmet night after night. And he looks too young to have seen what my father saw in France—'

''Arry, you risk to sound quite reactionary—'

'Can I say something?' said Sam, quietly so they had to stop and listen. He reached over and put a hand on his daughter's arm. 'I'll wear their tie if they want. I've been made to wear worse in the past. Your young man arranged this evening so's we could all meet and sound each other out, so to speak. Only, I'll need help with it.' He smiled, and with that smile the tension eased around the table. 'Harry, my girl, would you come with me? All them years of school uniform you'll know what to do.'

'Of course, Dad.'

They were walking towards the toilets when their waitress came up to them. 'You can use our cloakroom if you like, seeing as you can't both of you go into the same washroom,' she said confidentially. 'I'll show you.'

Sam and Harry followed her, and were themselves followed by some curious glances from other diners, attracted by the girl with the elegantly poised head, and the tall man in a utility suit and a Gypsy's red *diklo*.

'Don't mind bleddy Baines,' whispered the woman as she opened the door. 'He keeps telling us he only took this job because we lost India. He was an army batman there, you see. But *I'll* make sure you have a nice evening.'

'Thank you, lady, I'm sure you will,' said Sam. The waitress looked up into his smiling face, and let out an agitated little cry. She muttered something about menus and fled.

'Dad, I've never known anyone manage to pull the way you do, and you don't even mean to!'

'I only meant to be polite,' said Sam, bewildered. 'Can't be easy working for Baines.'

'Come on, let's get you trussed up then.'

Harry stood back eventually and surveyed her work, grateful at least that her father was wearing a shirt with a collar. 'They've never made a fuss in the chapel,' she added.

'That's 'cos God ain't a head waiter.'

Laughter eased the disappointment Harry felt looking at the change in her father's appearance. With the flash of the *diklo* at the open neck of his worn spotless white shirt, the ten-year-old suit and trousers, his 'best', had had a certain rakish style – *panache,* as Max later called it. Against the formality of the plain blue terylene tie, his other clothes looked tired and scruffy. Sam and Harry made their way back to the table where grapefruit segments awaited them.

Max looked up. 'Ah! Now I think they will allow us to eat in peace. Sir, 'Arry said you saw service in my country.'

''Twas in Picardy. I thought the people kind and friendly, though in some ways they'd it worse than us.'

Back in her place, Harry exhaled slowly, and picked up her spoon.

*

Harry called at the Flying Horse after breakfast on the Sunday morning, as arranged, and found her mother sitting with their suitcase in the entrance hall.

'Where's Dad?'

'He's gone out. He's probably talking to the milkman about his horse, same as he was yesterday. We've plenty of time, haven't we?'

'Oh yes. Perhaps they'll look after that suitcase behind the bar and we can have a walk.'

'I should go to chapel.'

'Oh Lord, I never thought, Mum. Derby Road's a bit far off.'

'Don't worry, Harry. I'd rather talk to you and tell God about it afterwards. Sit down for a minute, until your dad comes back.'

Harry pulled a chair closer to her mother and sat down.

'You have no idea how happy I am to see you so happy here,' went on Ellen. 'That park – the university – is so beautiful. And you and Anna have a lovely room.'

'We did tidy up a bit for you.'

'I guessed you had! She's a great friend to you too. The kind that would defend you against all comers. She has something of your Aunt Judy.'

'You miss her, don't you?'

'I do. But I know she thinks about me – and all of us – even if she's on the other side of the world. Whereas you—' Ellen's voice quavered a little. 'You'll perhaps only be going as far as France.'

'I won't, Mum. Or rather, if I do, it won't be with Max.'

'Oh!'

'I'm going to break with him, Mum. You and Dad have made me see that I have to.'

'*Us?* We've let you down somehow?'

'*No!* Absolutely not. I can just see him more clearly because you two are here. I know what love should look like – the kind

151

of love you and Dad have. I don't love Max, Mum.' Harry registered the look of relief on her mother's face, quickly suppressed.

'What did Dad think of him?' asked Harry.

'You know your father.' Ellen tried a smile. 'Nobody could be good enough for you, though he did think Max quite a gentleman. What he said to me though, after we'd had that nice meal, was that it didn't matter what either of us thought. Your opinion was the only one that counted.' Ellen stopped, looking beyond Harry in the direction of the door. 'Here he is now.'

*

A few days after her parents had gone home, Harry stood in the corridor of the French department desultorily reading the notices pinned into cork, without really registering what they said. Her attention was on the murmur of voices behind the closed door of Max's study. She glanced at the bland white face of the clock at the end of the corridor. *Those hands haven't moved. It must have stopped,* she thought. No, she saw the second hand click on, in that odd way it had of darting forward, then pulling slightly back. Then at last came a louder clunk – the hour. She tried to focus on an announcement of a travel bursary from the British and Foreign School Society, her attention instead on the scrape of chairs and the click of the door, before Max's students billowed out, not noticing her, still engaged in earnest conversation. One lingered in the doorway though, a beautifully coiffed blonde girl dressed not unlike Harry herself. However, even at that distance, as a child of rationing, Harry could see that there was more cloth in the swing jacket draped on the girl's shoulders, that the leather of her moccasins was suppler, the worsted of her slacks finer. The girl held her books in the crook of her left elbow. She took two steps backwards into the corridor and then Max emerged, smiling, amused, as with her free hand his student emphasised some point by patting his forearm again and again, her voice high with enthusiasm edging into hysteria. Max looked round then and spotted Harry.

'You must excuse me, Miss . . . Miss . . .'

'Harcourt,' said the girl, her tone flattened.

'It is just that I see my fiancée waiting for me.' He inclined his head, and Miss Harcourt set off in the opposite direction, her shoulders hunched. He strolled up to Harry, and bent to kiss her cheek. She pulled away.

'*Arry!* You are not jealous, surely?' He looked pleased.

'Not a bit of it! Why did you have to be so unkind? You *knew* that girl's name, didn't you?'

'Of course.' He grinned. 'But her adulation is so fatiguing. An hour with her looking at me like a calf and giggling . . . don't tell me that you are angry with me on her account?'

'No – yes – not only.'

'You are un'appy because your mother and father have gone, and so you wish to make your poor Max suffer. May I say though that I found them utterly *charmante* – your mother so refined – more than most Englishwomen I have to say—'

'Max, *shut up!*'

'What did I say? Come, let us go and eat and you can berate me all you like, on a full stomach.'

'Do *not* make fun of me!'

Max raised his hands in mock surrender. 'I would not dare!'

'Nor patronise me, nor them! Oh God, Max, I'm sorry, and you'd paid for their stay. They hadn't expected that.' *Nor wanted it, I'll bet.* 'They went to settle the bill and were told it was all taken care of.'

'I wished merely to make a good impression.'

You cannot buy them, or me, thought Harry, glowering still.

Max pulled her arm under his. 'Come,' he said, 'I shall order a taxi and take you into the country today. I think at Newstead they can feed us. And you can tell me if I pleased your parents.'

'That I can't tell you, honestly.'

'*Non?* They did not talk to you about me? They must have some opinion, surely?'

'They're bound to. Only they know me better than to say so.'

'And you didn't ask?' he said, nettled. 'Do I not matter to you, then?'

'You do – that is to say – Max, let's just go outside. I don't want to talk about this in here, with people going past. And I don't want to go to lunch either.' They'd reached the head of the staircase. Harry pushed through the double doors and pattered quickly downwards.

''Arry! Wait!'

Out in the fresh air he grabbed her arm. 'When we are married, will it always be like this? Am I not to know what I have done wrong?'

'"When we are married". Max, I haven't said I *will* marry you.'

'*Agace-pissette!*[16]'

'What?'

'I am sorry – but you make me mad, 'Arry!'

'Max, let's sit down for a minute, on that bench. And please, listen to me!'

He sank down onto the bench, but when she sat beside him, he budged up so that their thighs touched. Without meaning to, Harry felt herself recoil, but saw that Max didn't seem to notice. He'd grasped her hands, holding them one on top of the other between both of his, and was squeezing them tightly. She tried to pull away but his grip tightened.

'You're hurting me!'

'Not nearly as much as you hurt me!' he said. 'We were agreed—'

'Were we?' said Harry, bewildered, blundering about in her memory to find what it was he could have construed as agreement. She took a deep breath.

'Max, I admire you a very great deal.' She watched him tilt his head back, a gesture that made her think of a horse – not one of Tom's placid drays, but a thoroughbred with the East Kent Foxhounds – a comparison which was no advantage to Max.

'I cannot marry you, Max.'

'They have told you not to.'

'No one has told me anything I should or shouldn't do.' *Except you.*

---

[16] Cock-tease.

'Then why this, now?' His face came so close to hers now that she felt his breath hot and slightly damp on her cheek. As he hadn't let go of her hands, she dipped that cheek to her shoulder, an action that made him draw back. It was a relief to Harry to break eye contact, even so briefly.

'It's because of them, though.' She felt her nose prickle, and her eyes filled.

'You do not wish to be far from them. You have found it hard, being here without them. That is normal. We can talk about that.'

'No!'

'At least be honest with me about what I do wrong.'

'Nothing! Max! It is because I cannot love you as they love each other!' she cried.

'Oh 'Arry!' He released her hands and took hold of her shoulders. He was smiling now. 'Do you not see, most beautiful girl, that you have said to me a marvellous thing? You want to love me long, you see? Like them, thirty years.'

Harry shut her eyes, trying to think.

Max leaned in and kissed her.

She cried out, pulling away. 'Max, don't.'

Unruffled, he said, 'I quite understand. You have been through a terrible experience. You are afraid to love. So only the best will satisfy you – the love you see between your mother and father. *I* can give you that, 'Arry. I will soon be gone to Grenoble. You will have a letter from me every day. Then when I come back I shall ask you again, and you will see, you need not fear.'

Harry saw herself at her desk by the long window of the room she shared with Anna, hemmed in on all sides by pallisades of long white envelopes bearing Madeleine stamps.

'I can't promise the same – I mean a daily letter.'

'Of course not. Your studies . . .'

'Max – *I do not love you enough.*'

'You say that now. But when I come back . . .'

'All right, Max,' she said. It was easier to acquiesce. 'When you come back.'

*

'Drink your cocoa, Loverish, and tell Aunt Anna all about it.'

'Oh Anna, I don't know how you have the patience.'

'Face like mine, dearest, the nearest I'm going to get to a grand pash is hearing about yours. Only it's not, is it? A grand pash, that is.'

'I don't know what's the matter with me. He's like the hero of one of those little novels they sell at the newsagent's. The kind we used to read at school to find out about love. Only I don't know how to be the heroine.'

'I've read them too. They bring joy to lots of lonely women, those books. He's handsome, rich, exotic, overbearing. The pair of them start by hating each other but that emotion leads to the other one by page forty-six and a happy-ever-after by forty thousand words.'

'I don't *hate* him. But it's as if he wilfully misunderstands what I'm trying to tell him. I think there *was* a point at which I might have fallen for him, without reserve, I mean. Only I held back. I was scared. He *is* scary sometimes. His students seem to adore him, but it's more awe than affection. But I was probably more afraid of my own reaction.'

'You're still frightened of the sex thing.'

'Yes. Of course I am. What if I married him and found I hated him touching me?'

'I've said it before. With the right man you wouldn't be. If Max was that man, you'd know – even without sampling the merchandise.'

'Oh Anna . . .'

'Stop trying to make him that man. It's not fair on either of you.'

'If he would even slow down a little, it might help. I feel cornered. But each time I try to tell him he needs to let me breathe, it just makes him worse. He keeps asking me what he's doing wrong, but the way he says it, it's as if the fault is mine, not his.'

'You know what I would do. Let him go to Grenoble, and then see how you feel about him. If you miss him, well, that's one thing. If what you feel is mostly relief, then write to him. Say that the distance has helped you make a clearer judgement. A *cher Jean* letter.'

Harry smiled damply for the first time that evening.

*

A few weeks later, on a mild May morning, Harry again stood on the London-bound platform, this time to see Max leave. His tin trunk had preceded him, weighted with books. After they'd got out of the taxi he'd summoned a porter, overtipping the man as he had the driver, to put his suitcase and briefcase into the first-class compartment.

'I can see from your face I do another thing of which you do not approve, 'Arry.'

'Going first class, you mean?'

'That too. Other men have only to read their newspapers and fill in those coupons. *I* have work to do, and so must have comfort. In time I am sure you will not complain, because you will share zese things wiz me. In time you will be glad to put away your sewing machine, and your mugs of cocoa.'

I like making clothes, and drinking cocoa.

'And not being burdened means I can put my arms around you, 'Arry,' and he did so, bending his head to kiss her firmly and insistently on the mouth, darting his tongue between her teeth. Briefly, Harry forgot the annoyance he had just caused her, and gave herself up to the romance of the moment. Max was rich, yes, and handsome, and thrillingly foreign. Under the canopy of the railway station she saw him as other girls did, and enjoyed the kiss, enjoying it because she knew it would have to stop, that a whistle would put an end to it.

Max boarded the train at last, but stood in the corridor outside his compartment, pressing his hands against the window. Harry stood still as a lighthouse as the train drew away, though other girls and men flowed past her, drinking up the last dregs of bittersweet departure. Though she watched the train out of sight, her thoughts were already on her end-of-year exams, and the journey to Canterbury that would follow soon after, a third of the adventure of university already over.

'Ey up, duck!' cried a cheerful voice at her elbow, breaking into her daydream. 'Train's gone and man with it. 'E looks like 'e'll comm back, though.'

Harry smiled faintly at the man who had been Max's porter. 'Yes, I expect he will.'

Picking up the weariness of her tone, the man said, 'That's if yuh wannt him to, o' course.'

*

The first letter arrived eight days later, posted only hours after Max had reached Paris. There were three envelopes for Harry that day; she glanced at the handwriting on each before taking them up to her room. The first one she opened was in a childish hand, the pen pressing deep into the lined paper – from her godson, her brother David's child. He'd enclosed a photograph of himself proudly holding the box that contained the Meccano set he'd been given for his birthday. Luke looked almost exactly like the little boys in the image on the box: gleaming, neatly parted hair, wearing a pullover his mother had knitted, a pressed white shirt, short trousers, long socks and sturdy lace-up shoes. The child complained that his father played with the set as much as he did. Harry read the letter twice, her eyes misting over.

The second letter, on delicately scented Basildon Bond, was from Ethel Shaw.

I have spent some weeks in hospital but have been most neatly sewn back together again. Margaret Spellman knew but I urged her not to mention this to you as you have had your end-of-year examinations to face.

I do not think I can manage the bicycle just yet, but if you like we could catch the bus to Whitstable to our old haunt the Red Spider and see if the scones are still as delicious as they were when you were a schoolgirl.

Harry felt more than a twinge of regret: she had sent her old teacher a mere two postcards and had seen her only briefly during the Easter holidays, when she had put Miss Shaw's drawn appearance down to tiredness, and forgotten about it by the time she was back on the train.

The first letter Max had ever written her was short, but passionate.

I should say I will count the days until I see you, but instead I want that you should fill those days. Come to Paris, Harry. It is little distance to Dover from your parents' home and I would meet you at Calais. I have been walking all over my beloved Paris imagining being here with you, and wondering where we might live. I see you so vividly that yesterday I was convinced that a woman watering the plants on her balcony in the Île de la Cité was you, and almost shouted at her in anger when she turned her head and her features did not arrange themselves into your face. I have told Maman about you and she is prepared to be charmed. She wishes to have a day of you to herself in which to dress you . . .

Harry undid another button on her blouse and tweaked the front of her bra – her clothes felt hot, confining, tight. She took a deep breath and fought down her sense of suffocation. Just then there was a scuffle at the door and Anna strode in.

'Ah!' she said, looking at Harry's face.

*

'Summertime in Paris, though?' said Anna. 'Not to be sneezed at.'

'I *can't*. I hope and pray that poor Miss Shaw *is* really better, but . . .'

'She is your alibi.'

'No, that won't do. It'll have to be something else. I don't even want to *pretend* that she's worse than she is, because it gets me off the hook. It's too much like tempting fate.'

'You could just be honest. And you could also say you've a long-standing engagement in North 17 – with me. Can I have that stamp, by the way? Dad's found a dealer and has got everyone collecting them; every little bit helps the Incurable Jews.'

*

In his lodgings in Chippendale Street, Ned Stones was about to pull his shirt over his head without undoing all the buttons, when he remembered his landlady had complained that they were a 'faff' on laundry day, and please to remember next time. His vest followed his shirt, and Ned regarded himself critically in the mirror above the basin. Dora's voice came into his head, and he shut his eyes momentarily with the pain of it: 'Yuh've lovely skin, yow 'ave,' she'd said, her fingers delicately stroking his torso. *I never wannt to forget yow'*, he thought, and wished he'd gone for overtime that weekend rather than face time alone with himself. His mates had asked him again if he would rejoin the football team, but he'd shaken his head and said, 'Not ready yet,' knowing they'd give up eventually. He was pleased though that at Raleigh his hands had remembered their tasks, and that he'd soon recovered the speed he'd achieved before his call-up. The problem, he knew, was that this left his brain to wander where he wished it wouldn't go.

He plucked at the skin of his chest. *Yur white again, yow are. Like yow wor never away.* But Dora's face, and the jungle, with all it hid, were still there when he turned off the lamp. He'd found it helped to leave the curtains a little open, to let in the street light, and to think of the people he'd see milling about the city shops in the morning. They made him feel safer.

CHAPTER SEVENTEEN

Nottingham
April 1958

'Have you a moment, Miss Loveridge?'

Harry was already about to follow the other tutorial student out, but she turned in the doorway at Dr Holt's uncharacteristically hesitant tone.

'There's a Rag Week meeting, but I'm sure they can wait,' she said, closing the door and taking her seat again.

Holt steepled his fingers. 'Do stop me if I speak out of turn. I spoke to you last year, if you'll remember, urging you to think about staying on here after you graduate.'

'Certainly I remember. I haven't stopped thinking about it.'

'Oh? I might have grounds for optimism then ... it is only that I thought your plans had altered rather.'

'My plans?'

Holt cleared his throat. 'My colleague in French – Dr Arago.'

Harry felt the heat rise to her face. 'Plans?' she repeated hoarsely.

'I may have got the wrong end of the stick. Are you not engaged?'

'Certainly not! Is that what Dr Arago said?'

'I see that I am really rather a poor historian,' said Holt, with an apologetic smile. 'I tell my students – you among them – to always look for the evidence, and fail to follow my own advice. That Dr Arago said he intends to marry you does not mean that a marriage is bound to take place.'

'Dr Holt,' said Harry quietly, 'I have never agreed to marry anyone, and thanks to what you have just said, any hopes that Dr Arago might have had in that regard are well and truly dashed. I cannot tell you how grateful I am to you for telling me this.'

'And if I may say so, I am greatly relieved. I am not your father, Miss Loveridge. Alice and I have only our boy, and he is still too little for such matters, but in a fatherly way I felt some concern that even someone as vibrant as you might be eclipsed by Dr Arago's shadow, and never be allowed to bloom as you should, let's say. I know that Dr Fryer shares my misgivings. I thought, though, that perhaps I was motivated by selfishness – the desire to keep a gifted student . . .'

Harry blushed again, but this time with pleasure. She couldn't stop smiling.

'I know these are very early days,' said Holt, 'but the stronger a research proposal that we come up with, the easier it will be to find funding. Whatever you choose must be something that will absorb you completely, something original – a rich seam that has been missed by other researchers . . .'

Harry hesitated.

'You have something in mind, I think?'

'"Diverse and many outlandish people calling themselves Egyptians",' quoted Harry.

'Henry VIII's Egyptian Act, unless I'm much mistaken. So gratifying to know not everyone sleeps in my lectures,' he said. 'There's an earlier reference to the court of King James IV of Scotland, in 1505, I think. Miss Loveridge, we need longer to talk about this, and I know there are others waiting for you, so why don't you make an appointment through the departmental secretary – tell her I've asked you to do so if she puts up a fight . . .'

*

Harry still felt as though she walked on springy turf, as she pushed open the door of the private bar. The faces inside swivelled towards her.

'Oh, there you are, Harry. *You* look cheerful.'

'Do I?'

'Thank goodness you could make it. We want your photograph for the front of the rag mag,' said the convener. 'Something that'll make everybody sit up and take notice.'

'Why do you want *me*?' said Harry, pulling up a stool.

'Well, you're a lot better looking than any of us,' he said.

Harry rolled her eyes. 'What'll I be doing in this photograph? I'll tell you right now it won't be a shimmy dance.'

'Look at this first,' said another student, pushing a folded copy of the *Nottingham Post* across the bar table. *Vandals tip paint over lions in Slab Square,* Harry read. She looked up, eyebrows raised.

'The idea is that you go there with your paints, and well, you paint the lions. On a piece of paper, or canvas, or whatever. Then someone – well, one of us, obviously – sees you doing it and goes to a call box to ring the plods. They come piling down when they hear that "someone is painting the lions", only to find you sitting sweetly at your easel and we get our photograph.'

'So I get into trouble, then.'

'Why would you? They won't know which wag thought it would be a good idea to ring them up. Loads of people set up an easel there.'

'I'd be telling lies though.'

'Yes, well, there is that.'

'I've never painted anything in such a public place. Parks are all right.'

'It's for a good cause. The Children's Hospital.'

'Buy me a drink, then.'

'You drive a hard bargain.'

'Haven't said I'll do it yet, have I? I've got to think about it.'

*

Harry struggled to the rear of the bus, her painting bag containing Vanlo's easel weighing on her shoulder and her collapsible stool in her right hand. 'Let me help yow with a' that, mi duck,' said a middle-aged man, 'else yuh might fall and hurt thissen.'

'Ah' raight, I'll not ring the bell till the young lady is safely down,' called the conductor.

'Thank you,' said Harry, getting down and turning round to get her things. She noticed the flattened nails and the blue smudges beneath the skin of the man's hand as he passed down the heavy bag. A miner. Smiling up at him, she saw the same marks on his face. *He sees daylight only Saturdays and Sundays.*

'That was very kind of you, sir.'

The miner smiled, the conductor rang the bell and the bus rumbled off.

Once off the bus, Harry set off across the square and, with a deep breath, started setting up the easel four feet away from the lion she was going to paint. *I hope they don't forget that phone call,* she thought, *because I'm going to feel a right* dinilo[17] *if I've to sit here for very long.* She smiled to herself. *Dinilo. One of Dad's words.* She went on smiling, remembering that in three days time she would be meeting Dr Holt again, to talk about her future.

Twenty minutes later, she'd forgotten the phone call. The lion's pharaonic head and frown was taking shape on the page. *I'm not bad at this. I should do it more often. Funny bib they've given him instead of a mane. Like steps. I like his crossed-over paws though.* She frowned in concentration. *What about a big red bow round your neck? Sitting on a child's bed between Dismal Desmond and a Chad Valley teddy bear, with a Kewpie doll in your paws? Sorry, Lion, not very dignified.*

---

[17] Idiot.

She dipped her paintbrush in the waterpot. There was a shuffling behind her followed by an intent silence. *Some people haven't anything better to do than gawp.* She was aware now of a knot of students on the steps just beyond the lion, but knew she had to keep up the pretence that she didn't know what they were doing there. *I hope they've not forgotten their blasted camera. And where* have *the police got to?*

She sighed, and examined the lion's scowling expression for clues. *I expect you'd like to be back home on the veldt,* she thought. *That is, if they have lions in South Africa.* She frowned, realising that she knew rather more about South African politics than about the country's geography or fauna. *Not right, that, is it? There've been animals there for a lot longer than there've been Boers.* She remembered reading the names on the obelisk memorial to the South African wars in Forest Recreation Ground, wondering at the time if anyone else ever did.

'Bloody 'ell!' said a voice behind her. '"Painting the lions in Slab Square," they said. "Vandals! Best get down there quick!" they said. As if we've got noat better to do!'

Harry turned round on her stool and looked up into the sweating face of a police sergeant. His younger colleague had his hand over his mouth but she could see his eyes crinkle. Beyond them a knot of people were gathering: a courting couple, an old lady in what looked like bedroom slippers, and a tousle-haired youth in an open-necked shirt.

'We're going to do yow for wasting police time, young lady!'
'What, for painting a picture?' cried the youth.

'Yow mind yer own business or yuh'll be booked too!' said the sergeant, without turning round. The young man shrugged, and smiled at Harry.

'Bloody students!' said the sergeant. The younger policeman made a show of taking out a notebook, but his shoulders were shaking.

'Go on, lad, book her!' The sergeant stomped off in the direction of the police box.

The constable turned over a page. 'First name, miss?'

'Harry.'

'Harriet on Sundays, I s'pose.'

'No, Harmony.'

You could be called Albert and you'd still be gorgeous. Hell, give it a go, man! 'Oh! You must be a peaceful sort of girl, then?'

'Me! Not a bit of it!'

'Leave 'er be, can't yow? What 'arm's she doin'?' said someone at Harry's shoulder. She glanced round into the face of the young man in the open-necked shirt.

'You've already been told to stay out of it!' retorted the policeman. Turning back to Harry, he continued in milder tones: 'Who put you up to it, miss?'

'Put me up to what? I didn't know it was a crime to paint in watercolours. It's a nice day and I felt like a bit of fresh air. If someone chose to report it, that's nothing to do with me. It's them that's wasting police time, not me.'

The policeman tore the paper from his pad and crumpled it.

'Can't say I believe you. But you've given me the best laugh I've had in ages.'

'Is that all, then? I'm not in trouble?'

'For painting a picture? No! That old bastard is always playing tricks like that. Taking the details and then leaving a poor sod to stew thinking he'll be called up before the magistrates, when Sergeant's already used the paper for kindling. Can't say it's what I joined for. Will you come back . . . to finish the painting, I mean?'

'I might do.'

'Mebbe I'll see you again then?'

'Maybe.'

The policeman opened his mouth to say something more, when he was interrupted by a shrill whistle from the direction of the police box.

'Oh bogger. I'd best go. Goodbye . . . Harry.'

'Goodbye.' Harry started unpinning her work from the easel.

'Thought he'd never go,' said the young man.

'Oh! You still here?'

'I must be. Aren't yur going on wi' the picture then? Yur good, yow are.'

'No. I've done my bit. I can finish it at home. And look over there – they've got their photograph.' Harry waved at a gaggle of students on the steps of the Council House. One of them raised a camera aloft.

'Tellin' porkies to a policeman,' he said. 'Oh dear! I'd never've known!'

'*He* did.'

'Yow a student, then?'

171

'That's right. Second year. Oh, where will I empty this?' she said, holding the waterpot.

'That flowerbed won't mind. Fancy a cuppa, do yow?'

'I ought to get back. I've an essay to write.'

'Don't wannt to be seen wi' a townie?'

Harry stared at him, taking in dark blue eyes, the unruly brown hair left slightly too long on top, but free of Brylcreem and, *thank heavens,* with no attempt at a quiff.

'For that, I think I *will* have that cup of tea. But only if I can have a buttered scone with it.'

'Cream and jam, madam?'

'Of course!'

'Well, comm again termorrer! I wor goin' to tek yuh to the Kardomah, but I think it'll need to be Griffins. Ever been there?'

'Never.'

'Me neyther.' They both laughed.

'My auntie had a job cleaning in there,' he said. 'They've a place up on the top floor, apparently. She and her pal used to tek their sandwich boxes and sit at the table pretending to be ladies, and the night watchman put a tea towel over his arm and acted the waiter. All in the middle of the naight, nobody to see 'em. Don't think they let any of the staff in as customers, even if it is their day off and they've the money to pay for their tea.'

'I'm not sure I *do* want to go there then.'

'Just this once. Just to see if they stop us and accuse us of pinching things.'

'Go on, then.'

*

'Only teacakes left!' he said. He screwed his face up and came out with a passable Kenneth Williams adenoidal sneer. 'Shocking, I call it!'

'Tea cakes are fine. *You're* a good mimic. Do any acting?'

'Acting?' He laughed. 'Acting up, more like. Nope, I've been working in Raleigh since I left schoowel, 'part from when I wor in army.'

'Where did you serve, then?'

'Got my knees brown in Malaya. Don't suppose I'll go anywhere abroad ever again. Don't suppose I'll get further than Mansfield, comm to that. What about yow? Southerner, int ya?'

'Don't hold it against me. Kent. I grew up on a farm. My dad's the foreman, and my mum teaches in the village school. Infants mainly.'

'Lucky man. My fayther has spent his life dairn pit – a village outside Nottingham yuh'll not have heard of. Mam's a housewife, and I'm in lodgings about a mile from here. I go and see them odd Sundays. I'm Ned Stones, by the way.'

'Harry Loveridge.'

'Loveridge? There was a lad o' that name in schoowel wi' me. He wurnt there for long. He woh smart, but cudnt write his own name hardly.'

'Nor could my dad. Not until he went to prison.' She watched his reaction.

'Better that than leave a bloke kicking his heels.'

I think you might pass the test. 'Yes. A clergyman taught him. A prisoner, not a chaplain. He was in for fraud – the vicar, I mean.'

Ned Stones gave a low whistle, and heads at the next table turned, but looked quickly away when Harry glared at them.

'Am I allowed to ask what your old man 'ad done?'

'Of course you can, as he didn't do it. Horse stealing.'

A middle-aged waitress appeared at Ned's elbow. 'Will there be anything else, sir?'

'I'm ah' raight. Harry?'

'That was very nice, thank you,' said Harry.

'Well, it's just that we need the table.'

'We can tek a hint,' said Ned. 'Let's go downstairs, Harry, and see if they've finished raking our footprints out o' that squishy carpet, shall we?'

*

Standing outside Griffin & Spalding, Ned said, 'Can I see you again?'

'I don't see why not.'

'Oh. Well, what about same time, same place, Sat'day next?'

'Without the easel and the clobber.'

'Might have to share yuh wi' PC Plod, o' course.'

Harry frowned. 'I'm not sure if I want to share myself with anybody, thank you.'

'Sorry. I don't mean—'

'It's all right, Ned.' She smiled. 'I'd a nice time today. I even managed not to get myself arrested.'

'I'll see yuh onta bus, then.'

*

'Sphinx-like Harry,' said Anna that evening. 'How did it go?'

'Sorry, how did what . . . ?'

'Miles away. Painting the lions. What did you think I meant?'

'Oh that? Rather well, I think.' She got up to fetch her painting. 'I've still to finish it.'

'Oh, I say! You've talent.'

'Pity I nearly got arrested.'

'My godfathers! Who by, the Sheriff of Nottingham?'

Harry laughed, and told her story. But Anna stopped wiping her tears of laughter and sat up attentively when she described the teacakes episode.

'You'll not be telling Max, I'd guess.'

Harry hesitated. 'It was just a cup of tea. But I said I'd meet him again next Saturday.'

'*Mazel tov!*' exclaimed Anna, and got up to kiss Harry's forehead.

CHAPTER EIGHTEEN

The Gaumont

'Just as well yuh got your painting done last weekend. Fancy seeing a flick, Harry, to get uz out o' the wet?' said Ned, drawing her under his umbrella. His shoulders and the back of his raincoat were already glossy with the rain that blew at them sideways. The frail umbrella skittered and danced in the wind, threatening to fold upwards. She took his arm, feeling the solidity of him through her biker jacket.

'Why not?' she said.

'The Gaumont do? Summat cheerful called *The Bad Seed*. One o' mi mates saw it and said it wor a shocker.'

'Let's go and be shocked, then.'

*

Normally on entering a cinema Ned would light a cigarette as soon as the lights went down, but this time he wanted nothing to interfere with the scent of the girl sitting silently to his right. *I bet it's summat expensive.*

Ned rapidly got bored with the film, though not bored with the fact that he was sitting next to Harry. He'd hoped for something that would have had her shrieking and hiding her face in his shirt. He furtively slipped an arm across the back of her seat and leaned in to her ear. 'The scariest thing so far is Leroy's braces,' he whispered. Harry didn't stir. The screen turned bright, a sunlit scene, and in the pale light penetrating the fug of cigarette smoke he glimpsed her profile. Harry's eyes were closed, her lips gently parted. He put his free hand in front of her mouth and felt the warm regularity of her breath. She was fast asleep. He moved his right arm from the back of the seat to her far shoulder, clasping it gently. Ten minutes later, her body sagged sideways, and her hair brushed his neck. She felt as warm and relaxed as a cat. His heart thumped. *A fine girl, yow are. An' this is a bleddy awful film.*

Twenty minutes later, Harry stirred and noiselessly sat up. Ned withdrew his arm, although he kept it on the back of her chair, not touching her. Free of that delicious contact his neck and shoulder felt suddenly cold.

*

'Thank you for not kissing me, Ned,' she said, as they stood on the dark shiny street.

Taken aback, and not sure if she was joking, he said, 'Yow wor sleepin'.'

'You mean I was asleep and so I didn't know you did, or you didn't *because* I was asleep?'

'I dint, because I dint, that's all. It wurnt that I dint wannt to. I saw more of yow in there than that bleddy film, if the truth be known. Even in the dark I cudnt keep me eyes off yow. Harry . . . would yuh think about me and yow? Bein' my girl?'

'Oh, Ned,' she said, 'don't rush me.'

'I'm sorry.' *Yow daft bogger!* 'Cup of coffee then? I'll try an' behave.'

'I'm sorry I snapped. Yes, of course.' She took his arm.

'Kardomah do this time? I've spent most of mi money.'

'Yes. If you were Jesse Boot himself I'd say the same.'

*

'Nasty kid,' said Ned, over the Formica table.

'Where? Oh, the film, you mean. Even worse acting,' said Harry.

'Is it true, do yuh think, that yow can inherit madness? Same as me havin' me fayther's hair and me mam's eyes?'

'I don't know. Maybe for some – though I'm more inclined to think that it's what happens to people makes them mad. Something so unbearable you couldn't stay sane.'

''Mebbe you're raight,' said Ned, suddenly serious. 'Yow've eyther to forget summat happened, or yow've to get as far away from it as possible, before it teks yer over. Or if yuh can't forget it, yer remember it as if yow were standing to one side watchin' it 'appen to some other poor bogger instead.'

Harry stared.

'Yow'll be thinking yuh've just been to the pictures with a lunatic,' he said. In a quick, nervous movement, he pushed his hair up. It flopped over his forehead again.

'Something happened to you, didn't it?' said Harry. 'You couldn't talk like that if it hadn't.'

'Mebbe. Not really the best way to chat up a girl yuh really like, is it?' he said.

'The army?'

'Yeah . . .'

The waitress appeared with their coffees at that moment, breaking the tension.

'I'd rayther know about yow, though, than give yow a lot o' glum stuff about me,' said Ned, as the girl walked off. 'Is there just yow, or are there others where yuh come from?'

'I've two big brothers. I look like Tom, the eldest, but like David barely at all. *They* might of course be an argument for nature over nurture, for though they've been brought up the same way, they're very different. Two different dads, you see.'

'Your mam remarried, then?'

'Yes, she did, but you might say things happened in the wrong order. *My* dad made no difference between my brothers when they were growing up, and he doesn't now. David, my half-brother, though I don't think of him as a half at all, has a half-sister, my mother's age – from *his* father's first wife – but *she's* never made any difference between him and Tom, my eldest brother, though they aren't blood relations at all. Are you still with me?'

'I'm struggling a bit.'

'Judith's in Australia now. I suppose she's sort of my sister by marriage, but really she's like a mad aunt. I'm a bit like *her*, personality-wise, I'm told, though we're not related at all. Oh Ned, your face is a picture!'

'I should think so. Yuh biggest brother is Tom but he's yer full brother, and then there's David, who is yer ayf-brother, and then there is yow?'

'Top of the class.'

'Um . . .'

'Mum was expecting, from Dad,' she said patiently. 'He got beaten up by his family and then ended up in prison, so he didn't know she was expecting and couldn't contact her. To keep Tom, she married a widower. Then she had David. Then Dad found her again.'

'So where's this widower now?'

'Dead.'

Ned raised his eyebrows.

'An accident. Mum says David is very like him, only not so stiff. I've known since I was about twelve that we weren't like other families, but really, I just think we're different because our mum and dad have always loved all of us, unconditionally.'

'What do they do, your brothers?'

'Tom is head drayman at a brewery. He's still in Kent. David's near Birmingham. He's a Methodist minister – used to be an army padre. He married a nurse he met in a field hospital and they've a little boy – my godson. Tom's wife left him when he was fighting in Italy. Then there was my sister and last of all me.'

'Are yow like her – yer sister?'

'Flora was more like Mum.'

'Was?'

'Meningitis. She was thirteen.'

'Bleddy hell, I'm sorry.'

'I feel sometimes – for Mum and Dad's sake – that I've got to make up for her absence, though I wasn't always a model pupil—'

'What, wi' *your* brains?'

'I'm no good at being told what to do. I just made sure I wasn't caught. A bit like Dad when he went poaching.'

'I hated schoowel. Failed the exam for the grammar. Mi little brother Jimmy dint. He got into Henry Mellish at Bulwell. He's a clerk in the pay office at Player's now. I earn more'n him, though, I think, but I've to get my hands oily doin' it.'

'I liked it more after I stayed on. Somehow when I didn't have to be at school, when I chose to be there, it was something else altogether. I know that doesn't make sense.'

'Meks perfect sense to me. Yuh wor in charge.'

'I suppose that *was* it. Being a bit older helped, and there was one teacher in particular who really convinced me life wasn't a lost cause.'

He looked incredulous. 'How could life be a lost cause for someone like yow?'

'Just a manner of speaking, Ned. You've not said anything about *your* mum and dad.'

'Them? Noat to write home about mebbe for most people – known each other sin' they were six. They've allus been good to me. But yuh could decide for thissen, if yuh'd like to comm out some Sat'day an' meet them?'

*

Sitting on the top deck of the bus out to the university, Ned stretched his arm across the back of the seat but took care to avoid touching Harry. He couldn't decide whether the evening had been a success or not, and it made him tongue-tied.

'I'm off next but one,' he said eventually.

She turned and looked up at him, smiling. 'Thank you, Ned, for a lovely time.'

'The film wor bleddy awful.'

'I wasn't thinking of the film. And I'm sorry I was a bit prickly.'

Kiss 'er, yer daft bogger.

'I like talking to you, Ned. And I will come out to meet your mum and dad.'

'I'd best go down now. Sat'day?'

*

'Well, Prince Myshkin, how was it?' asked Anna.

'The film? A fright.'

'Not what I meant, Lover, and you know it.'

'I like him. He makes me laugh. He's easy to talk to. He's . . . chivalrous.'

'You mean he paid for you?'

'No I *don't* mean that. I paid my own way, thank you, insisted on it.'

'Kissed your hand and put his jacket over the puddles?'

'No, silly! But he wants me to be his girl, as he put it.'

Anna leaned forward. 'Put your tongue out and say "ah", please.'

'Ah!'

'Sit still.' Anna gently pulled down a lower lid. 'A hopeless case, I'd say. That's *amore.*'

'It's ... *marvellous.* I mean, to know I could feel like this about someone.'

'Stop jigging about for a minute, though. I picked up your post.'

Harry's face fell.

'Just two of them this time.'

'I have tried to get him to stop.'

'You've an even better reason now.'

'I know. But I don't want to tell him about Ned. It feels sort of ... private. I don't want to use him as an alibi. It mightn't work out.' She looked momentarily anxious. 'But even if it didn't, just to have felt for a while like this – it's extraordinary.'

'Devil's advocate question. If this pash about Ned doesn't go anywhere, would you want Max instead?'

'No. Absolutely not. I'd want to be alone.'

Dear Max,

I have thought long and hard about what I am about to write ['No you didn't,' said Anna. 'You went by instinct.

Trust it.' 'Ssh, Anna, let me at least finish it!']. I have been immensely honoured by having known you. You have made me feel that I was worth something when I had been treated quite otherwise. ['Did he really?' 'No, Anna, you did, and Mum and Dad, and Miss Shaw. Uncle Vanlo and Spellie too. But Max is proud.'] This distance between us has allowed me greater perspective, and I hope you will respect and recognise that. It is not only that I resent the assumptions you made about us as a couple and expressed this even to your colleagues in the History department. It's because I realise that I cannot love you as my mother and father love each other, nor ever will. I cannot see myself as part of your world, and don't want to be shaped to fit it. Please release me from any understanding we may have had, or that you think we may have had ['Much better. Now just say something nice but not conciliatory, and for heaven's sake don't say anything about wanting to be friends.'] I will always hold you in the greatest esteem and wish you success in all areas of your life, and hope that you find the woman you deserve. I am not that woman.

Yours sincerely
Harry Loveridge

CHAPTER NINETEEN

Kimberley

May 1958

'I'm not taking you unless you wear them,' said Harry, holding out the goggles and helmet usually worn by Anna.

'I won't be able to smell your hair!'

'You couldn't anyway if I've got a helmet on too. Where are we going then?'

'Kimbly – says Kim-ber-ley on the sign. About six miles out on the way to Eastwood.'

Riding pillion, Ned shouted instructions to Harry against the rush of the wind and the roar of the bike. He was both exhilarated to feel her so close, his thighs encasing hers, his chest against the tautness of her back, and anxious about the coming meeting. He wished the journey could have been longer. Harry slowed as they entered the small town, and she thought how different a place it was from the villages in Kent, with its sterner, taller buildings of brick, lumbering Methodist chapels, streets that climbed and fell.

'Down the next left!' yelled Ned. 'Pull over by the blue door.'

The bike puttered to a halt on the downward slope of a street of terraced houses. Harry pushed up her goggles and unbuckled her helmet, ruffling her hair.

'Give me a minute till I stop looking like a panda,' she said, rubbing the pressure rings around her eyes.

'We ran out o' bamboo shoots just this morning. Will roast beef and Yorkshire pud do instead? '

Harry laughed and took his arm. 'I'm glad to eat anything provided I've not had to make it,' she said.

'Not much of a cook, are yuh? Don't know how yow and me'll manage then.'

'I do. I'll get you a recipe book for your birthday.'

'We'd best go and live near a chip shop then,' said Ned, feeling reckless. The look on Harry's face quelled him.

Seeing his expression, she squeezed his arm in reassurance, then looked beyond him up the street, aware that they were being observed more or less openly, by three or four women standing on whitened doorsteps. 'What are *they* looking at?'

'Yow of course. Bein' wi' me, I mean. Never any need to tell 'em ote. They mek it up for theirsen.'

'Makes me want to give them something to talk about. Should I leave the bike here?'

'Mebbe take it around the back. It'll come to no harm but yuh mightn't want every little shaver in short trousers trying out the saddle. And it'll be worth it to see mi Mam's face when I bring yuh in the back door when she wants yuh to see the parlour first.'

*

'Oh Ned!' exclaimed his mother, wiping her hands down her apron before untying it. 'Yuh could've given me a chance to mek missen look decent.' Freed of the apron, Mrs Stones patted her perm, though Harry thought it already looked stiff with spray, and held out her hand. 'Hello, mi—hello young lady.'

'Harry'. She shook Mrs Stones's rough, cool hand.

'See,' said a male voice behind her, "e wurnt 'avin' uz on.'

'Don't mind 'im, dear . . .'

Ned's father appeared at her shoulder, a shorter, thicker-set version of his son. *That's how he'll be twenty-odd years from now.* Henry Stones also shook her hand, a powerful grip. The man's face bore the unmistakeable random tattoos of his years below ground, the blue-grey dust engrained in some fearsome scars branching through and above his right eyebrow and across his forehead.

'Like mi miner's medals, do yow? Not that ah looked a lot better before the accident. Lucky it wor only that prop or ah'd not be talking to yuh now.'

'I think you were lucky it didn't hit you in the eye, Mr Stones.'

'That's what ah reckon an' all. Yuh never know the time nor the place, like it says in the Bible, but ah was spared. We're chapel, Miss . . .'

'Miss Loveridge, but I'm Harry. So are we. At least Mother is. Father jokes that he likes the Tin Chapel best on the days when it rains. That way he can't hear the preacher and can think about something else.'

Stones laughed. 'What accent is that you 'ave, then?'

'Kent.'

'We'd a shop steward comm from one of Kentish pits. Pretty militant they are too dairn there, 'e told me. Yuh dad underground too?'

'No. He works on a farm.'

'Lucky man. 'E'll 'ave better lungs than mine.'

'He would do if he didn't smoke so much.'

'What's 'e prefer?'

'Old Holborn. Mother calls it Old Socks. She makes him go outside.'

'Ah should do that an' all!' cut in Ned's mother. 'Henry, stop tekkin' over the poor lass. Tek 'em through the front instead and let me get organised back 'ere.'

'Can't I help, Mrs Stones?'

'No yuh can't,' cut in Ned. 'Harry here int allus this mild,' he said to his mother. 'An' I can tell yuh, she can't cook. Said so herself.'

'I can fetch and carry, though. And stop showing me up in front of your mum and dad.'

Ned and Harry followed Henry Stones through to the crowded front room. A gate-leg table had been pulled out and covered with a linen cloth squared with crisply ironed creases.

'She's put out the best china,' murmured Ned. 'We usually only see that at Christmas.'

Ned's father bent over a wooden cabinet. 'See this,' he said over his shoulder as he opened its doors. 'Got it for the Coronation. All the neighbours comm in.' He straightened up, revealing a grey cambered television screen.

'On the never-never,' whispered Ned. 'Reckon he's still paying for it.'

'Noat wrong wi' my hearing, yowthe,' said his father. 'Yuh should watch it sometime. Very educational.'

'Prefer the wireless, Dad. And the gramophone. I've got them in my old room upstairs. Take you up after, Harry? *Ow!*'

Harry saw out of the corner of her eye Henry Stones's approving glance as she deliberately trod on Ned's toes. *Whatever we do,* she thought, *I want no one to know.*

*

'Yow were a star, Harry.'

'They're nice, Ned.'

'If mi dad's chapel, though, then my name's Neddy Seagoon. Worships his pint too much.'

'Mum's old-fashioned chapel. Won't drink at all, but Dad likes his ale. As soon as it was legal he got me to take him and Uncle Vanlo to the Red Lion to buy the first round with my pocket money. Mum will come too, but she'll just have a ginger beer.'

'I thought I'd crap missen when he asked yuh was yer dad a pikey.'

'It's how he said it, Ned. It's not a good word, but for him it was just a word, the way he used it. Like, "Does he have a bicycle?" Well, maybe not quite. It'd been different if he'd asked me why I wasn't wearing hoop earrings and where'd I keep my crystal ball. What *did* you tell them about me?'

'Only that yuh wor a student. What scared them most was that yuh might be stuck-up, though they dint say that straight out. More, "She'll not be raight impressed wi' a pit cottage, then!" They were happier when yuh said yuh'd grown up on a farm. I 'ant told 'em 'bout motorbike.'

'Your dad liked it though.'

'He did a'raight! I just about fell off mi perch when he asked if he could ride it down the back lane. I'd never seen him like that, Harry. He wor like a boy.'

Arm in arm, they made their way in the direction of the cemetery. Harry couldn't help noticing that net curtains twitched but weren't dropped again, and two women with shopping bags at a gable end stopped their conversation and gazed frankly at them. Ned greeted them with, 'Ey up?' and got a nod and a murmur in response. Harry felt their eyes on her back until the street curved and they were no longer in view.

'Do they always stare at new people like that?'

'It's not yow – it's me,' he said. 'There's reasons I live in Chippendale Street that aren't to do wi' gettin' to work on time.' They began the walk up to the cemetery, the highest ground in the town, where on a knoll a squat Victorian chapel crouched, surrounded by bristling tombstones.

'Yuh can see raight down into Derbyshire from here,' he said, his free arm sweeping across the landscape. 'I used to comm here when I woh a little lad, thinking I woh on top of world. An' sometimes when I just wanted a bit of peace – to hear meself think.'

An elderly man limped past, a spaniel trotting beside him on a loose lead.

'Ey up, Dan!' said Ned.

'Ah' raight, Ned?'

'How's the leg?'

'It does me,' said the other, rapping his left thigh with his knuckles, making a hollow sound.

'He's ah' raight, is old Dan,' said Ned once the man was out of earshot. 'Very patient wi' me when I wor a nipper. I wor fascinated by him only havin' one leg. Left the other one somewhere in France. He worked in the pay office at Dad's pit.'

'Were you ever going to be a miner?'

'Not if Dad could help it, not after his accident. "No son of mine's gooin' to live like a moudiwarp," – a mole – he said. And Raleigh's ah' raight. Noisy and oily, but yuh can see daylight through the roof.'

'But you said you didn't leave here because of Raleigh.'

'Will yer sit dairn a minute, Harry?' He led her over to a bench. It bore a little brass plaque to a Mrs Simmonds 'who loved this view'. He sat next to her, their thighs just touching, and put his arm along the back of the seat, as he had on the bus, but he didn't look at her.

'Not really in your league, am I?' he said quietly, looking down across the fields.

Harry turned, watching his profile move slowly to full face. She raised a hand, tracing the line of his jaw, then splayed her fingers, one of them catching on his mouth. He shifted on his seat, and both arms came around her.

'Oh Harry . . .' He kissed her softly, his lips closed. Harry breathed deeply; her shoulders tensed. Ned drew away.

'Sorry, I . . .'

'Don't be, Ned.' *He's nice. He's not them. Why should they spoil this too?* She put a hand on the back of his head, and lifted her face to kiss the corner of his mouth. She felt his smile against her lips, and then he was kissing her again, and the moment went on, and on, and Harry thought, *I can be happy. I too can be happy.*

When it was time to go, they walked slowly around the chapel. At its far side, Harry pointed across the landscape to a sharp-edged rectangular tower on a neat man-made mound.

'Kimberley's answer to the Leaning Tower of Pisa,' said Ned, 'only some duffa from Corporation dint read instructions raight and built it straight. That's our new water tower. Puts us on the map a bit, anyroad.'

*

A week later, Harry met Ned by the gatehouse at Florence Boot. She felt her heart surge at the sight of him, his hands in his pockets, his hair flopping over his eyes.

Ned straightened up when he saw her, and smiled.

'Ey up!'

'What's the right reply to that?' she asked.

'Ote you want it to be,' he said. 'This'll do,' and he kissed her.

'Can we go for a walk round here?' he said eventually. 'That's if yer don't mind bein' seen wi' me.'

192

'Don't be silly! Look, girls,' she called out, turning back in the direction of Florence Boot, 'this is Ned Stones!'

'Give over, yow!' he said, laughing.

'Let's go down towards the lake,' said Harry, taking his hand.

*

Later, she said, 'You've gone very quiet.'

He glanced at her. 'If we're gunna walk out, there's summat y'oughter know. That's if yer want to be wi' me, I mean.'

Harry stopped. 'Why else do you think I'm here now?'

'It's just . . . there was a woman,' he began.

'I thought there must have been,' said Harry gently. 'Those two that were staring at us last Saturday as good as said it. Where is she now?'

''Bout thirty yards from where we wor sitting in the cemetery.'

'I don't understand . . .'

'Cancer,' he said. 'When I wor in Malaya.'

'Oh, Ned, I'm sorry.'

'A married woman.'

'Oh.'

'Wi' kids an' all. Three.' *I can't judge him for that,* she thought, thinking of her mother and father.

'Let's sit down ower there, an' hope them geese leave us be.'

Harry joined him on the bench, close by him but not quite touching.

'Is that why you took me up there last week?'

'Yeah. I thought I could tell yuh after yuh'd said abaht your own mam and dad – not bein' like the usual . . . only I lost my bottle . . . y'aren't angry wi' me?'

'How can I be angry about a poor dead woman? And children without a mother?'

'Oh Harry . . . Her bastard of a husband never put up a stone to her. Hit her in life, forgot her when dead. I lost it a bit, out there wi' the bleddy army. Mam wrote to me. I thought she dint even know, but it turns out everybody did. Husband included. Sometimes I feel as if it's me that killed her, not being there at the end.'

'But perhaps thinking of you helped her, Ned. That she'd had some happiness being with you, I mean.'

'That must be the kindest thing anyone's ever said to me.' He took her hand. 'I'm not proud of it. Going with a married woman, I mean,' he said.

'Did you love her?'

'Oh I loved her ah' raight.'

'What was her name?'

'Dora. Do yuh really want to know all this?'

'If she mattered to you, yes.'

'Only, nobody's ever asked me. Asked me why I wor a bleddy fool, but not about *her*. She wor married very young, seventeen at most must've been. Mebbe she'd had to. I know she dint care for her stepmother, so she probably went for any port in a storm. Her husband was in the army – a regular. But I think she wor lonelier when he wor on leave than when he wor away, if yuh see what I mean. It started when he was posted to Libya. I was in up to mi lugs wi' her by the time some stiffneck from the barracks had seen her having a drink wi' me in Nottingham, and took it upon hissen to tell the injured husband – the one who'd spent most of their married life belting her. Her kids called me "uncle" . . . they were good kids, too.

'Mam told me afterwards he'd comm looking for me, but I'd had mi call-up and was away getting scalped by an army barber. And as soon as I'd done mi basic training, I woh shipped out east. I've her letters still. When they stopped coming, I went just about mad out there. Only afterwards I realised she ant wanted me to know she wor ill. The last letter said she loved me but it was better I forgot her. That she wudnt ever leave her husband, because o' the kids. I'd have tekken them on. I wish to God I'd been able to – heaven only knows how – because it would've been better for them. Once she died the husband went completely off the rails, Mam said, and upped his drinking as if he thought he wor getting prizes for it. He cudnt look after the nippers. The two boys went to Gordon Memorial. At least they had each other – have, I mean. They must still be there. I don't know where they put the little girl.' He ran a hand over his face. 'Oh well, I've told you now. I s'pose yuh'll like me less.'

'I think I like you more. You wanted to do what Dad did – he took on David and made him his own.'

'Another reason why I thought I could tell yow. Don't suppose *yow've* any skeletons to rattle, have yuh?'

'Me? Oh, depends what you'd call skeletons. There was a man I met here: Max. But I didn't love him. I know what love should be . . . I've seen it in my parents. I can hear it now, in you, saying you'd have taken that lady's children too.' As the shadows lengthened and the day cooled, she told him about Max.

'What'll yuh do when he comms back?'

'Nothing. I've told him as plainly as I can that it's over. It never really got started, you see.'

'There's more I'm going to have to tell yuh, Harry. But I don't think I could face it today. I want to remember this afternoon as it is. Just about perfect.'

'Me too, Ned.'

'Can I kiss yow?'

'I'd like that.'

As they got up from the bench, Harry said, 'Next time we go to Kimberley, let's plant some flowers at least.'

'I shoulda thought o' that. Yuh'd do that wi' me?'

'I would. Next time. I'd best go back now. It's getting dark and I've some reading to finish.'

*

Under a lamp post at the mouth of Chippendale Street, Ned peeled himself reluctantly from Harry's back and freed himself from helmet and goggles. Harry slipped off the Bantam and did the same. She was about to fluff up her hair when Ned stopped her.

'Let me,' he said, putting his hand to her head. 'Tufty Harry, you're beautiful. Mind if I kiss yow again?'

She smiled up at him.

He took her face in his hands and kissed her long and deeply, but holding his body clear of hers. 'Bigod yer nice, yow are,' he finally whispered in her ear. 'I could mek a bleddy fool of missen over yow.' He pulled her closer, a hand in the small of her back, but felt her stiffen in his arms as their bodies touched. He thought he'd burst with the effort of concealing his desire from her.

'I'm sorry,' he muttered. 'Yuh so bleddy lovely. Git dairn, Percy!'

'It's all right,' said Harry, touching his cheek briefly.

'I'd invite you in,' he said, 'only Ma Bowers dunt allow lady visitors. Probably because if her lonely old commercials saw someone like yow it'd be too much for them and they'd croak on the spot. And I don't suppose yuh'd comm anyway.'

'One day I would, Ned. Just so I could see where you live, then I could think about you there, when I'm not with you.'

'I'll tidy up then. Heck, I don't want today to be over. Will we have other days like this?'

'Oh yes, Ned, as many as you want.' In a few swift movements, her goggles were back on and the strap of her helmet clipped closed beneath her chin. He watched the slim straight figure glide up the road until lost to sight, before he fumbled in his pocket for his key, still warm with desire.

*

Anna was sitting in an armchair in a pool of light from the desk lamp, her head bristling with curlers. She looked up from her book and smiled at Harry's entrance.

'Put the overhead light on, Lover, and let's have a proper look at you.'

In response, Harry ran over and hugged her friend.

'What's this for, Harry?'

'I'm sorry, Anna!'

'What for?' cried Anna, in genuine surprise. 'Being in love?'

'Yes. I mean, no. For leaving you alone again on a Saturday night.'

'Don't worry about me. Actually, I had a lovely time. I was downstairs in the bar for much of it, arguing with some wretched Home Counties deb about why French settlers in Algeria are *not* deserving of Western support. The only time when Max might have been useful, and he wasn't here.'

'I've told Ned about him. But I couldn't tell him about the hop field. Oh, Anna, what happens if we do "go steady"?'

Anna dipped her head and looked at Harry over her glasses.

'And then you tell him about those brutes and all bets are off?'

'Yes . . . but not just that.'

'If he drops you because of them he's not worth having – if that's the case you could congratulate yourself on a lucky escape.'

'What if I tell him and he says it makes no difference but it still makes a difference to *me*?' Harry was close to tears.

'Oh, poppet, don't cry! You mean, after you've hung your white dress back on its hanger and put your new nightie on you find you *can't*? Or you don't like what he's doing? Is that what you mean?'

'Um . . . yes. That's exactly what I mean.'

'How English you and I are. Neither of us have actually mentioned the dreaded "sex" word but we both know what we're talking about. Well, I'm not Marie Stopes, or the great Kinsey, but I'll tell you what I'd do, when the time was right.'

'How will I know that? When the time is right, I mean?'

'Let's not rush that fence. Go by instinct. But if I were you, I'd ignore all the old biddies who'd tell you otherwise, and try before you buy.'

'Oh Anna! What if he doesn't respect me afterwards?'

'That's a very maidenly blush, Harry. And a very ladies magazine response. I'll never understand why a girl should fear not being respected when she's only done what the chap has begged her to do.'

'But it's what happens, isn't it?'

'Look, hold your horses. You've seen him a few times.'

'I know . . . and I've already told him not to rush me.'

'Good . . .'

'He's very polite. I had to tell him to stop asking me every time he wanted to kiss me.'

'*Better!*'

'I think, though, he's quite passionate.'

'And *I* think it's time I met him. Bring him to a guest night.'

'Oh . . . I . . .'

'He's let you into *his* world. The least you could do is let him have a glimpse of *yours*. The main problem you'll have is keeping the population of Florence Boot off *him,* if he really is the gentleman you've described.'

'I suppose you're right . . .'

'When haven't I been? Cocoa time? No, stay there, I'll make it. Oh, I'm afraid there's a letter for you.'

Ma chère Harry,

I can understand that distance is a strain but I am distressed that you listen to others who disparage me. I am convinced that in time your mother and father would learn to like me and know that I want only what is best for you. We cannot expect them to give their approval immediately. The day we have daughters and they are courted, I am sure I will not give mine freely. However, I do remind you that you gave me your word that you would wait for me until you graduate, and then give me an answer. All relationships must have their moments of doubt, although I can reassure you that there are no doubts on my side. But then I am older than you.

Je t'embrasse, toujours,

Max Arago

Harry had written her reply by the time the milk had boiled.

Dear Max,

I meant exactly what I wrote in my last letter. It is a privilege to have known you but we do not have a future together.

Sincerely,

Harmony Loveridge

'Telegrammatic,' said Anna. 'That's good. In fact why don't you send it as a telegram?'

'Bit expensive, and impersonal. I also don't like the idea of going to the post office and letting the world read what I have to say. Oh, this is so vexing! Could I have been any clearer than I was the last time?'

'Don't let it spoil today, Harry.'

Harry took a deep breath. 'I won't. You know, Anna, that time Ned and I walked down from the cemetery I thought Kimberley the loveliest place I'd ever been. A cluster of streets, a few chapels and that ripe fruit smell of the brewery. We didn't even say much on the way down, but I felt as though I was walking into my new life.'

'In Kimberley?'

'Why not in Kimberley? I meant with Ned, though.'

CHAPTER TWENTY

Dining room, Florence Boot Hall
May 1958

'I wonnt know what to say,' said Ned, running a finger under the collar of his shirt. 'And I've mebbe tied this too tight.'

'Just be you, Ned,' said Harry, loosening the tweed tie. 'Hold two fingertips in there so's I know you can still breathe.'

'Your bit of rough?'

She rested her fingers on his cheek. '*Are* you rough, Ned? All I know is that you're the nicest man I've ever met, aside from my father and my uncle.'

Anna came in then, calling, 'Hands off till after dinner! I managed to find one, boys and girls.'

They turned round, their faces close together, to see Anna striking a toreador's pose, and waving an elderly undergraduate gown.

'I've not got to wear one of them hats too, have I? said Ned.

'No, only this old bib,' said Anna.

Ned put the gown on over his Burton sports jacket. 'I'm really not sure about this.'

'Everybody'll be wearing them,' said Harry. 'You'd feel awkward if you didn't.'

'I'll feel bleddy awkud the minute I open me gob.'

'You'll be a hit, Ned,' said Anna. 'Harry'll be on your right, I'll be on your left. Between us we'll fight off all comers. Shoes polished and petticoats starched, everybody? Let's go down now and get the best seats in the house.'

*

'I wonnt know what to do eyther,' whispered Ned at the door of the dining room.

'Same as us,' said Harry. 'Stay standing until they all sit down after grace. The way you use a knife and fork'll be more elegant than the food anyway.'

'That reminds me. Yuh look bleddy nice in that skirt. Not seen yer in one before.'

'Hardly wear the things because of the bike,' Harry lied, not wanting to admit to the real reason.

Ned kept his eyes on the back of Harry's head as he followed her to one of the long tables, aware that curious faces were turning in his direction.

'Your fault for being such a handsome rogue,' said Anna, right behind him.

'Oh gosh,' said the youth opposite Ned, 'another man. Blessed are we amongst women.'

'Pardon?'

'Sorry, left-footer joke.'

'Left what?'

Seeing Ned's baffled face, the girl who had brought the young man said, 'All Jack means is that he's glad he's not the only boy. Only he ties everything up so. It's reading Politics that does it. What's *your* subject?'

'My subject? Like *What's my line?*'

Both she and her guest started laughing.

'This is Ned,' said Harry. 'Meet Caroline.'

'Bicycles,' said Ned.

'Ned's a captain of industry,' put in Anna.

'I'm not,' said Ned. 'I don't come to work in a Bentley. I make them. The bicycles.'

Caroline's mouth formed a perfect oval.

'You mean you're *from Nottingham*? You work at Raleigh?'

'Well, I'm from Kimberley, so near enough. I expect the people that've cooked what we'll eat – yes, I'm sure I'm going to like it, Harry, and where I come from we're taught to leave nothing – and the ones that clean your bedrooms and weed the flowerbeds, come from Nottingham too. And yes, I *do* work at Raleigh. Been there from when I left school, apart from National Service. It's a good job. They treat me well. It's a lot better than going down the pit like my dad does, anyroad. I'm not saying I'll do it forever, mind.'

'Where I come from you have to clean your plate too. And *my* dad's been in the steelworks in Workington since the General Strike just about,' cut in Jack, going a little pink.

'You never told me that!' pouted Caroline. 'You said something about the Lake District.'

'Because I didn't think you'd have even heard of Workington, Caroline. But you can see up to the Lake District from where I live. Dad mightn't be William Wordsworth but I'm proud of him all the same. And I worked at Moss Bay Steelworks a bit myself after the scholarship exams. It was better earning some money than kicking my heels to the end of the school year.' He turned back to Ned. 'Dad didn't want me to though. He was afraid I'd get a taste for the money and not come here to university. So Raleigh's all right, then?'

'It's good enough to be going on with.'

'I saw this little news film once in Workington Ritz. *How a bicycle is made.* They never said where it was but it must have been here.'

'It was,' said Ned, his voice unexpectedly shaky with pride.

'Which bit do you do, then?'

'I'm in the frame shop just now, but I've been all over. The place I liked best was assembly. It's what it sounds like, when all the parts of the bicycle come together. Some bits are of course already part-assembled. They've been soldered, polished, enamelled, all the rest of it. And then somehow you miraculously make it into a bike. It's better than Meccano. But because I've worked at just about all the other stages – apart from the drawing office – I know how each bit that comes into my hands has been made, how all them lads in overalls and grease have each done something that slots into one perfectly balanced thing. I wouldn't mind the drawing office, but you have to have qualifications to be in there. Same if you have one of those jobs in head office where you've got to wear a suit and tie. I've just my apprenticeship.'

'You could get the qualifications, couldn't you?'

'Not me. Me and school didn't agree.'

'Snap,' said Jack. 'Only I had a teacher that wouldn't give up on me. And anyway, being a student is as different from school as you could imagine.'

*

His tie loosened, and his sports jacket over one arm, Ned put the other around Harry's shoulders. 'I enjoyed missen, honestly. I wurnt sure I wor going to, not wi' all that dressing up and standing and sitting and grace and being served and all that. But what a picture that Caroline's face was when her boyfriend said his fayther was in the steelworks!'

'I wonder what those two are talking about now?'

'I wonder *how* he's talking to her? When he started on with all that stuff about left-foot jokes – well, I still don't know what he was on about – he had this posh way about him – you know, speaking in a kind of code that only the ones in his gang are going to understand. But when he got to talking about his dad, and about that fire last year up at Windscale and all the milk being thrown away and the workers being blamed for it when everyone in Workington knew otherwise – well, he must've been talking the way he does back home, because yuh could see from Caroline's face that she'd never heard him speak like that before. If yuh get educated, Harry, do yuh have to stop being who yuh used to be?'

'Not if you know who you are. Only if fitting in with the crowd is the most important thing in your life.'

'That's a good answer, Harry. I'm going to think on that. Then I'd better get on this sturdy Raleigh bicycle and get missen back to Chippendale Street before Ma Bowers sends out a search party. That's if yuh'll kiss me goodnight?'

'There's something I want to ask you first.'

'Yeh?'

'When you were talking to Jack in there, you spoke differently.'

Ned hesitated. 'Not so Nottingham, yuh mean.'

'Yes. Why?'

'It's the army did that, Harry. I know how to talk proper – what they told me was King's English at school – it'd be Queen's English I s'ppose now. But when I got out, and got home . . . I wanted to go back to how it had been before I went away. As if them things had never happened.'

'Dora?'

'No not Dora . . . I'll not regret her. Summat else. I s'pose yud call it a defence. And not only. Wi' yow being a student and all I wanted to see would yer like me for me.'

'I like you for you, Ned, however you talk. But has your defence worked?'

'Not really, no.'

*

A week later an actual post-office bike rumbled to a stop outside Florence Boot.

Harry, I understand your deflation. I will return from Grenoble soon so that we will talk about this.

'A real telegram. Harry,' said Anna. 'Now what?'

'I feel hunted.'

'Perhaps it's time to mention your gamekeeper, then.'

Dear Max,

I don't know how to be clearer than I have been. I think it only fair to tell you I have met someone else. He's not the reason for my first letter ending our relationship – I didn't know him when I wrote it. But he exists, and the way I feel about him blocks any way back for us. I wish you had accepted what I said before so that I didn't feel obliged to tell you this.

Sincerely,

Harry Loveridge

*

A month later, Harry and Anna had packed their clothes and books, taken down their pictures, walked past the denuded noticeboards and handed their keys in at the porter's lodge.

'Two years already gone by, Lover.'

'The best of my life.'

'Oi! No tears. There were enough of them when you said goodbye to his nibs last night.'

'Not seeing him for three months either . . .'

'At least you'll find out what kind of letter-writer he is.'

'Thank heavens the other ones have stopped, anyway. I thought they never would.'

'You can break the news to Dad yourself tonight, if you want. Tell him there'll be no more Madeleine stamps.'

'I'm looking forward to meeting him and your mum.'

'They're all right. I could have done worse.'

'You still coming out to Canterbury afterwards?'

'Try to stop me.'

CHAPTER TWENTY-ONE

Shakespeare Street
July 1958

In Harry's absence, Ned found himself drifting back to his old Saturday afternoon habits. He caught the bus from Chippendale Street and wandered around Slab Square smoking moodily, cross with himself because he'd promised Harry he'd cut down or stop altogether. 'My dad has this dreadful cough, but I think he's afraid to go to the doctor with it,' she'd written in the letter folded into his trouser pocket. He leaned against one of the lions, looking at the people crossing the square in the fitful sunshine.

'That's where I saw her first, sitting there with her little easel. God, I miss her!' he muttered. An old woman sitting on a bench looked up at him curiously. *Talking to yourself already, Ned, and so young! I'll go and look at the newspapers in the library. There'll be enough nutters in there already that they'll not notice another one.* He set off in the direction of Shakespeare Street just as it started to spit rain.

The weather had driven a number of men indoors, to stand at the long sloped newspaper counter. The Saturday afternoon staff, Ned saw, were keeping their distance from the pervasive odour of wet dog. *I've money to buy my own,* he thought, looking at the bank of stapled newspapers, and wondered what other part of the library he could explore.

Try through here, mebbe. He walked past the staircase foot and through the tunnel marked ENTRANCE into the airier space of the lending library. Here, there was no more encouragement to sit down than where he had just been. *Like one o' them supermarkets Mam hates so much, only wi' bowks,* he thought. He looked out at the fanned rows of bookcases, and the nearly motionless figures standing rapt between them, then back over his shoulder at the bulwark of the oak issue desk. As he'd thought, he was being observed. He noticed that the pattern of the parquet floor changed, a herringbone apron demarcating the librarian's domain from the square blocks on which the stacks stood. The place smelt of beeswax and old paper.

'Can I look at them bowks?' he asked the bespectacled young man sitting behind the ENQUIRIES sign. A slight frown acknowledged the fact that Ned had spoken too loudly.

'You can borrow them as well, sir, if you have a reader's ticket.'

Ned couldn't place the man's accent, though he'd heard all kinds in the army. But instinct told him that its owner had worked to disguise it. *Perhaps yuh can't sound common and work in here.* He completed the form he was handed.

'I'll just need a proof of address.'

Ned hesitated, then remembered the crumpled letter he carried. Harry. The first and only person who had ever written to him in Chippendale Street. He'd left it in its envelope to preserve it and every scrap of handwriting of hers. Even the fact of her writing his address pleased him.

The librarian glanced at the envelope with efficient indifference and gave it back.

'You can choose three books today, sir, and I can prepare your tickets whilst you do that, or you can come back and pick them up on Monday.'

Encouraged by the man's consistent politeness, and the insistent rain spattering the quatrefoil windows, he said: 'Where's the history bowks?'

*

'"To frighten me I have received at least one hundred letters, telling me not to come here today, for that if I did, my own life would be the sacrifice",' he read. The cloth binding of the book was warm from his hands.

'Sir?'

He looked up to see the librarian standing by his elbow.

'Didn't you hear the bell? We're closing in five minutes. I have your tickets ready.'

'Can I just have this one?'

The youth glanced at it and smiled for the first time. '*The Chartists*. Good choice.'

'Oh.' Ned had picked up the book only because that word on the spine had been familiar to him from that one teacher he had warmed to, but Feargus O'Connor's rousing speech at Kennington in 1848 had caught and held him and he wanted to read more. He followed the librarian over to the issue desk.

The man stamped the book and handed over the remaining two tickets and said quietly, 'Willie Gallacher's speaking in the square Saturday morning next. In case you're interested.'

'I think I might be. Thanks.' *Is he that communist bloke?*

'I'm going to go myself as I'm off that day. I've to hope the boss doesn't find out.'

Ned grinned. 'I've one like that an' all! And here was me thinking all yow educated people were keen on that sort of thing.'

'There's education, and there's privileged education.'

'I suppose . . . that's what my girl is allus telling me.' Ned had already resolved to go and hear Gallacher, thinking it would be something he could write to Harry about. *Summat that would mek her see me as a man who thought abaht things.*

'Yow in a hurry to get home, then? Fancy a pint first?'

The librarian hesitated. 'Oh, I . . . well, yes, why not? I'll be about ten minutes shutting up here, so I'll meet you at the front gate. Looks like the rain's stopped. Name's Sid. Sidney Probert's my Sunday name.'

'You know mine, of course. You wrote it on my tickets. But everyone calls me Ned. Yow'll not go telling anyone my name's really Edwin though, will yow?'

Sid smiled. 'I'm good at keeping secrets.'

*

213

'Here you are, Shippos Pale.'

Sid lifted his glass. 'Thank you.'

'Like it, this librarian work?'

'Love it.'

'How d'yuh comm by it?'

'There was a reading room where I grew up, the gift of some philanthropist. There weren't books at home, see. The thought of following my dad down the pit horrified me.'

'Yur dad's a miner too?'

'Yes. Taff Valley born and bred.'

'An' yow've this job?'

'Shouldn't I?' said Sid, smiling.

'I dint mean it like that. It's just that we've allus gone underground. Only after an accident he wor set on me an' my brother doin' summat else. But I'm still in Nottingham, and I still see them every Sunday dinner, so it's not like I've comm as far as yow.'

'I told them I wanted to be a teacher, though I think I was as scared of a room full of children as I'd have been of the dark and the gas underground. Mam and Dad were proud of me for wanting to teach, poor things, but all I wanted was to get away from home.'

'Well, I've been away from home. Not that I got to choose. Malaya.'

Sid eyed him over his glass. 'But you came back.'

'To Nottingham, yes. Dint know where else I might go. Cudnt settle at home though. Not after that.'

'Bad?'

'Yeah . . . yuh could say that. Yuh must've got some in as well.'

Sid grimaced. 'Catering. Two wasted years in Catterick, bored to tears. I'd my degree – I'd hoped for the Education corps.'

'But yuh said yuh dint wannt to be a teacher.'

'No. But better than greasy cooking pots – and adults would be different. The army told me I was too timid for teaching.'

'Yuh don't sound timid to *me*.'

'I'm here because you asked me. I'd find it hard to ask another man if he wanted to go to the pub with me. It's always easier to just stick my head in a book.'

'Well, yow can help *me*, then. I want to impress my girl.'

Sid smiled. 'I've never heard that reason before. Most of my readers either want to escape from something, or they believe – and there's something in it – that they can read their way out of poverty.'

'I'm not poor, Sid. I get good wages at Raleigh,' said Ned, bridling.

'I'm sure you do. I expect they're better than mine.'

Ned raised his eyebrows, but only said, 'I'm bored, mind. I could stay with it and one day they'd make me foreman, but really nothing much would change. And if I did get promoted, what would I be? I'd be like them . . . them that does the bosses' work for them, but I'd never *be* one of them. I'd still be owned.'

*

Harry knew she ought to be grateful. There were far worse summer jobs a student could do than work in a department store, and one of the chapel ladies had recommended her. She'd been

KATIE HUTTON

told it was an honour to model expensive dresses. But the days were made long by so much hanging about – that, and missing Ned, and the books awaiting her at home.

On cue, she pushed through the curtain, her starched petticoats rustling, and walked along the strip of carpet to come to a halt in front of the two women, striking the pose the floorwalker had taught her: hands on hips, elbows back, shoulders thrust forward emphasising the hollows above her collarbone. Harry put one foot before the other in a balletic pose, and lifted her chin, looking into the distance. She didn't smile; Mrs Holman had read somewhere that Mr Dior told his mannequins not to – it was too bourgeois. Dutifully, Harry cultivated a look of genteel boredom, and wished herself back on the perfume counter.

'This gown is the latest Parisian style,' said Mrs Holman, in the strangulated vowels she put on for the customers. 'The New Look *par excellence* but you would be buying British. A taffeta underskirt and over it genuine Nottingham lace ... Miss Loveridge, Madam does not wish to see you scowling!'

*

'Dad!' said Harry that evening, 'I don't think I can stand Lefevre's much longer. Find me your dirtiest job to do after dinner. The one you've been putting off doing. I've got to get those silly women out of my head.'

'What about changing the oil in the tractor?' said Sam.

Ellen turned round from the stove. 'Mrs Holman will be cross with you if you spoil your hands, Harry.'

'We've Swarfega, haven't we? Anyway, my hands are for doing things, not looking pretty. I could ask them to put me in stores, instead. They might give me my own boiler suit there.'

'Put you in a boiler suit, my Harry,' said Sam, 'And it'll be the next big thing. All them ladies'll want one too.'

'Oh *Dad!*'

*

'Ey up, Ned. Good weekend?'

Ned looked up from his lathe. 'Jim! I wor looking for yow.'

'Yuh were? Most of the time it's the other way about,' said the shop steward.

'Who's Willie Gallacher?'

'Got yuh interested at last, have we? He's an old communist. Scot. A friend of Uncle Joe. Lost his seat to our Labour man a few years back but all that does is free him up to get on his soapbox, which is probably where he's happiest. Too Stalinist for my liking, but if yuh only have to work forty hours before yuh get overtime, Ned, it's got a lot to do wi' him. Going to Slab Square on Saturday, are yow?'

'Thought I might.'

'We've our meeting Thursday too. Might yuh comm to that too?'

'Mebbe.'

*

The speech over, the crowd dispersed, spreading out across the square like ripples in a pond into which a stone has been dropped from a great height. Ned and Sid walked up Friar Lane, having earlier decided on a pint in the Salutation.

'Penny for them?' said Sid.

Ned looked up. 'Sorry, I was elsewhere. I'm . . . disappointed, I suppose. A bloke like that gets yuh all worked up, and the rest of the crowd too, bar them hecklers . . .'

'He'd an answer for them too.'

'Yeah. When we wor standing there, though, it was like we wor all part of summat bigger. Only we're not. It ended there – everybody goes off and gets on with his own business same as before.'

'Do *you?*'

'Well, he gave me plenty to think on – I can't believe that the Russians have it as good as he makes out. Else why aren't there Russians coming here to tell us abaht how marvellous it is there? Because they're not let out, are they? But that bit he said abaht who owns the wealth and who produces it – that meks yuh think. We've the upper hand now only because there's not enough people to do the work that's on offer. I know that even if I was to get the push at Raleigh – which I won't, because I'm too good a worker and they know it – I can walk into just about any factory in this city the same day. But if things was to go dairn again, the way my dad said it wor before the war, the boot'd be on the other foot. And the Bomb – I thought we needed to protect ourselves, but where's the protection if we all of us go up in smoke?'

218

'Better red than dead, then?'

'Yeah, probably. Everybody says this is a democracy, but there are times I feel as chained as if I was on one of them tread-mill things.' Ned instinctively ducked beneath the overhang of the upper floor of the old pub, and pushed through the door into the smoky fug of the public bar.

'It was bread and circuses in Ancient Rome. We've got beer and football,' said Sid, as they settled at a corner table.

'And my dad's pool coupon. If he did win, I don't know what he'd do with it all. Leave the pit, of course, and hope that emphysema doesn't get him before he's had enough time to go fishing and dig his allotment.'

'It hardly solves the problem, does it?' said Sid. 'Doing the pools, I mean. A few lucky individuals benefit, but the bank always wins. My dream's a different one – that the work-ing man should have more time to himself, and less worry. And more choices. You only get that if certain things are taken care of: education, health, libraries too. My own dad wouldn't ask for much – just the opportunity to rest his feet on the fender more often, and read those tracts the minister gives him.'

'Gallacher is the real thing, though, in't he?' said Ned. 'He'd understand that. Somebody's got to dig coal or we'd all starve. Don't mean the miner shouldn't have as decent a life as he can.'

'Gallacher understands it better than the toff politicians, even the ones that are on our side. Attlee, for instance. Not upper class, but privately educated and all that. Got his views intellectually, not from bitter experience. Bevan's my hero, even if he isn't what he was.' Sid's Welsh cadence grew stronger. 'We've got a health service based on a miners' aid society set up only about ten miles from where I was born! I'm so proud of that. I'm with Bevan on the prescription charge. It should never have happened – the thin end of the wedge.'

'Another one, Sid?'

'Yes, but it's my round.'

When Sid brought over their pints, Ned said, 'Yur proud of where yuh came from, but you've left home.'

'It was growing up in the shadow of the pit did it, Ned. It's there, up above those little houses, and the slag looking like it's only waiting to slide down on our heads. I went no more than about twenty miles away, to Cardiff, but it was a different world. Tiger Bay – people of every shade. Merchant seamen. I knew I'd never go back.'

'Don't they miss yuh at home?'

'*Mam* says they do. He doesn't know how to say he does, according to her. My two brothers are underground. My sister has married a miner. Conditions are better than they used to be, but Gallacher is right: in the hard years my father had his hours cut and there was nothing to be done about it. It was that or nothing. So for me it was the big wide world – well, libraries, anyway.'

'Do you miss *them?*'

'Of course. And not just them. People look out for each other in a place like that.'

'They do here too – yuh'd not see much difference probably if yuh went to where my two live. It's the city that's different, mebbe.'

'Or the lives we choose to lead. In my lodgings there's me and a couple of students, plus the commercials. *They* must have a tough life, for all their airs and patter and moustaches. The police came round about one of them a few nights ago.'

'What had he done?'

'Nothing except go and die somewhere. Apparently he used to come to Nottingham once or twice a year with his stockings or whatever. The last time he came he asked Mrs Watkins to look after a little box for him. She thought nothing of it, and put it on the top shelf of the pantry. Never opened it to see what it was. Well, after he croaked, the police came to get the box. It was his wife's ashes.'

'The poor bastard!' exclaimed Ned.

'Loneliness is a kind of poverty too, isn't it? At least there was nobody as poor in that way in Aberfan.'

Ned studied his pint. 'At least he'd been married. I'd like to be, one day. But I'd hate it if my wife died before me.'

'"But of that day and hour, knoweth no man."'

'Impressed.'

'All those Sundays in chapel, that's all.'

'My girl's chapel, or was.'

Sid eyed him warily. 'Strict?'

'Yuh mean does she let me kiss her?'

'More or less. In the Zion Methodists anything like that was definitely dirty, dangerous and don't.'

'It's not the chapel bit that's the problem. I just can't see how I'd ever be good enough for her. Yow got a girl, Sid?'

'No. Don't think I'm the marrying kind. But tell me about yours. You've not even told me her name.'

'Harry.'

'Oh. They wanted a boy, I suppose.'

'Already had tow of 'em. Short for Harmony, though Harry suits her better. I'd like yuh to meet her, Sid. I . . . I'd like her to think I'd friends like yow. Not just my workmates.'

'I'll take that as a compliment,' said Sid, slowly. 'I'm not sure though that you're being fair to your mates. Or to her.'

CHAPTER TWENTY-TWO

Nottingham
October 1958

'Max is back, Anna. He's left me a note.'

'Ah! Just when you thought you were off the hook.'

'Right through the long vac I was wondering if he'd write to me. The porter's lodge forwarded all my post but there was nothing from him. I'd started to relax.'

'You hadn't really. All those diversions to avoid the French department.'

'It's not just the French department. Am I to avoid going to my ban the bomb meetings, or to hear visiting lecturers as well? He's asked me to go to dinner with him, so that, as he says, "we may say *adieu* as civilised people". He says he has no regrets at having loved me and that he will never forget me. And please would I respond quickly, as he is suggesting Thursday night "as I do not wish to interfere, dear Harry, with any other arrangements you have made". I think I might go, Anna. I'm bound to run into him somewhere otherwise, and if I do this, it'll be a lot less awkward.'

'Up to you, Loverish. But if you do, name the place you'd like to go to. Just in case Spellie and I have to come and rescue you.'

'You don't think he'd do anything strange, do you? In a public place? Perhaps I'll suggest the Flying Horse, so he can't lavish a fortune on me again. I'll write and let Ned know, of course. Only Thursday is the day after tomorrow.'

*

Mrs Bowers always put her lodgers' post behind the squat little Bentima mantel clock in the dining room. That is where Alfred Twigg went after his breakfast on Wednesday morning, to find a card from his aged mother in Derby wishing him a happy birthday, and a letter from his estranged wife. He frowned and took them upstairs. It was only after he had shaved and cleaned his teeth that he realised he had accidentally picked up a third envelope, addressed to Ned Stones in a decisive, feminine hand.

Enclosed with his wife's letter was a photograph of a toddler taken in what looked like a public park. *He's got her eyes, her smile.* Alfred put the deckle-edged rectangle in a tin Kimberley Ales ashtray and took out his lighter. As the photograph of the little boy with the neatly brushed hair, the toy rabbit and the long socks curled and collapsed into powder, he read the mother's latest plea. *I'm not asking for my sake but for Peter's. Unless you let me have a divorce, his father and I will never be able to do right by him.* Alfred swore and crumpled the letter, adding it to the embers in the ashtray. It flared up unexpectedly, and had to be doused with water from his toothbrush glass. *Trust you to go on causing trouble, you bitch! Living the life of Riley while I'm in this grubby room – a man of my talents.* He opened the sash, and making sure there was no one in the backyard first, tipped the soggy black fragments out of the window. Checking his pockets for keys and wallet, and taking a last look around the room before he went to his work in the wages department at Raleigh – starting an hour later than the manual workers, and wearing a shirt and tie – he spotted the letter for Ned lying on the bed. He didn't dislike young Stones so much as resented his boyish good looks, and the amount he earned on piecework, *compared to what I get with all my night school certificates,* so stuffing the envelope hurriedly into the drawer in the rickety desk, he muttered, 'I'm doing you a favour, lad, though you'll never know it. Keep clear of women. They're all whores. The ones you have to pay are the only honest ones amongst them.'

*

Harry dressed carefully and unostentatiously, in what Anna called 'your secretary look . . . the one where you smile demurely when your boss is in his cups at the works do and tells you his wife doesn't understand him'. These were not the clothes Max most admired on her, and thus they were a deliberate choice: a tweed pencil skirt, low court shoes, a starched, contrast-stitched linen blouse Ellen had made, and a neat fine lambswool cardigan with pearl buttons – *ladylike, and just very slightly forbidding.* She put her mackintosh over her arm and picked up her brolly.

*

Max was waiting downstairs by the porter's lodge. There was a bench he could have sat on, but instead he was pacing, and looking at his watch, though Harry knew she wasn't late. She caught sight of him through the swing doors, and thought, *he's a handsome man,* and marvelled at how detached she felt.

'Ah, 'Arry!' He took her hand and, bending his head, kissed her knuckles. 'I am honoured. Please, come this way,' he said, opening the outer door. *It's only politeness, of course, but he behaves as if he has forgotten it's me that lives here, not him.* Outside, she turned in the direction of the bus stop. Max called her back.

'No, 'Arry, I will drive you. See? I brought my Renault back with me this time. She is very *jolie,* is she not?'

'Oh . . . I'm not sure.'

'You know I am a gentleman. I think also it will rain, and you will get wet either going to the bus stop or on the way home. And you are not dressed for your bike, I think.'

No, and I do not want you riding pillion. That's Ned's place.

'All right, then,' she said eventually, grasping the door handle.

'No, 'Arry, the other side. Unless you wish to drive.'

*

The first course passed in polite enquiries, after Max's comment on the food: 'still these grapefruit segments everywhere one goes'. Harry told him about her summer job promotion from shop assistant to ladies wear model. Max listened inattentively and at the first opportunity expanded on his work in Grenoble.

'So,' he said, as Harry cut up the last of her fillet of sole. 'I think we have still what you call the elephant in the room? Am

I permitted to prod dear Babar a little and hope he does not stampede me?'

'Go on,' said Harry quietly.

'You are "in love" at last, are you not?' His fingers danced apostrophes in the air. 'Someone who is worthy of you, if such is possible?'

'I have met someone, yes.'

'Another student, I suppose.'

'No.'

Max's bantering manner evaporated. 'Not another lecturer?'

Harry noticed a tug at the corner of his mouth, as though he was biting at his inside lip.

'No.'

'All this *non, non,* 'Arry! Why do you make me guess? Is there something wrong with him? Is he some other woman's husband?'

'*Max!*'

Several heads turned. The waitress ostentatiously appeared at the table.

'Are you both happy with your meal?'

Max was about to answer but Harry cut in with, '*I* enjoyed it a great deal. But perhaps you could bring us our coffee now, please – no, no dessert. We will be going soon.' She turned back to Max. 'He makes bicycles. His father is a miner. Apart from when he was a soldier, he has always lived in Nottingham.'

'You have given yourself to him, then ... to this factory hand. Men of his class expect it.'

Harry gasped, and put her hand to her cheek as if he'd slapped her.

'You have no business saying that. I would like you to take me home as soon as we've drunk our coffee.'

The waitress appeared to take their plates, and the coffee arrived as Harry was dabbing her lips with her napkin.

'Would you bring us our bill, please?' said Harry.

The girl trotted back seconds later, the bill in her hand. Max snatched it from her without a word.

*

Ned swore, the bicycle bumping to a halt. He was already in a foul mood, wet through. He'd had an enjoyable evening with Sid in the Salutation but had misjudged the weather and then found that his front lamp was flickering, near to death, but he'd thought if he went fast he could get home before it went out altogether, and not be troubled by any passing policemen. Not now. He swung off the saddle and prodded the front tyre. *Floppy flat. No point in even getting the kit out, and I can't do ote when it's silin' dairn anyroad.* He lugged the bicycle onto the pavement and plodded on under the drizzle. Partway along the road he decided to cross over. The wind was driving the rain sideways, and the far pavement looked marginally more sheltered. Turning his face to the oncoming traffic, he waited until a furniture van passed, but the unfamiliar make of the car behind it attracted his attention. *Looks like one of 'em cavalier spaniels like my Auntie Doreen wanted. Turned up nose and saucer eyes. Funny number plate. Foreign, must be.* Curious, Ned forgot to stand back from the kerb, and as the Renault swished past him, a spray of dirty water flashed over his trouser legs and his shoes. Ned blinked through the rain and his heart sank. Sitting in what he took to be the driver's seat, was Harry, her face pale and stiff.

She never even saw yuh, lad. Never told yuh she had a car, eyther. What else ant she said, then? And who the hell was that bloke int wi' 'er? That posh French bloke, or someone else altogether?

*

As he drew up in front of Florence Boot Hall, Max spoke at last.

'I would just ask that you come to my office and take away the few letters you wrote to me,' he said, not looking at her.

'There's no need, Max. You can just burn them.'

'No, no, I wish you to have them. I insist – I assume you would prefer to come to my office than to my rooms.'

'Oh, yes, of course.'

'I usually receive students on Wednesday afternoons.'

'Yes.'

'I shall expect you then.'

'Goodbye, Max.'

'*Adieu.*'

*

Once outside the Gaumont, Harry shivered and turned up the collar of her coat. The crowd at the earlier showing had flowed out, and another flowed in, alive with Friday night relief. She looked at her watch, rubbed a cold stockinged calf against her other leg. The toes of her shoes were dark with rain. She felt sweaty, despite the chill, though she'd had a long hot shower before going for the bus.

'Ey up, mi duck!' called a voice. She turned her head, though realising as she did so that the speaker couldn't be Ned. A teddy boy, carrying an umbrella to protect his carefully modelled quiff, smiled and said, 'Stood yer up, has he?' a little too loudly, and she saw he wasn't alone, but playing to an audience of three friends.

'Like that, wouldn't you?' snapped Harry, and stalked off in the direction of the bus.

*

Ned meantime had cycled, on a firm new tyre, not in the direction of the Gaumont, but out to Kimberley. He wheeled the bicycle round the back and in through the gate into the yard, propping it unlocked beneath the kitchen window. He pushed open the back door, to find his mother sitting alone at the kitchen table, nursing a cup of tea. She looked up in guilty surprise. Ned realised he couldn't ever remember her sitting down and relaxing. *Perhaps she only does that when she's alone. And now I've ruined it for 'er.*

'Ned! What are *yow* doing here on a Friday night? Wurnt yuh s'pposed to be tekkin that nice lass to pictures?' said his mother.

'Nope, 'cos she int a nice lass,' he snapped. The look of disappointment on his mother's face only made him angrier with Harry.

'Oh dear . . . want a mash, lovey?' she said, getting to her feet.

Ned looked into the tired, kind face.

'Yeah, thanks . . . thanks Mam.'

'That's ah'raight, lad.'

'Where's me dad?'

'Pub.'

'Silly question. When did he last take *yow* out, Mam?'

She wiped her hands down her apron. 'Me? Oh, not sure ah can tell yuh that. Mebbe Queen Victoria was on the throne.' She tried a smile.

'Leave that tea. Weer's thi coat?'

'*Ned?*'

'Nelson and Railway. Ah can stand mi old motha a ayf of shandy on a Friday naight, can't ah?'

*

'She woh driving a car – never even knowed she 'ad one. With some bloke in the passenger seat. Drenched me and never even saw me. Leastways I 'ope she dint. That'd be even wairse.'

'Sure it wor her, Ned?'

'It wor her, a'raight. Funny-looking car – foreign. Wannt another one?'

'Yes plaise.'

Standing at the bar as the barmaid waited for his stout to settle before she topped it up, Ned watched his mother sitting at the corner table. *Poor soul,* he thought. *I hope I never tek a woman for granted the way Dad does her.* He carried the drinks over to the table.

'What were yuh 'opin' for when yow an' Dad got married?' he asked.

His mother took a gulp of her shandy, her eyes wide over the top of the glass.

'Same as any lass wannts. 'Usband and fayther for kids, Ned. And 'e's allus provided, can't fault 'im for that. 'E allus gives me the needful out o' 'is wages, before 'e sets off for pub.'

'Summat for thissen, though?'

'What do yuh mean?'

'I mean, what people 'ope for when they get married. Love, companionship, that sort of thing.'

'Well, it's what you do. Nobody wants to be an old maid. Your dad was 'andsome, believe it or not. Ah wanted a family, like any lass. Mebbe not the way ah got one, about-face as yuh might say. Though ah did want a little boy first, one that looked like yer dad. And that's what ah got. As Mrs Stones too, in the maternity ward. Better than the mother and baby home.'

Ned lowered his glass.

'Don't look so surprised, lad. Ah'm hardly the only one round here where "you may kiss the bride" was only shuttin' the stable door.' She looked both sheepish and proud. 'Sorry. Not 'ad a drop sin' Christmas. Went straight to mi 'ead. Ah wanted a home of my own, anyroad. Not much fun being one o' eight.'

'S'pose not,' he said, thinking about his grandmother, in her two-up two-down, alone now except for daft Uncle Paul.

His mother hit the table with the flat of her hand. 'Ah know what ah'd been meaning to say. It wurnt her car, Ned.'

''Ow do *you* know?' he said. 'Not that ote yuh'd say now would surprise me, Mam.'

'Yur Aunt Jean was in the Wrens. She wor over in Germany for a bit . . . forget the name of the place . . .'

'Kiel.'

'That's it. She lont to drive there. But she won't drive here, she says, because they lont 'er another side o' the road – she said wheel was on left in Germany. Mebbe it's the same in France – wurnt that man French? His car'll be laike them German ones.'

'In Malaya it was same as here.'

'It would be, wudnt it? Malaya's British.'

'Oh God . . . well, even if it wurnt 'er car,' he said slowly, 'she shouldn'ta been in one with some other bloke. Not if she's my girl.'

'Yuh jumped to conclusions about 'er driving, Ned. Yuh maight be putting tow and tow together and mekking fowertain about a' the rest of it.'

'Bogger.'

'I think yuh should see me home now, Ned. And termorrer goo looking for 'er and say yer sorry for standing 'er up, but tell her why yuh did.'

'Ah'm a stupid bastard, aren't ah?'

'Most men are, Ned,' said his mother, and drained her glass.

*

233

They'll be ringing the plods if I hang around here much longer, thought Ned, as another group of girls trotted briskly past where he sat on the low wall. *I'll have bleddy piles too. I coulda gone fishing today. And I don't even know that she's here. Even if I get up and look for that bike of hers, there's no guarantee she's not gone off somewhere on bus instead.*

He shifted his buttocks on the unrelentingly cold wall, and looked down at the toecaps he had buffed that morning in Harry's honour. Other feet came marching along the gravel path – just one pair – but this time they stopped and their owner faced him. Ned's eyes travelled up past sensible brogues, laced up with fringed toggles, lisle stockings, and a heather-coloured tweed skirt suit that to him looked as impregnable as a suit of armour. Grey waved hair framed a severe, but intelligent face. Sharp brown eyes held his gaze from behind tortoiseshell frames.

'*You're* not a copper!' he blurted.

'I should think not, young man. But as warden my rule is law here, nevertheless. May I ask what you are doing here?'

'I was looking for a young lady.'

'We have plenty of young ladies here. Was it one in particular you were after?'

He saw a twitch at the corner of her mouth, and flushed.

'Yes. But she's not expecting me.'

'Indeed? What did you want her to do, this young lady of yours? Open her window and let down her hair?'

'It's not long enough, Miss . . .'

'Spellman. Well, that's the modern girl for you.'

'Miss Spellman.' His face was on fire.

'So what do you want with her, this young lady, if that's not an impertinent question?'

'Noat – nothing, I mean – I just wanted to say I was sorry.'

A smile broke over Miss Spellman's austere face. 'You must be very stiff sitting there. I've been watching you from my office. If you wish to leave the young woman a message you may. I shall be sure that she gets it. I cannot of course guarantee what response you will get. Follow me.'

Recognising an order, Ned got stiffly to his feet and trailed after Miss Spellman through a fanlighted doorway and into a spartanly clean but imposing entrance hall. Ned thought about the last time he had been here, for the guest dinner, and sighed.

Miss Spellman was standing waiting, holding open a door for him. Most of the room was occupied by a large oak desk, but the remainder was as bare as the hallway, save three crammed bookshelves and some framed academic certificates. The lino looked as though it was polished weekly, and the nubby covers stretched over the two easy chairs either side of the fireplace, though old, looked clean.

'Do make yourself comfortable, Mr . . .'

'Stones. Ned Stones.'

'I'll bring you writing materials. Let's grab one of those tomes and – oh, you'd better put a magazine on top to save the binding.' She pulled out a substantial volume and handed it to him. *So now yuh know what a tome is, Ned.* He sank obediently into one of the chairs. Miss Spellman took from a drawer of the desk a copy of *Punch,* some sheets of writing paper headed up 'Florence Boot Hall' and a fountain pen.

'Now which of our young ladies am I to deliver your letter to?'

'Harry Loveridge.'

'I thought it might be. The infamous painter of the lions in Slab Square?'

'That's where I met her first . . .'

'I remember *you,* of course. Perhaps I should have said so. You came here on a guest night last term. You can be quite sure she was in on that joke, Mr Stones. It wouldn't surprise me if she'd come up with the idea herself. I shall leave you to get on with your letter.'

Miss Spellman retreated behind her desk and Ned stared at the paper, his head swirling with rage at himself. *Yer stupid bastard.* In the quietness of the room, the rustling of Miss Spellman's papers and the insistent tick tock of a small pendulum clock was amplified. *Like that jungle at night.* The fountain pen lay inert in his hand, slick with sweat.

Tick tock tick tock.

He looked up, for Miss Spellman had stopped writing and was smiling gently at him over her spectacles.

'I'm sorry, I . . .' he mumbled.

'You're angry with yourself, from the look on your face. Write that anger down and you'll get on all right from there.'

'I think she's got another bloke.'

'Why should that stop you? Faint heart and fair lady and all that.'

'A man with a car. Foreign, probably.'

'Ye-es. I think I know who you mean. Don't look so down-cast, Mr Stones. He's clever enough, but a mite didactic.' Seeing Ned's expression, she clarified. 'Tends to hold opinions he is convinced are right, and says so.'

'What, bossy, you mean?'

'One could say that perhaps.'

'With *Harry*?'

'As I said, if I were you I wouldn't let him put you off.'

*

Three frantically written pages later he looked up, his heart thumping. *One of the reasons I'm cross with myself, Harry, is that I'm behaving as daft as that French bloke. You told me how he tried to own you. And I've just done the exact same thing and taken the hump with you because I had a flat tyre and soaked trouser legs.*

'You'll need an envelope,' said Miss Spellman, holding one up.

'I'm not sure if I should ... I mean I think I've gone on a bit. I've never written such a long letter before. Not even from Malaya.' *Poor old Mam.*

'I'm hardly an expert, Mr Stones, in the ways of love. I am perhaps more of an expert on Miss Loveridge however. Give her your letter as it is.'

He folded the pages awkwardly, *all thumbs, Ned,* and reached for the envelope Miss Spellman had left on his side of the desk.

'Why did you want to help me?' he said.

'Because I was watching you through the window. I saw that you needed it. And, if I'm not speaking out of turn, I saw how Harry looked at you when she brought you to the guest night. There isn't much one misses from that high table. Put her name on the envelope and she'll have it as soon as I find her.'

*

Ned walked at a brisk pace away from the campus. The phrases that had gushed onto those pages reverberated in his head. *That day in Slab Square it was like the rest of the world just blurred and all I could see was you.* There was self-pity he knew he'd regret. *Why would a girl like you look at a man like me? You could have all the men you wanted and all their fancy cars. Why'd you want a lathe operator in Raleigh even if he does earn good money? He only knows to piss it up a wall anyroad.* Then, *Even my Mam thinks I'm a right idiot.* A hot wave of bitter jealousy engulfed him again. *I couldn't bear seeing you with another man.* And frank remorse: *Whatever I thought, I shouldn't have left you standing out there in the rain.* He finished with *Your Miss Spellman's very kind, but I don't suppose you'll ever forgive me. I don't suppose I would, in your pretty shoes.*

A second bus passed him as he marched through Old Lenton, but he'd wanted the walk *to work my thoughts off. Heaven knows how I'll get a wink of sleep tonight. Beer, I suppose.* A gentle drizzle damped his hair; he turned up his coat collar and walked a little faster. He turned left up Gregory Street, preferring the route through fallow fields, knowing that they were earmarked for new housing. *That'll be my luck, wurnt it? Settle dairn wi' a 'nice girl' and pay off a three-bedroomed semi before I drop dead. That's if I can find a 'nice girl'. Difficult, as that's the last thing I want. I want Harry. I want my bolshie bleddy Harry.*

A furniture van lumbered past. Then there was the roar of a motorbike. He kept his head down, but twenty yards ahead the bike puttered to a halt and its slender rider dismounted. *It's her! It's* not *her, yuh just want it to be. No, nobody else has them showground curlicues painted on her fuel tank.* Harry stood there waiting. For a moment he didn't know whether to approach or to hang back. *I bet I'm in for a bollocking, but at least she's here.* She was still wearing her crash helmet and goggles, and a scarf around the lower part of her face, but there was something in the tension of her shoulders that indicated impatience. *My Harry.* She waved something at him – another helmet.

'Hello, Ned,' she said, pulling down the scarf. 'It's stopped raining. Trust me enough to get on the back?'

'Not yet. Tek that bleddy helmet off a minute, will yuh?'

'If you want.'

'I do. Goggles too.' She did so, placing them with the helmet on the seat of the bike.

'Bleddy hell, Harry. I'm a daft bogger but I love yow.' He took her by the shoulders and kissed her, and went on kissing her despite the hoots and yells of passing motorists. At last he broke away, then nuzzled her neck, drinking in the scent of her skin. 'God, I could eat yow all up, I could!'

'Let's go somewhere where we won't be entertaining half of Nottingham. Put your armour on, Ned.' She put her own goggles and helmet back on with practised speed, but when she saw him struggling with the buckle, said, 'Let me do that.' Ned's heart sang for joy just feeling the touch of her cool fingers under his chin.

He clambered up behind her, thrilling to the feel of his opened thighs embracing her bottom. His hands slipped round her waist.

'Where are yuh tekkin me?' he asked. *It doesn't matter, as long as I'm wi' yow.*

'Newstead,' came the muffled reply.

How lithe she felt, how strong, even through the motorcycle leathers, yet so slender. The wind rushed into his mouth and he remembered an early train journey to Derby, to his first away football match, when his father had had to pull him away from an open window. The cold air buffeted his thoughts, chasing away the doubt. He shut his mouth, gasping, and leant against Harry's tensed back.

By the time they reached Newstead he was in a state of mortification, however. *I'm as hard as a board. She can't have missed that.*

He turned away from her and unbuckled the goggles and helmet. He put the goggles inside the helmet and, facing her, held it in front of his fly. Harry was ruffling up her hair and laughing.

'I'm not going to kick you, Ned, even if you do deserve it. Fancy the tea shop, or want a bit of a walk?'

'A bit of a walk, mebbe, then the tea shop.' He wanted her alone, not amongst crowded tables and lurking waitresses. 'Yuh read my letter then.'

'Miss Spellman found me in the library. I think she likes you.'

'I like *her* – a nice woman.'

'And I like your letters. I liked them so much that sometimes Mum or Dad or Uncle Vanlo would come into Lefevre's with them, so that I'd get to read them on my tea break and not have to wait until I got home. They turned some boring days happy, I can tell you.'

'That wor nice of 'em. Told them a bit about me, did yow?'

'Told them *a lot* about you.'

'Will I get to meet them then?' He thought his face would ache if he smiled any wider.

'You will.' She held out a hand.

'I love yow,' said Ned, and took it.

'So do I. Love you, I mean.'

'Oh, Harry . . . don't say anymore till yuh know everything abaht me.'

'I've been wondering about that, ever since the day in the cemetery. I've something I'd better tell you too.'

'There's that bench over there. Let's hope the rain keeps off. I don't think I could say them things over teacups an' scones.'

CHAPTER TWENTY-THREE

Newstead
October 1958

'There woh all sorts in army. The sergeant kept telling us it wor a great leveller. I can tell yuh it wor no more a leveller than the bleddy Grand Lodge in Goldsmith Street. Who got a commission and that. There wor the grammar school boys pretending they wor like the toffs – the public school boys – to hear 'em – as if it was only a mistake they wurnt eating in the officers' mess and all that. But there was one in our hut – this was before we woh sent east – that shouldn'ta been in the army at all. He wor picked on. I think he wor a nancy boy, but if he dint know it, the others did, or decided they did. Some o' the borstal types thought it wor fun to tek a rise out o' the way he spoke. I comm in one evening to find 'im crying in his underpants, and they wor all wet, and them all standing round laffin. I'd no idea what they'd threatened him with – still don't. I saw red then, an' took a swing at the one that wor laffin most. I bust 'is nose. Sergeant comm in to see what all the row wor about, and I got confined to barracks and fatigues. The poor nancy never comm back from his next leave. I hope he wor invalided out, but there wor a story went abaht that his mother found him hangin' in the wash-owse.'

'Oh no!'

'I never knew what really happened. But the ones that were tormenting him dint cause any more trouble around me after that, an' the NCO comm and thanked me on the quiet.

'Dad said I wor lucky. I'd see the world, he said. Dad's allus been dead keen on anything in uniform, which is funny for someone who never wore one hissen. Wanted me to be a scout an' all.'

'At school they encouraged us to go into the Girl Guides. I liked that idea no more than I liked hockey. All much too jolly.'

'I think it wor easier for them public school types. Apart from getting commissions, they'd been used to square-bashing at school. And bein' away from 'ome too. But if any of that wor a leveller, it wor the medical. Yuh shoulda seen uz, Harry, stripped to the skin, most of us looking about as appealing as a bundle of spring onions. An' after I'd given my sample the doctor grabbed my tackle and told me to cough – stop laffin, Harry! Have *yow* ever tried to pee only a little bit, and then stop?'

'No. But I've had check-ups I haven't liked.'

'What is it, mi duck?'

'Oh, nothing really. I suppose we all have to put up with unpleasantness sometimes.'

'Harry?'

'Go on, Ned.'

'Yuh still want my war stories?'

'I've heard my brother Tom's – only because he was in the actual war, in Italy.'

'The actual war? If yer fightin' someone, it feels real enough. Malaya did.'

'Sorry . . .'

'Don't be. I wor allus getting into bother, though, ending up in the glass'owse.'

'The glasshouse? Were you gardening?'

He laughed. 'No, that's just what they called chokey. Don't know why as there was precious little daylight in it. I'd've done anything to get a chance to look out.'

'Funny you should say that. Dad was in Lincoln as a conchie. He was forever in the punishment cells because he tried looking out of the window, or looking up at the sky when they were marching round the yard.'

Ned whistled. 'The bastards!'

'He did sign up in the end, as a farrier. Anything to get out of being locked up.'

'I think I'd like yer old man.'

'He'd like you, Ned. I should warn you though, he's a bit protective of me.'

'Yuh mean he'll want to know if my intentions are honourable, or whatever it is they call it in bowks? What's that funny laugh for, Harry? They are, y'know.'

'What is this, Ned? A proposal?'

'If yuh like . . . oh, Harry, of course it bleddy is! Only I'm not holding yuh to an answer yet. Too much to tell yuh still.' He ran his hand through his hair, and it stuck up in all directions. 'I think you're gorgeous. And clever. Yer far too good for a bloke like me. And, if yuh don't mind me saying so, yuh've the finest arse I've ever seen.'

'You know something, Ned? I don't think I do mind.'

'So I can kiss yow again, then?'

'Of course you can. But since we've talked about Dad, I think I should have told you that where he comes from and everything, a kiss means something. It's not just something that people do in the lane at the back of the Red Lion.'

'Hell, if I kissed yuh in the lane at the back of the Red Lion, it would!'

'Here will do though.'

*

'Go on, Ned. I interrupted you.'

'Yuh can interrupt me that way for the rest o' your life if yow want to, Harry! But before yuh say yes or anything else yuh might be sorry for after, hear me out. Yuh said that about glass'owses and gardnin'. Well, funnily enough, I *wor* gardnin' some o' the time. That was one of their punishments. I cheeked an NCO and I wor made to weed some officer's little patch of God's earth – only with a fork. An eating fork, I mean, not a garden fork. The other squaddies laughed fit to piss theirsen whenever they came past. If it wurnt that it wor latrines. Oh hell, talk of watter and it starts silin' . . . Let's get indoors. I'll tell yow another time.'

*

On Sunday evening, Alfred Twigg hung the suit Mrs Bowers had pressed for him on the outside of the wardrobe, and pushed up the sash to get rid of the odour of mothballs. He'd spent a most unsatisfactory day. The only bright moment was the morning service at Lenton Methodist, and another glimpse of that pretty dark girl a couple of pews in front. That morning he stumbled over the words of the Lord's Prayer, realising that some of those phrases he had repeated automatically since Sunday School actually meant something: 'As we forgive those who trespass against us . . .' *I know I can never forgive Mabel. But it's not the kiddie's fault.*

He grasped the handle of the desk drawer and pulled. *Bloody thing's sticking again. Must be all that rain last night.* Eventually, he rattled it open, only to see the letter addressed to Ned Stones lying on top of the writing paper he used for his dutiful correspondence with his mother. *Is it against the law to interfere with the Royal Mail?* He picked up the envelope and tossed it onto the bed. Then before he could change his mind, he took out the pad of writing paper and wrote:

Dear Mabel, Go ahead with the bloody divorce if you want it so much; I'll not oppose you. I'll even stand up in court and give evidence if it's needed, but tell your solicitor to arrange things so that we don't have to meet. As long as I don't have to see you or hear from you ever again I shall be happy. The ten shilling note is to buy something for the little lad. I wish him the best of luck. He'll need it with the parents he's got.

Having clambered back up to the moral high ground, Alfred Twigg slept well that night.

In the morning, Alfred waited on the landing until the post had rattled through the letterbox at half past eight and been picked up by his landlady, before descending to breakfast. The others had already eaten, and Ned had left long before to beat the factory hooter. Mrs Bowers called out from the kitchen, 'Ah'll mash your tea fresh, Mr Twigg, and 'ave a cup missen.' He glanced at the mantel clock. The morning's post was already there; with half an eye on the door to the kitchen he pushed Ned's letter in amongst the others.

CHAPTER TWENTY-FOUR

Chippendale Street
November 1958

Harry got down from the bus and walked into Ned's arms.

'Hello, duck!'

'Quack!'

'It's nice out, int it, for this time of year? Fancy a walk in the Rec before the flicks?'

For answer, Harry took hold of his hand.

'Your letter turned up eventually, by the way. I'm sorry I wor a pillock, Harry.'

'Stop saying you're sorry. It's all right.'

'Well, seeing as it is—' he let go of her hand and caught her around the waist instead '—I've a suggestion for you. Ma Bowers is away at her sister's in Bolsover. Remember how yuh wanted to see where I lived? I could sneak yuh in ayfter film. The other lodgers'll eyther be out gallivanting if they've any sense, or they'll be shut in their rooms drinking theirsen into a lonely grave.'

'That's all very well, Ned, but what had you in mind once we're in your room? It's a serious question, so stop grinning like that.'

'I know it is. As we're going to get married sooner or later I want to be completely honest with yow. I've nightmares, Harry. I've had them since I comm out of army. They're one of the reasons I don't live at home – I dint wannt Mam and Dad hearing me. In lodgings full of blokes it doesn't matter so much. Groans and yelling in dark I mean. Ma Bowers is allraight about it – John Bowers wor shipped back from the Somme not raight in 'is 'ead, so she's well used to blokes shouting the odds in their sleep. He never did comm raight and now he's dead. I wondered, if I sneaked yow in some time, and – um – yuh lay dairn beside me, if I would still wek up like that.'

'So you'd frighten the life out of me as well as out of yourself? Oh, Ned, I don't know if you realise what you're asking me.'

'I'm sorry. It wor a stupid thing to think yuh'd agree. Tek it back, as if I'd never said it. Plaise, Harry.'

She looked up at him. His anxiety made him look suddenly older. 'You really meant it, didn't you? About the nightmares.'

'God yes, Harry. They're real enough.'

'Let's turn back. We can go to Forest Rec again another day.'

'Yuh want to go home,' he said hopelessly.

'I do. I want to get my toothbrush, my cold cream, and a clean blouse and underwear. And I need to warn Anna to cover for me. In case I'm missed at breakfast, that kind of thing. And after we've been to the pictures we'd better go and eat something or my tummy will keep us awake.'

'Harry, yuh don't have to . . . it wor a stupid suggestion.'

'It wasn't. You want to find out something about yourself. It might be that I need to do the same. And about us.'

∗

Harry looked round the room, taking in the cream wood-chip walls, the bare picture rail, a washbasin with the towel rail attached and a bevel-edged mirror above, the Utility gentleman's wardrobe, a Rexine-seated chair and an old-fashioned, iron-framed bed – a small double, inexpertly made.

'With Ma Bowers being away, I've had to mek it,' he said, following her glance.

'Oh *Ned!* Didn't they teach you how to do corners in the army?'

'Taught me lots there. I've been tryin' to forget it ever sin,' he said quietly.

'Not successfully, if you're having nightmares.'

He twitched as though stung.

'I'm sorry, Ned, that was pretty crass of me.' She sat down on the rumpled counterpane, as if testing the bed with her weight.

'It's ah' raight, Harry.' He sat beside her and took her hand. Harry felt his nervousness in the pressure of his fingers.

'*Where* was it you said the toilet was?'

'I dint. Out the back. All the owd 'owses are like that.'

'I shouldn't be surprised. Ours is too – at home, I mean. I think I must be getting soft, living in Florence Boot. But how will I get there and back without being spotted?'

'This,' said Ned, reaching under the bed.

'A *potty?* Oh Ned, even when we are married, I will never, ever use a potty in your presence.'

'Glad to hear it. Or rayther, not to hear it. I've thought about that, though. When yow need to go, I'll go dairnstairs and out the back missen, so's yuh've a bit o' privacy.'

'Practicalities, Ned. What about emptying it?'

'I'll do that. Put a towel ower the top if yuh like. I can't believe your pee is wairser than mine.'

'Oh, Ned ... I've just sat through a film I can't remember anything about.'

'Me neyther.'

'We're about to spend a night together in this lumpy bed.'

'Yes – that's if yer sure. I can still put yer onta last bus – nay, I'd comm wi' yow and then walk back.'

'No. I didn't mean that. I mean we're having a sort of rehearsal for living together and all we're doing is talking about wee. You know, Anna once asked me what I wanted in a man. I said he'd have to be kind, and he'd have to make me laugh.'

'Yer not laffin now, though.'

'I'm not. But that's only because I'm nervous.'

'Me too, Harry.'

'One day, though, we're going to laugh like drains about this. Aren't we?'

Ned knelt in front of her then, and slowly laid his head sideways in her lap.

'We will. I love yow, Harry. I'm never going to get tired of saying it.'

251

'Even if I tell you I've just realised that I'll have to go back for my pyjamas?'

'Oh . . .' He looked up. 'And I don't have any – last time I wore any was in the blessed army as well. I wor goin' to sleep in my underpants. But I've summat I can lend yow.' He got up and went to the wardrobe.

'I've this nightshirt. It's an old one o' Dad's – all the miners had 'em once,' he said, shaking out the folds. 'Much too big for yow. Put it on and yuh'll be in no danger from me. I'll not be able to find yow.'

'Turn away then.'

'I'll go to the jakes. There's a towel here. An' soap on the basin. I'll tek the paper so yow can tek yer time.'

Once the sound of his footsteps on the stair had faded, Harry stood up and undressed rapidly, without looking at herself, and, standing naked at the basin, she washed and cleaned her teeth. She ran her fingers over Ned's shaving things, and noticed that the fibres of the toothbrush in the mug were fanned from over-use. *What will it be like to see these things of his every day?* She picked up the voluminous night shirt and fought it over her head. It crackled with starch, and whoever had laundered it last had used too much blue bag. Then she opened the wardrobe and appraised herself in the mirror inside the door. *I look about ten years old.* She glanced in, noticing that Ned had arranged his clothes neatly, exactly as the labels screwed to each drawer suggested. A suit, his sports jacket, a pair of corduroy trousers and three plain white shirts hung in the well of the wardrobe, and a pair of polished black lace-up shoes stood on newspaper beneath. Next to them in a small stack were three library books. Harry bent down, and picking one up, read the spine.

Footsteps outside, then a pause, and a soft knock. Harry quickly put the book back, clicked the wardrobe door shut and opened the door.

'Oh look at yow!' he murmured, delighted. 'Want to get in first? Only don't go peeking at me getting undressed.'

Ned sat down on the edge of the bed with his back to her, looking down at his socks. *Yuh can take* them *off, anyroad, wi'out the osses getting frit.* He felt the movement of the bed beneath him as Harry got in.

'Decent?' he asked, alarmed by the tremor in his voice.

'Yes. You can look now if you want.'

He turned, and couldn't help smiling. She lay there with her arms on top of the counterpane, engulfed in the oversized nightshirt, her hands almost hidden by the length of the sleeves.

'I've never seen anyone as good to look at as yow.' He lifted one of her hands and kissed her knuckles. 'Do yer mind me wi' no shirt on?'

'I grew up on a farm, Ned.'

'I'll keep my underpants on, promise.'

He twitched his braces from his shoulders, then pulled his shirt over his head. Harry watched beneath her eyelashes as his vest followed. Ned's back was lean and muscled, but white from working indoors.

'I thought I told yuh no peeking,' he said, smiling over his shoulder. Harry felt a sudden spurt of love for him, that vulnerable naked back, the ruffled hair.

'Go on, turn away, or I'll never get mi breeks off,' he said. She obeyed, hearing him grunt as he struggled with his trouser buttons, and then felt the bed heave as he stood up.

'Yow keep looking away, till I get washed.'

Harry turned on her side, and fidgeted in the bed to disguise the intimacy of the sounds coming from the basin.

'Ah'raight, now.'

Harry looked round.

'Oh, Ned . . .' *He's beautiful.*

Although he was not completely naked, Ned crossed his hands in front of his groin. His hair was tousled, slightly damp at the temples.

'You look like a picture in a book I had at school,' said Harry.

'I do? What sort o' schoowel were *yow* at, then?'

'It was a marble statue – of a Greek god. You're like him, perfectly proportioned. Only . . .'

'What?'

'You're a bit hairier. And you're wearing underpants.'

Ned laughed. 'That's 'cos it's a bit colder in Nottingham than Greece, probably! Can I get in?'

They lay side by side, neither daring to touch the other.

'Like an old married couple already, int we?' he said shakily.

Harry put out a hand, encountering the warmth of his thigh. She pulled back, as if burned, but his hand reached down and held hers. Then he turned onto his side to face her, and leant over and gently started to kiss her, relieved that she kissed him back, but nevertheless holding his body carefully away from her. *Don't muck it up now, Ned!* Tentatively, Harry raised a hand to the nape of his neck. His heart pounding, he put his arm over her. Too late, he felt her stiffen, her hands grasping his shoulders, holding him back.

'Stop, Ned. Stop it.'

He pulled away. 'Sorry.'

'Don't be. It's nothing you've done. It's me.'

Ned propped himself on an elbow. Harry's eyes were closed, but tears seeped out. There, in the privacy of that quiet room in Nottingham, she'd caught the scent of hops, the pressure of a hand over her mouth,

'Harry . . . Harry. I'll not touch you. I'm sorry.'

'It's not you . . . I'm not a virgin, Ned.'

Ned hesitated. 'Nor am I.' *So she wurnt straight wi' me about the French bloke after all.* He felt his throat tighten. *It's not that she's done it already. It's that she dint tell me before. I don't know what difference this'll mek yet, but I do know I want nobody else.* Miserable, he bent to kiss the tears away.

'No . . . stop. Please listen.' She put both palms flat on his chest.

'You're telling me to make sure I *don't* make love to yow,' he said slowly.

'"Make love?" Oh, Ned, that had nothing to do with it.'

He tentatively stroked her cheek. '*I* love you, Harry. Forget that other man.'

To his horror, Harry started to sob without restraint. Ned put his arm over her and eased her towards him, stroking her back through the voluminous linen folds, as though she was a baby with trapped wind. She tucked her head beneath his chin;

he felt her breath warm on his collarbone. 'It's ah'raight, Harry, it's ah'raight.'

Harry sniffed, and shuddered. 'It wasn't Max. It never was. I was raped, Ned. Two men raped me. I was still at school.'

'Oh . . . oh, Harry, my girl. Oh, Harry. The bastards.' He rocked her back and forth. 'Oh, Harry!' He found he was crying himself, but the pain he felt for her was also tempered by relief. He hated himself for it. *She never lied to me. It's me that's a bastard too. She's tried to tell me before, only I never let her.*

'I expect yuh don't want to talk about it.'

'Actually, I do. I want you to understand.' Quietly, steadily, Harry recounted the whole story to Ned's breastbone: the attack, the police surgeon's questions, Sam and Vanlo's mission to the Resolute.

'So they're free? And that silly woman married the bastard?'

'She's to be pitied, Ned.'

'And you're not?'

'Don't need pity. One day I'll get my own back – on them and others like them.'

'Yuh will, won't yuh?'

'Ned, thank you for listening.'

'I'm just sorry I dint before.'

'It'll not make a difference, will it?'

'To me? No . . . no, Harry.'

Silence. Eventually, he said, 'Want me to get up and turn the light out?'

'Yes.'

Lying down again, he said, 'Will yuh be in bother for stopping out?'

'Perhaps. But Anna will have thought of something.' Harry stifled a yawn.

He stroked her hair in the darkness. 'I'll need to think of summat too. There's a woman coming in from next door to do the breakfasts who doesn't know us but does know there are no women here.' He waited for a response, but none came. Harry was asleep. Ned kissed her forehead. His eyes became accustomed to the gloom, for he had left the smallest of gaps between the curtains, as was his habit. He lay awake for half an hour, watching her profile. *You're mine. I want yow allus to be next to me.*

*

Ned woke at six, aware of rustling in the room, but kept his eyes tight shut and concentrated on breathing regularly. Harry was on the potty, trying desperately to angle it so she made the least noise. *She int wanting to wek me,* he thought. The furtive, but unmistakeable sounds of her relieving herself filled him with immense tenderness.

An hour later, he pulled on his trousers and pushed his bare feet into his shoes.

'Ned?' said Harry, her voice full of sleep.

'Just going to tek a leak. So's *yow* can.'

CHAPTER TWENTY-FIVE

The Boat, Priory Street
November 1958

'Pass me those matches, Lovergirl, would you?'

Harry pushed the box across the table in the college bar. Anna drew deep on her cigarette, leaving a ring of her bright red lipstick round the filter. Holding her right elbow in her left hand, she blew the smoke up at the ceiling, her eyes narrowing.

'Now what? Does he want to make an honest woman of you?'

'Yes.'

'Is he kind and does he make you laugh?'

'Ye-es,' said Harry, a laugh in her own voice.

'Do you love him? Silly question, I know, but one does like to be thorough.'

'I do. It's funny how you just know when you've nothing to compare it to. I never let myself love Max, you see. I was afraid to.'

'Because of the hop field.'

'Not only that. It's because he never seemed to have any doubts about any opinion he held. I always ended up feeling rather browbeaten with him. There was a bit of me that said, "Watch yourself, Harry. Don't let your guard down." So I didn't. The trouble is, if you don't let your guard down at all, love never gets in.'

'But Max did – let his guard down, I mean.'

'Yes. That's exactly what he did. Falling in love for him was losing control. And having done that, he had to convince himself he was right. He never thought there was any danger to him, until it was too late. He kept saying so in his letters.'

Anna looked at the ash cumulating on the end of her cigarette. She'd forgotten to smoke it. She waved her hand, and the ash shivered into the saucer.

'What have you done with them?'

'Burned them.'

'Did you ever go back and get yours, by the way?'

'Oh crumbs, I forgot completely. Oh dear ... I'll go on Wednesday. Remind me, would you?'

'I will. But let's think about Ned. If I was a *shadchan*—'

'Pardon?'

'A marriage broker, where I come from. I'd be asking about his prospects.'

'His *prospects?* He can spend the rest of his life at that lathe if he wants. I'm not sure he does, but I'm more sure that he doesn't know what else he'd do if the world decided to stop riding bicycles. He's never been so unhappy that he's persuaded himself to do anything else.'

'"Work is the opiate of the people."'

'That was religion, not work.'

'Just testing, Harry. For some people work *is* religion. William Morris said something about how there would never be revolution in this country, because things might get bad, but they'd never get *so* bad that people would risk their skins by taking to the streets. That's Ned, isn't it? He's decided, like so many men, that if he's well enough paid, and housed, and fed, then the bargain is good enough to accept unremitting boredom between one factory hooter and the next. But, I've a not so hypothetical question, Harry, given the circs . . .'

'Go on. Though I think I can guess what you're going to say.'

'Will Harmony Loveridge, Dr Holt's brightest student, be happy to be the wife of a factory hand?'

'I'd be happy to be the wife of *that* particular factory hand. Only . . . I'd be happier if he was doing something he loved.'

'I see . . . Harry, going back to that *shadchan* business . . .'

'This is Nottingham, Anna, not Czarist Minsk. And you're up to something.'

*

Knowing no more than that Ned lived in Chippendale Street, the following Monday evening Anna told Harry she was going to borrow a book from a girl in Nightingale Hall. Instead, she hailed the first bus in the direction of town and, lighting a Woodbine to give her courage, walked into the public bar of the White Hart. *No Ned.* He wasn't in the private bar either, but locking eyes with the man with the least wavering stare of all those in the place, asked 'Where are the other pubs around here?'

'Let me buy you a drink and I'll tell you.'

'Help you remember, will it? Good evening to you too.'

'There's the Boat,' said a barmaid, coming in to clear the tables. 'No use asking this lot. They can't find their way to the netty most nights, never mind managing to point Percy in the right direction when they get there.'

Five minutes later, heads turned as Anna pushed her way into the public bar of the Boat, and looked for Ned through the fog of smoke and noise. He was sitting at a circular table with two other young men. He was immediately on his feet.

'Anna!' he cried, looking beyond her. 'Where's Harry? Has something happened to her?'

'Harry?' said one of the youths to the other. 'Never said ote abaht that one.'

'Harry's absolutely fine,' said Anna. 'But have you a minute, to talk in confidence?'

'Oooh!' chorused Ned's companions.

'That's if Laurel and Hardy can spare you, of course.'

'Here, lads,' said Ned, putting some coins on the table. 'It wor my round next. See yuh in morning.' He took Anna's elbow. 'It'll be quieter in the back bar.'

'I'm sorry to have interrupted your evening,' said Anna, once they were settled with their beer in front of them. Anna pushed her packet of Woodbines across the table.

'No, thank yow. I've given up. Harry's worried about her dad that way. And don't be sorry. I'm glad to see yow. In fact, if yuh hadn't comm looking for me I'd have probably comm looking for yow.'

'Oh?'

'I need advice.'

'I'm listening.'

And for the next hour, she did. Afterwards, he waited with her at the bus stop.

'I'm honoured that you told me, Ned. But you've got to tell her yourself. She knows about the nightmares, but it's wrong to let her think you get them about the poor lady that died, or that lad that was bullied.'

'It's for them too.'

'If you don't tell her, Ned, then you're not letting her choose. You'll probably even worry she finds out. And they'll have won. The people who put you in that situation – a boy, thousands of miles from home.'

'It was supposed to make a man of me, Anna, not a monster!'

'Ssh!' she said. 'You're no monster. No more than she's the rubbish those two swines treated her as.'

'But I've to carry it with me the rest of mi life.'

'So does she – what happened to *her,* I mean.'

'But it wurnt her fault!'

'Was what you did yours, man?'

'If I'd been able to confess it, do some time, it'd have been better.'

'Tell her.'

'And lose her?'

'I don't think you will, Ned. Oh, there's the bus now.'

'Dint *yow* have summat yuh wanted to ask me?'

'It was nothing of any importance.'

*

'*You* were a long time, Anna.'

'Turns out we had a lot to talk about, Harry. More than I'd expected.'

'Serious, by the looks of things. I'll get the cocoa.'

*

'Tow to Kimberley, plaise,' said Ned to the conductor. He put his arm along the back of the seat and leaned closer to Harry, peering into the trug she held on her lap.

'They're nothing fancy,' she said. 'And they'll not need much maintenance. Just regular watering if we ever have a dry spell.'

'There's a standpipe at the back of the chapel. I can ask Dan. He knew her, after all. Funny little faces they've got, pansies.'

'The wild ones are called heartsease,' said Harry. 'They might have medicinal qualities – Dad would know. Or it might only be that they're cheering to look at.'

'They are that. Mind if we don't tell Mam and Dad what we're doing? I'll just need to nip round the back and into his shed for a trowel.'

*

'We're lucky it rained last night,' said Ned. 'Ground's nice and soft. Pass me the next one?'

Ned eventually sat back on his heels. 'That's better. More like somebody cares,' he said in an oddly distant voice. 'Look. Them little heads nod when there's a breath of breeze, as if they're talking to each other.'

'They do, don't they? When the blooms shrivel, pinch them off. Then they'll flower again. They won't last for ever, though.'

'But it's a start.'

Harry looked down at Ned kneeling there. 'I'm going to leave you alone for a bit,' she said. 'I'll go and sit on Mrs Simmonds's bench.'

CHAPTER TWENTY-SIX

Kimberley
November 1958

Harry sat and turned her face up to the scudding clouds. Despite the crisp air, she thought of summer days of childhood when she'd lie in the warm grass and look up at the wide Kentish skies. A slow tread on the gravel path brought her back to the present.

Ned sat down.

'I've talked to her. Time I talked to yow.' He turned towards her, and hid his face in her neck. 'Afterwards yuh mightn't want me to talk to yuh ever again.'

'Try me, Ned.' She stroked his hair. 'It's something that happened out there, isn't it?'

'Yeah ... I wor in a camp out there, square-bashing, like my life depended on it, though what that had to do with going into the jungle I don't know. Making me into a man, they said. Cudnt see the bleddy point, polishing kit and dubbining mi boots for them inspections, when if the sergeant wanted to find summat wrong and cudnt, he'd invent it. The bastard dint like my face, anyroad. I hadn't heard from Dora in weeks, and I

265

could never write back. Who'd I write to? Then this envelope comm to the barracks when we was still in Singapore, and I recognised Mam's handwriting, and 'cos it wor hers, poor old thing, I wor cross. I wanted it to be Dora's. So I never opened it until later. When I did it was to fahnd out Dora was dead, and that Mam wor sorry, but she wanted me to hear it from her and not some other bogger – not her word. What she meant was the husband. Turned out they all knew, of course. He wrote an' all. Accused me o' killing her. Of giving her the tumour! An' how I shoulda thought of the nippers. Told me not to show my face in Kimberley again or he'd push it inside out for me. I still don't know who gave him my address as it wurnt Mam.

'From Singapore we were sent to Malaya. Jungle-bashing. Fighting our way through undergrowth and forest where yuh'd barely see proper daylight sometimes, the trees were that high and thick – me full o' rage and grief. No heat like it – mawled by it we wor, sopping wet the whole time, dripping sweat. None of the training prepared yuh for fighting an enemy yuh cudnt see – the woods were teeming wi' 'em. We'd local trackers, o' course. The officers kep' telling us that they wurnt "our equals" but if it ant been for them yow and me wudnt be talking now. Naights were wairser, dark so solid you cudnt see your own hand in front of yuh. And snakes. And trench foot. Yuh know what I used to long for most, Harry?'

'Safety?'

'That and a proper bath. I wanted most of all to be standing on the terraces at the City Ground, in the rain, watching Forest lose at home. Just something normal to get worked up about, yuh know?' He sniffed loudly.

'Ned . . .'

'I hadn't a clue what we wor even doing there, not till this Jock lad in our platoon put me raight. He wor a communist from somewhere near Glasgow, a miner who'd joined up only because he thought tow years of summat different had to be better than the pit. Archie told us we were only there because some big nob had been assassinated by terrorists, and because the rubber plantations and tin mines were too important to the British.

'We got good at catching the terrorists – better than they were at gettin' *uz*. It wor near enough a game – to finish off more o' them than they got of us. Sometimes we'd catch 'em, or if we only managed to wound one, we'd truss 'im up over a pole and we'd carry 'im to the nearest field hospital. Pointless that – 'cos he'd be nursed back to health only to be put on some sort of trial, for terrorism, and after that he'd be hanged.'

'You killed people?' said Harry softly.

'I did.' He spread out his hands and looked at them as if they didn't belong to him. 'That is, I pulled the trigger. I know I could just say "it woh him or me" and that would be true, o' course, but my only thought by then was we should've cleared out. I mean, where do Englishmen think they get the God given raight to own a country the other side of the world and tell the fowk there what to do? The first time I had what they called "a kill" I wor as sick as a dog after. I'd never even seen a dead pairson before, let alone one wi' a bullet through his head and his eyes still open. My platoon commander called me a "jolly good chap" and said not to worry, it wor allus like that the first time, and he got the other lads to move the body – we'd to tek 'em to the nearest outpost, you see. Army fashion, everything got its docket, even a corpse.

'I dint like that at all, the idea that I might get used to killing other human beings. I said so to Archie, and he told me that when he was at schoowel up there in Scotland, they used to punish the nippers with this forked leather belt, not the way they do it here, with a cane in the headmaster's office, but in front of the class. Archie said he could remember the first time he saw one of his mates being belted; he thought he was going to wet hissen, it wor that horrible. But the next time it happened – and he went on to get belted many times hissen, he said – he realised he was looking forward to the show. Think about that, Harry. Did that mean I was going to start enjoying killing some poor bogger I dint know?'

'Ned – Ned, you're shouting . . .'

'Christ, I'm sorry . . . but then I'd to get missen worked up to do it all over again.'

'Of course you had to. To stop being killed yourself.'

'That's true. Nothing like the will to live to bring out the wairst in a man. The platoon were my mates too – they had to be. We'd never've got out of the jungle alive otherwise. When we were moving at naight, the only way we could keep gooin' was to hold onto the kit of the man in front. The first man o' course was a Malay tracker. I can't sleep in blackness, yuh know. I have to keep the curtains open a bit for the street light.'

'I noticed that . . .'

'If I don't, I wek up feeling like I'm falling sideways, out of line, into that horrible darkness.'

'Then we'll always sleep, Ned, with a gap between the curtains—'

'Don't say that yet, Harry . . .'

'Have you stayed in touch with any of them?'

'No. I'm not a great one for letter-writing and that, but that's not why.'

'You are with me, though. I treasure your letters.'

'Well, that's different.' He squeezed her hand. 'Funny, that, int it? Your life depends on them, and theirs on yow doing your bit. But if I saw any of 'em again it'd be like being back in the jungle. Archie wrote to me once. I've still got his letter somewhere. Not very nice of me not to send him even a Christmas card, was it? We did all get back, though one lad lost a leg, but the poor bogger thanked me for saving his life.'

'What happened?'

For a full minute he said nothing. Harry stroked the hand she held – it trembled.

'We were in a shitty mood. It had rained, warm rain like it is out there, nothing that would make yuh feel cleaner or fresher. Rain in that jungle was greasy as well as wet, and yow felt the wairse for it because afterwards yuh wurnt any cooler, it was just more humid than before. We'd hardly slept so we wor lathered – tekkin it in turns to keep watch, but when it was my turn to get some rest I wor too tired and wound up to sleep. My head was on my rolled-up kit, but that was soggy too – everything was. My feet were sodden, itchy. There was the usual night-time racket, but behind it I wor sure I could hear summat else – a squelchy sound of someone creeping around. One of the platoon – Horace – woh snoring – heaven knows how he managed it – we'd to wek 'im up continuously, because a noise like that could cost us. But noat happened until daylight, and we were hacking our way forward again. We reached a river, but we were so bushed that we dint realise it till Horace, who wor at the front with the guides, sank into the mud just about up to top of the entry—'

'Where?'

'Oh, up to his tackle. We'd to pull him out. There was that much undergrowth in the way he dint see clear to the watter. We cudnt hear it eyther, it was so sluggish – oily looking – and we were so busy swatting off them bleddy droning insects. Between them and snakes yuh could be etten alive in a place like that.

'It was when we were wading through that river – it came up to our chests and of course we all had our arms held up to keep our weapons clear of the drink – that the shooting started. It turned out that there was only tow of 'em hidden on the far bank, but when yuh can't see them you don't know that, and even though their shots had went wide, all hell broke loose. The guides were over first, of course, and being better trackers than us catched the first one easily enough – killed him I mean. But there had to be at least one more, and we spent the next however long it wor hunting him in pairs, fanned out. That's when yuh know yuh mustn't lose yer compass, or yuh'll lose everything including each other.

'I don't know how long it woh – it could've been twenty minutes, or an hour and a ayf – when a bullet whizzed out and got Fred in the thigh. I should've realised then we wor dealing with an amateur. He hadn't aimed high enough, and had fired too early. If he'd thought about it, he could've waited till we'd turned and got both of us in the back. When Fred fell screaming, I was that mad I ran forward yelling – the way they trained uz to in bayonet practice but the last thing I wor s'posed to do in jungle – and, by luck, if yuh can call it that, pitched right into the commie before he could point his rifle at me. It wor just some kid, or at least that's what I thought, not that they have what yuh maight call beards anyroad. He squeaked an' dropped his gun, put up his hands. I could hear Fred behind me still, not screaming now but groaning – the others were with him by then and trying to stop the bleeding. His leg went septic later and they took the lot off up to the hip in the field station. I raised my rifle, Harry, and shot the commie raight between the eyes, though he wor kneeling there with his hands up. I can remember everything about that face – the green peaked cap wi' the red star sewed on it.'

Ned put his free hand over his face. Muffled, his voice went on. ''Course I wor made out to be the hero of the hour. What a good shot, they said! All they saw wor that corpse lying there with the rifle alongside. And I did the strangest thing. I sat on the ground and yawned and yawned. I cudnt stop missen. I wor all of a shake too, starvin' cold.'

'That's shock,' said Harry, remembering.

'The only pairson that knew the truth was Archie, and he kept telling me that if we'd tekken the lad alive he'd have been tried and hanged anyroad, same as all the others. He wor trying to mek me feel better, and all I could think on, in spite o' poor Fred, was I'd killed some mother's son and I wor a lathe operator from Kimberley who'd no business bein' out there. They've got their independence in Malaya now anyroad, so what the hell were we even doin' there? What wor the point?

'Afterwards, we went back the way we comm, wi' Fred in a fold-out sling thing, his face like putty, and the tow stiffs tied wrists and ankles to a pole. Corporal asked me if I wanted to do the honours, seeing as it was my kill, but Archie stepped in and said he'd carry in my place.

'Only when the corpses had been looked at back at base I fahnd out it wurnt a man I'd killed. It wor a girl. Harry, I shot an unarmed woman.'

'Ned—'

He went on as if she hadn't said anything.

'I woh tekken so poorly after that – sweats, racing heartbeat, the lot – they thought I'd got malaria. I took the Paludrine they give me but of course that just made me feel worse, itchy everywhere and some of my hair fell out, so I told 'em to think of summat else. Eventually, they told me I wurnt going back in the jungle. They give me a clerk's job at base. Yuh wouldn't think it, hands like mine, but I can write quite neatly.'

'I know. I've your letters.'

'The adjutant meant to be kind. My job was to go through the stuff o' lads that had copped it, just to mek sure nobody's mam and dad got anything sent back that might upset 'em, or the widder a letter from the other woman, that kind of thing.

There's not much left of a sowjer when he's dead, just a bundle of letters if he wor lucky enough to get them, half a packet of smokes, and whatever he'd got from the regimental barber in the hope of finding a friendly girl in Sepang. "Makes you feel better about being alive, doesn't it, Trooper?" the adjutant would say to me. Never have worked out why *I'm* supposed to be happy just because some other poor bogger has gone to kingdom come ahead o' me. And before yuh ask, a friendly girl in Sepang was prescribed as part of the treatment for *me!*'

'What?'

'Maight as well tell yuh the lot now, Harry. I wor in that field station with this MO bloke thinking he wor some sort of psychiatrist and tellin' me to do exactly what the army and the padres were allus preaching against. He'd interviewed me after I'd fahnd out my kill was a woman and got the whole story about Dora. He told me I wor transferring my guilt on to my job as a sowjer. But I dint just feel guilt. I felt grief. The MO had the cheek to say that if I used it raight, my anger'd mek me a better fighter. I told him I'd never wanted to be any kind of sowjer, good or bad, and he told me to remember I wor an Englishman. In the meantime, he said, he needed to give me what he called "hair of the dog", and he wurnt meaning the drink, eyther. Sent me off with one o' the other lads to a brothel. I went, Harry, because I wor bored. I wurnt even thinking about sex, honest I wurnt. I just thought abaht the drinks they'd give me.'

'But you went.'

'Yow'll finish with me now so I maight as well be hung for a sheep as for a lamb. 'Course I did. I maighta been a grown man,

Harry, and I'd done grown man things like shooting a girl who was on her knees with her hands up and sleeping with another man's wife, but time off base was time off base. Yuh did things in the army because everyone else did, same as when yuh were at schoowel, only more dangerous and wrong than being egged on to do things your motha would tell yuh not to, like peeing ower the seat of some other kid's bicycle because somebody said he never washed . . . And of course I did want to know if I'd forget the whole bleddy mess that way. I dint of course. There was this girl – quite little, like most of the Malays – mebbe seventeen, stroking my arm and smiling up at me with her head on one side. And there wor an old woman watching us from her corner, smoking a bleddy pipe, she woh. I got the idea that the girl would get into trouble if she dint hook me, so I went up that rickety staircase with her. I cudn't do ote . . . I remember I tried to kiss her but she wudnt let me. I thought that was a bit odd given what we'd comm up there to do.'

'I don't. Kissing's perhaps more intimate, Ned.'

He looked at her. 'Mebbe you're raight. I'd never thought o' it that way – faces being what yuh really recognise about a person, I mean. Anyroad, I looked at her properly then. Yuh know what she made me think of? A child that wants to go out and play on a Sunday afternoon but can't because her mam and dad are that kind o' godbotherer that don't like it. An' looking bored, and somehow not there, made her look younger. I wondered if she *had* a mam and dad. I wondered if she'd ever got to play when she wor a nipper. And I . . . well, I faded away to noat. I pulled the dirty sheet over her and left the money. That was me, my hair of the dog. The poor kid looked like she dint care one way or the other. So I comm downstairs feeling like a dirty bastard and no more over Dora than I wor before.'

Ned gently eased her hand away.

'I wish I'd not had to mix yow up in a' that, and not just because yuh'll not want me now. But, thank you for listening, Harry. I mean that.'

'Couldn't you have said something at home? To your mother, at least?'

'Could yuh tell yer own motha yuh wor a murderer, Harry?' He didn't wait for an answer. 'She'd had a bad enough time about Dora. There were some would cross the road and not talk to her because of me carrying on with a married woman, though she dint tell me anything about that till long after. It wor hard work to get into the bed she'd made for me for as long as I can remember, smelling of whatever it is she uses to wash the sheets, after doing what I'd done.

'They woh all plaised, of course, when I wor demobbed. Dad took me for a drink and everybody said how lean and brown I wor. Mam would look at me sometimes, though, when the pair o' them were sitting watching that blessed telly, and she'd say afterwards things like "Yuh not wi' us, are yuh, duck?" and she was right, I wurnt. I went back to Raleigh and fahnd the room in Lenton and everybody behaved as though noat had happened. Back in there it was as if tow years of my life had folded up like a piano accordion that was broke but nobody had got round to throwing out. I could've sworn them were my same tools waiting for me just where I'd left 'em. It made Malaya unreal – summat that comm creeping out from behind the curtains at naight-time. Only of course it wor allus real.

'When I'm in that factory it's that noisy sometimes yuh can't hear ote anyone says, and that's wairse, because I can hear my own thoughts. I work like stink there – I get some of the best piece rates in the place, I think, but it's only because I'm still fighting through the jungle. Then I look round at it all and ask missen "Is that it? Am I to stick this place out for the rest of my natural, same as the others?" I could jack it all in, but it'd just be some other factory, some other foreman, wudnt it? And I'd still have the nightmares. God help me, Harry, I'm only an ordinary bloke, from an ordinary little town like Kimberley.'

'I don't think you're ordinary at all, Ned.' She took his hand again and he let it lie there.

'Marry me, Harry.'

'I would. I'd marry you tomorrow. Only I'm afraid.'

'Of course y'are,' he said bitterly. 'What sane woman wudnt be?'

'I don't mean I'm afraid of *you*.' Harry looked down. 'I'm afraid of *me*. I'm afraid of – oh dear – the physical bit. That I might reject you, that way. Hate you, even.'

He said nothing, but with his thumb gently stroked the palm of the hand that lay in his.

'Oh Ned, that's nice,' she said, with a little jump of delight in her voice.

'I'll never, ever do ote yuh don't want. And yow can have all the time in the world, Harry. I'm patient.'

'I love you, Ned.'

'Oh Harry ... mek me better ...' He took her face in her hands and kissed her.

She nestled against him. 'My degree first.'

'Of course. I want to be there when they give it yow.'

*

Sitting on the top deck of the bus going back to Nottingham, Ned glanced around to be sure the other passengers were out of earshot, then asked, 'Would yo comm back to Chippendale Street again sometime?'

'Meaning?'

'Meaning we can see how we are wi' each other – I mean without – I'm not much good at this, am I? I mean just to get used to each other a bit. That naight yuh comm I slept better than I had in ages. And I've slept better sin', just thinking about yuh bein' there.'

'But if I were to say stop, what would you do?'

'Stop, of course.'

'Promise?'

'I wudnt pretend it would be easy,' he said, with an attempt at a smile, 'but I'm not a brute.'

'Kiss me, Ned.'

He closed his eyes, and gently touched his lips to hers, paused, then pressed his mouth to hers again. He realised he was holding his breath, fearing a sign of reluctance, or withdrawal. He opened his eyes, to see hers closed, her lashes thick and dark against her cheekbone. He fought the urge to push his tongue against her lips, to open them. He wished his breathing wasn't so loud, so heavy.

God, I want her!

'Look out, yow tow!' said a voice. 'Yuh'll miss yer stop if yer not careful. Save it for the pictures.' The conductor called out again as he set off down the stairs. 'I wor young too once, believe it or not.'

*

''Arry!' Max got up from behind the turmoil of his desk. ''Arry! At last!'

Harry didn't move, ignoring the wave of his hand towards a chair.

'You're looking well, Max.' *He doesn't though. He looks gaunt, and the way his eyes glitter you'd think he'd taken something.*

'And you, *ma petite Gitane.*'

'I came for my letters.'

He opened a drawer in the desk and brought out a small bundle tied with string. Despite the disorder in which he worked, Harry noted that he'd been able to locate them straightaway.

'I shall have the post at Yale this time next year, as good as signed for. You'll have your finals, then—'

'Max. Max. Stop.'

'*Comment?*'

His face grew as stiff as parchment. 'You are not still seeing your factory hand?'

'It would be the same whether I was or not. I am, though. But this was never about another man.'

'If it had at least been one of my colleagues, I could have given you Arago's view of his intellectual worth. Instead, you want to experiment with someone who wipes his oily hands on a rag before he touches you.'

'Max, will you *shut up!* I am going to marry him.'

'*Putain!*' He strode around the desk and reached for her. Harry backed against the door, fumbling for the handle, but his right-handed punch crashed into her left eye, and his weaker left fist jarred against her right cheekbone. She screamed, as much in shock as in pain, and at that moment the door pushed against her back, catapulting her forward into Max's arms in an involuntary embrace. Blood from her nose spattered his shirt.

'What *is* going on in here?' said a voice, more peeved than concerned. Harry raised her hands, pushing Max away, and turned round.

'Good God!'

*

Ned crossed Slab Square to their appointment between the stone lions.

Hang on, that's Anna. So where's Harry, then? His heart felt cold in his chest. *No, not after she said she loved me . . .* He heard himself say, 'Ey up, Anna!' with feigned jauntiness. 'Where's our Harry?' Then to his shock he saw that Anna's eyes were puffy, and her mouth pale and set, free of her usual lipstick.

279

'She can't come,' said Anna, putting a hand on his arm. 'She wants to know will you come to her.'

*

Anna closed the door behind her with uncharacteristic softness, leaving them alone. Harry leaned back on the bank of pillows, and closed her purpled eyes, but Ned felt the renewed pressure of her fingers around his.

'They've arrested the bastard, surely?'

'Oh no! But I've to see the Dean on Monday.' Then she started to cry. Ned leaned forward, his cheek against hers, his arms round her shaking shoulders.

'Ned . . .' she sobbed into his neck.

'I'm here, I'm here, Harry.'

'That night . . . when I was attacked . . . this has brought it all back. The doctor came out. *He* was kind. It was a bit of a blur – he gave me a sedative, you see. But I remember him saying "Not all men are brutes. There are many who are good and kind." But what did I get? Another brute! Max was frightening to look at even before he hit me. And the things he said . . . I don't mean about me, but about you.'

'Let me try, Harry,' said Ned. 'To be good and kind.'

'I'm sorry, I didn't mean . . .'

His voice trembled. 'I can leave Chippendale Street. I could find us a couple of rooms and a kitchen. We can be married – quick with the registrar if yuh like, and do the works wi' all the cousins an' confetti throwing after yuh've got your degree. I want to protect yow, Harry.'

'Oh Ned ... There's a bit of me that really wants to do that. I love the idea of you and me in rooms of our own, or even huddled up in Chippendale Street with that potty. Only, I came here to go to university, and to live a university life. I've loved it – I still do love it. I want you to come to see me get my degree, Ned, the way we talked about, and then I want us to choose the day that'll be ours forever. And every morning after breakfast you'll go off to Raleigh and I'll be Mrs Stones, Dr Holt's new research assistant ... I'm damned if Max Arago is going to decide any of that for me!'

'Y'aren't tellin' me the pig'll still be working here?'

Harry shook her head, wincing with pain. 'Spellie thinks he'll be made to leave – I mean before he's due in America.'

'Think on it, though, Harry. Yuh know the offer's allus there. And I'd pitch a tent below your winder year-round if it'd make yuh feel safer. Only ...'

'Ned?'

'Mebbe not Raleigh. Mebbe summat else.'

*

'You must understand, Miss Loveridge, that I have to put the interests of this institution – the common weal, you might say – above all other considerations,' said the Dean. He raised an admonitory finger. Harry felt like biting it off. 'That does not mean that I wish to belittle the seriousness of Dr Arago's attack on you.'

Harry glared at him through the purple and yellow bruising. 'You'd better not!'

Ignoring this, he said, 'Allow me to gather the facts, if I may. You were engaged to be married to Dr Arago, I understand?'

'You understand wrongly. We were . . . walking out together, I suppose, before he went to Grenoble. Then I broke it off by letter.'

'*He* is making noises about breach of promise, Miss Loveridge.'

'*What?*'

'He hasn't a leg to stand on, of course. I did consult the university's lawyers.'

'Did you talk to them about the likelihood of an arrest for assault?'

'Actually, since you mention it, I did. That would be most inconvenient, was their view. For your own sake, given that we expect you to get a first. Court schedules are no respecters of examination timetables. It would be most disruptive. And though you and Dr Arago are *not* married, the police would most likely treat this as a domestic incident, and would be reluctant to get involved. I mean, if they were to investigate every lovers' tiff, they'd have no time to chase after criminals, would they?'

'So men who hit women are *not* criminals? God help us all, then,' said Harry. 'You want me to shut up. What happens to Max? Nothing?'

'Ah, well, there we can help, Miss Loveridge. Dr Arago's academic contribution has been immensely valuable in the few years he has been here. It is time that he moved on, of course. The academic community will work to enable that. He will be relieved of teaching duties in the meantime, enabling him to concentrate on research. For the little time he is still here, we are looking at ways to restrict his movements, so that you are less likely to run into him accidentally. We do not envisage any such arrangement to be anything other than temporary. Indeed, we are considering telling his next post that we are prepared to release him early.'

'I see. So my bruises have actually helped his career. They've got him exactly what he wanted.'

CHAPTER TWENTY-SEVEN

Lenton, Nottingham
November 1958

'Sorry, Ned, just me again,' said Anna, coming into the private bar of the Boat on a damp Monday evening.

'How is she?'

'A bit better than when you came up on Saturday. She said she was coming until only an hour ago, but she's still wary of going out. We just have to be patient.'

'She can have all the time she wants. What about going to lectures and that?'

'She's got more guards around her than Marshall Tito. Spellie's got us on a roster. She's never alone. And her mum and dad are coming on Friday. You've not met them yet, have you?'

Ned took a deep breath and a deeper swig of his pint. 'I 'spect her dad'll scare the life out o' me. A lot to live up to the way Harry talks abaht him.'

'He wouldn't, you know. He's not fierce at all. He's probably one of the gentlest people you could ever meet. A fine-looking man – I'd call him noble, even. That's if you can say that about a man of sixty in a shapeless old hat, mended clothes and no collar to his shirt most of the time. But I think the only clothes that wouldn't suit him would be a uniform. Her mother's very ladylike – not stuck-up ladylike – sweet and kind. She's a beautiful woman too.'

'Where she gets her looks from then.'

'Actually she looks like him.'

Ned laughed. 'Perhaps I would like him, then. Wonder what he'd mek of me?'

'If you love and care for his daughter, that's all that will matter to him. It's really their marriage you'd need to live up to.'

'Oh?'

'I don't know what Harry's told you, but he risked everything to be with her mother. I mean everything. Beatings. Separated from his own people for ever. Prison. A murder charge—'

'*Hell!* I knew he'd been in clink but thought it was summat to do with a nag.'

'It's all right, he didn't murder anyone. Couldn't have done. He wasn't there and it turned out to be an accident after all. But it wasn't just that. He walked away from a way of life, Ned, the one his people had followed for generations and generations. The fact he's been rooted on a farm in Kent for thirty-odd years is a sort of uprooting for him. What I'm trying to say is that Sam Loveridge gave up something precious to be with his wife. Harry doesn't say it, and perhaps she doesn't even know she's thinking it, but maybe she's waiting for you too to sacrifice something – for her.'

'So what you're saying is that what I'd be giving up wudnt be much seein' what he did, is that it? A steady job, people I know, places I've allus known?'

'It doesn't suit you, sounding peeved like that. You've said yourself how bored you get, same old same old week after week.'

'It feels safe – normal – after Malaya.'

'I should think it does. But do you want it to be the same, ten years from now?'

'Can't say I do.'

'So do something about it. If not for Harry, for yourself.'

'It'd be for Harry. But what? I've only my apprenticeship. I'm not qualified for ote else.'

'Get qualified.'

'Now you're having me on, Anna. I can hardly go back to schoowel, can I?'

'No. But you could try night classes.'

'Oh, I'm not sure . . . after all this time . . .'

'You'd be in with people like you, not boys in short trousers. And you'd study what you wanted. Not what you had to. Charles Dickens, if you felt like it. Or why in Raleigh the people who make the bicycles aren't paid more than the chairman who gets chauffeured everywhere.'

Ned laughed. 'Yuh sound like the union men. But it won't change ote. I might be a lathe operator who reads bowks but I'd still be a lathe operator.'

'Ned, you're a man aren't you, I mean besides being a lathe operator?'

'Yeah!'

'Harry's man.'

'I 'ope so.'

'Just say you do marry her, and you've kids one day. What would you want for them?'

'The world, of course . . . All right, Anna, I take your point. I'll find out. There wor summat on noticeboard at work abaht Evening Institutes. Only, would yer do me a favour?'

'Go on.'

'Don't tell Harry. I'd like it to be a surprise.'

'Our secret, Ned.'

*

'It was Miss Spellman's idea,' said Harry, unlocking the door of the guest flat and standing back to let her parents in. 'Normally it's used for visiting lecturers. She didn't want me going back and forth between here and town, even with Pinkerton's Posse in tow.'

Ellen turned and stroked her daughter's hair.

'I'm all right, Mum, honest,' said Harry, managing a smile. 'The bruises are fading already.'

'I worried about you going so far,' began Sam.

'Looks as if it makes no difference where I am, does it? In the hop field or two hundred miles away,' she said, and burst into tears.

*

Ned got to Florence Boot early, but paced between the gate-houses rather than go any closer. More than once he'd thought

287

of going to see Anna, in search of encouragement, but reminded himself he'd faced worse than two people she'd kept telling him were kindness itself. *I'd best not bodge it . . .* He straightened his tie again, remembering his mother shaking out the folds in the best tablecloth, and telling him for the fourth time, 'Front door, mind!'

And suddenly there they were, and Sam was striding over to the startled Ned, to grasp his hand and look him frankly in the eye.

'I hope you'll always be good to our Harry.'

'I'll try, if she'll let me, sir.'

*

Part-way through the meal Harry and Ned exchanged conspiratorial glances. Ellen had followed Ned's mother through to the kitchen to help bring in the sweet, and Sam and Henry had pushed back their chairs and were deep in a discussion of the provisions of the Homicide Act.

'Ah wor all for the drop till the Christie business,' said Henry Stones, 'but they can't bring back that poor bogger Evans.'

Sam, who had come closer to the noose than he was ever going to admit, said mildly, 'And if a man's dead, he's no way of turning a corner.'

'Summat more cheerful for the dinner table, Henry, plaise,' said his wife, coming back in with bowls of apple crumble. 'Tek Harry's da to the Railway ayfter and talk abaht it there instead.'

*

'Ah can see yur lass's all bartled up,' said Henry quietly, setting their pints down.

'Bartled?' said Sam.

'My way o' spaiking. She 'owds it all in.'

Sam's face cleared. 'She dunt want us worryin', that's why, poor maidy. Wants us to think she's stronger'n she is.'

'Wannts bostin', that bogger – skelping a lass!' said Henry, with sudden force. Seeing Sam's renewed puzzlement, he waved his fists illustratively. 'Brek 'is nose for hittin' a woman,' he explained. Sam saw that three or four of the quiet drinkers, men Henry had nodded to when they came in, were looking in their direction.

'Ah'raight, lads,' said Henry. With a murmur, they went back to their pints.

Lowering his voice, Henry said, 'They're all good blokes, them. Pay 'im a visit, they would – gi'im a raight good clonkin. Yuh've only to ask.'

'I wanted to do that,' said Sam, with a sick feeling of déjà vu. 'Me and my bruv, and my boy Tom. My Ellen talked me round. We'd all end up in stir, she said. But I'll remember your kindness to my girl.'

'Well, we laike Harry . . . near enough as much as Ned does,' said Henry gruffly. He nodded towards Sam's pint glass. 'Wannt to swag that dairn and go and see allotment?'

*

Ned and Harry had also gone out, to Mrs Simmonds's bench.

'They like you, Ned,' said Harry. Her head was resting on his shoulder, and she felt his sigh of relief.

'Said so, did they?' He turned, touching his lips to her forehead.

'No, they didn't need to. I can tell.'

'I wor that wittled. But Mam cudnt wait to get uz all aht of 'owse. Yu could see she wor wanting a proper yack wi' yours. Only . . .'

'What?'

'I've been a' this time wi' yuh an' not kissed yuh yet.'

'Go on, then.'

*

Walking back down to the house, Ned remembered a promise he'd made to Anna. The day had gone so well he felt he could take on anything.

'Them essays yuh write . . . how is it yuh do them?' he asked.

'Them? What do you want to know about that for?'

'I'm interested in what yuh do, that's why.'

'Well, I don't know about anyone else. What I do is to read an awful lot – history is often a bit like politics, only older, so you have to get both sides of the story. I make notes of things I want to remember, or to quote later. The books bristle like hedgehogs with all those slips of paper. Then when I think I've got an idea in my head of what I want to say, I try writing it. It's a bit of a dog's breakfast to start with – contradicting myself, things like that. So I have another go, and somehow, the whole thing starts to slot together. I mean, history happened, but

THE GYPSY'S DAUGHTER

I'm not just recounting the facts. I'm understanding why they happened as they did, and why things could happen again. Because nothing happens by accident.'

'Hmm. Like building a very complicated bicycle, then. The way yuh describe it, history's also about moving parts, only loads of 'em. All of 'em have to fit together raight, if anybody is to go anywhere.'

'It's a good analogy. Can I use it in an essay?'

Ned laughed. 'Yuh joking, int ya?'

'Not at all. Not if we want to build a world that doesn't make the mistakes of the last fifty years. If for once we could design something that works.'

'Funny yuh should say that. I allus thought the drawing office was the place to be. I'm fascinated by that – how you can put summat down on flat paper, and it turns into a three-dimensional machine, summat yuh can actually mek. Ever sin' I wor old enough to comm into Nottingham on my own I've gone ormin' abaht the place looking at the buildings, all that mass of stone and brick, even Chippendale Street, and thought, that was once just an idea in some bloke's 'ead. They could *see* it, before it existed. That man that did the drawing never picked up a trowel much less got lumps of cement on hissen, but what goes up there is his.'

'Did you ever think of being an architect?'

'Go on wi' yow! Only in my daydreams.'

'Ned, what do you see when you look forward? Like that architect, who has an idea in his head, and then he gets it down?'

'I *don't* really look forward, or at least I haven't till now – that is, apart from looking forward to things being finished and out the way – like army, for instance. It'll be Raleigh, I s'pose,' he said quietly. 'That or some other factory. But I wudnt care which, Harry, if my future had yow in it.'

*

'Hello, Stones,' said Sid, looking up from his statistics.

'Hello, Probert,' said Ned. 'I'm being a responsible citizen, like you said, and bringing that book back early.'

'*The Struggle for Mastery in Europe.* Thank you – we've a long waiting list for it still,' said Sid, taking the book from him. 'What are you looking so worried about, boy *bach*?'

'My girl, of course. Fancy the Salutation when yuh've finished? And listen to my woes?'

'Yes, and yes. Not that I'll be much use. I'm no expert when it comes to women.'

*

Two hours of talking and five pints had made Ned progressively less eloquent and more despairing.

'If she wants *you*, Ned, it won't matter *what* you are,' said Sid, a reiteration of what he had been saying in one form or another all evening.

'I'm sorry, Sid, I'm one of them blokes as is really boring when he's had a skinful. I mean, yuh must've had disappointments thissen.'

Sid wouldn't meet his eye. 'You could say that.'

'So what *yow* do abaht her?'

'Oh, Ned . . .'

'I'm a bastard, int I? I'm a right bastard,' said Ned, suddenly maudlin, throwing his arm around Sid's thin shoulders. 'I've gone on and on about my own worries, and never let yuh get a word in edgeways. What happened, Sid?'

'Nothing. National Service got in the way.'

'Dear John letter, was it? Yow up in the frozen wastes of Catterick and her finding someone else to kep her warm?'

'Not quite. It was someone I met when I was *at* Catterick.'

A lopsided smile stole over Ned's face. 'Dark oss, int ya? A camp full of men and about three typists to go round, and yuh're one of the lucky ones!'

'Not exactly. I thought I'd get flung out, but instead the one I loved got posted away. And that was the end of it.'

'Posted away? But women don't do National Service, do they?'

'You're right, they don't.' Sid looked straight at him, and to Ned's horror and shame, he saw his friend's eyes were full of tears.

'Bleddy hell, Sid, I'm sorry, me and mi great ommocks . . .'

'Your what?'

'Size nines.'

'It's all right. It doesn't matter,' stuttered Sid. 'I think I'd best go, Ned. Work in the morning and that. I'm sorry I couldn't help you about Harry.' He gathered up his coat and pushed his arms into the sleeves. 'Just love her and hope for the best, that's the best advice I can give you. Because you can.'

'Sid, wait! Sid! Yuh've not finished your pint!'

*

'I've upset Sid, Harry,' said Ned, letting the sugar slide off his spoon and into the taupe depths of his coffee. He'd have preferred to walk around the town but insistent rain had driven them into the Kardomah. 'I went on and on at him about *yow,* and when I had the wit to ask him about *hissen,* after being sorry for *me* all naight, then his eyes got as wet as those puddles out there. He said I should count missen lucky to be able to love yow.'

'Poor Sid,' said Harry.

'Harry . . . I don't know how to say this.' He fidgeted. 'I like Sid, yuh see.'

'And?'

'I think . . .'

'What, Ned?'

He hesitated, looking out the window.

'You're saying you think your friend was trying to tell you he was homosexual,' said Harry, equably.

'If I'd 'ave let 'im, yes.' he whispered, smiling briefly at the two middle-aged ladies at the next table who'd been watching him with their coffees poised midway to their mouths. They looked away quickly, cups clattering in saucers.

'I've never had to deal with ote like this before. They don't have any like him in Raleigh, anyroad.'

'Of course they do, you dope! They're hardly going to make a song and dance about it, are they? Not when they could go to prison for it.'

Ned lifted the teaspoon out of his cooling coffee. 'Poor Sid,' he said. 'Harry, would yuh comm with me next time I go to meet him?'

'I'd like that. Would he mind meeting Anna too?'

*

Ned put out a hand, awkwardly, something he had never done before with Sid. Reaching across the issue desk, Sid took it, just as awkwardly, but Ned felt a firm, dry grip. *Not what I'd expected.*

'I'm sorry,' said Ned. It came out more gruffly than he'd intended.

'For what?'

'For being a blather 'ead. For not listening to yuh when yer wor wanting to tell me summat.'

'I don't know that I did. But I've come nearer to telling you than anyone else.'

'Easier over a pint?'

'I think perhaps I'd rather walk. If that's all right with you? If you don't mind being seen with me?'

'Daft bogger.'

Sid raised his eyebrows.

'In a manner o' speaking,' said Ned, and to his relief his friend laughed. 'Harry and me go up to the Rec usually. She wants to meet yuh, by the way.'

*

'My heart can break same as anyone else's,' said Sid. 'Not having anyone to talk to about it makes it worse though.'

'It must do,' muttered Ned.

'Sit here, shall we?' Sid indicated a bench by the side of the avenue of trees.

Looking not at Ned but across the park, Sid said, 'It was like having a secret garden – me being with him, I mean. Somewhere walled, with a rusty gate hid behind some brambles. Inside there was a little wood, wildflowers. And . . . he was there. He! You wouldn't think, would you, that a tiny pronoun like that was so difficult to say. And I could go there, and think about him when he wasn't with me, in my own head I mean.'

'Where is *he* now?'

'I've no idea. He never wrote to me, though it would have been risky.' He looked down at his knees. 'I never really did know if I was loved back.'

'I was in the glass'owse more times than I've sneezed, I think. There was someone in for . . . for what yow did, in there.'

'Perhaps I was "lucky" then.' Sid's fingers danced apostrophes in the air. 'It being hushed up. The only way I thought I could cope was by destroying my secret garden – in my head, I mean.'

'How did you do that? If I get an idea in *my* 'ead, I can't shake it out again most times.'

'You have to put something else in there instead. You were here with the bombs, weren't you?'

'I was out at Kimberley. But I got took in to see the mess.'

'You'll know what I mean then,' said Sid. 'You think something is so familiar – some big building that's been there for a hundred years or more, blocking out a chunk of sky. Then one night the sirens go off, there's a raid, and then it's nothing but rubble, or after a bit some rosebay willowherb.'

'Some what?'

'Bombsite weed.'

'Trust you to know the proper name for it.'

'It's the kind of thing librarians are expected to know. Anyway, when you look at a bombsite that was once a place you knew, for a while you can just about remember what it used to be like. But when somebody goes and puts something else up in its place, you struggle to picture what used to be there. So . . . I destroyed my secret garden myself. I dug up the trees and the flowers. I pulled down the walls brick by brick. That's how I coped – cope, I mean.'

'So what's left?'

Sid gave a bitter laugh. 'I put a bus depot there. Laid the tarmac, built the shelters that stink of pee by Sunday morning. There's never a minute's peace there, all coming and going, and hooting and petrol fumes. At night it's full of winos, trying to find somewhere out of the rain.'

'Yuh've quite an imagination!'

'I write things, sometimes. Poems, mainly.' said Sid modestly. 'Only I don't show them to anyone either.'

'Yuh can't get into trouble for poetry, can yow?'

'I expect you could, if people thought your poems were bad enough.' They both laughed. 'But I'd be in proper trouble for the other thing. If I met someone else, and was caught, and prosecuted, I'd lose my job. Everything.'

'Wurnt there some inquiry a bit ago that said that should change?'

'Wolfenden.'

'That wor the name. After some lord or duke or somebody got twelve months.'

'That started it, yes. A lord, a landowner and a journalist. I read the journalist's memoir when it came into the library. It's a funny thing about our job, that the readers expect us to have read just about everything so we can tell them what to borrow.'

'That's why yuh have to wear them specs!'

'I'd have read every word of Wildeblood anyway though. I can't remember the words exactly, but he says somewhere near the end that all he wants for himself, and those like him, is to choose whom to love. There were a lot of requests for it, from all kinds of people. But it's a class thing too, Ned. Wolfenden got going because those men who were sent to prison were something in public life or had some social standing. I don't suppose any of that would have happened for a miner's son from Aberfan.'

'Mi mam said it wor a crying shame, I remember. She said the police would do better catching burglars or men who stole old ladies' handbags.'

'Wildeblood said the police are rewarded for the number of arrests they make.'

'Like piecework then?'

'I suppose it is. And it's a lot easier to catch a homosexual than it is to catch a burglar.'

A spatter of drops hit the path in front of them. They were still protected by the trees, but not for long.

'We'd best go,' said Sid.

'Or yow could think us up a bus shelter!'

'Thank you for listening, Ned. You've no idea . . .'

'Yer ah' raight, Sid. Yow can trust me.'

'The Sal after all?'

'Why not? In fact, I want to ask your advice abaht summat – seeing as you're the all-knowing librarian. I was thinking about night classes.'

'I'm hopeless when it comes to technical things.'

'I know about *them*. It wor summat else I wanted to ask abaht. But our secret, mind.'

'Snap.'

CHAPTER TWENTY-EIGHT

Florence Boot Hall

February 1959

Harry saw her pigeonhole was bristling with post. She smiled at the porter as he said, 'Here yuh go, Miss Popular!' and handed over the bundle. A bumper day: the lilac Queen's Velvet envelope she recognised before even seeing her mother's neat, sloping hand, another plain white one with Aunt Amy's handwriting (though her news would characteristically be less about her than about Uncle John), a postcard from her brother David (he knew she pinned these up in her room) and an invitation from the local Labour Party to a meeting about prescription charges. Another slip of paper fluttered to the floor. She bent and scooped it up, thinking it was a circular, only to see that the folded piece of paper was typed with her full name: 'Harmony Loveridge'. She unfolded it.

'I am watching you,' was all it said.

She stared at the paper, feeling the blood drain from her face.

'Something the matter?' said Mr Davies.

'Did you see who left this?' she said, holding out the paper.

His eyes widened. 'No, but I thought there was summat odd about it at the time. The postman had just been in and left a pile of things on my counter. I'd started sorting them, turning my back now and then, of course, to put them envelopes in their place as I went. That paper was in amongst the letters, about halfway down. I just thought someone must've given it to the postman on his way in. Oh, you look like you need a brandy, duck.' He lifted the counter. 'Come in the snug a minute.'

Harry sank gratefully into the worn leather armchair, refusing the brandy but accepting a cup of tea. Tim Davies set his kettle to boil and positioned his own chair by the door so that he could see out to the counter.

'Did you read it when it came?' asked Harry.

'It wurnt addressed to me. I just left it folded up as it was. But whoever it is ant done much to hide hissen.'

There was a noise at the counter and he went out for a few minutes. The kettle started singing and Harry stood up to turn down the gas ring and open the tea caddy. She smiled at the sight of the tea bags; Harry hadn't succeeded in persuading her mother to give up leaves.

'A cup for you too, Mr Davies?' she called out.

'Yes please, duck!'

He came back in frowning slightly. 'Ah' raight if I tell Roddy when he comms to relieve me? So's he can keep his eyes open?'

'Yes, please do.'

'I think you should tell Miss Spellman too. It's a nasty piece of work, whoever did it. We can't be too careful, with there just being young ladies in here.'

'Perhaps you're right ...' said Harry. From nowhere, she could suddenly smell the cloying scent of the hop field. It went as soon as it came.

'Are you sure you don't want that brandy?'

'Quite sure.' She tried a smile.

'Any idea who it might be? That French fellow that gave you the black eye?'

'No, it couldn't be him. He's in America now.'

'Good riddance. I never did like him hanging around here, even before he did what he did.' He frowned. 'Mebbe it's just someone's silly prank – someone that's got it in for you because you got a better mark. Or some girl who fell out with you over a bloke.'

'I can't think of *anyone,* nobody who'd do that, anyway.'

'Will you tell Miss Spellman yourself or will I?'

'I will, but would you mention it to her too?'

'Yes. Now you look after yourself. Try not to be alone.'

'The truth is, I've learned not to be already,' said Harry.

*

The following afternoon Ned paced between the lions trying to think up something light-hearted to say about Harry's lateness. Then he saw her, walking briskly over from the bus stop, and something in her expression told him that a joke wasn't in order.

'What's up, mi duck?' he said, bending to kiss her.

'Sorry I'm late, Ned. Somebody slashed the tyres of the bike.'

CHAPTER TWENTY-NINE

Colwick

February 1959

'Do you have a minute, Stones?'

Ned was tucking his notebook into his greatcoat pocket and putting the lid back on his pen. The other class members were buttoning up against the cold air that gusted in from the open door of the church hall.

'Yes, Mr Staley?'

'You asked some pretty pertinent questions in class this evening.'

'Oh. I was worried yuh might think I was being cheeky.'

'Quite the opposite,' said the tutor. 'One is honoured, of course, to see all those bent heads, assiduously writing down every word. Our school system, however, has too often taught passivity and failed to encourage debate.'

'I was allus getting into trouble for answering back. Schoowel *and* army.'

'Well, I'm glad you did answer back, as you put it. I want you to write something for me.'

'*Write* summat? I've not done that for ten years and I wurnt any great shakes then. I mean, I can *read* the bowks yuh talk abaht, but I cudnt write like them to save my life.'

'I don't want you to write like them. Write like yourself. Like what you said this evening, about how we can't trust early historians because of who was paying them to write the books, and you said that was just the same now, depending on who owned the newspapers. Had you ever thought of local politics, Stones?'

'Me? Not really. I'm a union man, though, and the shop steward has tried to get me more involved.'

'And what brought you here?'

'I wanted to impress my girl.'

Staley laughed. 'What better reason could you have?'

'Well, it's more than that, in a way. Somebody asked me once what I'd want for my children – the ones I don't have yet – and I dint want it to be just the same as what I have, or my dad has. Not that Raleigh is bad . . .'

'I'd be a poor socialist if I were to say there was anything amiss in an honest day's work making something as useful and beautiful as a bicycle.'

'But there must be more to life than that.'

'"To do nothing but grumble and not to act – that is throwing away one's life."'

'Who said that?'

'William Morris. I'll lend you something of his. But only after you've written something of your own for me.'

*

'Miss Loveridge?' Roddy, the other porter, leant over his desk. Harry turned. There was a note of caution in the man's tone that put her on her guard.

'There's been a delivery for you.' He held up a jug she recognised as having come from the dining hall. It contained a blaze of flowers – variegated chrysanthemums.

'Oh, they're pretty. Who brought them?'

'A florist's boy – from Colwick.'

'I know somebody who lives in Colwick, but I don't know why Sid would be sending me flowers.'

'A friend, is he?'

'A friend of a friend. When did they arrive?'

'Just after you went out this morning. I put 'em in water to give 'em a bit of a chance. I wet the little envelope by accident so I'd to take out the message and dry it. Only with what Tim Davies was saying.' He handed over a smudged piece of paper.

'You did right,' whispered Harry.

'I took the liberty of telling Miss Spellman. She thinks we should tell the police.'

You have been warned, said the damp card.

'What'll I do with them?' asked Roddy.

'They're lovely flowers, but I don't want them. It's not their fault.'

'You wouldn't mind if I took 'em home?' he said hesitantly. 'Mrs Roddy likes her chrysanths.'

'I think that's a lovely idea. Is Miss Spellman in, do you know?'

*

The florist's card lay on the polished oak of Miss Spellman's desk.

'My grandmother told my mother that when they'd been living in London, their Italian neighbours had said chrysanthemums were the flower of death,' said Harry.

'Hmm. They're a hardy bloom. Perhaps they're good for cemeteries. Any Italian connection?'

'None that I can think of.'

'We might be right in assuming that the flowers are meant to be sinister – with a message like that they were meant to frighten. I think we should assume a connection with the damage done to your tyres. But whoever this is has overplayed their hand. May I go and enquire myself at the florist? Or ask your Ned to do so? No, not Ned. He's too close to you. Whoever this is might wish him harm too. But above all *you* must not go. I know you might think it absurd that a florist's in a busy part of Nottingham would be watched, but that could be exactly what our mystery man is doing.'

'You think it's a man.'

'I think it's Dr Arago, Harry.'

'But how can it be? He's in America.'

*

'It's not pleasant, I can see that,' said the sergeant. 'Most likely the work of some crank. But we've nothing much to go on, ma'am . . . Miss Loveridge.'

'I have a building full of young women entrusted to my care, Sergeant,' said Miss Spellman.

'We can hardly put them under police guard, though, can we? We've not got the resources even if we wanted to. If you really want to find out who this is, we'll have to wait and see what he does next. Seeing the police will only make him more cautious.'

'"What he does next?"' echoed Harry.

*

You are not to worry about me, wrote Harry to Sam and Ellen. *The police want to wait and see. Miss Spellman though has the nose of a bloodhound and wants to investigate further. In the meantime she has put the entire hall on alert. Anna came into our room the evening after the flowers arrived and I nearly shed my skin from fright, so now everyone who needs to see me knows there's a special knock. We lock the door when we go to sleep, and at other times, which we never used to feel the necessity for. But I know I am loved, even by girls I thought I didn't know very well.*

*

'Ned has talked again about us marrying and going into rooms together,' said Harry. 'Only if whoever this is found out, Anna, I'd be more vulnerable there than in Florence Boot. He'd be going to work and I'd be on the bike heading over here on my own. And I'd miss sharing with you.'

'Not if you were living with Ned you wouldn't!'

'I would. This is *our* special time too. Anyway, I'm not letting poison pen man – or woman – decide how I live.'

'That's the spirit. All right if I go down and have the last cig of the day, Harry?'

'Oh, I don't mind if you smoke it out of the window. If you don't mind cold air at bedtime.'

'Not at all. Helps me sleep.'

Anna crossed to the window and raised the sash, and, with elbows planted on the sill, struck a match. Blowing it out, she threw it down into the darkness. Her sudden stillness attracted Harry's attention. Anna's cigarette was idle between her fingers, as she stared down into the near darkness. Harry came closer, but kept back from the window.

'What is it?' she whispered.

Anna reached her free hand back and patted the air for silence.

Harry's throat tightened. She swallowed. A moment later, Anna shrugged, stubbed out the unsmoked cigarette and pulled down the sash.

'Sorry about that, Loverish. Just a bit on edge, you know. I thought I saw that bush down there move. Well, it *did* move, actually. Probably just a fox after rabbits.' Anna closed the catch on the sash, though to reach the window from outside would have needed a window-cleaner's ladder, and pulled the curtains closed.

*

'Yes, I remember the order, ma'am,' said the florist. 'The instructions were so precise.'

'Could you describe the man, Mr Calladine?' asked Miss Spellman.

'Oh, it wurnt a man. It wor a child.'

'A *child?*'

'Yes, a little girl, about nine year old. I remember thinking that there wurnt many who'd have trusted someone that age with that much tin.'

'Did you know her?'

'No. I'd never seen her before. She gave me an address in Hucknall – written on a piece of paper, same as the instructions. It'll be in the book. I cudnt think why anyone would comm all the way to Colwick – there must be florists closer than here.' He reached down the ledger and thumbed back through the pages. 'Here we are: Arkwright, 4 Gypsy Row, Hucknall – I wudnt be telling you this, only you are obviously a respectable person. And here's the address of the lucky lady. I explained that University Park was a bit out of the way for our van, so the delivery would cost more. The child – a trusting little thing – put all these notes on the counter and said I was to take whatever was needed. I did that, but only that. Someone less honest would've helped hissen.'

'You've not got the bit of paper still, by any chance?'

'Dolly writes everything into the book as it's too easy to lose scraps of paper. She'll have put it into the stove long since.'

'How did she speak, this little girl?' asked Miss Spellman.

'Oh, Nottingham. Just an ordinary little girl she was. Short hair and a print dress, ankle socks.'

'Mm . . . perhaps his landlady's child,' said Miss Spellman, half to herself.

'Sounds like the bloke was trying to cover his traces, mebbe? You'd expect that more around St Valentine's though. Important that you find him, is it?'

'Indeed it is. Thank you, you've been most helpful.'

*

The man who walked out of Nottingham Victoria onto Milton Street that cool evening was identifiably a stranger. He was broad built, his swarthy face healthily fleshed, a strong man in middle-age. He carried a canvas bag over his shoulder that would have been recognisable to many men who had fought in the last war. Some would have known how it had got its bleached appearance – the relentless blazing sun of North Africa. He wore an old army battledress, but he looked too old for National Service, and could not have been a raw conscript even in the last conflict. His boots were those of a labourer. Those who glanced at him might have thought him a countryman, but also identified some wariness in his look that suggested he knew well enough how to defend himself in a town, somewhere he was not known, and had hands tough enough to do it.

Yet after a moment's reflection, it was clear that the man knew where he was going. To begin with his pace, moving down into the city, was impeded by the flow of clerks and shop assistants on their way home. He turned into Slab Square, then followed Friar Lane, skirting below the Castle, until his route became Lenton Road. He ignored the teeming buses, wanting instead to get his bearings, and the best way to do that was on foot. It was dusk, but the road was well lit. He was well into his stride by Abbey Bridge, and beyond the brick-built streets he could see the tower of the university rearing against the horizon.

Yet it was in the rolling parkland of the university that the stranger's sense of direction deserted him. Some new planting of trees, reordering of shrubs was enough to do it. The map in his mind no longer corresponded to the landscape he saw before him. After he'd wandered over the same ground twice – just the feel of a gravel path, or the inclination of a grass verge was enough to tell him he'd done so, more than the milestones of the blocks of residences now draped in shadow – the man stopped a youth on a wobbling bicycle.

'Beg pardon, but where's Florence Boot?'

'The women's hall? You'll be lucky. Must be about locking up time I should think.'

'I'll manage.'

'Yes, well, I expect you will,' said the cyclist, unable to see the other man's face beneath his workman's cap, but impressed by his size and an accent he afterwards pondered over but couldn't place. *Not a townsman, but not a gownsman,* thought the boy, who had had hopes of Oxbridge. *I should try to remember him – in case someone asks. Odd, anyway.*

'You're close,' he said. 'Turn up there, and you'll see a couple of lodge houses, I suppose you'd call them. Like a gate. Go through there and then right again. But, as I say, I think you'll find you're late.'

'Thank you, brother.' The traveller touched his cap in an oddly old-fashioned manner and walked on, and patted his

311

breast pocket where he'd hidden a little pencil map of Florence Boot Hall, a cross marking the spot where he intended to make his vigil.

*

'Goodnaight, lover!' murmured Ned, his lips below Harry's right ear. They were standing at the entrance to Florence Boot, the light casting their joined shadow onto the asphalt. Inside, standing by the porter's desk, where Tim Davies was already jangling his curfew keys, Anna cleared her throat with theatrical loudness. Sid was already outside, ostentatiously dropping the two bicycle chains he had just unlocked and clipping on their lamps.

'Just because Spellie likes you, Ned, doesn't mean you get to keep everybody up.'

He lifted his head, laughing. 'Bogger off, Anna, there's a dear!'

*

'No, leave them bikes a minute, Sid!'

'Why?'

'I just wannt to go round and get her to comm to the winder.'

'Go on, then. I'll wait for you here.'

Sid watched his friend's dark shape disappear around the side of the building, noiselessly, for Ned walked on the grass verge deliberately.

Seconds later, he was back – panting.

'What—'

'*Ssh!*' hissed Ned, grabbing his sleeve. 'By Christ, *he's* there!'

'Who?'

'Him! Whoever it is who's been bothering Harry. Under her winder, looking up.'

'You're joking!' Sid felt his stomach lurch coldly upwards. 'Is he doing anything apart from looking?' he stuttered.

Ned registered his friend's fear in the stronger Welsh cadence.

'Well, I don't think he's catching rabbits, anyroad. C'mon, there's tow of us. I'll knock 'im over. Yow can sit on his legs. Then we'll have to shout the place down.'

They crept around the corner of the building, scuttling behind a hawthorn.

'There he is!' hissed Ned, motioning Sid to stay still. The clouds cleared and the stranger's face was illuminated by the moon. Even in that pale phosphorescence they could see that he was not a young man; resignation had set into the lines of the face, the strong jaw.

He was looking straight at them.

Ned swore softly, and in that moment the clouds shifted, greying their target. 'Now or never,' whispered Ned. 'And yell like an Apache. Someone'll call the busies then.'

They tore across the grass, ululating. Ned cannoned into the stranger; only afterwards did he ask himself why he hadn't considered the possibility of a knife. Winded, the man sat down heavily on the damp grass, and Ned tumbled over him, pushing him unyielding onto his back. Only when he was down, Ned lying across his chest and Sid squatting on his knees, did the stranger fight back, bucking and kicking. They could see him now as clearly as if they fought on a theatre stage, for lights had flashed on one after the other, sash windows were thrown up, and faces smeared with cold cream looked down on the struggle in round-mouthed surprise.

'My . . . *Harry*,' grunted the man.

'I'll "my Harry" yow,' gasped Ned. 'An' yuh'll explain thissen to the coppers when they get here, an' all!'

'Let him go!' commanded a high, clear voice above them.

'I've only just got 'im!'

'And I'm telling you to let him go! That's my uncle Vanlo you've got there.'

'Oh hell, Harry. Oh bleddy hell . . . ah, hello again Anna,' he added, as a head partly nubbled with rollers appeared at Harry's shoulder.

'No home to go to, Ned?' said Anna.

Ned scrambled to his feet and helped Vanlo up.

'Look,' cut in Harry, 'there can't be many girls who don't want three men fighting below her window—'

'Give us one, then, Harry!' cried a voice from one of the other windows, to general laughter.

'—only you're keeping up the entire building.'

'*We* don't mind!' came a voice.

'But, Vanlo, what *are* you doing here?'

'Protectin' you, was the idea. I'm good at following people about. Them two friends of yours are hopeless. Crashing about like bulls, they were. I was going to keep watch here – until I was interrupted – and when you was up and about in the morning with the other girls, then I'd go and find me somewhere to kip.'

'Oh, Vanlo! Look, they might be clumsy but they're all right really.'

'Oi!'

'Quiet, Ned! See if you can't find somewhere for Vanlo to sleep tonight, and let's talk about this tomorrow. I'm going to have to do some explaining to Spellie as it is.'

'But I've come all this way to look after you, my Harry!'

'That means everything, believe me,' said Harry, her voice wavering. 'And you will. But if you lurk under these windows you'll probably get arrested instead of . . . instead of whoever it is.'

'I might be able to help,' said Sid, speaking for the first time. 'One of Mrs Watkins's commercials has cancelled and she's a room free.'

'Sensible Sid. I suppose you walked here, Vanlo?'

'Just from the train.'

'You love. Here, take the keys to the bike, and do your best not to overtake Sid.' Vanlo caught them with one hand. 'And here's the helmet Ned wears. Promise me you'll put it on. I wish I could come down and give you a hug, but we're all locked up.'

'It'll wait.'

CHAPTER THIRTY

Nottingham
February 1959

From behind the bulwark of her kitchen table, Sid's landlady regarded Vanlo warily. Sid's lungs and legs still hurt from the effort of cycling ahead of a near-idling motorbike.

'Well, if he's a friend of yours, Mr Probert . . .' she said doubtfully. 'Are you a . . . working man, Mr . . . ?'

'Buckland, lady. Vanlo Buckland. I do all sorts of works. If there is anything I can help you with, by way of thanks for your hospitality . . .'

Vanlo Buckland, mouthed Mrs Watkins silently. She took in the old-fashioned collarless shirt, the knotted red silk handkerchief in place of a tie, the battledress blouse *(don't mean ote, that. The dealers have more of 'em than they can handle),* the shapeless moleskin trousers and workman's boots. Flattering herself she was a good judge of character – *after all these years keeping house for single gents* – her eyes came to rest on his face: *he looks patient, that's what he looks. He's clean, anyway. That's the main thing, even if he int quite the standard of my usual gentlemen. I know who he is! He's Barker, to a T!* Barker was a long-dead Labrador, called so because he had never, in fact, barked very much.

'I've a vacancy for a few days, as Mr Probert has told you. One of my commercial gentlemen is indisposed,' she said, trying out a word she had read in a magazine story. 'Sent me a telegram, he did.' She inclined her head towards the mantelpiece, where that document sat in full important view. 'I don't allow smoking in the bedrooms, or at the dinner table. You will find this is a very quiet house. As he's a long-standing resident, and it's a bit late for me, I shall ask Mr Probert to show you to your room.' She creaked to her feet, and fetched a set of keys from a wall hook. 'Number four.' Then dropping the elevated style she adopted with all her new 'gentlemen', she turned to Sid and said: 'Mek thissen and yuh friend a cup of tea, duck. Voice like 'is ah'd say 'e's comm a long way today.'

*

'I needed this,' said Vanlo, holding his cup clear of the American cloth covering the table. Sid hadn't bothered with saucers – a thing he would never do in Mrs Watkins's presence. Sitting opposite Vanlo, Sid was at last able to make his own observations. He clutched his cup with both hands, not wanting the older man to see that they trembled.

'You're Harry's dad's brother then?'

'In a manner of speaking. Not exackly how they'd have it in the town hall, mebbe.'

'Oh?'

'Sam had a wife before he met Harry's mother. I'm *her* brother, only I've always felt more like I was his. But Sam and Ellen's my family.'

'Not married yourself then? Children?'

'Not the marryin' kind,' said Vanlo with a shy smile, his dark eyes holding Sid's gaze. 'An' all the children I need are Sam's and Ellen's.'

'Oh. And your sister? Do you ever see her?'

'Nope, though I 'spect she knows where I am by now. She's not a bad sort, really, only her and Sam brought out the worst in each other. That is, brought the worst out in *her*. Sam dunt have a worst side that you could bring out, no matter what you did.'

'You're very fond of him, then,' said Sid. His tea suddenly tasted bitter, his stomach cold.

'It's all right, Mr Probert,' said Vanlo. 'Everyone loves Sam. Men, women and *tickners*[18] and the *grai* in the field.'

'Pardon?'

'*My* pardon. I'm tired, so the old words come out more easy. I meant little 'uns, and horses – dogs too. Mebbe you'll get to meet Sam yerself one day. You'd like him too.'

'Maybe I will,' said Sid, and gulped his tea. He knew with what was surging through him now, he would sleep badly, but he didn't mind. It was joy. He got up. 'I should show you the ropes. She's had a bathroom built on through there – she's very proud of it. A bath is one and six. You arrange it with her. The students here don't bother; they sneak into halls or the

---

[18] Children.

sports pavilions and get theirs free. The khazi is out the back, of course.'

'I'd best go there next.'

'The flush isn't very good. She keeps saying she'll get someone to fix it.'

'No Mr Watkins then?'

'He calls in from time to time, but no, he doesn't live here. I don't know the story, but I think he did something that meant he'd overstayed his welcome. You weren't thinking of applying for the vacancy, were you?' Sid tried a jaunty smile.

'Me? Oh no. The lady wunt find me much use, I should think. But I can manage a bit of plumbing.'

*

'I'm on the second floor, up under the rafters,' said Sid over his shoulder, as Vanlo followed him up the narrow stairs. 'Watch yourself here – the runner's a bit loose. Yours is the first front.' His voice fell to a murmur. 'I'll not turn the landing light on. The others'd see it under their doors.'

Sid fumbled at the lock of number four, aware that his palms were damp and his heart beating uncomfortably loud, as he prickled with consciousness of the dark shape at his shoulder. He walked in and, flicking the switch, illuminated an iron-framed bed, an old-fashioned washstand and a rag rug on the dark-green lino. The only decoration was a garish framed image of a cottage garden, with the words 'A little while and Ye shall see Me'.

'With luck not just yet,' said Sid, gesturing at the picture.

'Oh . . . yes,' said Vanlo, puzzled; only afterwards did Sid discover that his companion could barely read. 'It's a nice room. Clean,' he added.

'I'm right above you,' said Sid, pointing at the ceiling. 'I'll say goodnight, then. Breakfast is at half past seven.'

'I've no timepiece. Live in the country and you can reckon the time by the animals. Would you call for me?'

'Gladly.'

'Goodnight then, and thank you, Mr Probert.'

'Sid.' Awkwardly, he held out his hand.

'Sid, then,' said Vanlo, taking it. They stood facing each other, until reluctantly the younger man drew his away.

*

Sid wound his alarm clock and held it close to the bulb of the bedside lamp he'd bought himself for reading, so that its dial would glow its phosphorescent comfort in the darkness.

'Could I be wrong?' he whispered into the darkness. He went over all the phrases Vanlo had used, alternating between treasuring them and picking them to pieces. *'Not the marrying kind' . . . 'the lady wouldn't find me much use' . . . am I clutching at straws? And if I'm not, what do I do? He's as old as my dad, nearly.* Sid fidgeted with delighted apprehension. *Or is he a decoy?* Lying on his back, he looked up at the skylight, a dark rectangle tinged with the yellow of the street lights. *No, you're being silly. He's Harry's uncle. He's come here to protect her, that's all.* He realised with shame that he hadn't even thought about Harry's nemesis, once Vanlo's identity had been established. Yet he had to be out there, somewhere, in that sleeping city, planning his next move.

*

The next morning Vanlo was dressed and shaved when Sid called for him, his black eyes shining with a wakefulness the younger man envied him.

'This is Mr Buckland,' said Sid to the men already seated around Mrs Watkins's expanding table. A commercial in shirtsleeves lowered his newspaper and nodded. The two students said, 'Morning!' and went back to their bacon and eggs. None of them expected the newcomer to be there long.

Yet all of them noted that evening that the toilet flushed fiercely again and the loose bit of Brussels matting on the staircase had been nailed firmly down.

*

The murmur of voices ceased as Miss Spellman swept in to high table, followed by her guests. The girls seated at the trestles scrambled to their feet in a squeal of chairs scraped on parquet. Black academic gowns were hoicked back onto shoulders, over neat pretty dresses and the occasional set of pearls either real or paste. Then all eyes turned to see who would be dining on top table tonight. There was indeed some confusion about who was to sit where, but Miss Spellman swiftly resolved this and pronounced sonorously: 'For what we are about to receive, may the Lord make us truly thankful.' A ragged 'Amen' rose from the rows of girls, followed by the din of sitting down, but this time their faces remained turned towards the high table. Miss Spellman remained standing, a fork in her hand to rap for silence again.

'Before we are served, ladies, I would like a moment of your time to introduce my guests. This is not a usual proceeding, but these are not usual circumstances, and most of the time you would not in any case thank me to present to you a retired Classics scholar or a local clergyman.'

There was a spattering of polite laughter.

'As you know, there was a disturbance here the other night, though happily there was nothing sinister about that particular incident, even if it is connected with that rather more troublesome matter you have been informed about. I urge you, as I have before, to continue your vigilance and to report anything untoward, no matter how minor you think it is, to myself or to the gentlemen in the porter's lodge, who are our first line of defence.' Miss Spellman's gaze passed over the young faces, coming to rest momentarily on where Harry sat beside Anna – who had put a protective arm over the back of her friend's chair. Harry was the only girl in the room who didn't look back at Miss Spellman.

'The police continue to counsel caution and plain common sense.' She paused, and, looking at the men sitting silently either side of her, smiled for the first time.

'However, I am pleased to say that we *shall* have some assistance. This gentleman on my right is Miss Loveridge's uncle Mr Vanlo Buckland, who has come from her home and intends to stay in Nottingham until the perpetrator is found . . .' Vanlo, half throttled by one of Sid's tweed ties, shifted inside his borrowed academic gown and nodded in the direction of Miss Spellman's listeners, whilst not looking any of them in the face. Beyond them, outside the long windows, he could see the rabbits gathering on the grass, and half wished himself with them. *Not to catch 'em ... I think I'd rather* be *a rabbit than wear these* togs.

'On my left, we have Mr Ned Stones, whom some of you will know as Miss Loveridge's friend ...' Some smiles greeted this description. 'And beside Mr Stones, is Mr Sidney Probert. Those of you who lodge in town and study in the public library will probably already have come across Mr Probert. As a general rule, ladies, I advise the cultivation of librarians. They are of immense use to us at all times in our lives. Not often, though, are they called upon to be ... What shall I call him? A bodyguard ... a detective? Or collectively, the three musketeers?'

More polite laughter greeted this. Vanlo remembered a film night at the camp in Egypt. The others had complained they weren't getting Vera Lynn 'instead of some lousy old flick', when he'd fancied himself as Onslow Stevens, playing Aramis.

'So you should not be surprised if you encounter any of these three gentlemen in hall, perhaps at times when you might not expect to see visitors. I need hardly say that the same latitude will not be extended to others; these are, after all, extraordinary circumstances. Ah, I see that the soup is ready to be served. Pea, I would guess by that aroma ...'

Miss Spellman sat down, the last words of her announcement met by a collective moan.

'I've never felt so important in my entire existence,' whispered Sid to Ned.

'Pity all them nice young ladies is wasted on you, duck!' he whispered back.

'*Ssh!*' said Sid, nevertheless delighted.

At their table, Anna murmured, 'Aren't you hungry?'

'No,' snuffled Harry, 'But I am loved.'

*

'In my experience, gentlemen,' said Miss Spellman to the three grouped in front of her in the comfortable chairs of the senior common room, 'there is no such thing as an "ordinary little girl", which is how Mr Calladine described the child who ordered the flowers on this Mr Arkwright's behalf. I think little girls grow into extraordinary young women, if you can get to them early enough and convince them of it. But ordinary, or extraordinary, we've not been able to find her.'

'And I looked up Gypsy Row in Hucknall in the directories,' said Sid. 'There is no such place.'

'It was altogether too pat, wasn't it? Though it does suggest that our quarry knows quite a bit about Harry. Even if he's in America, I can't quite shake the idea that Dr Arago is behind this.'

'Even if there was such a place, whoever he is wasn't forced to be living there,' put in Ned. 'He'd hardly be stupid enough to give his own address.'

'Agreed,' said Miss Spellman. 'Not stupid, but possibly unhinged, which means sooner or later he'll do something foolish anyway.'

'But if he *is* in Hucknall, I can ask a colleague of mine in the branch library to keep an eye out for anyone new. It's not a big place,' said Sid.

'Would you? Discreetly?' said Miss Spellman.

'I'm good at discretion.'

'Arkwright,' said Ned, talking to his glass of port and wondering if he could acquire a taste for it.

'Common enough name,' said Sid. 'And bound to be false.'

'Agreed. But let's suppose he's got to comm up with a name to tell the nipper,' said Ned. 'He's pretty sure she can't be traced, so any name she'd be able to pronounce would do, and a name that florist wouldn't think twice about.'

'Arkwright *Street,* maybe?' said Miss Spellman.

'That's what I was thinking. It's perhaps where he lives,' said Ned. 'The kind of place a bloke would look for lodgings if he came in to Midland Station – not Arkwright Street itself p'raps but the streets roundabout. Some of the London trains comm that way, and from Manchester in the other direction.'

'You think he's from outside?' asked Miss Spellman.

Ned sighed. 'I don't know ... Somebody who bears a grudge ... but who would? Know anyone, Vanlo?'

'Nobody. Harry'd have more cause to bear a grudge herself.'

Ned and Vanlo held each other's gaze for a moment.

'If it *is* someone who lives near Arkwright Street,' said Sid, 'and from what you're saying that'd be a fine needle in a haystack for us to look for anyway, then why go to Colwick for his flowers?'

'Same reason as he said Hucknall was his address,' said Ned. 'It's not close. He could though follow the river to get there, or just wander through the streets till he was far enough away from where he started from. It'd be a walk of two miles, mebbe two and a half.'

'He couldn't be wandering all that way with the child, could he?'

'No, so he must've found her nearby,' said Ned. 'Bribed her with a doll, or summat. Most of 'em aren't daft enough to take sweets. After all, it's not as if he's tried to get her home with him – only into a shop and *away* from him.'

'We're inventing all of this, Ned,' said Sid.

'I know. But them flowers are real enough. We've got to think of summat, else all we can do is wait for him to make his next move. How long is it you can stay, Vanlo?'

'As long as it takes,' said Vanlo. 'If you can point me in the way of some work though – anything I can do with my hands – you'd be doing me a favour. Else I might be begging at the kitchen door here in a week's time.'

'You won't have to do that, Mr Buckland,' said Miss Spellman. 'Please let me know the moment you are in any difficulty.'

'I'll ask in Raleigh,' said Ned. 'It'd just be labouring – unloading steel and that. You look strong enough, anyroad.'

'I'd be grateful – to both of you.'

*

'Oh ... Roddy ...' Harry held on to the counter, white to the lips. The porter looked up, closing the ledger he'd been writing in.

'It's another one, is it?'

She nodded.

'This time with a stamp on it – sent yesterday, at the main post office.'

'Don't suppose he's signed it?'

Harry held out the piece of paper, her hand shaking.

What you did, is insupportable. You must pay.

'No, I'm not going to touch it,' said Roddy. 'I don't know much about them things, but in *Dixon of Dock Green* Jack Warner says the fewer prints there are on the evidence, the better.'

'Dixon of what?'

'That new police series on the telly . . . here, put it all into this big clean envelope, and comm in the back here for some hot sweet tea, while I look for Miss Spellman.'

Harry took the smaller envelope and the half-sheet of paper it contained by their corners, and dropped them into the larger one as though they burned her fingers.

*

'Cat and mouse,' said Miss Spellman to a shaking Harry. 'The first note was slipped in right here at Florence Boot. So he was here. Then he turns up in Colwick, claiming to be living in Hucknall, right out the other side of the city. There's Ned's theory that he lives around Arkwright Road. And this was posted in the centre. If this was a detective story, he'd be getting closer and closer. But he's not as logical as that. I know I've asked you this before, but other than Arago, do you have *any* idea who this could be?'

'I wake up in the small hours asking myself that. I end up waking Anna too sometimes, but she's very patient. She goes to the pantry and brings me a glass of milk. I even wondered if that child said Arkwright because that's what she heard instead of Arago.'

'Except that it was written down.'

'Oh yes, so it was. But it can't be him. He's in America, where he always wanted to be.'

'Without the person he wanted to be with, though.'

'I can't think of anyone else. I've been through everyone.' Harry's shoulders slumped. 'There's what I told you yesterday – those two who attacked me.'

'But you said they *didn't* go to prison. They've no real motive for vengeance. *You* have, not them,' said Miss Spellman.

Harry started to cry. A box of tissues was pushed across the desk. *Just like Miss Shaw. And I'm back where I started from.*

'And frankly, Harry, from what you told me neither is clever enough for this, nor sufficiently unhinged. There's also something odd about the language of this most recent note.'

Harry blew her nose. 'I thought that too. I wouldn't say "insupportable". I'd say "unbearable", wouldn't you?'

Miss Spellman's chair creaked as she leaned forward. 'Harry, I am minded to find out just how Dr Arago is getting on with that American fellowship.'

'But if it isn't him, and I get in touch with him, he might get the wrong end of the stick.'

'*You* are to go nowhere near him. I shall speak to a friend in French. Then invent some excuse – some books left behind that we think might be his. I'm sure Clarice will be discreet, Harry.'

CHAPTER THIRTY-ONE

Florence Boot Hall
March 1959

'I asked to have the senior common room to myself this evening,' said Miss Spellman, looking around at her visitors. Vanlo and Sid sat on a small settee, a foot of space between them. Harry occupied an armchair, with Ned proprietorially leaning on the back. Anna had another chair to herself, but was carefully pouring measures of sherry.

'There are rather too many of us to squash into my office, you see.'

'You've got news, then?' said Ned.

'I do indeed, Mr Stones. As some of you already know, my colleague in the French department was able to tell me two things, in addition to writing on our behalf to Max Arago's university. One is that "insupportable", though a genuine English word, is also the French translation of what we'd more commonly call "unbearable". The other question I had for her, on a hunch merely, is the significance of chrysanthemums. Harry's grandmother learned in London, long before most of us were born, that for Italians they are the flower of death. It is apparently so also in France.'

She cleared her throat. 'I also asked Clarice to write to Dr Arago. She did, but heard back from his head of department – his former head of department.'

There was utter silence in the room.

'Mr Probert, would you mind reading this aloud?'

Dear Dr Forbes,

I am sorry to have to tell you that Dr Arago's fellowship came to a premature end some weeks ago; he was persuaded to resign rather than, in effect, be fired. Although his time with us started with great promise, unfortunately Dr Arago's health declined quite precipitately: he became aggressive, unpredictable and obsessive, going from upsetting his students to making them fearful – especially our women students. He disintegrated almost before our eyes. In Dr Arago's interests as well as our own, we persuaded him (eventually) to be examined by specialists. Whilst there were still times when he appeared to function normally, it would seem to be in pursuit of the abnormal. In other words, he would seek redress, with all the appearance of logic, for slights either imagined or exaggerated, making him impossible to work with. To bring this unhappy episode to a close, we voted an additional month's salary to Dr Arago, for the purposes of buying his passage back to Europe. It is my understanding that he intended to return to Paris. He has not though provided us with any forwarding address.

I am sorry to have to give you such tragic news. Dr Arago is a very talented man and it has been most distressing to witness his collapse . . .

'So it *is* him,' murmured Harry. 'I think perhaps I always knew it had to be.'

'I shall ring the sergeant,' said Miss Spellman, 'and trust that he doesn't think we have been treading too heavily on his toes. I wish, Mr Stones, that it were possible for me to adapt your suggestion that Harry move into rooms with you as your wife, and instead have you move into Florence Boot Hall until Dr Arago is found and given the treatment and support he evidently needs. However, I should never hear the end of it if I did; I would be accused of putting a rabbit in charge of the lettuce.'

*

When Harry entered Florence Boot library three evenings later, not to study but to unwind by playing the sleek Steinway in the far corner, it was to find just two other girls reading at the long table, and taking desultory notes.

'Do you two mind?' she asked, gesturing towards the piano.

'Go ahead,' said Caroline. 'It'll help me concentrate.'

'Something restful,' said the other girl. 'Not one of your noisy Russians.'

'I've got just the thing,' said Harry. She lifted the lid of the piano stool and rummaged. 'Liszt's Nocturne No. 3 in A flat major.'

'Take it away, Rubinstein!'

Harry took a deep breath and placed her hands on the keys. The music was in front of her, but she knew that once she began, she would probably not need to look at it. The Liszt was one of her mother's favourites, but how different it sounded on the silky keys of the Steinway, in contrast to the cottage piano at home. Harry felt calmer than she had in weeks. The shadowy figure who haunted her dreams now had a face. She knew who she was up against, and why, and the knowledge made her feel armed.

One of the girls passed near her. There was a whisper of cool air as she opened the French window on her way to smoke a cigarette. Miss Spellman disapproved of 'her' girls smoking. 'It's not ladylike, it makes your hair smell and ash gets everywhere.' For security, the window only opened from the inside. Harry's fingers flowed over the keys. She shut her eyes and swayed slightly.

Two minutes later, Caroline ground out her cigarette and hid the butt in a flowerpot. Coming back in, she closed the French window as softly as she could, to not disturb the glissade of sound that rose beneath Harry's hands, so softly that she didn't realise the catch hadn't clicked. Reverently, she tiptoed over to the table where she had left her books and gathered them up. Shortly afterwards her companion followed her cue.

They were halfway up the staircase to their room when the music abruptly ceased.

*

Roddy was making his rounds outside the building when he looked up towards the library and saw the lights left on, though the room was empty. He frowned, and made his way up to the windows, muttering something about 'bet those young ladies don't behave like that at home'. The French window was open, and the lid of the piano was up, but the sheet music lay about the floor. He stood looking in, then turned and said uncertainly into the darkness, 'Comm in now, I'm about to lock up,' but no furtive smoker appeared from behind the shrubbery. He sighed, and went in, to gather up the pages and put them back in the piano stool. Turning the light and his torch out, he went back to the window and once more looked out into the darkness, but nothing stirred.

Twenty minutes later, he was in his cubbyhole behind the reception desk, tidying up, he told himself, but in reality lingering longer than was necessary, for something about the abandoned piano hadn't seemed right. *The girls are usually better behaved than that . . .* He heard the rapid slap of bedroom slippers on parquet, and got up to see who was moving so purposefully at such a late hour.

'Miss Segal!'

In a worn man's paisley dressing gown tied with a fraying cord, Anna looked more unkempt than usual. 'Her cocoa's cold,' she said. 'I can't find Harry anywhere.'

'Where've you looked?'

'Everywhere. The laundry, the JCR, the dining hall – only that was already locked. I've just been in the library, thinking she'd maybe not realised it was after eleven.'

'I think,' said Roddy, 'we'd better fetch Miss Spellman.'

*

Snuffling, Caroline blew her nose into the policeman's large ironed handkerchief. 'I'll wash it and bring it back,' she said.

'Don't worry.'

'I'm sorry,' she said again. 'I just wanted a smoke!'

'It's not your fault, miss. You can have another one in a minute, as soon as I've got your fingerprints. Though if he's clever he'll have used gloves.'

Caroline, Sally and Roddy duly had their pads inked, and an inevitable confusion of other prints was found on the handle of the French window – which someone in a quiet laboratory in Epperstone Manor subsequently failed to match to any known villain.

*

Harry opened her eyes, but shut them again immediately. She couldn't see clearly and trying to focus only exacerbated her dizziness. Under the blanket, she clenched and unclenched her fingers, and wriggled her toes. She explored a little further; *he's left my underthings on, anyway.* But her furtive movements didn't go unobserved. There was something unexpectedly pleasant in the air – the aroma of strong coffee. She heard a rustle, some muffled footsteps, and then the sound of a body sitting heavily in a chair somewhere close to her head – there was a squeak as it shifted on the linoleum.

''Arry!' Max whispered. 'Will you drink this? I have put sugar – I think it is too bitter otherwise, even for you.'

I'm going to have to look at him eventually. Harry opened her eyes. She hoped that the blankets disguised the rapid rise and fall of her breathing.

'It's not like in the films, is it?' she babbled.

'*Comment?*'

'When you put that pad over my nose and mouth, I mean. I was supposed to go limp straightaway, wasn't I?'

'You fought,' he said admiringly.

'Yes,' she said, turning to face the wall, her head pounding. She wanted to fix in her mind the details of the room, but more than that, she wanted to avoid the sight of the gaunt man with the obsessive eyes. 'But you were strong. And a higher dose might have killed me.'

'Look at me, Harry.' Hearing the hard note in his voice she thought it best to obey. His face had stiffened; the side of his mouth was puckered – a gesture she remembered from that last meeting in his office.

'Why would I want to kill you when at last you are mine?'

Harry stifled a cry.

'Will you drink this coffee before it is cold? And then perhaps we can talk about our future.'

'How do I know you've not drugged it?'

He stared at her, unblinking, as she felt the air thicken around her. 'Watch me.' Max picked up the cup and went over to the basin in the corner, tipping its contents away.

'I will make more of it, for both of us. And you will choose the cup you drink.'

He went out of the door, locking it behind him. Harry listened. She heard steps going down a thinly carpeted stair, a door opening below, then silence. Harry's eyes darted around the room, taking in the washbasin in the corner, with a spotless white towel hanging on a rack alongside, a folded-down gate-leg table, two chairs. The uneven walls were distempered white, the small window deep in its embrasure made of panes too small to wriggle through, even if she managed to break any of them. Through the glass she could make out scudding clouds. She peered at the window frame. It had been fitted with a bolt, and that bolt was padlocked.

Harry tried to sit up, but her head felt worse, and she thought she might be sick. Lying back on the pillow, she strained her ears for the sound of cars, but heard only birdsong. *So I am in an old house, and in the country.*

The door was unlocked, and Max came in carrying a coffee-maker, two small cups and a sugar bowl on a tin tray.

'Where did you get that stuff from?' she asked.

'The coffee?'

'The chloroform.'

'I borrowed a white coat and took it from the biology lab. They are so disorganised they won't have noticed.' He put the tray on the table.

'Max, I will have that coffee. Then you can tell me how long you mean to keep me here.'

'That is entirely up to you.'

How can it be up to me, when you've brought me here against my will? 'What do you mean?'

He smiled. 'When you agree to marry me. You have left your factory-hand, of course?'

'Of course.' *Oh Ned, forgive me for saying this. I just want to stay alive.*

'*Très bien* . . . as I thought, he was only a juvenile trick to test me. So we can leave here, and tell all those nice people who are wondering where you are, that this was merely a romantic flight, and we shall apologise for any disturbance we may have caused. Now, I shall pour first for me, and drink it, and then bring you yours.' He picked up the coffee-maker, standing to one side so that she could observe everything he did. Then he came over to the bed, putting her cup on the floor, and said, 'Let us put the bolster behind you, so that you may sit up.'

Gritting her teeth, Harry heaved herself up. She caught a whiff of his coffee-scented breath as he bent over and rearranged the bedding. *Please do not touch me.* He handed her the cup, then sat down in the chair, his eyes on her as she drank.

'My mother and father will be worried,' she said.

Max frowned for a moment, as though this possibility hadn't occurred to him. Then his face cleared, and he said, 'I will bring you paper and a pen. You can write to them, tell them you are safe wiz me and that you have good news. Yes, I think this is the best idea. They will show your letter to the police, of course, who will no doubt smile, and shake their heads over the madness of lovers, and go back to catching murderers.'

'You have it all worked out, don't you?' said Harry faintly.

'I had planned this for some time. But the letter to your parents is *your* contribution, 'Arry. It is a good idea, *n'est-ce pas?* And, as I said, how long you are here is entirely your choice.'

Harry shut her eyes.

''Arry?'

'Max. You will have to bring me some clothes.'

'Ah!' he said, springing to his feet. 'I thought of that too!' He went out, leaving the door open this time, and she could hear the sound of a key turning nearby. Max returned with arms full of linen garment bags. He deposited these carefully over the back of the other chair, and pulled the table into the centre of the room, opening it out. Dizzy still, Harry managed to sit up straight, tucking the blanket under her armpits. Without looking at her, Max said, 'You will have fine undergarments too, and shoes. These dresses – and you – deserve them.' He lifted the uppermost bag onto the table, unzipping it. There was a slither of silk satin, and Harry gazed round-eyed at the most beautiful garment she had ever seen, a shimmering oyster cocktail dress with a narrow waist and a skirt so full that it scoffed at all those years of rationing.

'I think it will fit,' said Max. 'I checked the size of that old coat you are so fond of whilst you were in the Ladies' room, months ago. If it does not, it can be altered in the *atelier*. The master himself is dead, of course, but his assistants carry on his work. Maman is a client, naturally.'

'I thought gowns like that were made to measure.'

'They are. These are the ones worn by the *mannequins*.' He laid the dress on the bed where Harry sat, and she glimpsed the label: three feathers and a tailor's scissors, and the name Jacques Fath.

'Max,' she said gently, 'I don't even know where we are, I don't know where I am to wash, and I don't even have a change of underwear, but you want to dress me in Paris fashions?'

'Lend me your . . . I do not remember the English word. Your *soutien-gorge.*'

'Max, there is no need for this.'

'You misunderstand me. I promise not to put my hands on you until we are married. I wish only that you give me that garment so that I can get others in the right size.'

'Where will you go for them?' asked Harry, thinking of Griffin & Spalding and how Ned had joked about the staff having to brush their footprints out of the carpet.

'Nowhere I am known,' he said, smiling. 'I shall go to Sheffield. I shall tell zem I want to make a surprise for my wife.'

Harry shut her eyes. 'Max, I don't feel well. I want to go to the bathroom. I want to wash. I want my things . . . my books. But after warm water and soap, what I want most of all is to sleep.' *What I want most of all is to think and make a plan, especially if you're going to be away in Sheffield.*

Instantly solicitous, he said, 'My poor 'Arry. I shall show you. It is not how you will live – the dresses, which tomorrow you will put on for me, is how you will live. I have remembered nightwear at least.' He turned back to rummage amongst the garment bags, as she watched him, producing eventually a pair of silk pyjamas.

'They look like something Joan Crawford would wear,' she said.

'So why do you not sound pleased?'

Harry's hands clenched, hearing the edge in his voice. 'Oh, I like them. I just have to get used to all this . . .'

'You can 'ave all the time you need. As I said, 'ow long we remain here is entirely your decision. Here, take this dressing gown, these slippers. Then I shall show you everything, and what you may do, and not do, for as long as you choose to stay here.' He turned aside, as Harry wrapped the dressing gown over her underwear.

'Oh . . . I think you'll have to help me . . .' A wave of nausea rose up and hit her as she swung her legs off the bed. She raised her hands, and Max took them. *He behaves as though were were about to dance.*

'How long will I be feeling like this, Max?'

'It will pass,' he said, confidently. *Perhaps I can pretend it hasn't. Perhaps he will bring me a doctor.*

She leaned on his arm as he took her out on to the landing. The walls were panelled in dark-stained wood to dado level, with old-fashioned sepia woodchip above. She could see the marks where pictures or photographs had once hung. The place was dimly lit from a window above the staircase, the light filtered though red, blue and yellow Victorian stained glass. Harry ran through how she would describe the place: *it's an old house, for the walls are thick and the windows small, but it's been altered over the years. It's remote – a bit eccentric. No one would build anything like it now. I think it has been loved, and that once many people lived here.*

'You may not go downstairs,' said Max. 'I shall know if you do. In any case, the doors of those rooms are locked, and so are the outer doors.'

'I shan't want to.' *Not with invisible thread tied across the stairs.* 'Just the thought of steps, feeling as giddy as I do, makes me want to be sick.'

'The bathroom is here,' he said, opening a door. 'Not the most modern design, but there is everything you need.' He hesitated.

'I shall manage.'

'Knock when you wish to come out, then. Otherwise I shall have to knock and come in myself. I have the key here.'

He quietly closed the door behind her and she heard the lock click. Harry subsided onto the edge of the ancient, claw-footed bath and started to cry, stuffing a fist into her mouth so that if Max was listening outside, which she was sure he was, he wouldn't hear her sobs. *Better if I turn on the tap,* she thought. She did so, unleashing a cacophony of unearthly groans and bangs and a spluttering of water, which, however, was crystal clear. *He's planned everything,* she thought, eyeing the row of toiletries on the shelf above the tub. *Even that bottle of Tweed.* Harry remembered Anna's remark about a 'gilded cage' and out loud said, 'How right you were,' but hearing a shuffle outside the door, stopped. She wondered what Anna was doing now, what any of them were doing. She thought of Ned's shaving things on the washbasin in Chippendale Street, and how she'd meant to buy him a new toothbrush.

On the floor near the basin Harry found a small carton of washing powder, which she used to rinse out her underthings before hanging them on a towel rail. The normality of that action in such an abnormal situation gave her some momentary comfort.

The bath was even better; the water was surprisingly hot, and smelled metallic, but lolling in its steamy embrace Harry was at last able to weigh up the evidence. *I am to write to Mum and Dad. He'll read the letter, of course.* As she lay there, the words she would write took shape in her mind. Words that would look innocuous, but Sam and Ellen waiting for the postman couldn't fail to know that there was something terribly wrong lurking behind the words that pretended to reassure them. *I'll ask after Mittens, only I'll call her Tiddles.*

Her body clean, Harry's mind felt clearer and the pounding in her head reduced to a dull ache. The room was full of steam. In Florence Boot Hall there was a notice in the bathroom requesting that the window be opened after use, no matter the weather, 'to avoid the build-up of condensation'. Florence Boot Hall already seemed days, not hours ago. *Thought, Harry, then action.* Standing on the wooden toilet seat, she was able to stretch across to the tiny window, set deep in the wall. Its four small panes were set with frosted glass. *Who on earth would be spying on anyone in here?* But the catch gave. Harry took a deep breath of the mild air, the smell of wet grass. *If there are fields, someone must work in them, surely? This window is too small though – a well-fed cat might think twice.* She could see obliquely the tops of trees along the horizon. *Chestnuts, by the look of them. Hang on, though, what's that?* She remembered Ned's words, as clearly as if they'd had that conversation only days before: 'Kimberley's answer to the Leaning Tower of Pisa,' he'd said, 'only some duffa from Corporation dint read instructions raight and built it straight. That's our new water tower.'

Harry dried herself, put the pyjamas on, and knocked softly on the door to be let out. It was immediately unlocked.

'You must be hungry,' said Max. 'I have already prepared the table.'

'Not really,' she said. 'Now I am clean, what I want most of all are books.'

'Make a list,' he said. 'I shall obtain them for you.'

'From the university?' she said, incredulous.

'I am not so foolish. Sisson & Parker.'

'Oh . . . don't do that . . . I might not want them.'

'*Comment?*'

'What I meant was, these would be books I haven't read before. I won't know yet how useful they'll be and I don't want you going and buying them just yet. I should look at loan copies first.' She added, astonished at how calm she sounded: 'There's a big public library somewhere in the centre. I expect they'll have them.'

'Eat, and then you can write your list. And the letter for your charming mother and father.'

CHAPTER THIRTY-TWO

Shakespeare Street, Nottingham
March 1959

Sid sat at the issue desk trying to compile monthly statistics for the town clerk's report. This was usually a job he enjoyed, especially when he got to choose what went on the list of unusual requests from readers, a list that always made him smile although he had been told by his po-faced boss that its purpose was serious: 'to indicate changing social trends, especially since the advent of television, and to bring to the public's attention, as well as our paymasters, the complexity of our calling'. Sid dutifully noted: 'How to sculpt in Perspex'; 'the history of sausages'; 'where are the mountains on the moon?'; 'recipes for the manufacture of sasparilla and horehound', but his heart wasn't in it. The police had said to him, as they had to everyone concerned, that life must go on as normally as possible, and to remember that the search for Harry was in good hands. He sighed when he recalled how he had passed his lunch hour, standing outside the library entrance whilst Ned paced.

'Why aren't they putting up more bleddy posters, Sid?'

'I've seen plenty. Four in the library at least. I've heard they're breaking into sheds and – um – digging up every bit of disturbed ground. But they say they're waiting for his next move.'

'He moved, ah' raight! Moved and took her with him. And I wannt to kiss every nosey parker and curtain-twitcher in Nottinghamshire for looking out for her. Because I feel as if I'm walking on a tightrope above a hundred foot drop all the blasted time. Even if I'm only walking up Listergate. I went to work but kept dropping things so eventually they sent me to the sick bay and that bloke from Personnel comm to talk to me. Said he was sorry for "having no experience of matters like this". I should think he bleddy dint!'

Sid tried again to calm his own nerves with a hopeless little fantasy he'd invented. Harry had been found safe and well. She and Ned, himself and Vanlo, had got a bus into the countryside to have a picnic. Ned and Harry had gone to lie in the grass beneath a hedge and gaze into each other's eyes – a sense of delicacy about his friends, along with a gentle nudge of envy, prevented him imagining anything further. He and Vanlo had walked on, Vanlo saying quietly, 'They need time to themselves,' whilst the look in his eyes as he gazed at Sid was 'so do we', and they'd slowly made their way towards the cover of a little copse, hands dangling at their sides but never quite daring to touch.

He was roused from this reverie by the dark shape of a reader looking down on him. By the look on the man's face Sid wondered if he'd been standing there a while.

'I do apologise,' he murmured.

The reader didn't acknowledge this. 'I require zese books,' he said, holding out a list. 'Where may zey be found? I have looked at your cataloguing system but I fail to understand it.' From the man's tone, it was clear to Sid that this was the library's fault, but it was his accent that put him on the alert. Sid forced himself to speak as though nothing was amiss.

'I am sure I can help. But the quantity here exceeds the number of tickets we allow.'

'Tickets?'

'You are new to Nottingham, are you, sir? Well, all we require is a proof of address . . . a utility bill, a bank statement . . .' He tailed off, for the reader was already heading for the door. 'I . . . excuse me, sir . . .'

Sid looked again at the list. They were all history texts. Foolishly, he wanted to run after the man and say, 'We do have the Trevelyan, of course, but for reference only.' Then he saw what was wrong with the names and titles written there, and with the blood pounding in his head, he forgot the notices demanding silence he'd so often had to point to. The statistics for Mr Owen fluttered to the floor, and the flap to the issue desk banged, as Sid hurtled through the doors and along the corridor to the entrance hall.

He kept telling himself, *perhaps you're mistaken.*

In the entrance hall people he didn't see in his haste stood aside to enable his white-faced flight. His instinct was to follow the man, but he was aware of his incongruous appearance, shirtsleeved whilst everyone outside was putting up brollies against the rain. Then the decision was made for him, for by the door one man deliberately put himself in his path. With a cry of frustration, Sid tried to dodge around him, only to find immovable solidity, and large hands holding his shoulders. He looked up into Vanlo's concern.

'It was him! I'm sure it was!' gasped Sid. 'He wanted to borrow books, but ran off when I asked for his address.'

'Come on. Let's see if we can see the bastard.'

*

'There – that's him,' panted Sid. Max stood out, not because he was running, but because of his relentless, purposeful weaving through the home-bound crowds on Shakespeare Street. Sid had spotted him not a moment too soon: Max was about to disappear over the lip of the street.

'You get hold of the sergeant, Sid, and Miss Spellman.'

With a squeeze of Sid's shoulder, Vanlo set off in pursuit, with that easy, long-limbed stride that marked him out from all those who bent over desks, drawing boards or lathes. Sid drew breath, remembering that Ned would be here soon. The three of them had intended to meet, as much to give each other support as to share developments.

Only when Sid turned back into the library was he aware of how wet he was. His hair was slick against his head, his shirt clinging to him. His boss's face swam into his vision. 'What *is* going on, Probert?'

'Your telephone, sir. I must ring the police.'

*

Twenty minutes later, Ned walked into the storm.

'Is this the man you saw?' a constable was asking Sid, showing him a photograph gleaned from the French department.

'Yes – thank God!'

'Eh?'

'I was afraid I was wrong.'

'And who is this?' said the policeman, looking up at a white-faced Ned.

'Ned Stones, Miss Loveridge's . . . um . . . we're walking out together,' said Ned. 'I've just seen your men at the canal at the end of my road, talking to the boatmen.'

'They'd only be asking them if they've seen anything unto-ward. There've been a couple of developments. The suspect has tried to borrow books.'

'Bowks? Where is he now?'

'Sit down, lad. We can probably assume your girl's alive.'

'Look at this, Ned,' said Sid, holding out the book list. The paper had got damp from the rain, and some of the letters were smudged, as though the writer had dripped tears on it.

'Careful, now, that's evidence,' said the policeman.

Ned leaned over without touching it. 'It's her writing,' he said. 'Harry . . .'

'I saw straightaway the names were spelt wrong,' said Sid. 'Look, this should be Trevelyan, but she's written Trewelyan. And here – MacAulay is written MacAuly, leaving out the last 'a'. Not the kind of mistakes Harry would make, I'd have thought.'

The policeman tore a sheet off his notepad. 'Write them all down, sir. The wrong ones, and the missing ones.' He looked at Ned. 'She's clever, your girl. And brave.'

Ned put his face in his hands and started to cry. As if on cue, the city librarian's secretary put her head around the door.

'I think we could do with some hot, sweet tea here, if you wouldn't mind,' said the policeman.

'Certainly, sir.' Her head bobbed out of view.

*

'They'll find her, Ned,' said Sid. 'Especially as I think she's about to tell us where she is.' He looked at the collection of odd letters he'd written on the piece of paper, and they looked back at him. There were some repetitions: he checked he hadn't recorded anything twice . . . no, *w* occurred a second time, likewise *e,* and *r.* Few people after Nottingham's wartime bombing would want to claim any affinity with Germany, he knew, but that didn't change the fact that so much of English was Germanic . . . *-er* thus a common suffix, and there were two of those. Suddenly, as though the letters moved around on the page of their own accord, Sid saw the answer. He lifted his head. 'Water tower,' he said.

'She means Kimberley,' said Ned, astonished. 'Of all the luck.'

The policeman lifted the receiver on the desk. 'Swingate Water Tower,' they heard him say, 'any abandoned buildings or recently let houses. A big radius. Yes, you can see the damn thing for miles. The girl's uncle may have got there before us, of course.'

'Yuh've got to let me help, sir,' said Ned, as the man put down the receiver. 'I'm from Kimberley. I know the place as if it was the back of my hand.'

*

The unmarked car was parked across the entrance to the lane. The officer in the passenger seat turned round to face Ned.

'All of this is up for development,' he said, waving an arm to encompass the fields and hedgerows.

'Three bedroom semis with inside bathrooms. Dad wanted to go on the list for one but Mam wudnt have it.'

'Means the house shouldn't have been let out at all. It's condemned. They'd some trouble getting the old girl out of it and into a home. She was clinging to the door jamb, I'm told. Family'd been there for nigh on two hundred year. And now it'll be gone before she is. Nephew thought he'd make some easy money, seeing as the fellow only wanted it for a few weeks.'

'So what now?' said Ned.

'What now is that you do exactly what we tell you to do, to the letter. No heroics – they could cost your girl her life. Strictly speaking, we're not even sure if we have the right house, but it's the only one within a mile's radius of the water tower that's been let out in the last four months.'

'To a Mr Arkwright.'

'Precisely, though the nephew said he couldn't be one hundred per cent sure he was the man in the photograph we showed him. Mind you, he started by denying the whole thing, so mebbe finding himself in a hole he just kept on digging. We've got to bear in mind though that there's always the slim chance that we're about to surround some innocent member of the public.'

'Plaise,' said Ned, 'she's been gone three naights a'ready.'

'All right. You're just a motorist who has broken down, nothing more. All we need to know is if that's the house. So no pushing past him, or even trying to see in. If you get the door slammed in your face, as you probably will, just walk off. Keep your ears open as much as your eyes. Are you *quite* sure Arago doesn't know you?'

'I don't think he's ever seen me,' said Ned, thinking of Max's car sweeping past him in the rain, soaking his trousers.

'The object of the exercise is to frighten him into moving. It's much easier if we can get them both into the open air than if they're holed up inside.'

*

Ned hunched into his coat as he approached the farmhouse. It came into his head that this was a story he might tell his children one day, a thought that made him go cold with fright. *What yuh do now might decide if you ever do have nippers, Ned.* He looked up at the first floor, at the Victorian stained glass window above the front door, incongruous in that much older façade. He glanced up at the chimney pots, for a moment thinking he'd seen something moving. *Trick of the light, or some bird. Try not to be so frit!* He forced himself then not to look anywhere but towards the front door, aware that if he was being observed the last thing he wanted was to appear curious. Out of the corner of his eye he noted a Morris Minor parked to the side of the house, with a local registration. He repeated the letters and numbers over to himself, so that he could recite them later. *He'd have had to have a car to bring her here.*

At the front door he paused, and took a deep breath. He remembered what the policeman had said, about keeping his ears open. All he heard though was the faint caw of rooks in the trees three fields away, and, more distantly, the rumble of a baker's van. There was a little window to the right of the door, but any view to the inside was obscured by a large vase. *Feels like the place is listening to me. Or that's only mi nerves.* A letter box was cut into the door at about waist height, and there was a bell push on the door frame, both so in need of polishing that it was impossible to say what metal they were made of. He pressed the bell, but the thing rattled uselessly, and there was no answering ring he could hear. Ned scuffed away some fallen leaves, raised his fist and knocked smartly on the peeling door.

Do like they said. Count to thotty before knocking again, or yuh'll do it too quickly. Oh God . . . there is someone in there . . . sounds like he's shiftin' furniture abaht. Oh . . . it's stopped now. Is that feet comming dairnstairs? Bleddy hell, he's behind the door. What's he doing? Ned glanced apprehensively at the little window, and as quickly away again. *If he is spying on me, I'd best pretend I don't know it. I'm just a motorist with a pranged car. And this is a lonely house with a madman in it. Oh Harry! It's like a bleddy horror flick, this!*

Ned heard some scuffling behind the door, and a key being turned. He held his breath. There was silence, and another turn of the key. *Sounds like he's locked it again.* The letter box rattled, and Ned jumped to one side. *What if the bastard has a gun?* His stomach quivered. *Yer six miles from Slab Square, Ned, not Kuala Lumpur.* He watched, fascinated, as the flap creaked inward.

'What do you want?'

'I . . . I'm sorry to bother you, but my car broke down,' babbled Ned. 'I was wondering, have you a phone? Just to call the garage.'

'*Non!* Go away.'

What's that banging? Keep him talking, Ned!

'I don't want to be any trouble, mate. I've the same car as yourself. If you could just tell me where I can get hold of a mechanic and I'll push off—'

The flap creaked closed. Holding his breath and wishing his heart would stop racing, Ned laid an ear against the dry wood of the door. He could hear footsteps retreating, then running, *upwards by the sound of it,* then muffled shouting. Two voices. *Christ, that's her! That's her!*

Ned turned and ran. He'd not gone five yards from the door when some small missile hit him sharply in the back. *What the—?* Without thinking, he looked round. The door was still closed, the house front impassive. But on the roof, one hand around a chimney stack, was a man, silhouetted against the sky. With his free hand, he was waving something at Ned. *So that's where he got to. Vanlo's up there with a bleddy catapult!*

*

Two policemen detached themselves from the hedgerow as Ned pelted down the lane. Other heads bobbed up in the neighbouring fields. 'She's there,' he panted. 'Banging, and shouting.'

'Is he armed?'

'A catapult!' gasped Ned.

'*What?*'

'Not *him*. I never saw no gun. But her uncle's up by the chimney pots. He's a good shot – wi' pebbles, I mean.'

'Bleddy hell! *Right, men!* But don't touch the bloke on the roof!'

*

'You will come now!' bawled Max. 'We have to go!' He had hold of both of Harry's wrists and was forcing her down the stairs. The heels of the hated stilettos he had made her wear caught in the Brussels matting; she kicked them off and was half dragged, half carried downwards, the wide skirt of her dress with its stiffened underskirt swishing against the banisters. *Where the hell is he going to take me now, in this blasted cocktail dress?* Harry thought to herself, as he dragged her out towards the car. She saw him look round wildly.

'He's gone,' he muttered.

Harry was already praying they would get stuck behind a tractor, or a milling flock of sheep, so that she could burst out of the car in her torn stockings. *Why did whoever that was have to come banging on the door before they'd time to work out my message and come and find me?*

By the car, they struggled, Max taking a hand off Harry to open the door, at which point she tried to pull away, but his remaining hand held her wrist with such force that she thought she could feel the bones grinding against each other. The bruises would take weeks to fade. The car open, he pushed her into her seat, crushing the stiff grosgrain of her skirt as though it were a piece of sacking. Then he slapped her face, hard. Harry gasped with the shock: every response to him in the days of her captivity had been calculated to keep his violence at bay. But then Max's face bobbed towards her, his eyes widening in surprise, his mouth opening in a soundless 'oh!' He put the hand he'd just struck her with to the back of his head, then brought it back, staring at his bloodied fingers, and then at her, as if she had caused his injury. She heard a tiny thud, followed by the sound of something like a pebble hitting the ground, and he started, letting go of her wrist. Harry bounced forward, both feet landing simultaneously on the rutted grass, and hurtled down the path, her head bowed 'like a charging bullock', the policeman whose solid torso stopped her in her tracks was later to say.

'Miss Loveridge, I presume? Where on earth are you going all got up like that? And no shoes?'

'Oh!' said Harry, and grasped his arms to stop herself falling. Shock took over, now that she was free. The policeman picked her up as easily as if she was a doll, carrying her down the lane against the tide of running men in blue. Afterwards she wondered why she hadn't looked around her, having been penned up for what seemed so long. All she remembered of that lane was the feel of the policeman's tunic jogging against her face, and an inch from her eyes, a button, domed, with a raised design of a crown.

'I'll put you down in a minute,' rumbled the voice above her. She heard a car door open, and then someone calling her name.

'Ned!' she cried.

'Careful, mate, don't drop her!'

Laughing and weeping with relief, Harry glanced up at the sky as she was rolled into Ned's arms. She thought it had never looked so blue. Nor had his eyes. And then she started to shake.

*

'You're free,' whispered Ned, his arm around her shoulder, his other hand holding hers as they sat in the back of the car taking them swiftly into Nottingham. He kissed her forehead, an eye towards the men sitting in the front seats. 'What's the thing yuh most want to do in the world raight now? After they've finished with uz at the station, I mean.'

'I want to go back to my room. I want to see Anna and Miss Spellman.' Harry twisted round, looking out of the back window as Swingate Water Tower grew smaller and smaller. 'Where's Uncle Vanlo?'

'Mr Buckland will need to give a statement too,' said the officer in the passenger seat.

'Oh, yes, of course.'

'And?' said Ned.

'Then I'd like to have a shower, and put on normal clothes.'

'That's natural, I s'ppose. And I'd best call in at the works, tell them I'll be back termorrer.'

'Ned! I meant you to come with me.'

'What, into the shower too?' he said, nuzzling her neck to hide his expression of relief.

'Behave! But kiss me, would you?'

'I'll kiss yow within an inch of yer life, if yuh'll let me.' He wondered if he was going to cry.

Three minutes later, he said, 'Yuh do look the business in that dress. Only it's not really yow.'

'I'm glad you think so too – that it's not me, I mean. There are half a dozen like it back there. I expect this one'll be labelled "exhibit number something or other".'

'Good grief. Do yuh get to keep 'em? We'd have to start going somewhere posher than Kardomah.'

'I don't know what'll happen to them. Maybe they could be auctioned for the Children's Hospital, or something. "Swingate Farm kidnap Paris couture," should get them running.'

He laughed. 'Yuh're quite a woman. Joking ayfter a' that.'

She held his hand tighter. 'No, Ned, I'm trying to hold it together if I'm honest.'

'Oh Harry . . .'

'I can't wait to put on my favourite jeans,' she rushed on. 'That linen shirt with the open collar Mum made, that I've starched until it could walk around the room on its own.'

'What about that wide belt that meks your waist look like my hands'd meet round it? An' that little scarf – in that get-up yuh make Margaret Lockwood look like Margaret Rutherford.'

'My *diklo,* as Dad would say – oh, *Dad.*' She lifted her head, speaking more loudly in the direction of the front seats. 'Has someone been in touch with my mother and father?'

'They will have,' said a voice from the front. 'Procedure. We've let Canterbury know.'

CHAPTER THIRTY-THREE

Sneinton Police Station
March 1959

Sid's interview was quite brief: he described Max coming into the library, his odd manner and his abrupt flight.

'What'll happen now?' he asked.

'With Arago? The police surgeon's with him now, but they've sent to Mapperley Asylum for someone to take a look at him,' said his interviewer. 'They might decide he's not all there, you see. Not realising he'd have to give an address to borrow books might even be a symptom of it. He'd got things all planned out, but was so single-minded he overlooked something that'd be obvious to you and me. You deserve a medal for cottoning on, and then for unscrambling the lady's message.'

'Thank you, but until your colleague showed me Arago's photograph I was afraid I'd got it all wrong – it was just his accent and the funny spellings. I didn't really have time to convince myself I was mistaken.'

'You're quite a team, though, you and Mr Stones – and that Miss Spellman. The Gypsy bloke, though . . . that could have gone very wrong. He had Arago pinned down like a beetle on its back, though, by the time us lads got there.'

'I couldn't possibly have stopped Mr Buckland. I thought he'd follow Arago some way, and then come back. We . . . we're in the same lodgings. I was worried sick when he didn't appear last night, and wasn't there at breakfast. And now you tell me he was camped on the roof.'

'We were worried ourselves. About a double murder, to be honest. You don't look like you got much sleep yourself either last night.'

'I didn't. Where is he – Mr Buckland, I mean?'

'Two doors down. Being interviewed, same as you.'

*

'It's all quite irregular,' said the sergeant, wiping the back of his hand across his forehead, 'but I suppose we've you to thank for him not getting into the car with her and running any of us down.'

'Just did what I promised my bruv and her mum I'd do, that's all,' said Vanlo, sitting on the opposite side of the table. 'You really writing all of this down?'

'Your brother? Thought you said your name was Buckland.'

'In-law I suppose you'd call it. He's my bruv anyroad.'

'So how did you manage to follow Arago without being seen, then?'

'Comes of all that poaching,' said Vanlo, without thinking.

'I'll not write that down, mebbe.'

'Oh ... yes, thank you. Well, I'd gone to the library to meet my friend Sid that works there.'

The policeman raised an eyebrow at this. 'Mr Probert? How long have you known *him* for?'

Vanlo was suddenly still, alert. 'Only days, really. He's Ned's friend – Harry's young man. Mr Probert got me my lodgings.'

'I see. So you went to the library to see him—'

'Yes, only he was tearing out of the place like the Bad One was after 'en, so I followed 'en out and we saw the professor fellow going up the street. Arago hopped on a bus at the square, and so I hopped on too. Went upstairs, so I went up too, sat a few seats behind. I heard the fare he asked for, so I asked for the same. Problem was when we was in open country, I couldn't very well get off at the same stop as 'en or he'd want to know why. So I waited till he'd got off and the bus was moving again, then pretended, being a stranger and that, that I'd missed my stop. Conductor was all right – he rang the bell some special way and the bus stopped then and there and off I hopped. I'd seen which way the man went and them hedges was good and deep and the path not straight so it wunt hard to keep 'en in sight without 'en cottoning on to me. Then I'd to go the long way round the back so's he'd not see me from the house. There was this shed thing built up against the wall, so I climbed onto that and then up a drainpipe. On the roof I could see the lie of the land, so to speak. That was yesterday, o' course. I'm sorry I ain't shaved, but I got my kip up there – it bein' an old house there was a sort of walkway between them chimney pots, and fortunately it was a dry night. I didn't sleep much as I was on the alert for anything going on in the house, so I'm a bit stiff today, that's all. Got used to a comfortable bed in Nottingham, that's my problem.'

'You ever thought of a career as a cat burglar?' asked the policeman, half-admiringly.

'Wouldn't tell you if I had. But I haven't.'

'What did you plan to do, then?'

'Find out if she was there, first of all, and that wunt hard. I heard 'em talking, The noise goes up them old chimneys like smoke. Couldn't always make out the words but I could hear from how she talked to him she was being very careful – nothing to rile him.' Vanlo shifted in his chair, exhaling. 'I was going to wait. Get him when he came out.'

'With that catapult?'

'With that or with my own hands.'

'Get yourself into trouble, that way.'

'I'd do anything for my niece. I couldn't know you was all on your way.'

'You're all saying much the same thing. Seems to be quite a girl.' The man stopped taking notes, and laid down his pen. 'I expect you get plenty of rabbits with that catapult.'

'Might do.' Vanlo smiled. 'You going to take me in for that?'

'Better things to do.'

*

Vanlo found Sid waiting for him in the entrance to the police station.

'They kept you a long time.'

Vanlo sat down beside him on the bench. 'They was interested in my climbing, and my catapult.'

'I was so worried . . . After I'd worked out Harry's message, they sent me home. I told Mrs Watkins I was feeling peaky and that I wouldn't have any supper. Then I went upstairs and lay on my bed waiting for you to come in.'

'How would you know it was me coming in and not one of the other fellows?'

'I . . . I know your step.'

Vanlo looked down at his hands, resting on his knees. 'I like that, Sid. That you know my step, I mean.' He glanced towards the counter. 'I think you and me oughtn't to be here when Harry and Ned come out.'

'Don't you want to wait for them?'

'No, I think we should leave 'em to each other. Know any pubs round here? Then I ought to go and ask pardon of Mrs Watkins for being a dirty stop-out.'

*

Harry and Ned stood outside the police station on Colwick Road, looking at each other.

'That looks like a comfier outfit, anyroad,' said Ned.

Harry looked down at a battledress blouse, a small man's old collarless shirt, dungarees with the trouser-ends rolled up, and a pair of boy's lace-up shoes. 'It was the best they could manage, they said, but I quite like it. They offered me a lift, but I told them I wanted to go with you.'

'Can I see yuh back 'ome, then?'

'Of course,' she said, and took his arm.

*

'Anna's been gone a long time,' said Ned. He was sitting on the end of Harry's bed, whilst she had taken her desk chair and turned it to face him. 'Don't the rules say there has to be a gooseberry?'

'Yes, but Miss Spellman has gone out too. I saw her from the window ten minutes ago, with her coat on and carrying a briefcase.'

'Harry ...'

'I think they just thought we ought to be alone for a while.'

He got up then and came and knelt at her feet, putting his head sideways in her lap. She stroked his hair gently. *What now?* she wondered.

'Not here, not like this,' said Ned, as if he knew what she was thinking. He lifted his head from her lap, looking up at her.

'No.'

'But somewhere?'

'Maybe.'

'Oh, Harry,' he said, getting up and taking her hands, pulling her gently to her feet. He kissed her, then, holding her against his shoulder, his hands slipped under the battledress, and beneath the straps of the dungarees, moving up and down the curve of her back through the man's shirt. He grasped a fistful of it, and whispered, 'Can I? Just this?' He felt her head nod against him.

He pulled the shirt up, and explored the nubs of her spine, the taut, smooth skin of her back.

'Yuh like velvet, yow are!' he whispered. Then he kissed her again, his eyes closed, and pulled her closer to him, his fingers fanning out to edge beneath her waistband, and upwards to span her ribs.

'Only if yuh're sure, mind.'

'Ned,' she said, tilting her head and looking at him directly. 'I've never been so sure. Poor bloody Max ...' She saw him wince. 'Being there with him, listening to his endless demands – round and round and round again. If I hadn't had you to think about and how much I wanted to see you again, I don't know how I'd have managed to keep as calm as I did. I tried to tell them everything, in the police station, as much as I could remember. They had a good way of questioning ... it's as if they drew a curtain back and I could see a picture I thought I'd forgotten altogether. It was only when I was sitting there talking to them that I remembered what happened before the chloroform. I was there on the piano stool playing from memory, with my eyes closed, but there was a particular phrase coming up I sometimes have trouble with so I opened my eyes to look at the music, and there was a shadow across the page. I didn't have time to turn round before the cloth was across my nose and mouth.' Her voice tailed away.

'Tek yer time. Yuh don't need to tell me if yuh don't want to.'

'I do. I went over and over again in my head all the things I wanted to say to you, that I hadn't ever said to you, while I was trapped in that house. The police told me that with Max I'd done the right thing. I made him think I was agreeing with eve-rything, hoping he'd relax, be less vigilant. I nearly asked him – I shiver to think about it now – if he was going to hit me again. But I didn't have to. He warned me that he would, but only if I provoked him, like the last time. He did, of course, when I was trying to stop him forcing me into the car.'

'Bastard!'

'It was a wild try asking him for books, and anyone else but Max would've noticed there was something wrong with those names; they'd have known straightaway that Trevelyan is never written Trewelyan. It was always a risk – but it was my only chance of getting a message out. Imagine if another librarian had been on duty, and had looked at all those spelling mistakes, and never realised they were deliberate? Or worse, if they'd said something snooty about academic standards drop-ping, and then he might have realised something was up. But I had to try!'

'Thank God yuh did . . . yow could still be there, or wairser.'

'What's the matter with me, Ned? Why did those men attack me in my father's backyard? And then why did I get kidnapped by a man everyone told me was a catch, and dressed up and made to parade around for him, a man who was convinced that all I needed was adulation and Paris frocks to get me to see the error of my ways? Why is it that some of the cleverest men are the stupidest?'

'Like that old Greek bloke that woman rode around on as if he wor a donkey?'

'Aristotle?'

'Oi, don't look so surprised! I can read bowks too, yuh know.'
He paused. 'I've summat to tell yuh abaht that, by the way.'

'Go on.'

'Nope, later. Harry, there's nothing wrong wi' *yow*. Tow
brutes and a nutter. Not your fault!'

'You know what happened when I was in there?' She turned
her face into his shirt and he had to strain to hear her.

'Only what yow wannt to tell me,' he said slowly. *If that
bastard has raped her too, I swear, I'll get through all the locked
doors of any prison or any asylum, and I'll do for him missen!*

'They say that a girl should be pure. That if she gives herself
to a man he'll not want her again afterwards.'

'Harry—'

'I don't know how true that is. It sounds like an unequal
bargain to me. The man ought to be ashamed of his unkind-
ness. When Max left me locked up alone in that house, I
thought I mightn't get out of there alive. He'd hurt me before
and the next time he might strike harder, or I might hit my
head on something if he knocked me down and do for myself
that way. The odd thing was that when he was there in front of
me I feared him less, because then I'd a chance to make him
think I was going along with him. Anyway, what I'm trying to
say is that you'd told me you loved me, and I love you, but I
was shut up in there and we'd never—'

'Harry—'

'Sorry.'

'Stop staying sorry. Comm away wi' me. Somewhere nobody
knows uz.'

368

'Yes. Only . . .'

'Only?'

'Not straightaway. Mum and Dad are coming up again. Once Vanlo gets home.'

'I'm sorry. I wor rushing things – again.'

'No,' she said, laying a finger on his lip. 'No you weren't. Now what was it you had to tell me about reading books, Ned? Though I've half an idea already, I think. People don't make friends with librarians by accident, usually.'

'It wurnt only to do wi' Sid. Anna too. And in a way, your Miss Spellman, and that lad at the dinner table. But mostly to do wi' yow. I've been gooin' to night classes.'

Harry watched with a rush of love as heat rose to the tips of his ears.

'I wanted yow to be proud of me, Harry.'

'Oh, I *am* proud of you, Ned. With or without books.'

He smiled in a way that made him look younger to Harry. 'I've been told I'm quite good, even. My essays.'

CHAPTER THIRTY-FOUR

At Mrs Watkins's

March 1959

Sid stood in the open door of number four. Vanlo had his back to him, putting his few belongings into the bag open on the stripped bed.

'Hello, Sid,' he said, without turning round.

'How did you know it was me?' said Sid, coming into the room.

'I always do. I know your step, same as you know mine.'

'You're going then?'

Vanlo turned round. 'Yes. Our job's done. I'll go and catch my train. I've done what I came for – *we've* done it. Our Harry's safe.'

His throat tight, Sid said, 'I'll miss you, Vanlo.'

'Shut the door a minute.'

Sid closed it softly behind him. He'd read so many times that expression 'his heart leaped', that it was with some surprise he felt that sensation in his own chest, and realised it was no hyperbole.

'I'll miss you too, Sid.' Vanlo put his hand on the back of Sid's neck.

Afterwards Sid tried to remember in detail what happened next: at what point the comradely hug of farewell turned into a frantic embrace.

'I thought you'd never catch on,' murmured Vanlo, when at last their flushed faces separated and they were gazing at each other in delight and surprise.

'I was too afraid of being wrong. Don't go, Vanlo.'

'I got to. Harry's dad can't come and see her if there's no one to work the farm. You ever bin to Kent, Sid?'

'No.'

'They've libraries there too. A nice big one in Canterbury where I go to look at the newspapers 'cos they never hurry me there – I'm very slow, see. After I've tole Ellen and Sam about this—'

'*This*?'

'You, me and Ned. Takin' Max, I meant,' said Vanlo with a flicker of sadness. 'I'd like to tell the whole world about you, but you know I can't. Will you come though?'

'Try to stop me!' said Sid, trying not to cry. 'Oh, Vanlo! Look . . .' His voice shook. 'I took a day's leave, thinking you might be going. But you'll want to say goodbye to Harry, of course . . .'

'I done that. Last night.'

'What time's your train?'

'The time I catch it. I'm not partickler.'

'Then, would you let me see you off?'

'I'd like that mor'n anything. I mean you bein' the last person I see here.'

'When do you have to be out of this room?'

'Half past nine. Mrs Watkins said to leave the keys on the hook. She had the shopping to do.'

'Everyone else has gone to work too. Vanlo . . . would you come upstairs?'

'I thought you'd never ask me.'

*

'I feel safe here, in your arms,' murmured Sid, curled against the hardness of Vanlo's chest.

'Nicest that's ever been, and that's a fact,' said Vanlo.

Nevertheless, Sid felt a pang of jealousy as intense as pain.

'Have you . . . Did you? Stupid question. You're that much older than me – and the way you . . . sorry, Vanlo, it's none of my business.'

'That's all right. Not much, if the truth be known. London, when I ran away. I was just a boy then, in them lodging houses. There was a couple of lonely gents that kep' me for a bit. One of 'em cried when I said I was going off to Kent. I'd to find Sam, see. And I did. But Sam dunt know any of that. Most times I've been on my own. There was the war, o' course. Egypt. But in London a fellow tried to put the blacks on me once, so I've had to be very careful.'

'*No!*'

'Not so loud. A public jakes. No, I hadn't gone there on the prowl; I needed a leak. Sam was waiting for me upstairs. Hate those places but in a city you've not got no choice. What's wrong with a nice clean hedge when it's about to rain? The fellow told me he was a *gavver*—'

'A what?'

'Policeman. Dunt know if he was or not, but he said he'd take me in if I didn't empty my pockets for 'en.'

'And did you?'

'I knocked 'en over, bloodied his nose. Then I scarpered afore he could get up.'

'Couldn't you have got the law yourself?'

Vanlo laughed. 'I heard of someone as did that, and the blacker got six months stir. *He* got a year.'

'Oh God . . .'

'What about you, then?'

'I've only one story to tell. It was in the army. They separated us – sent him somewhere else. That was about all. I think I was lucky.'

'The way you say it you dunt sound so. Broke your heart, did he?'

'Yes. It was the army that separated us, but I think he'd have left me anyway. Ned and Harry are the only others that know.'

Vanlo's arm tightened. 'Will you tell them about us?'

'I *would* like to tell them – I'd like to tell the *world*. But I can't. And I'd not tell anyone unless you said it was all right. Anyone know about you?'

'No. I'd thought about saying something to Harry's mum, but I never have.' He smiled. 'I tole Sam's old dog, an' the ones he had before 'en. Mebbe we oughter go carefully for a bit. But I got my own *vardo* where I am – my own wagon, that is. I'm still in it, though it never goes anywhere. It's in the corner of a pad-dock, where Harry's bruv keeps a couple of horses. But about this . . . it's never bin like this for me, not ever.'

'Like this?'

'I'm not good with words, not the way Harry is, or you. You've been to college, like her, haven't you? I can barely write my own name. But what I mean is that there was never love in it them other times, Sid.'

*

A week later, in the Boat, Sam put Ned's pint down in front of him. 'My Vanlo tole me what you did,' he said.

'Nothing to what *he* did, sir.'

'Sam, remember. That's if you dunt want to call me Dad.' Harry and Ned exchanged happy glances.

'It was me taught him the catapult,' went on Sam. 'Know how to use one yourself?'

'Not well . . .' said Ned.

'So I'll teach you too. Where are we staying this time, Harry?'

'Same place as before. As Miss Spellman's guests.'

'That's kind of her. We mun meet this Sid, too. Clever boy. Your uncle Vanlo's taken with him, and he's slow to make friends. Always has been a bit shy.'

CHAPTER THIRTY-FIVE

Lincoln
April 1959

As the train pulled out into open country, Ned fumbled in his right pocket, hiding what he had been looking for in his palm. Harry was sitting next to the window on his other side, her right hand loosely in his left. Leaning against her shoulder, he could see the rapid movement of her eyes reflected in the glass.

'Ah' raight, Harry?'

'Oh . . . yes.' She looked round at him.

'Yuh wor miles away.'

'I know . . .'

'It's over now.'

'I know . . .'

'I've summat to give yow,' he said. 'Got it out of Ma's sewing box. Give me your hand – the other one . . . Harmony Loveridge, with this curtain ring, I thee wed.'

'Oh Ned! But it's a good fit!'

'Not bad, is it, Mrs Stones? But are yuh sure about this, duck? The staying away?'

'I'm sure. What did you book?'

'Summat simple. A room above a pub.'

'That's perfect. The kind of place Mum and Dad like to stay.'

'Actually it wor him gave me the idea.'

'*Dad?*'

'Not directly, of course.' Ned flushed. 'He told me that with his people – that wor how he said it – a young couple would run off. He said they'd have to marry when they comm back. He wor smiling when he said that. I dint know where to put mi face, so I said summat like "Did it matter where they went?" and he said no, if a man had a wagon, he'd go with that. If he hadn't, a room above a pub was good for courting.'

'Oh, Dad . . . he's as good as given you permission, Ned.'

'I don't think he meant I was just to tek yuh away for a Sat'day naight and mek free wi' yow.'

'No. He definitely didn't mean that.'

'So I can marry yow.'

'I think he meant you'd better!'

'My girl.' He kissed her.

A minute later, she said, 'You've had a haircut. Your neck's all stubbly.'

'Had to,' he said, flushing. 'Needed some supplies. "Anything for the weekend, sir?" I'd to go somewhere I hadn't been before. The usual bloke in Kimberley's a Catholic so he wudnt do.'

'Oh yes . . . of course.' Harry tilted her face to his, and they kissed again.

*

'It's good it's on the second floor, anyroad – quieter,' said Ned. He'd insisted on hauling both Harry's bag and his own up the narrow back staircase. 'Mine host said we're the only people up there tonight. He never bothered his head about any awkud questions eyther.'

He caught his breath on the little landing. 'Bathroom looks like it's in here.' Harry glanced in. It was simple and clean: a shower stall and a lavatory. A spare toilet roll sat on a shelf, under a pink crocheted skirt belonging to a doll whose arms were held out, a bright smile painted on its plastic face. Harry thought it a thing she would never have in her own home, for the doll was neither particularly useful nor beautiful, but her eyes prickled, for she knew she would never forget its cheerful, silly expression, its outstretched hands.

She turned round. Ned was rattling the large key in the lock of room number two. The door creaked. 'Wait a minute, Harry.' He left the bags on the landing, and picked her up, just as he had held her when the burly policeman at Swingate Farm had handed over his burden.

'Welcome home, Mrs Stones,' he said, nudging the door open with his foot and carrying her in. He deposited her on the bed as carefully as if she might break, and looked down at her, smiling.

'Harry, I want yuh to know summat. If yuh'll let me, I'll pick yow up like that again. But it'll not be to tek yuh into a two-up two-down in Nottingham, with the jakes out the back.'

'I wouldn't care if it was, Ned. That's not what counts,' she said, puzzled at the look on his face. 'I don't *need* a posh place, any more than I needed Max's frocks.'

'What I really want to say, Harry, is that it mightn't be Nottingham. So yes, it might be a two-up, two-down, only in some other place.'

'Leave Nottingham? But why?'

He sat beside her and took her hand. 'I know you're staying on, because of Dr Holt an' all. I've been to see Miss Spellman again. She allus said I could.'

'Spellie?'

'Yes. But it's your help I'll need, Harry. I'm not sure I raightly know what I'm doing. I've been trying to find the courage to tell yer. I've been given this chance, yuh see . . . I got a letter tow days after yuh wor fahnd.' He reached inside his jacket pocket.

Harry wordlessly took the white envelope, noting that it had been well handled, and that it had an Oxford postmark. She unfolded the no longer crisp letter inside, aware of Ned's eyes on her, and read.

'Ruskin College,' she said eventually. 'Oh Ned, I am so proud of you!'

'Yow had a lot to do wi' it,' he said shyly, taking her hand. 'And Sid . . . and Anna . . . and Miss Spellman. The way she looked me straight in the eye, was interested in me, when she fahnd me hanging abaht waiting to see yuh that time. And, of course, Mr Staley – my tutor – at night school. I've a bit more work to do to prepare – well, I wannt to, anyroad – before I go in October.'

'That'll make two of us. I can't believe I'm going into the last term. The air is already starting to crackle in Florence Boot.

Damp towels on foreheads and tense little voices calling from window to window: "Are you revising, Gertie?" I hope Anna's got shares in Player's, the amount she's smoking. But, Ned, this news of yours! – I don't know, it just gives me more impetus. And here's the union about to sponsor you. Does that mean you'll go and work for them afterwards?'

Ned paused. 'I could do, mebbe. I'd like to talk to yuh abaht that. But it's not what will *I* do but what *we'll* do after.' He watched her carefully. 'It's only a year. I don't want to go back into the frame shop, but if I can do summat for any one of them nine thousand souls who obey the hooter in Raleigh every bleddy morning – or in Player's or Birkin or Aristoc or Boots for that matter – but want there to be summat else in their lives before they croak, then I want to know how to do it. How to find the right arguments, rather than just what I feel here,' he said, tapping his heart. 'Staley explained summat to us the first class I went to. He said he wurnt there to cram us full of facts, so's we could go on *Double Your Money*. He said he wanted to *educate* us. He took that word to bits for us then and there on the blackboard, getting more chalk on hissen than on it, the way he allus does. I expect yow got Latin in your schoowel?'

'Oh yes,' said Harry.

'Well, we dint get any at mine, so it was all news to me. How that word meant "leading out". Bringing out what a man – or a woman – already has. Helping him to be what he's able to be, only the rest of the world has told him otherwise since the day he could ask questions and got a clip round the ear for his efforts. Mebbe one day I could be someone like him – like Staley.' He glanced round the room, his eyes coming to rest on the slope of pillows under the counterpane.

'Sorry, Harry.' He nuzzled her ear. 'We dint comm here for me to get on my soapbox.'

'Ned, I'm delighted. How couldn't I be? Have you written back? It's says here you need to reply to them.'

'I wanted to tell yow first.'

She gently disengaged her hand and stood up. 'I want to wash my face first, then I think we should go and buy an envelope and paper and a stamp. See a bit of Lincoln, find a café where you can sit and write to them, and then we should celebrate.'

'And after?' he whispered.

She leaned over and gently guided his head towards her breasts, ruffling his hair and stroking the back of his neck. She said to the top of his head. 'Just as I said, celebrate. I love you, Ned.'

*

'I like this,' said Ned, stroking the dark tufts in Harry's armpit. 'It's sort of . . . foreign. There's a lad at work has a picture of that Sophia Loren taped up inside his locker. She's in a swimsuit and has her elbows up. I thought she woh the sexiest woman alive – that's until I met yow of course. And it reminds me of this . . .' He slipped his hand under the crumpled sheet.

'Ooh! No, it's too sensitive still.'

'Sorry.' Ned propped himself on his other elbow and looked down at her.

'Max told me I wouldn't be able to wear those dresses without getting myself a razor.'

'Max is in Mapp'ley,' said Ned, smoothing the crease between her brows with the ball of his thumb. 'It's all over, Harry.'

'It is, isn't it? I just have to learn not to be frightened. And to trust you.' She covered her eyes with the back of her hand. 'Not to push your head away like I did.'

'I meant it when I said I'd be patient, and stop whenever yuh said to.'

'I just didn't know what you were doing down there.'

'I could do it again in a bit.'

No sound, but a nod.

Ten minutes later, he said, 'Yer so ... lovely ... when yuh put your arms above your head ... yes, like that. Giving yourself to me completely.'

*

In the grey light from the gap in the curtains, Harry turned towards Ned's slumbering body, outlined like a mountain range against the pale horizon of the far wall. 'I wish you could have been my first,' she whispered.

The mountain shifted. Ned bent his head to kiss the corner of her mouth.

'Good mornin', Mrs Stones. I *wor* yer first. The first to love yuh. I'm hoping yow'll let me be yur last.'

*

Weeks later, having shaved so closely that he'd cut himself, Ned sat in an allocated seat next to Ellen and Sam under the wide, shallow vault of a hall in North Circus Street, amongst hundreds of other murmuring parents and lovers.

'It looks like one of our grander chapels,' said Ellen, nodding towards the great organ, on a dais between two vivid stained-glass windows. A man in black tails was taking his seat before it.

'That's what it is. The Wesleyans have it the rest of the time. Temperance meetings, and that,' said Ned. Ellen looked pleased.

Sam leaned across, smiling. 'But I'll need a pint or two after all this,' he said. 'Once I've given you back your tie.'

Ned opened his mouth to answer, but in that moment the organ swelled into life, and everyone present got to their feet, and heads turned as a tall, silver-haired, long-nosed man in a gold-tasselled mortar board, the train of his gown held up by a pageboy, advanced up the aisle. Ned blinked, wondering about the weight of the mace the man carried.

Later, he was determined to be the last one clapping as Harry, and later Anna, detached themselves from the throng of black-gowned graduands and demurely stepped forward to receive their degrees. For a flicker of a moment, Ned saw himself making the same journey, but pushed the thought away. On Monday, he reminded himself, he'd be back at his lathe. *Not for long, though.*

*

A week later, Harry walked with her mother through the hop fields.

'Are you sure you want to do this, Harry?' asked Ellen.

'I have to try, Mum. I stayed up at John and Amy's last September because I couldn't face seeing the hoppers here. Poor things, it wasn't *their* fault.'

'Plenty of people asked about you.'

'And I missed them. Some of the regulars I've known all my life. But this year I'm going to stay here, because if I don't, those two have won, you see? They'll have decided how I live my life. And I've been through so much that I feel better able to cope with it.'

She stopped, and looked around her. 'It was about here, I think. But it's so different now. I never will stop marvelling at how a place as quiet and still as this is now can turn into such a bustle and noise come September.'

'Do you remember what you said to me at the time, about never letting a man near you again?'

Harry sighed. 'I'd hardly forget it! I did think that for a long time. I told both Max and Ned, partly to see how it made *me* feel telling them, but also so that I could see their faces, see how they'd react.'

'And?'

'Max asked if I'd fought back,' she said in a tight voice.

'And Ned?'

'Ned cried, and comforted me,' she said, remembering that night in Chippendale Street.

'He's right for you – not that it's up to me.' Ellen hesitated. 'What *did* happen to Max in the end?'

'He's in Mapperley – the asylum, I mean. It's a humane regime, apparently. Dr MacMillan is an enlightened director.'

'*You've* not been to see him?'

'No, don't worry, Mum. And he's a long way from being let out. Spellie – Miss Spellman – has been, as a concerned colleague. They've put him on some drug to stabilise him. She said MacMillan wanted to find a way forward that would curb his fixations but not slow his remarkable brain.'

Ellen's hand went to her cheek. 'I wish you'd told us more at the time.'

'I didn't want to worry you, and I didn't want Dad to feel he'd failed to protect me a second time. *He* needs to convince himself that none of that was his fault. It took *me* a while to understand that it wasn't mine. But I can't tell you how pleased I was when Uncle Vanlo came.'

'He says a friend of his is coming from Nottingham to see him.'

'He means Sid – you remember, the librarian. Oh, *good*.'

'You never met my grandfather Oliver, Harry. But there's a lot of him in you – without his hardness, I mean. You're determined. He was a principled man in his own way, and you are too, but he never let that be leavened by kindness. I mean, he would stand up for people in the abstract – the rights of the working man, education for poor children – but he had no tolerance of human failure. He even raised a gun to your poor father once, and he'd have given away your brother Tom and not had a twinge of conscience.'

'I never knew the bit about the gun!'

'Your father won't talk about it. If he'd let Sam speak to me then instead of chasing him away so much unhappiness could have been avoided. David's father wouldn't have drowned. But David himself wouldn't be here.'

Harry slipped her hand under her mother's arm. 'Is David like his father – as a person, I mean?'

'In many ways, yes. I'm not surprised he went for ordination; Harold was a preacher. He has his voice. He was a good man, but he knew I couldn't love him. I respected him. Sometimes I only tolerated him. I always loved your father, even when I thought he'd abandoned me – which of course he never did. I have only ever loved two men.'

'Two?'

'The other was my fiancé, killed in 1917. I don't think they ever met, but your father was posted to the same place. It must have been hell on earth. My poor, innocent Charlie. Harold – David's father – tried to tell me that it was God's work and that I must accept it, same as he'd had to accept widowerhood. I *hated* him for that. But if Charlie hadn't been killed, you and your brothers would never have been born. If Harold hadn't fallen in the mill race, then I wouldn't have been free to be with your father. So perhaps Harold was right after all. I sometimes wonder . . .'

'Mum?'

'I hope that Charlie, and Harold, are in a happier place. They deserve it. I remember them both in my prayers, and I know that your father prays for poor Harold. Only, I wonder how it will be, one day, if we all meet again in heaven. We are told that there are no marriages there – or rather, that no marriages are *made* there – and we should be so taken up with praising God that we wouldn't notice the lack of them, but I find it hard to think that earthly love should be extinguished in heaven, or at least relegated. I mean, isn't Paradise a manifestation of God's love for us?'

'I don't know how much I believe now, Mum.'

'I know. But to behave as if you do is no bad guide. To love your neighbour, to be just, to help the widow and the orphan. These are good principles.'

'And to battle against injustice and exploitation of the working man?'

'That could be my grandfather speaking! Yes, Harry, that's a calling that would please God. There should be a life before death, not just after it, not an endless struggle to survive, as if your emotional ration book is as thin as the real ones were. Love is the biggest part of that.'

*

Two weeks after Sam had seen Harry onto the train back to Nottingham to start work under Dr Holt's supervision, a letter came to French's Farm. The first thing Sam thought was that it was about Mrs Lasseter, who had been too frail to come hopping that year. He saw the smudgy East End postmark, and feared bad news. Sam turned the grubby envelope over in his hands, studying the address, the way the fountain pen had dug in, nearly making holes. The address was in capitals, and

KENT had been underlined twice. The back of the envelope was blank. He put it down on the table and went to fill the kettle. *I should wait till Ellen's back from school, mebbe.* He frowned. That would mean another three hours or more. He took a knife from the drawer and slipped it under the flap. The cheap paper tore raggedly.

'*Dear Mr Loveridge,*' it began, under an address he didn't recognise. Loveridge was printed, as were two or three other longer words in an otherwise childish and untidy cursive. 'Daughter' stood out. His skin prickled.

I hope you will remember me, sir, when you came with the other gentelman to find me at the Resolute though I was a bit dusty with you. I was about to be marrid and had other things on my mind but I kep your bit of paper becos I said to myself Ada you never know do you. Well I am marrid and I've my Tommy who is two and means nobody no harm tho whatever he does his father gets angry and I'm his mother so I do the best I can to take the blows for him poor little beggar. I should of listened to you sir but you dont do you not when you know you've a baby coming and want to keep him. Even Bert's auntie God rest her tried to warn me . . .

Sam put the paper down for a moment and wiped his eyes.

I belive you now sir, and am hartily sorry I didn't earlier for he has gone and done to my sister what he done to your daughter when I was in the park with Tommy. Vera is only sixteen and she has never had a man. The only mercy is that he has not got her in the family way but I said enough is enough and her and me and Mother have been to the police and that pore girl has suffered all over again nearly as bad as what he did to her but I spect you know all about that with your daughter. He is a bad un and if he was to be put away it would be a mercy for all of us because in the Scrubs he cant hit me nor Tommy. Of course he says my sister wanted him — the liar she is only a baby realy — and the sergeant says it would be his word against hers all in an open court with them all staring at her and I wouldn't be allowed in the box with her to hold her hand. Only if there is somebody else would say he done it to me too then there might be some hope and I wonder would your daughter want to speak up maybe not after all this time and she maybe has a nice man to love her now I dearly hope so.

I am sure you must be a kind man if you come all that way to Poplar to warn me. I am sory I never seen the hopping place where you live it must be lovely like Mile End Park only bigger but I never got to go as I was always needed at the Resolute well men always want to drink dont they. I miss the Resolute I saw a bit of life there but Bert said not for a marrid woman and anyway there is Tommy.

Your respectful servant,
Mrs Ada Evans

*

'What's wrong, Sam?' Ellen was shrugging off her mack when she caught sight of his face.

'This came,' he said. 'Tell me what we mun do, Ellen. But whatever happens, I'd like this Ada and her boy to come here for a week or so. Give her a holiday.'

Ellen read the letter twice, then carefully folded it up and put it back in its envelope. 'It's not our decision, Sam. There is a part of me that thinks . . . well, Harry's come fighting back. She's beaten those two, by making a life for herself. And outwitted Max. But . . .'

'She *is* a fighter, our Harry. More'n that little maidy of sixteen is, prob'ly.'

'I think she'll want her day in court.'

CHAPTER THIRTY-SIX

London

December 1959

'You ready, my Ellen?'

'The bus won't come for half an hour, Sam.'

'I know. I'd just rather be at the stop miles early than a minute late and miss the train.'

'All right. Have you seen my gloves?'

*

Sam stared out at the wintry landscape hurtling past, it seemed to him, though the train was travelling at only fifty miles an hour. He and Ellen sat opposite each other, alone in their compartment.

'They've still got the old wagons,' said Ellen. 'All they've done is paint over "third" with "second".

'It's like a little house, this,' he said. 'A front door and a back door each side and warm and comfortable in the middle. And no corridor, so nobody can come in and bother you when you're between stations. You could do what you liked in here.'

Ellen shot him a quick look, but Sam's expression was entirely innocent.

'But if someone does get in at the next station, Sam, you're stuck with them.'

'Well, if they do, best make 'em welcome. Only ... I hope today we're left alone, Ellen. So all I've to think about is getting to John's and seeing our girl.'

'I am afraid though, just as the sergeant warned us, that she'll be put through the wringer. She knows we'll be there hearing all of it, but I think she'll find it easier to keep her nerve if we don't look as though we're pessimistic ourselves. Sorry, I don't think I'm explaining this very well.'

'No, you are, my Ellen. Come and sit next to me.'

He put his arm around her shoulders and pulled her in tight.

'Don't suppose I'm allowed a smoke, am I?'

'*Sam* ... you were going to try ...'

'Let me roll it, then, and I'll smoke it out the door when we get to Ashford.'

He removed his arm and rummaged for his pouch. Ellen nestled against him. *I don't like the way he coughs, but I do like that tobaccoy smell he has. It's how I knew he was there, waiting for me in Surman's Wood all those years ago.*

*

Harry's determinedly cheerful chatter about her life in Florence Boot, her forays into the countryside on the Bantam, Ned's letters from Oxford, how much she missed Anna, now reading

391

submissions for a London publisher, dominated the evening meal in John Quainton's manse. Nobody mentioned what was looming the following morning. As the empty pudding bowls were cleared away, Sam got up and said, 'Mind if I go for a smoke?'

'I'll come with you,' said John Quainton. 'For the walk – not the smoke.'

*

'How do you think our Harry will manage, brother?' asked Sam, as the two men paced the wet streets.

'She's a remarkable young woman, but you know that, of course. Courageous.'

'She came to yours last night. What'd you talk about?'

'Same as this evening. Anything but the case. Not that we tried to avoid it. More that we let her decide what to say. She talked about her young man a lot.'

'Is he coming, do you know?'

John hesitated.

'I rather think she hasn't told him – he's in Oxford so she could keep it from him. Perhaps she wants to see this through herself, though she said she's going to see him after Christmas, before going back to Nottingham.'

'She said that to us too. We're all going to go. That's after we've been to Chingestone.'

'*Chingestone?* When were *you* last there?'

'More'n thirty years ago. Dunt remember the date exackly, though I remember everything else about it. I'd just been let out of Winchester.'

'I remember.' John was silent for a moment. 'My sister's never been back either, has she?'

'No. Too feared to, even for her mother's funeral.'

'It was so cruel, all of that. Yet everybody seemed to think it was the right thing at the time. Even I didn't speak up when I should have.'

'You listened to Ellen, though. Nobody else in her family did.'

'You were steadfast, Sam.'

'That was all I could be.'

They walked on in companionable silence, until John said, 'Harry told me last night about what she's doing back at the university. She said – this is more or less it – "I'm working on something to do with my dad's people, Uncle John. I have to travel a bit – libraries in Liverpool and Leeds, for instance. The problem though is that others have written the books about them, mostly, and they write what they think they see, or want to, not what's really there."'

Sam turned his face away, his eyes hot with tears. He fumbled for his handkerchief, wiping his eyes whilst pretending to blow his nose. 'I couldn't read nor write till I was in Winchester,' he whispered. 'And then after, what your sister taught me.'

'I know,' said John gently.

'And now my maidy is going to write books herself. I'm that proud of her, John.'

*

'More like a big church, this,' said Sam, looking up into the dome of the entrance hall of the Old Bailey. 'Like St Paul's. All them statues and marble and paintings.'

'Makes me think of a mausoleum,' said a pale Harry. 'The public gallery is up there. I have to go this way. I'll come and find you as soon as I've given my evidence.' She hugged John and Amy first, then Ellen, and lastly Sam, before walking briskly away to where a solicitor's clerk was waiting for her. The man held a door open, and then she was gone. Holding hands, her parents took the direction Harry had indicated, and found themselves with the Quaintons ushered into the steeply raked public gallery. Without speaking, John and Amy separated, so that when they were all seated, Amy was at Ellen's left and John at Sam's right.

'I'm glad we got here early,' whispered Ellen, looking down into the court to where two clerks were laying paperwork up on the judge's bench. 'That usher told me the public gallery fills quickly for these cases.' She felt Sam flinch next to her, and took his hand. His palm was damp.

'Entertainment for them!'

'Ssh!'

'Sorry. I'm nervy, bein' in such a place. Never seen one as grand as this, mind.' He glanced behind them, hearing other spectators clattering into the benches. 'Like a big chapel, ain't it? Only we won't get sermons.'

'Let's hope that the truth is told here as well.'

*

With ten minutes to go, the well of the court was bustling, and the public benches were full of excited murmurs.

'Theatre!' muttered John. 'There's a woman back there with opera glasses.'

His heart pounding, Sam looked across to where the jury members were filing in. His eyes as sharp as they had been in his old poaching days, Sam studied each face and began to give them names. *That way I'll remember 'en. Same as I did when I couldn't read nor write.*

A fellow in a shabby suit sporting a moth-eaten moustache and a row of First World War medals he called Reginald. From the colours of the ribbons and the slight lurch with which he walked to his place, leaning on a stick, Sam worked out that the man had left something of himself, if not an entire leg, somewhere in Flanders. 'Esther' was a fine-looking dark-haired woman of about forty; from the set of her felt hat and the fur collar of her coat, Sam ascribed to her a constrained childhood in the East End followed by migration to the suburbs. A pinched-looking young clerk with darting eyes was Eustace. A balding, middle-aged man creaked into position next to him. *That perfessional-looking gent with the watch chain and the stoop prob'ly pulls teeth the rest of the time.* With a memory for smells as strong as it was for faces, Sam felt the ghost of a scent of oil of cloves, and ran his tongue around his own teeth. *Clarence, I'll call 'en.*

'All rise!' bawled a voice.

*

Sam's fists clenched as the man in the dock rose to his feet. *Cocksure, cheap ... what was it John called him? A bounder. Well, he ain't bounding now.*

'How do you plead?' said a voice.

'Not guilty,' came back in a nasal whine. Sam closed his eyes.

Vera Porter was the first in the witness box, looking too young for her cheap peplumed costume. The clerk stood in front of her, holding the Bible, murmuring instructions. Sam saw the girl flush, then fumble with the buttons of her cotton gloves. The court fidgeted as she struggled to pull them off. Finally, she took the oath in a faltering voice.

Sam couldn't look at her as the prosecuting counsel got her to tell them what had happened on that afternoon that had seemed like any other, when she'd expected her sister to come round but instead Bert Evans arrived on a half-day holiday, a man she had thought she could trust, 'because he was family, wasn't he?' she said, in high-pitched, perplexed tones. Sam listened to her recount her mounting disbelief at what Bert did next, at how he laughed at her tears and pleadings, and how he told her he'd beat her if she didn't shut up and let him get on with it in peace, and how nobody would believe her if she kicked up a fuss.

'What did you do after he'd gone?'

'I took my undies out the back and rubbed salt into the blood. They was my good ones.'

'Thank you, Miss Porter, I have no more questions.'

Sam looked up.

'Oh!' she said, and with a timid smile turned round.

No, maidy, the worst is still to come.

'Do you have a sweetheart, Miss Porter?' began the defence barrister, unsmiling.

'I've Dan.'

'Dan. How old is this Dan?'

'Nineteen, sir.'

'Works, does he?'

''Course. In a greengrocer's in Hoxton.'

'And how long have you been consorting with this boy?'

'We've been walking out for about six months, if that's what you mean.'

'I suppose I do. Where do you go, when you "walk out", Miss Porter?'

'The pictures if we've any money. The park if we don't, or if it's a nice evening.'

'Hmm. Alone with him?'

'Well . . . yes. We're steady, ain't we?'

'Going to marry you, is he?'

No call for you to sneer! Sam heard John Quainton grunt in annoyance.

Vera Porter flushed, and her eyes darted around the room. 'He wants to . . . as soon as we're old enough, that is to say, he wanted to afore . . . I don't know.'

'"Afore" what, Miss Porter? Before you allowed him to take liberties with you?'

Sam joined in the collective gasp that arose from the public benches. The barrister glanced in their direction, but Sam could see he was unfazed. *Rattled her – that's what you wanted, ain't it?*

'*No!* I meant "before" Bert Evans did it to me.'

'"Before Bert Evans did it to me." Who, exactly, "did it" to you, Miss Porter, and in what order? Let's see, first this Dan, then Bert Evans?'

'No, I never said that! I never!'

'Don't shriek, Miss Porter. We can all hear you perfectly well. Let's leave aside for a minute who did what to whom and in what order. So you have your swain working in the greengrocer's in Hoxton who doesn't always have the needful to take you to the cinema, and here you have your brother-in-law, twenty-five years old, already finished his apprenticeship as well as his two years honourably serving his country as a national serviceman, now earning a good wage as chargehand in the carriage works at Stratford. Quite the man, then. Could give you money for the best seats in the cinema every night of the week. In fact, my client has told me he has long been in the habit of giving you little gifts, Miss Porter, isn't that so?'

'Well yes, but that don't mean—'

'Fine nylons, the last time, I believe. Things you could wear with your – let me see . . .' He consulted his notes. 'With your "good undies", the ones you put on because you knew your brother-in-law alone was coming to see you for the purposes of being intimate with you.'

'No!'

'You see, my client is an honest man. He doesn't deny having intercourse with you. He says you wanted him to.'

'*No!*'

'When you went to the police station with your sister and your mother – eventually – and only, it would seem, because your sister arrived just as you were tidying yourself up, and you had to come out with a story quickish   '

'*No,* it wasn't—'

'I concede, Miss Porter, that my client is not entirely blameless. For the purposes of the law, though, he is guilty of no more than moral turpitude, "doing it", as you so elegantly put it, with his wife's younger sister. At most, we might call him a seducer, but in accepting all his gifts over a period of some months, Miss Porter, it would appear that you were quite happy, indeed, to be so seduced.'

Sam flung unspoken curses at the barrister's head as he watched the crushed figure of Vera Porter being helped out of the witness box.

The police surgeon gave his evidence next. Sam listened with his head down, clutching Ellen's hand, until the sound of her ragged breathing made him look up to see tears. He took out his handkerchief and silently dried them, but his action made them well up even more.

'The tags of her hymen were present,' intoned the doctor, 'and there were smudges of blood on her thighs. The patient complained of considerable discomfort.'

'Any lesions, lacerations?' asked the prosecuting counsel.

'Slight, but considerable inflammation. The girl had until very recently been *virgo intacta*.'

The defence barrister rose, but spent some long seconds adjusting his gown before glancing at the doctor standing waiting in the witness box, as though he'd forgotten the man was there.

'You told my learned colleague Mr Tolney that the physical signs of intercourse were, to quote you, "slight",' he said.

'Not quite.'

'Did you in fact find *any* evidence that the complainant had undergone anything other than the normal experience of having sexual relations for the first time?'

'As I said, there was considerable inflammation and the patient complained of discomfort.'

'Yes indeed, as might any girl at her first encounter with a man. You did not, in fact, find any signs of violence, bruising?'

'I did not, but may I say—'

'No, you have answered my question.'

'Mr *Bell*,' warned the judge.

'I beg your pardon, Doctor, do continue.'

'Miss Porter weighs seven stone. She may have decided that opposition was futile.'

'"May have", you say. Supposition on your part, Doctor, hardly evidence.'

'She was distressed enough that I had to administer a bromide before examining her.'

'Ah! Tears of remorse! Thank you, Doctor.'

Must be her turn now, thought Sam, watching the doctor put away his glasses and shuffle out of the witness box, chastened. But it wasn't, or not yet; the morning was already over.

*

Just after midday, the little group shivered outside on the pavement.

'Ellen and I have brought sandwiches and a flask,' said Amy.

'There's a bomb site just there by St Paul's,' said Sam. 'Nobody'll mind if we drop our crumbs there. And five minutes beside a church med help our Harry.'

*

As the little group walked back, Sam murmured to John, 'How d'you think Miss Porter did up there?'

'I could say that Bell is an unprincipled wretch, of course, but he'd argue he's just doing his job.'

'Them things she took from 'en don't help her any, though how she could have refused them coming from someone she thought was her bruv, I dunt know.'

'That bit about serving Queen and country always goes over well, even if Evans had no choice about doing it.'

'I wonder what he did, then. Korea or the Catering Corps?'

'Frankly, Sam, I hope it was the Catering Corps. I don't like to think of a fellow like that with a gun in his hands and a lot of unarmed villagers.'

CHAPTER THIRTY-SEVEN

Old Bailey
December 1959

'The prosecution calls Mrs Ada Evans!'

'*You can't do that! She's my wife!*' Bert Evans stood up in the dock, waving his arms, until two officers grasped him and forced him back into his seat.

'Mr Evans,' warned the judge, 'I advise you to keep quiet unless you want to appear again on a charge of contempt of court. Your wife does not *have* to give evidence. She has evidently chosen to do so.'

'Look at Bell!' muttered John Quainton. Sam did – he was conferring hurriedly at his desk with another man.

'He dunt look so sure of hisself now, John.'

Ada was deadly pale, but composed, as she took the stand. She wore a little felt hat on the back of her head, but no coat though the courtroom was chilly, and standing there she slowly and deliberately removed a flimsy scarf from around her throat. Without it, the square neck of her dowdy green dress exposed her throat. The sleeves of the dress finished at the elbow. She rested her arms deliberately on the lip of the witness box, turning her hands palm upwards. 'Oh God!' whispered Ellen, and a murmur swept the court as everyone else saw what she saw. Ada had rather shapely forearms and a neck more elegant than her clothes or hairstyle. Someone had dappled both her arms and throat with purple and yellow bruises. Across the room, Sam saw Reginald bristle and stick his chest out. His mouth formed some silent words. Clarence frowned, and Esther's thin lips opened and shut. Eustace sat up straight. *He ain't a dusty little clerk no more. He's riding into battle, he is.* Sam looked over at the dock, where Evans sat hunched and scowling.

Ada took the oath in an expectant silence.

'I am going to ask you to take us through the events of that afternoon, Mrs Evans,' Mr Tolney began.

'I've got a key to my sister's, but I always call out when I open the door anyway. We're all family. She lives with our mother. Or did – we lost Mother ten days ago. Vera works at home making gentlemen's trousers for Mr Makolsky, so I don't like her to get up from her machine in the middle of something fiddly. She usually takes a break when I come round, and we go to the kitchen and get ourselves a cup of tea. I heard this funny noise coming from the sitting room when I went in that day, so I left Tommy in his pram in the passage and went in. There she was lying in a heap on the floor, with her face pushed into the rug. She'd something screwed up in her hand – I got down beside her and got it off her. It was her knickers, and they was all damp – I mean like they'd been washed – well, she *had* washed them, she told me. She said she was hurting something terrible, and wanted the doctor. It was a bit before I got the story out of her. Poor lamb thought I'd think it was *her* fault. I got warned off Bert before I married him, but I wouldn't listen. He'd served another girl the same way, down at the hopping, see.'

Bell got to his feet. 'My Lord!' he said, appealing to the judge. 'My learned friend must surely know better than to allow such outrageous allegations to be made!'

'Mr Tolney, do ensure that your witness confines herself to the complainant's case,' said the judge.

'My Lord,' said Tolney. Facing Ada Evans, he said, 'You were telling the court about finding your sister in a state of distress. Please go on.'

'Well, he'd told Vera she wasn't to tell anyone or she'd be sorry. He'd pushed her face down into that rug, so she couldn't struggle, and she's only a little thing. He's a big strong man, boxing since he was ten. Anything will do 'im for a punchbag, 'specially if he's crossed.

'It was my idea to go to the police. She wouldn't, only I said, "You've done nothing wrong," but what persuaded her was that if she didn't, he'd come back for more.

'I've never stood up to him, never till that moment. I still don't know where I got the courage, though I know *why* I got it. I got a walloping when I came back from the police and found him raging about where'd I been all this time, asking where his tea was. I didn't tell 'im I'd been at the station, of course. I screamed at him for what he'd done and flung a skillet at his head – missed him though. I thought he'd kill me then, but he's not stupid – devious, but not stupid. He's never hit me in the face so's you'd see it. The nearest he's come to that is banging the back of my head off the wall. No sign of this when we was courting, o' course.

'I put Tommy in his pram and went to Vera's to sleep. He came round there in the morning when he woke up, and was shouting and swearing and banging so's you'd think he'd have the door down but pore Dan had called in on his way to work and he opened up and got knocked down for his trouble. Mrs Next Door called the busies, bless her, but they didn't do much, only threatened to take him in for breach of the peace. He didn't know then that they was at the station deciding whether to pull him in or not on *this* charge. If I'd told 'im the night before that we'd been to the police I wonder would I be standing here now. It was after they took 'im in and then gev him bail I got this beating,' she said, showing off her arms, 'though I never let on I'd gone in with my sister. He thought it was just her and Mother.'

'All this is most interesting, My Lord,' interposed Bell, 'but I cannot see what the Evanses' alleged matrimonial strife has to do with this case, other than provide Mrs Evans with another excuse to blacken her husband's character.'

'I must ask you again, Mr Tolney, to try to keep your witness to the point,' said the judge.

*

'Mrs Evans, would it not suit you for your husband to go prison?' Bell smiled slightly, his head on one side.

'I'd not get walloped, if that's what you mean, but we'd be hard up.'

'You'd not get walloped . . . might I suggest to you, Mrs Evans, that you are tired of your husband's society, disappointed in your marriage?'

'It's not that—'

'Perhaps you know another man you would rather live with than him?'

'Well, of all the—'

'No doubt, your sister's evident partiality for your husband – we have seen that she willingly accepted his gifts – gave you an opportunity to resolve your problem.'

'*No!*'

Ada Evans grasped the edges of the witness box.

'Mine are not rhetorical questions, Mrs Evans.'

'You can "suggest" whatever you want, Mister, until the cows come home. I dunno what that ret oracle is you're talking about, but I can tell you for nothing that I haven't put my little sister up to nothing. Her and Dan were walking out quietly: he's a good boy, and anyone with eyes in 'is 'ead, could see she thinks the world of him – what would make her accept that brute?'

'Devotion to her elder sister?'

'That's a disgusting thing to say! My husband *raped* my sister, Mr Bell, whatever you say, and that's the end of it. Yes, of *course* I'd love to see him sent down! That way he wouldn't be able to get his hands on some other pore innercent!'

*

'It must be her turn now, my Ellen,' whispered Sam, as a quivering Ada stepped down. He felt as though someone was squeezing his stomach, making it turn upside down. He tasted Ellen's ham and cheese sandwiches at the back of his throat. Then Harry walked out and took the stand.

Sam looked with pride at the slight figure standing up there, taking the oath in a clear, level voice. Harry's face was calm to the point of austerity, clean of makeup. She wore a plain linen blouse that he recognised as one her mother had made for her, and a neat costume. There was nothing of Vera's clumsy tawdriness. *Maybe Harry could take her under her wing, like, help her put her life right.* He remembered that day when Harry had twirled around the farmyard showing off her new haircut, and how he'd thought then that even her gymslip couldn't eclipse her natural gracefulness. Sam blinked, and wiped his eyes. *She's the same girl she was then, Sam. But so strong and brave they oughter make a statue of her.*

'Let me apologise in advance if the questions I ask you distress you, Miss Loveridge,' began Tolney.

Harry inclined her head.

'Have you seen the man in the dock before?'

'Yes. Bert Evans. He used to come to the farm where my father is foreman, for the hopping.'

'Regularly?'

'Oh yes, for years. I suppose he was there when I was a little girl, because once a hopping family comes, they usually come back, and French's is a good farm. I'd seen him come for at least ten years.'

'And the last time?'

'September 1955.' Harry hesitated.

'When you feel able, Miss Loveridge, would you tell the court what happened on that last occasion.'

With a theatrical flourish Mr Bell took out his watch and raised his eyebrows.

'There was a bit of a row, the last day of the hopping. The call had gone out, "Pull no more bines." Dad went to tally the bins – this is what he told me happened – and the one Bert Evans was working on was short. Bert was a bit the worse for wear, Dad said. Many of the men only come at the weekends, and Bert had come up on the Friday night, got drunk, and been late getting started on Saturday morning. That wasn't the problem, really, because the hoppers are paid by what they pick, not how long they've been at it for. He'd cheated, though. The bottom of the bin was lined with rubbish – leaves and such. Dad said he didn't make a fuss – that's not really his way – but he told him not to try that one on him again. It would likely have ended there if Bert hadn't then tried to put the blame on the Ackletons – that's another regular family. He said they must've changed over the bins when he was on his break. When he said that Dad told him the people he was down with would be welcome next year as he'd never had a quarrel with them, but Bert wasn't to come with them.

'By then quite a crowd had gathered, and maybe it's because there was an audience and Bert didn't want to lose face, that he shouted names at Dad, said he and the Ackletons were nothing but dirty pikeys, liars and cheats that shouldn't be put above true Englishmen. There were cries of "shame" and "leave it out", and Bert's friend George pulled his sleeve to try to get him to come away, but he pushed him off. Wester Ackleton stepped forward then and would've used his fists on Bert, only that Dad held him back, saying he didn't want the last day and the feast to be ruined for all the other hoppers. Bert lifted his jacket then and went off swearing and the other man went with him. Only they didn't go. They must've just hid.'

There was utter silence in court. All the faces that Sam could see were turned towards his daughter, all except Evans, who was looking upwards and trying to cultivate a sneering raised lip, and Bell, who was feverishly writing in a large notebook. Sam glanced at Ellen's profile, and saw her lips moving silently. Amy was holding her hand. Then he looked at John, who was leaning forward, intent, nervously pulling at his fingers.

'When did you see him again, Miss Loveridge?'

No father should have to hear what my Harry is telling him. I've to keep looking at her, because all of them people are, as it wunt do if she looks round and sees I'm not there for her.

As if from a distance Sam heard Tolney's quiet, insistent voice.

'Did you struggle?'

'I wanted to, but they had a knife.'

'Did you try to cry out?'

'No. I couldn't. The other one had a hand over my mouth. When he did take it away, it was only to slap me, and then . . .'

'Go on . . .'

Silence.

'Miss Loveridge?'

Sam closed his eyes, knowing he would never forget Harry's words. He opened them when in a thin wail she said, 'I thought he'd choke me!'

Next to him, Ellen whimpered.

'Then they changed over!' Harry crossed her arms on her chest, as if to protect – or hide – herself. Before Tolney could go on, Harry cried, 'Nobody believed me! The police said the charge would never stick. It was the word of two against one, they said. So they got off scot-free, and *I . . . I'll* remember what they did for the rest of my life.'

'Was this your first encounter with a man?'

'Yes,' whispered Harry. Sam glanced over at the transfixed faces of the jury. *I ain't sure they believed poor Vera. But I'd swear they believe you.*

'Thank you, Miss Loveridge. I have no further questions, though my colleague may do, but might the witness be granted a break, My Lord?'

'By all means.'

'Please, I can go on,' said Harry. 'Let Mr Bell do his worst. He cannot do me any greater harm than they did. If I might have a glass of water . . . ?'

*

'Are you quite recovered, Miss Loveridge?' said Bell.

'Recovered? Depends what you mean by that.'

'Quite,' said Bell, with a slight laugh. 'Now, in your evidence to my learned colleague you referred to the defendant as "Bert", am I right?' Before Harry could answer, he went on. 'You were evidently on quite familiar terms with him. It wouldn't be unusual, then, for a healthy young man to be sweet on a healthy young woman he knew and who called him by his first name, would it?'

'*Sweet?* I didn't like how he looked at me. Not him, nor the other one.'

'Well, it might interest you to know that "the other one" is dead, Miss Loveridge.'

'Oh no!'

'An accident at the docks. Crushed.'

Harry shut her eyes.

'Those can't be tears, surely? If what you told my learned colleague was true, I would have thought you'd be pleased.'

'He must have a mother and father,' said Harry. 'It's them I'm sorry for.'

'Most noble. Miss Loveridge, the jury knows little of you besides this dramatic scene you have just played to them. You are a research assistant at the University of Nottingham, I believe?'

'Yes.'

'You are also a graduate of that institution, is that right?'

'Yes.'

'Hmm . . . weren't you a little young to leave home, to be so far from parental care?'

'My Lord, I don't quite see the point of this question,' interposed Tolney.

'Indeed, what *is* your point, Mr Bell?'

'I am about to make it, My Lord.'

But before Bell could speak again, Harry said, 'I don't suppose it was any different for *you*, Mr Bell, unless you were educated at home with a governess.'

Laughter rippled around the court. For the first time that day, Sam smiled.

'Clever, Miss Loveridge,' snarled Bell. 'Perhaps we could get back to the matter in hand. You had, doubtless, more freedom there than you had at home. You could see whom you liked, go where you liked.'

'I was a scholarship student, Mr Bell. My mother and father didn't have the means for me to "see whom I liked, go where I liked". I was at Nottingham to study, and still am.'

'Most commendable. With friends, no doubt, like-minded young people of both sexes – all thrown together.'

'I lived in Florence Boot Hall, Mr Bell, and still do. Women's accommodation. Men are not allowed on the premises unless chaperoned. Spellie – I mean Miss Spellman, the warden – is very strict. I wanted my degree, and I got it. No one will ever be able to take *that* away from me.'

Scattered applause broke out on the benches behind Sam.

'*Silence!*' thundered the judge. '*Or the public gallery will be cleared!*' Sam heard rustling behind him as the crowd settled, but for the first time he thought, *they're with her. They ain't gawping now. They want her to win.*

Bell glowered at Harry, then lowered his head for his next attack.

'Quite. No one will ever be able to take *that* from you, you say. I understand, Miss Loveridge, that in people of your background, chastity is much prized. A matter of honour.'

'My background is that I went to grammar school, I was brought up to attend the Methodist chapel and my mother teaches infants.'

'And your father is a Gypsy.'

'*So what if he is!*'

'Do try to keep calm, Miss Loveridge. You've told the court that you've known the defendant – Bert as you call him – for years. On the last night of the hopping we have some carousing, carousing in which you took part, I believe, even though you claim you "didn't like how he looked at me", yet instead of going home you chose to wander off into the hop fields in the dark—'

'I wanted some time alone—'

'Might this not have been a signal to Mr Evans that he was to follow you?'

'*No!*'

'I put it to you that he *did* follow you, as arranged, and that his friend George, who is no longer here to defend himself, was not in fact one of the party, but could conveniently be called to mind when you had to explain why you came home dirty and, shall we say, dishonoured, and had to invent this story.'

'*No!*'

'You knew very well that your father had publicly rowed with Mr Evans, didn't you?'

'Yes, but—'

'Yet you had sexual relations with Mr Evans yards from your father's door.'

'No, it was—'

'And in doing so flew right in the face of the honour of his tribe!'

'*No! They raped me, both of them!*'

'What was your motive in giving evidence today, Miss Loveridge?' said Bell in a calmer voice. 'Was it revenge for the fact that despite Mr Evans having relations with you he went back to London and married someone else?'

'Did you not hear me? They *raped* me!'

Bell turned towards the judge with a weary air. 'I have no further questions.'

Up on the bench the judge was conferring with a clerk. Then, 'Do either of you wish to call any further witnesses?'

'No, My Lord,' said Mr Tolney. 'That is the evidence for the Crown.'

'Mr Bell?'

'My client is exercising his right not to give evidence.'

'If there are no more witnesses, then, this case will be adjourned until tomorrow morning.'

*

'Hev they finished with her, then?' Sam whispered to John.

'Yes, I think so,'

'I got to go outside. I can't breathe in here. Ellen?'

415

She was already gathering up her things, buttoning her coat and putting on her gloves. Sam looked at her pale, tear-tracked face. They eased their way to the end of the bench, John standing to one side to let them pass, and joined the throng of chattering people leaving the day's entertainment. Then, hand in hand, they came out into the domed atrium, and Sam said, 'It tears my heart to see you like that.'

'It's worse for her.'

'It must be.'

'I'm so proud of her, Sam.'

'So am I. Ah, there she is!'

Harry was waiting for them in the echoing space, a slight, lonely figure outlined against all that exuberance of veined marble, still where everyone around her was in constant movement. Sam's heart lurched when he looked at her. He wanted to tell her that he'd never let anything hurt her again. *I can't, though, can I? I couldn't protect her before, nor when that man took her off, and I couldn't protect her upstairs when she was standing up with all them people gawping at her. I don't even like that I'm a man right now.*

'Dad? It's all right. It's almost over.'

'It's me should say that to you, Harry.'

She took his arm. 'It wasn't so bad. I mean, it *was* bad, only it was made easier because I was so angry. Not just angry with him, and the other one, but angry for those bruises, and that poor girl who should have been able to trust him – and angry with those who didn't act the first time, because if they had then maybe he wouldn't have had the chance to do what he did again. But it was a *bit* like that time, in a way.'

'I see . . .'

'I mean, I was there, and everything. I could hear what they were asking me and I could hear my answers.'

'Loud and clear you was, too.'

'Only it was as if I was looking at the whole goings-on, not from above, exactly, more like I was standing to the side. That's what I meant when I said it was like the hop field. As if it wasn't really happening to me. Here's John and Amy – let's go and get our tea. Tomorrow perhaps we'll know what the jury thought of it all . . .' Her voice tailed away.

The little group emerged into the gloom of the December afternoon.

'There's a lad over there with the evening papers,' said Sam. 'Shall I get you one, Ellen?'

At that moment the boy cried his wares: '*Rape case latest! Read all abaht it!*', folding the uppermost copy ready for his next buyer.

*

'. . . remember that the defendant is not on trial for moral turpitude,' said the judge. 'Remember that you are trying him only for rape, the rape of Miss Vera Porter. If you believe him, that his young sister-in-law consented to his embraces, then you cannot convict him simply because you may not like an adulterer. Nor is he on trial for how he treats his wife. And finally we come to Miss Loveridge's evidence, on the basis of which some time ago a decision was made not to go to trial. That does not mean that her evidence was in itself invalid, nor that you should discount it. However, it is not your role to see justice done for Miss Loveridge, however compelling you may have found what she had to say. Because of the way the law works, though, what *is* appropriate for you to consider is the picture that has been painted of Mr Evans's character – namely, if you believe the evidence of the prosecution witnesses, of a man with a pattern of violence towards members of the fair sex . . .'

'*He* believes her,' whispered Sam to his brother-in-law.

'Don't let's get our hopes up,' said John.

They watched the jury troop out.

'None of 'em are looking at him,' said Sam.

Bert Evans was led down to the cells.

*

'Members of the jury, have you reached a verdict upon which you are all agreed?' asked the judge. The foreman was the man Sam thought of as Clarence.

'We have.'

'Do you find the defendant guilty or not guilty?'

Sam saw that Harry was watching not the judge nor the jury but the man in the dock. There was utter silence in the court. Sam was transported back to a day in childhood, where he lay in the corner of a field, in a border of lush grass untouched by the plough. He'd often remembered that moment. He was watching a drop of dew slide slowly, slowly, down a green blade. When that drop fell, he'd told himself, something momentous would happen. He lay silent in that quietly buzzing morning, until a shadow fell across the sun. His brother Noah, now lying somewhere in French soil. 'What are you doing, my Sam? They're wanting to *coor* the *drom* and dunt know where you'd got to. Your *togs* is all damp.' Sam had scrambled to his dirty, naked feet and followed his brother, and never knew if that drop ever fell.

And then it did.

'Guilty.'

Sam heard a tiny scream, as of an animal deep in the woods, struggling in a trap, but it was lost in the hubbub that erupted in the court room. He saw Ellen's arms around their daughter, and Harry sobbing like a child. Amy was the other side of Ellen, reaching across to stroke Harry's hair. He glanced at John, to his right. He was flushed, and couldn't disguise that he was pleased.

'Justice, Sam, she got justice. For herself, for those others.'

Someone was shouting for order, and the judge was gathering himself up for his final words. In the dock, Albert Evans was standing, truculent, sneering and unrepentant. Sam heard shreds of the judge's words. 'A heinous attack on a defenceless, innocent girl . . . a betrayal of trust . . . thank the witnesses for their courage in coming forward . . . a picture painted of a fiend preying upon young womanhood . . . you will serve the full tariff . . .'

*

In the damp, dead time between Christmas and New Year, the mid-afternoon train from Paddington was not busy, so they had a compartment to themselves.

419

Harry looked about her. 'They're not good, carriages like these,' she said. 'If I was in one with someone who attacked me, I'd have no escape but to open the door and fall down onto the track.'

'Oh my little girl . . .' murmured Ellen.

'It's all right, Mum, honestly. Look – I survived! And we had a lovely Christmas, didn't we?'

As Sam watched the countryside flash by, and Ellen quietly read a book opposite him, Harry settled in a corner seat and again took out Ned's most recent letter.

3 Walton Street
Oxford

Dear Harry,

I miss you an awful lot. I hoped we could meet at Christmas but I promised Mam and Dad I'd go back to them and of course you'd gone back to Kent. Mam writes how proud of me she is, and that Dad is too but won't admit it. They've even had a whip-round in the Working Men's Club to help me with books. I was afraid the nightmares would come back when I was back in my old room but they never did. They've not while I've been here in Oxford either – think on that! I persuaded them to let me have an extra pillow, and I go to sleep holding it as if it was you. I think of you on that bike of yours, and wish I was on it with you with my hands round that neat waist of yours, and your back all tense against my chest. I'd best not go on like that as I've promised myself to get an essay finished today and mustn't get distracted. I'll save up thinking about that until tonight after I've put the light out . . . after I've said goodnight the way I do every night to that painting you did of the lion in Slab Square, the day we met. I've got it hanging on my wall here.

I've taken to this place, Harry. Something happened when I was in that church hall back in Nottingham. It wasn't just what the tutor had to say but that he wanted to hear what I thought. That had never happened before – and for my part I'd always thought of history as being like a row in a public bar, only bigger – and of course it's not, and it is, at the same time.

When I was in Malaya we were led by officers who'd been at public schools, national servicemen like ourselves, only richer – lads who could afford to pay Mess bills. I remember one of them – not a bad lad in himself but never questioned why he was there and why he was top dog – told me that schools like his gave 'tone' and brought out 'leadership qualities'. I said I thought going down a mine was a better test of leadership, seeing as how everyone down there depended on everyone else, and mentioned Keir Hardie and Nye Bevan too – in case he hadn't heard of Keir Hardie. He gave this silly whinnying laugh and said that in his view the best thing was to take the schooling he had had and give it to a few select plebs (I think he said 'deserving working-class boys' but plebs is what he meant – and did he mean all the rest were not deserving?). That way, he said, they'd better themselves, but that society would collapse if everyone got let in – standards would fall, he said. He told me his school had a couple of 'foundationers' in every year and they were 'jolly good chaps too'. Well, society the way he likes it probably would collapse if more of the 'jolly good chaps' got to run it, and no bad thing either. What's different here in Ruskin is that it's not a question of picking out a few lucky campers and 'bettering' them. It's about giving a man the tools to go back into his own world and improve it for others. That's some responsibility, Harry, but that's also what the union men said to me when they told me I could come here, and the union would pay.

Only now I'm here I don't want it to stop. I was afraid, I'll be honest with you, about what it would be like. I still can't get my head around being in a college, which is why I'm only putting the street address on the top of this page. Perhaps I'll write 'Ruskin College' on the back of the envelope. One step at a time, eh? I've not told you much yet about the other men here, have I? They're like me. They're not bigger schoolboys like the students in the regular colleges, but miners, and foundry-men and shipwrights. There are some women too, but not many (and none as gorgeous as my Harry) as it's the unions that send the students so of course it's mainly men. That's a thing should change too. These men have done their national service too and for the first time in my life, I won't say I see the sense of what we were doing in Malaya, but I can now argue why we shouldn't have been there. I can't tell you what a relief it is to be able to talk about what happened out there and be understood.

We go to some lectures with the – I was going to write 'real' students, but what I'm doing feels real enough. Some of them are out and out toffs. They sound just like the announcers in the newsreels at the pictures – like that public schoolboy in Malaya. I'll never figure out how the human mouth can make such a contorted sound but I think, nay I'm sure, that the way I speak isn't what it was. Apart from the belted earls, some of the other students try to dress like us – corduroys and knitted ties – even though they're not like us and know they're not.

And now for my big news, Harry, and you need to be the first to know. My tutor says I should go on studying after Ruskin. I could even try for here, for Oxford I mean, but of course I want Nottingham, not because I'm afraid of the big wide world, but because I'd be with you, and it wouldn't be like crawling back to what I knew anyway, as my life would be as different as it could be from what I had before. Not that I'd abandon Raleigh altogether. The union men want me to go in and speak there, and in other factories. Staley said he'd see if he couldn't get me a bit of evening teaching.

Perhaps I'm going to wake up and somebody will tell me that I am Ned Stones from Kimberley and not to get above myself, and tell me that if I get a move on I could have overtime Saturday morning. If I don't get on with this essay, they might well be right.

I love you, duck. I'm not going to wake up from that, anyroad. Ey up!

Ned

CHAPTER THIRTY-EIGHT

Chingestone and Oxford
January 1960

Harry sat apart from her parents on the coach, knowing that this was their time. Hers would come next, in that city of spires, twelve miles north of the village they were bound for, the village where her mother had been born. The first sign that things were not as they were had come at Princes Risborough.

'When's the next train to Chinnor?' Sam had enquired, not finding it on the timetable.

'When was the last one, you mean? Sorry, sir, the line was closed more than two years ago. You won't get to Chinnor on the railways now unless you're a load of cement. There's a coach goes in twenty minutes.'

Harry could hear the low murmur of her parents' voices, though they were the other side of the aisle of the bus and two rows further up. Her mother was closest to the window, pointing things out to Sam, but whilst she couldn't make out what they were saying, she caught the anxious timbre of her mother's voice. *It must be thirty years or more. She was as young as I am.*

As the bus slowed on the way into Chingestone, she saw her mother's head turn, and a little 'oh!' escaped her. Harry followed the direction of her gaze. To the right she saw a row of flint cottages, pretty but unremarkable, and read the inscription carved above the door of one of them, not a house name, but the words 'Primitive Methodist' and a date. A tiny garden burgeoned with early snowdrops, and some tools and Wellington boots were heaped in the porch. Harry caught a glimpse of net curtains. The 'ranters' had long ago given up their chapel.

The bus rattled to a halt on the main street. Sam got down first, hefting the holdall, turning round to thank the conductor and help down first Ellen, then Harry. Her mother watched the bus depart, lips parted, and then look around her as if she had been put down in some foreign country.

'It's the same, Sam, and not the same,' she said in a wavering, high voice. 'I suppose we should go this way . . .' Harry listened to her mother's hesitant litany as she listed the people who had lived in the impassive Victorian villas, the flint cottages, who'd kept his harvest in which barn. 'The Wesleyan minister lived there . . . a nice man, but his wife a bit distant. And that was the Red Lion . . . I was never in there, but it's strange to see it's now just a house . . .'

'Let's find a pub you can go in,' said Sam. 'You could do with something after the journey, Ellen, even if it's just an orange juice. We med get some news that way.' The place they went into was simple enough: a long wooden counter, a darts board, some high-backed settles. It was a Brakspears house, as it had always been, but the landlord was a youngish man.

'No, I don't know him,' said Ellen to Sam's murmured question, as he handed her her glass. 'That is, he looks familiar only because he looks like people do around here.'

'Says "Munday" above the door.'

'There've always been Mundays here. There are two of them on the war memorial – twins.' Ellen's eyes were glossy-bright in the light from the low window.

'Mebbe we should go there next,' said Sam.

'Yes, to the churchyard – that's where we'll find them all.'

'Not before you two have had some bread and cheese. Or a pie.' He went back to the counter.

*

Harry held her mother's elbow as Ellen gazed down at a grave shadowed by the flint wall of the church.

'She was a good woman, your grandmother, though always in awe of her father-in-law. I'm glad she was able to spend her last years with your uncle John instead, and that he brought her back here to lie beside my father. I can just about remember *his* funeral – the long journey out of London with his coffin. It must have cost my grandfather a fortune, but he wanted his son to lie in his own earth. There was a bit of trouble because the vicar didn't like the Prims being buried in the churchyard. Those things are a lot easier than they used to be. But that's not why I didn't come to Mother's funeral, Harry. This is the first time I've stood at her grave ... because Grandfer outlived her. Here he is —' she walked to a neighbouring grave '—with my grandmother. Silent enough now, but he was a rousing preacher. He could put the fear of God into the most hardened men, but made many rejoice. Sam?' She held out her free hand to him; he clasped it. 'He can't touch us now.'

'Harold here too?'

'He must be. The Chowns were over there, I think, near that yew. Everything looks smaller than I remember it.'

They walked over, as a cloud obscured the sun and the shadows blurred. Sam spotted the grave first. 'He's here, with his first lady.' He peered at the inscription. 'Harry, can you make out what that says?'

'"O man of God, flee these things; and follow after righteousness",' murmured Harry.

'It's from Timothy,' said Ellen. 'Grandfer would have decided on that. Once I'd have been able to tell you chapter and verse.'

'I hope he's happy, wherever he is now,' said Sam, in an oddly muffled voice. 'Deserved better than he got.'

*

'Let her go alone, Harry,' murmured Sam, as Ellen walked slowly in the direction of the austere Portland stone cross that faced the road. They watched her bend, and touch the names. Ellen's mouth was moving, but they were too far away to hear the words.

'Charlie, is it?' whispered Harry.

'Yes. Her first sweetheart. Poor fellow dint get to lie in his own earth. She always wanted to take a handful from by his cottage and put it over him. Never has.'

'We could do that, Dad, take her there I mean.'

'That's an idea. So close to Dover in Patrixbourne that we should have done it before. You've a bit of the French, haven't you?'

'I have.'

'Ah, your mother's coming back. What's she doing now?'

'Looking at other graves.'

Ellen was pale but composed. 'They're all here,' she said. 'Dear Grace . . . old Mott. I never knew his name was Edgar, but that must be him. Reggie Horwood's there, with his mother and father. He died before them. I wonder who has the farm now?'

'Where'd you like to go now?' asked Sam, knowing the answer.

'The path, if it's still there. Surman's Wood.'

*

'It should be here,' said Sam, frowning. 'But it's a road.' He looked up at the ridge of the Chilterns. 'No, this is it, all right. They can't move them hills, can they?'

'They'd cut through them if they wanted,' said Ellen, looking at the grass verge where once there'd been a hedgerow teeming with birds.

They stood to one side as a Morris Minor puttered past them, then followed the smoke of its exhaust. Rounding a corner, they saw two more cars, parked outside neat rendered council houses.

'They've pretty gardens,' said Ellen, looking at Sam.

'Is that the wood?' asked Harry, pointing at a line of trees marching across the horizon.

'What's left of it,' said Sam.

They moved past the houses. An old man weeding his front garden waved.

'Med he know you, my Ellen?'

'I don't recognise him. I think he's just being polite,' she said, waving back. 'Unless . . . he looks a bit like the postman, but I'm not sure.'

Beyond the houses was a playing field, with goalposts and scuffed turf.

'This was Horwood's. Them cows were here, remember? Me and Vanlo must've come from where that fence is now. Only we came out of trees.'

'But where *is* the wood, Sam? There's only that copse, over there.'

Harry hung back, her heart wrung. She couldn't see what they were seeing, superimposed on this tidy reality, but knew that whatever they had remembered for so long was now dissolving before their eyes.

Beyond the playing field was a smaller, fenced area with swings, a seesaw, a slide. A mother was pushing a baby girl in one of the toddler swings. The child looked well fed, but bored.

'The stream, Sam!' Ellen's voice was high with distress. She ran towards the blackcurrant bushes that bordered the playground. Beyond them, a few beech trees clung to higher ground. 'I can hear it!' she cried. Sam took off after her. The young woman with the baby glanced round at them, and then gave the swing another push. Harry stayed where she was, watching her father put his arm around her mother, seeing her slump against his shoulder, and knew she was crying.

Eventually, she saw Ellen pull out her handkerchief and blow her nose, and they walked back to where Harry waited for them.

'It's fenced off,' said Sam to Harry. 'To stop the kiddies fallin' in. But the wood's gone. Just a few trees for trimming, like. Don't go looking. I'd rather tell you how it was, so's you think of it that way. A memorial, if you like.' He looked at his wife. 'Do you want to see your cottage now?'

'No. I don't think I could bear it. It mightn't be there anymore anyway, and even if it is, it'll be so changed. I'm glad we came, Sam, all the same. My home's been with you all this time. Now I know that's where my roots are too.'

'Too much weedkiller here,' he said.

'That's it exactly. Too much weedkiller and not enough life. I'm sure those people like their houses, and are comfortable in them. Inside bathrooms and everything . . .' She caught Sam's grimace. 'I don't mean we have to have one,' she added. 'I wouldn't go back to the old days, because they *weren't* always good. Children dying of diseases you can cure now. Old people sent to the workhouse and lasting only a week because they're separated from all they love. But those nice houses are the same as they are everywhere.'

'And nowhere left to stop a wagon.' He turned to Harry. 'We mun keep all of this here,' he said, striking his heart. 'What if we see about a bus to Oxford already, 'stead of looking for somewhere to sleep here?'

*

'You mean you haven't even told him you were coming?' exclaimed Ellen, standing on Walton Street.

'All we have to do is go in and ask for him,' said Harry.

'I'm with you,' said Sam, laughing. 'Lead on.'

Harry walked up the steps into the entrance hall and looked round. The place was clean and Spartan. There were no plaques on the wall, as there had been back at school, detailing the girls who had won places at Oxbridge, only some photographs: she recognised Nye Bevan declaiming to a rapt crowd, Keir Hardie's earnest face and neat beard, a group of Victorian gentlemen photographed in a garden. A middle-aged lady got up from behind a desk. 'Can I help you, dear?'

'I'm looking for Ned Stones.'

The woman's smile was genuine. 'Our Ned? He'll be back about half past five, I should think. Family is it?' she said, glancing over Ellen and Sam.

'Friends . . .'

'Why don't you sit in the common room? There are some cups there, a kettle and a tea caddy. Make yourselves at home . . . it's this way. Or you could sit in the garden if you wanted. It's very mild for this time of year, and if you keep your coats buttoned . . . or perhaps Mr Stones will want to show you around himself.'

*

Ned didn't see Ellen and Sam straightaway. They were sitting, whilst Harry was standing in front of the fireplace. With the wait, her bravado had deserted her, and she'd spent most of the last twenty minutes pacing the long room, every now and again resuming her position facing the doorway. Sam had pulled out his tin of tobacco and had rolled a cigarette, encouraged by the faint tang of smoke in the air and a tin Brakspears ashtray, recently wiped, but Ellen caught his eye. He put the cigarette behind his ear.

'You're as jumpy as a cat,' said Ellen to Harry.

'*Our* cat's about as jumpy as that cushion,' said Sam.

Harry looked beyond them then, to the eruption of male voices in the hallway. The Ruskin College students were returning from lectures. And suddenly, there he was, Ned, but not quite the Ned she'd known. *Older, a bit thinner in the face – well, it has been more than three months. More intense – more* dash, *even.*

'I thought . . . I thought it was some bloke from the union. I never . . . Oh Harry, I am right glad to see you!' He strode across the room, and she walked straight into his arms.

Something different about your voice, though. But mine changed, going to Nottingham. Everybody said so. Then she stopped thinking, closed her eyes, and gave her face up to his kiss.

A moment later, his hands stilled on her shoulders. She opened her eyes. His mouth still just covered hers, but she could see him looking beyond her, to where Sam and Ellen sat quietly, deliberately looking elsewhere.

Still a little flushed, Ned said, 'I'll just go and see the cook to get three added for dinner. Then perhaps you'd like me to show you around.'

'Mind if we go outside a minute?' asked Sam. 'Ellen's stopped me smoking indoors.'

432

'Of course. We'll go in the garden. Some of the tutors call it a quad, like the old colleges have. For me it's a garden. I'd put vegetables in it if it was mine. Like my dad's allotment.'

'I remember it. I'm not much good at the gardening. When I was young we were never stopped long enough in one place for it. My Ellen's better with the plants.'

*

Sitting on the bench, Sam rolled another cigarette, and tapped it on the top of his tobacco tin. 'Make one for you, Ned?'

'No, thank you, Mr Loveridge. I've stopped altogether. I nearly took it up again once I got here, to help with the studying, but I knew Harry wouldn't like it.'

'She's right. They're saying it's bad for us now. I'm Sam to you, remember.'

'Sam. Thank you, Mr—'

Sam laughed.

'So, Ned. Have you what they call honourable intentions by my daughter?'

Ned took a deep breath. 'I want to marry her. I just hope I pass the test.'

'Anything worth having deserves a bit of a struggle, mebbe. I think you've both had yours.'

'Her more than me. I need to earn her.'

'Like I did with her mother.'

'When I got out of uniform, all I wanted was for things to be normal again. To go back to the old life, as if I could pretend that I hadn't really seen – and done – what I did see and do.'

Sam nodded. 'I understand that. After what I saw in France.'

'But of course it couldn't be normal again. You can't undo, or unsee. And it's like you do it all over again, every time you think about it. There must've been loads of us like that, in Raleigh, carrying all of that inside, not talking about it. Drowning it in pints and bets on the nags. Harry came in and blew all that to bits. It was a hard bloody test. I wasn't going to win her unless I did something with myself. She's no snob, Mr – Sam – but she was right. She met my old man and poor Mam, and boy, she held her ground! More'n I've ever been able to do. I don't mean they were nasty to her – they weren't. They think the world of her – well, you've seen that. They just didn't understand why a girl would want to study. It wasn't part of their world. It took them some time to get used to the idea of *me* throwing up a steady job to come here – even though I kept telling them they'd take me back tomorrow at Raleigh if I wanted, if it didn't work out. So my choice was to live my life like Dad's, or follow Harry's example. It's not about "bettering myself", which most folk probably think means trying to be middle class. That's the most a lot of people hope for, nearly all of the time, but leave it up to the Pools coupon to decide it for them. What Harry wanted was for me to be a better *me,* but still me. Being obstinate, I couldn't see that at first. It took Anna to show me.'

'And now?'

'Well, there's a world that needs changing, Sam, or at least things that need to be fought against. The Bomb, fr'instance.'

'Her mother is getting together some ladies for the Aldermaston march at Easter. Harry bein' one.'

'There'll be some of the lads from here going,' said Ned,
delighted. 'Me being one too!'

'She talks about you a lot, Ned. An' her face just lights up.'

'She does?'

'Oh yeah . . .'

Sam looked away into the dusk. The evening was growing
chilly, and a miasma of boiled beef floated on the air.

'She's had a hard few days, Ned. Did she tell you what she
was doing, before we came up here, I mean? In London?'

'No, but I was wondering why she wasn't back in Nottingham.'

'She's going back tomorrow. But she got her day in court at
last.' As calmly as he could, Sam recounted the trial.

Eventually, he said, 'You'd have been proud of her too.'

'I wish she'd said . . . Doesn't she trust me?'

'She trusts you all right. It was for your sake, boy. She didn't
want to take you away from what you was doing here.'

'Oh Harry . . .'

A gong sounded in the distance.

'Oh, that's dinner. Not that I feel hungry.'

'Then we should go and eat. Food's too precious to be wasted,
'specially when it's eaten in good company.' Sam got to his feet,
ground his cigarette butt under his heel then picked it up and
slipped it into his pocket.

'You've passed, Ned. As long as you love my girl, and you'll
defend her always, even when she thinks she dunt need no
defending, you'll do.'

Ned laughed with relief. 'If she'll have me! I love her all right.'

'Only, do you remember how I tole you what used to happen, Ned, in the old days?'

'About the boy and the girl taking a wagon and going off somewhere for a bit?'

'Yeah. It dunt need to be far – the next village would do – because nobody went looking for 'em. O' course when they came back they had to get married, whether they'd been playing at being man or wife or not.'

'Did they? Play at it, I mean?'

Sam shot a glance at him, smiling slightly.

'Some did and some dint, I 'spect. Anyways, once they was back they'd take hold of each other's hands before everyone present and that would be them, wed before God.'

'But no church?'

'No need then. You're wed before God if he's up there looking down at you making your promises in good faith, same as if there's a roof over you when you do it. Easier for God to see you, I should think.'

'*Dad! Ned!*'

'We'd best hurry. It's this way, Sam.'

*

As bread and butter pudding was being distributed, Sam turned to Ned and said, 'I wanted to ask you . . . what happened to Vanlo up there? Apart from the catapult business, I mean. He's always been a quiet sort of fellow. But since he's come back from Nottingham he's something else altogether. He's ... *happy*. That's what he is. Never seen 'im like that.'

Ned hesitated. 'I couldn't really say, of course. I didn't know him before. Maybe he's just pleased he helped Harry.'

'Well, it's not worn off yet, anyways.' Sam glanced across the table, to see Harry deep in conversation with her mother. He dropped his voice. 'But coming back to our Harry, what I wanted to say is that there is that way of doing things, the running off I mean, only afterwards I'd want my girl to be married proper in the chapel all the same – you know, in a nice dress her mother helped her make. I'd want to walk 'er in, see 'er go to someone as'll love 'er and keep 'er and all that. And mebbe a nice tea afterwards.'

'I'd want it too,' said Ned. 'And what you said before as well. Only, instead of the wagon ... I mean, I've no experience of horses other than patting the nose of Shipstone's dray.'

'A good brew, is that?'

'The best, though you'd have to come back to Nottingham to try it.'

'You take me, lad. You were saying "instead of the wagon" ...'

'Would an old motorbike do? And a boarding house?'

'I should think so. They're easier to park, the bikes, and the *gavvers* can't do nothing about moving on a boarding house, can they?'

'I suppose not,' said Ned, relieved.

'Well then, you know what to do,' said Sam.

*

437

After dinner Ned said to Harry, 'Come with me to the common room a minute. I'd like to introduce you to the other lads. So that they can see what I've been going on about all this time.' He hesitated. 'Where are you going to stay?'

'Dad's booked rooms for us at the Old Black Horse. It's always got to be rooms above a pub for him.'

'Wise man. God, Harry, I'd love to sneak in there – or shin up the drainpipe – and keep you warm. I won't though,' he said, seeing her troubled expression. 'Not that I don't want to. It wouldn't be quite respectful – to you – to them. Your dad's told me what we need to do. I'll finish up here, and then you tell me the date you want.'

'Oh Ned! I don't have the words to tell you how happy I am!'

'Me neither.' He glanced round, seeing that Sam and Ellen were some distance away, backs tactfully turned. 'Kiss me?'

CHAPTER THIRTY-NINE

Canterbury
July 1960

'Oh Sid, it's really you, this place!' Harry moved through the little flat above the greengrocer's, running her hands over the books on the shelves her father and Vanlo had helped put up, smoothing the cloth on the gate-leg table.

'It's the first time I've managed to get all my things together in one place. There wasn't space in that room in Nottingham. My books were all in Wales, in boxes under the rafters.'

'And how's the Beaney?'

'I like it. Very different from Nottingham, but I like that there's a museum in there too. My colleagues are a bit more reserved than up there, but we rub along all right.'

'Lucky to get a job so quickly smack in the middle of Canterbury.'

'I *am* lucky. I think it all started when your Ned came in looking for a book to impress *you* with, and I've just gone on being lucky.'

Harry crossed to the window overlooking St Dunstan's. 'It's all chance, isn't it, Sid? Down there was where my parents met again after three years apart. Mum was standing on the pavement with my two brothers when the Gypsies came past on their wagons. They thought they'd lost each other for ever, though Dad said he'd never have stopped looking.' She turned round. 'Talking of luck, I've got something for you. Where did I put my satchel?'

'Maybe in the kitchen nook. Yes, here it is.'

Harry unbuckled the bag. 'I think you should have this.' She handed over a parcel. 'I hope that frame's all right.'

'What is it? Your graduation photo?' He ripped the brown paper.

'Oh heavens no! I've only put it behind glass because it's charcoal, so that it doesn't smear . . .'

But Sid wasn't listening. He was gazing at Vanlo's sleeping face, huddled in the window seat of the train bound for London. 'How did you know?' he whispered.

Harry smiled. 'I know my uncle, that's how. I see how he looks at you, when he thinks no one is looking at him. I should do another portrait of him. He looks younger now than he did when I made that drawing. He's happy.'

'Oh Harry!' Sid put the portrait carefully down on the table, and embraced her.

'Ned's asked me to be best man,' he murmured into her hair.

'And Anna insists on being bridesmaid!'

*

'Where's Harry, Sam? Her bike's not here.'

'She'll have gone away a few days, my Ellen.'

'Gone away? She never said anything, though!'

'She'll be back. Her and Ned.'

'Ned? When did *he* arrive? I thought he wasn't coming until Friday, with his parents. Thursday David's coming to make all square for Saturday, and Tom the day after . . .'

'You was at school. I tole him he dint need to come and tell me what him and Harry was going to do, but he said with all she'd been through he dint want me worrying. He'd be happier I knew where she was, and he's right.'

'Oh Sam! Our little girl!' Ellen went into his arms, her cheek against his chest. She felt him breathe in, and his chest whistle.

'For me them two is married, Ellen, as square as you and me. But I'll walk her into the chapel on Saturday, and be proud to do it.'

'She's got the one she always loved most, and loves her.'

'She has. Will the tea wait, Ellen? I should like a walk with you.'

HISTORICAL BACKGROUND

Harry Loveridge is a beneficiary of the 1944 Education Act, commonly known as the Butler Act, which grew out of a 1943 White Paper entitled 'Educational Reconstruction', explicitly linking education to post-war recovery. Amongst other things, the act ended the need for parents to pay fees for a child who has passed the eleven-plus to go to grammar school, thus increasing opportunities for girls and working-class children in general. As a result the percentage of young children attending higher education went up from 1% to 3%. Around 17,000 students were awarded first degrees in UK universities in 1950 – but even so, fewer than 4,000 of them were women. Fifty years later, that overall number had increased to 243,000 and women outnumbered men, with 33% of school-leavers going into higher education.

Student grants such as the one I had have now been legislated out of existence, but they did not exist in the form I knew either in the 1950s. State, municipal and county scholarships existed (the first of which were aimed mainly at those who were going to Oxbridge), and were hotly competed for through scholarship exams. However a student's success depended also on being able to stay on another year at school after A levels to prepare for those exams, and on the school's ability to prepare that student.

Florence Boot was the wife of Jesse Boot, 1st Baron Trent (1850–1931), who had transformed the business his father founded into the nationwide chain Boots and who donated the land on which the University of Nottingham was built. Florence Boot Hall was built in 1928 as a women's hall (it has been mixed since 2000), the oldest hall on campus.

Sid and Vanlo's relationship was a criminal offence at this time. The *Report of the Departmental Committee on Homosexual Offences and Prostitution,* better known as the Wolfenden Report, after the committee's chairman, was published in September 1957. Wolfenden's inquiry followed a number of high profile cases, including those of Lord Montagu of Beaulieu, the landowner Michael Pitt-Rivers, the journalist Peter Wildeblood and the writer Rupert Croft-Cooke, all of whom were given prison sentences of between twelve and eighteen months; Wildeblood and Croft-Cooke published their experiences of incarceration. Alan Turing was also prosecuted but attempted chemical castration as an alternative to prison. The Wolfenden Report recommended the decriminalisation of homosexual acts in private, but this was not made law for another ten years, and to begin with the age of consent was set at twenty-one years.

The first major Aldermaston march against the nuclear bomb took place on Easter weekend in 1958. The direction of the march was reversed in subsequent years, starting in Aldermaston and finishing in Trafalgar Square.

The trade unionist Willie Gallacher (1881–1965) did address crowds in Nottingham in the 1950s but not at the time I have described him being there; I hope I'll be forgiven the artistic licence.

Harry's summer job is in Lefevre's department store in Guildhall Street in Canterbury. The Lefevres sold their business to Debenhams in the 1920s. Harry and Ned have their tea in Griffin & Spalding, also sold to Debenhams in 1944. Both stores traded under their original names until 1973.

ACKNOWLEDGEMENTS

Firstly, I would like to thank my agent Annette Green for her continued, unswerving support, followed by Claire Johnson-Creek and all the team at Bonnier Books UK for making this book as good as it can be, Alex Silcox for copyediting and Gilly Dean for proofreading. Charlie Sanderson (voice artist), Charles Sanderson, John and Danuta Allsop, Elaine Stones and Martin Dawson gave me invaluable help and advice on Nottinghamshire dialect and locations. Steve Arundel and Roy Plumb of the Chinemarelian (Kimberley) Historical Society provided indispensable detail on Swingate Water Tower I really needed for the plot as well as providing the details of Ned's walk to the canal with his father, as the route they took has now vanished. The staff of the local history section in Nottingham Central Library gave me unstinting help and drew my attention to sources it hadn't occurred to me to look at. Sid is not a portrait of any of the library staff, but his list of queries is drawn from the library's annual reports for the 1950s compiled for the town clerk. If I've got the layout of the old public library (now Nottingham Trent University) right, it's thanks to the plans library staff showed me.

Special thanks are due to the member of staff at Florence Boot Hall who saw me skulking outside during the Easter Vac, took me in, and showed me round all the original features of the hall. If I have managed to evoke the place for people who have lived there, the credit is his.

I am immensely grateful to my fellow Memory Lane author Elizabeth Woodcraft for reading the court scene for me and correcting details of legal procedure. If mistakes remain, they are mine not hers.

Last but by no means least, I would like to thank my husband Carmine Mezzacappa for his unswerving patience and support.

Welcome to the world of Katie Hutton!

Keep reading for more from Katie Hutton, to discover a recipe that features in this novel and to find out more about Katie Hutton's upcoming books . . .

We'd also like to welcome you to Memory Lane, a place to discuss the very best saga stories from authors you know and love with other readers, plus get recommendations for new books we think you'll enjoy. Read on and join our club!

www.MemoryLane.Club
www.facebook.com/groups/memorylanebookgroup

Dear Readers,

I enjoyed writing *The Gypsy Bride,* the book that precedes this one, so much that I was sad when I'd finished it. I knew I was going to miss Sam and Ellen. But when that book was accepted by Zaffre I was asked if I would write another book for the Memory Lane saga list. I was stumped for an idea, but inspiration works in strange ways. I opened the fridge and ate some chocolate buttons and thought: a sequel – the next generation. I wanted to move forward into the 1950s because anything I have read or heard about that time indicates a sense of hope in the future, reconstruction after the desolation of World War II that wasn't just physical – for instance with the Butler Act opening up access to education in a way that hadn't happened before. At the same time there was still a certain stuffiness around sex, despite some relaxation during the war years. My mother and father went to Nottingham University in the 1950s, she on a scholarship, he on an exhibition, the first of their respective families to go on to higher education. Some of the incidents in *The Gypsy's Daughter* derive from stories they told me (for example the painting of the lions in Slab Square incident, and that poor commercial traveller who left his wife's ashes with his landlady).

Not only was I glad to be able to meet Sam and Ellen again and let readers know what had happened to them through telling their daughter's story, but I was also pleased to let Vanlo, Sam's brother-in-law, come into his own with his own love story, all the more poignant because at that time men like him risked blackmail or prison.

I hope you enjoyed *The Gypsy's Daughter* and *The Gypsy Bride* if you've read it. If you did, please do share your thoughts on the Memory Lane Facebook page.

Best wishes,
Katie

Recipe for Sweet Scones

This recipe for scones, like the ones Harry and Miss Shaw ate in the Red Spider, is one of my mother's. She got her recipes from a cookbook she bought when she was a newly-wed from a door-to-door salesman.

Fruit Scones

8 oz. flour
¼ tsp. salt
½ tsp. bicarbonate of soda
1 tsp. cream of tartar
1–2 oz. margarine
2 oz. currants or sultanas
Sugar if desired
Milk to mix
Egg to glaze

Sieve dry ingredients, rub in fat and if liked a little sugar. Add enough milk to give a soft dough, and place on a lightly floured board.

Roll or pat the dough out very lightly to the required thickness – about ¾–1 inch is usual.

Cut out, using a small, plain cutter, and put the scones on a greased tin, well spaced out.

Brush scones over with a little beaten egg and bake in a hot oven (450° F) 7–10 minutes.

· MEMORY LANE ·

Watch out for the upcoming saga from Katie Hutton . . .

ANNIE OF AINSWORTH MILL

It's 1906 and nineteen-year-old Annie Maguire is leaving County Down, Ireland. Driven away from home following poverty and bereavement, she's searching for a new start in life and moves to Cumberland, an area known at the time at 'Little Ireland', to work as a flax dresser in a mill.

Robert McClure grew up in Cleator, Cumberland. The illegitimate son of a wealthy land owner and a cook, he spent his childhood being moved from pillar to post and always felt like he doesn't belong. When he is asked to join the Protestant Orange Lodge he jumps at the chance, despite guilt at his Catholic upbringing.

When Annie and Robert meet they fall instantly in love. But when Annie gets pregnant there is opposition to their relationship within the local community and Annie is sent away to a convent to give birth. Can these star-crossed lovers overcome their cultural differences and build the family that they've both always dreamed of?

Coming July 2022. Pre-order now.

·MEMORY LANE·

Introducing the place for story lovers – a welcoming home for all readers who love heartwarming tales of wartime, family and romance. Sign up to our mailing list for book recommendations, giveaways, deals and behind-the-scenes writing moments from your favourite authors. Join the Memory Lane Book Group on Facebook to chat about the books you love with other saga readers.

·MEMORY LANE·